SATIN & GRIT

A NOTE.

Seaside Pointe is an interconnected series. For the best reading experience, please begin the series with book one, Blossoms & Steel.

Seaside Pointe is a fictional town set in the area of Skagit Valley, Washington. Most of the places mentioned are fictitious. However, there are very real places brought into the story too.

We are writers who research and know things. Any mistakes made are either intentional for story purposes or accidental because, well, as we said, "we're just writers."

Please forgive us if we've botched something up.

— XOXO M&M

Satin & Grit
Copyright © 2021 Michele G. Miller & Mindy Hayes writing as Mindy Michele
Published by Enchanted Ink Press

All Rights Reserved.

No part of this book may be reproduced in any form or by any electronic or mechanical means, including information storage and retrieval systems, without written permission from the author, except for the use of brief quotations in a book review.

This is a work of fiction. Names, characters, places and incidents are the product of the author's imagination or are used fictitiously, any resemblance to any actual persons, living or dead, events, or locales is purely coincidental and not intended by the author.

The author acknowledges the trademarked status and trademark owners of various products referenced in this work of fiction, which have been used without permission. The publication/use of these trademarks is not authorized, associated with, or sponsored by the trademark owner.

Cover design © Sarah Hansen, Okay Creations
Edited by Samantha Eaton-Roberts
Proofed by Jo Pettibone

ALSO BY MINDY MICHELE

Seaside Pointe Novels
Blossoms & Steel
Copper & Ink
Satin & Grit
Book 4 - releasing 10/14/21

Pratt Family Stories
Paper Planes and Other Things We Lost
Subway Stops and the Places We Meet
Chasing Cars and the Lessons We Learned

The Backroads Duet
Love in C Minor, Vol one
Loss in A Major, Vol two

Nothing Compares To You, a 90s novella

ALSO BY MICHELE G. MILLER

Last Call

The Prophecy of Tyalbrook
Never Let You Fall
Never Let You Go
Never Without You

From The Wreckage Series

From The Wreckage

Out of Ruins

All That Remains

Standalone FTW spinoffs

West: A male POV Novel

Into the Fire - Dani's story

After The Fall - Austin's story (17+)

Until We Crash - Jess and Carter's story (17+)

Havenwood Falls Series

Awaken the Soul, Havenwood Falls High

Avenge the Heart, Havenwood Falls High

Co-written with R.K. Ryals:

Dark Seduction, Havenwood Falls Sin & Silk (17+)

Sign up for Michele's newsletter

http://bit.ly/MGMNews

ALSO BY MINDY HAYES

The Faylinn Series - YA Fantasy

Kaleidoscope

Ember

Luminary

Glimmer

The Willowhaven Series - Adult Romance

Me After You

Me Without You

Me To You

Individual titles

The Day That Saved Us – Coming of Age Romance

Stain - Romantic Psychological Suspense

Sign up for Mindy's newsletter

http://bit.ly/mindyhayesnews

To our M&M's
Thank you for your support

...since I left you, I have been constantly depressed. My happiness... incessantly... my memory, your caresses... your... affection... solicitude... comp... forgetting... tinually a burning... me in my heart. When... all solicitude, all harass... shall I be able to pass... time with you, having... love you, and to think only... happiness of... saying, and... ing it to you.

1

Reid

New Year, New Me. A saying spoken mainly by poor souls who likely won't remember their resolutions in two weeks. *Ring out the old, ring in the new.* Words repeated to make oneself feel better about leaving behind one year and heading into the next. *Like a chapter of a book, your story is waiting to be written. Cheers to 365 days of blank pages!* Give me a break. That's like saying I'm gonna start working out—on Monday. Please, every day is a chance to rewrite the narrative. To change the way things go. Beginning with this damn tie.

"Damn hoity-toity Harrises." I yank the unruly checkered tie I haven't worn since Uncle Frank's funeral from around my neck and unbutton the top two buttons at the first red light I come to. *There.*

Why did I accept Loe's invitation to this party? Sure, she's technically my boss, but I have no obligation to spend New Year's Eve at her boyfriend's parents' house, of all places.

2 | MINDY MICHELE

We broke up over six months ago. The sting is still there, but I've come to realize it's more the sting of rejection, of wounded pride. She picked Kip Harris over me. But I wasn't in love with Chloe Lockwood. On my way to it, maybe, but there was always a barrier between us. Not some solid brick wall, but a thick plastic sheet I could never quite pierce. I tried. Over and over it stretched, making progress, but she never fully let me in.

And whatever. Good for her for finding happiness with Harris. He's not a complete prick like I thought. We've both grown up since our pitching rivalry on the varsity baseball team. Most weekends Loe asks me to help at her new land, Kip's there right alongside us—mud slung on his clothes, hair not perfectly coiffed—willing to take part in whatever Loe needs.

Maybe that's why I dug out my navy sport coat and climbed in my truck. Loe's entrusted me with the Lockwood farm while she preps the new land, the least I can do is go to a party when invited.

My truck isn't ancient or in poor condition. It's newer than Loe's classic Chevy, Betty, but the charcoal F-150 stands out like a sore thumb among the Audis and Mercedes lining Marvin Road. I pull up behind a pristine white Volvo and hop out, tugging at my shirt. Even unbuttoned the collar chokes me.

"I could be at home with Dad watching a bowl game with my feet on the coffee table." I watch my warm breath curl in the thirty-degree air as I slip on my coat and finger-comb my too-long hair. "Walking half a block to a party for millionaires. You'd think they'd at least have valet parking." I grumble the entire way toward the lights and sounds of a party well underway.

It's like Buddy the Elf puked Christmas all over the three-story mansion and yard. Though puked is a bit harsh. There's a lot, total overkill, but it's done up nice like they hired someone. The lights strung along the roof are tight and straight like a professional hung them, while wreaths and fresh garland deck the windows and porch. It's the most festive and lavish house in town. Nothing like the plastic reindeer and wayward twinkle lights Wade and I helped Dad put out this year.

I climb the steps, laughter and chatter filtering from around back and through the front door. It opens as I'm about to let myself in.

"Oh." Grace stumbles back, sparkling brighter than the lights hanging on the giant Christmas tree at the end of the front porch. A decorated tree *on the front porch*. Oh, to be filthy rich.

"Hey, Reid." Grace pauses in the doorway.

"Hi." I steal a second glance at a Grace Embry I'm not used to. She's dressed to kill in a flashy gold sequin jumper that leaves little to the imagination. She owns a clothing store, so of course she looks good, but I typically see her at the farm helping out during harvests. She doesn't look like *this* when she's cutting flowers.

Rubbing my chilled hands for warmth, I shift out of her way. "Ditching so soon?"

She shakes her head with a twitch of her light pink lips and slips past. "I'm just grabbing something from my car."

I allow the front door to close, my gaze following Grace as she floats down the marble steps, her heels clicking with each step. "From your car? I just made the two-mile trek from Marvin Road. Do you need help?"

Twirling around, her light blonde hair so white the strands glow under the festive lights hanging along the circular drive, she walks backward. "Two whole miles, huh?" She grimaces. "Actually, I'm parked right over there." She waves toward a cluster of cars in the driveway. The rear bumper of her silver Honda peeks out from behind Kip's Audi.

"Best friend benefits, huh?"

Grace lifts a hand in surrender, and I huff. I'd complain about mistreatment of the common folk, but with what she's wearing, she'd suffer hypothermia if she'd been forced to park as far away as I did.

"There's a ton of food in there." Her upbeat tone draws my attention from her impossibly long legs. "Go have at it. Free food, one perk of a party, am I right?"

I crack a smile. "Only if free alcohol is involved, too."

"It's your lucky night," Grace calls over her shoulder before she disappears between cars.

Exhaling, I rub a hand across my unshaven jaw and step over the threshold. It takes everything in me not to whistle as my eyes rove around the ornate rooms. I didn't grow up poor, but I definitely didn't grow up like this. My dad is an electrical engineer, not a commercial development tycoon.

There are so many people, I doubt Loe will know if I made it. Half of the town mills around the house while the other half is outside under heat lamps. I wouldn't be surprised if Mayor Pete is here. Denton Harris has that kind of sway in Seaside Pointe.

After I grab a plate of food from a long banquet table in the living room, I turn and spot Hayden and Brynn. We're not best friends, but it's better than standing in a crowd alone. Though the more I glance around, the more people I recognize. This party isn't for the elite only. Even May is here, her tassels and rhinestones shimmering in the Christmas lights. As I cross the room, Hayden turns in my direction and tips his chin in greeting.

"You actually showed." He doesn't mask his surprise.

I shrug. "How could I miss a chance to rub elbows with Seaside aristocracy?"

He chuckles and takes a swig of his beer.

Since we've been working together at Loe's land here and there, I've gotten to know him. He's a decent guy, and after what he did for Brynn last summer, I'm inclined to think I want to remain on his good side. I don't know all the details, but the Seaside rumor mill is alive and well. He saved her life and nearly killed a man doing it.

Brynn offers me a smile, but she's in another conversation with some guy in a suit as she holds Hayden's hand.

Hayden's voice lowers as he bends his head toward me. "I'm just glad I'm not the only one here who feels out of place."

"You're dating a Harris. This is your life now." I smirk.

He returns the smirk, the snug hoop ring in his nose twitching, but there's an easy acceptance in his eyes. Maybe Hayden doesn't think he fits in—the piercing and tattoos do make him stand out—but he will soon.

"Have any teaching opportunities opened up for you yet?" I pop a meatball in my mouth.

"Not yet. I'll probably stick around for Chloe for the season. It's hard going into the middle of a school year."

"You better be sticking around for the season." Loe sidles up to my side, Kip in tow. "I need my right-hand man. We've got more to do than we did over the summer and fall combined. Spring is going to be booming."

"If you need, I could send Denise and Meredith over there full time. Maybe we hire a couple more to help out on my side. We've got a well-oiled machine going, as you know. We can spare the more experienced for a few newbies."

"Yeah." Loe waves me off. "We'll figure it out. I don't want to worry about work tonight."

Unsurprising. When the Lockwood farm comes up, she's not keen on staying on the topic for too long. I don't know the last time she spoke to James. Probably not since their big blowup back in June. She doesn't bring him up, and he doesn't mention her. The estrangement is killing her. I know it is, but me handling the flowers on her parents' land is the best option at the moment.

Loe bumps me in the arm with her elbow. "I'm glad you came."

She looks beautiful tonight, decked out in a shimmery silk dress with her wild curls smoothed into an updo. I offer a polite smile. The jury's still out on whether I made the right choice. Kip acknowledges my presence with a head tilt but doesn't speak as he slips his arm around Loe's waist and tugs her into his side. Is he gonna pee on her next? She's yours, Harris. I get it.

"Where can I find one of those?" I gesture to Hayden's hand.

"There's an open bar over there." He points to the room across from us.

"I'm just gonna," I excuse myself with a toss of my hand.

I grab a beer and finish off my food while making the rounds, carrying on lukewarm conversations with people I've known most of my life yet rarely speak with. Exhausted, I head outside to check out the property from this side of the fence.

I wave at those I recognize on my self-guided tour of the yard. It *is* an excellent plot of land. I can't say I blame Lockwood for being pissed about missing out on it.

When I reach the edge of the garden area where the Christmas lights trickle off, a figure moves out of the shadows. A short, curvy, feminine figure.

Mia Mason.

Less than a year ago, I gave Kip crap about going to lunch with her. And yet, when Loe invited me here tonight, all I could think was how I'd like to see Mia again. She's practically a Harris. With it being the holidays, it made sense she'd be home from college. Though, I definitely wasn't planning on getting secluded with her in the dark.

When she helped out on Chloe's farm this summer, there was something about her, something different that wasn't there when I saw her with Kip. More mature, maybe? She was beautiful with her long dark hair and expressive eyes, but her demeanor appealed to me as much as her looks. No matter how many times I ordered my eyes away, they steered back. There's a spark when I look at her. Not a spark of romance or excitement, but this fire in her warm brown eyes that's hard to ignore. Like a bug to a hot lamp, I'm bound to get zapped.

She's eighteen. I'll be twenty-eight in two months. Nothing good would come of getting close to Mia Mason.

"Well, if it isn't Mr. Jump-To-Judgy-Conclusions." Her hips sway as she saunters across the grass in a barely-there dress covered by a fitted coat.

Yeah, I had that coming. "I said I was sorry. You can't blame me for misunderstanding the situation. It's not common to see a guy my age hanging out with a girl your age when you aren't family members. It usually only means one thing."

"Oh?" She sways closer. "And what exactly is that?"

I walked right into that one seeing as how I'm standing alone with her where anyone who stumbles across us could come to the wrong conclusion.

Changing the subject is my best bet. "What are you doing out here all by yourself?"

"I should ask you the same question." Folding her arms across her chest, she lifts a brow. "Don't you know it's rude to snoop around other people's residences?"

"Snoop?" I scoff. "In case you haven't noticed, there's a party going on a few yards away. People hanging out all around this place."

"Still doesn't explain why you're not closer to the party."

"Same goes for you." I'm a guest showing myself around. What reason does a young woman have to hide in the shadows? Unless…is she out here with someone?

Her dark-stained lips curve up at the edges, a hint of a smile, though it's pensive. "I'm more of an outsider these days."

"A semester away doesn't make you an outsider." I slide my hands into the pockets of my suit pants, shielding them from the cold. "Though, you are both a southerner *and* an east coaster now."

Mia feigns shock. Her overly expressive heart-shaped face lights up as those plump lips form a silent 'oh' and her innocent eyes go wide. A bolt of lust zings through my gut. *Eighteen, Reid. She's eighteen.*

She inches closer, her eyes scanning over me. "Imagine that, a girl my age who's so worldly."

Dangerous. That's what she is. The almost ten years between us isn't even the biggest problem. She's basically Kip's little sister. He didn't take a swing at me over Loe, but he'd definitely land a blow if I messed with Mia.

"College makes you worldly, huh? I guess I wouldn't know."

School was never my thing. I like working for Lockwood Blooms. Maybe I settled, but it's a decent career with decent pay and the crew is like family. I can't complain.

"You've been a townie your whole life?" Mia stops less than a foot away from me.

"Never been referred to as that before, but yeah. I guess I am. Seaside born and raised."

"Do you regret it? Never leaving, I mean." Her brows furrow. "Everyone pushed for me to go to college, but honestly, school feels like a giant waste of my time."

"College isn't for everyone, but I wouldn't write it off." I shrug. "What would you have done if not school?"

"Taken a gap year." Her stare shifts off into the distance, glazing over. "There are so many humanitarian projects abroad, or even here in the US. Or doing environmental conservation."

I should hold back my surprise, but I can't. "A do-gooder?"

"Is that such an unexpected thing?"

Honestly? Yeah. Mia looks like she should be on the arm of a wealthy man or on the internet with all the other WAGS of professional athletes. And that makes me sound like a complete and total dick, but it's true. That's what I get. Over and over, I misjudge her.

Circling back to why she's here alone, I double-check. "You're not out here with someone, are you?" I glance beyond her shoulder into the dark again. If he's smart, he's hiding. *I'd* hide.

"Just me, myself, and I." She raises her hands at her sides—flashing more of her bare thighs—before slipping them in her wool coat pockets. "I needed the air. So many people. So much happiness."

Her last words are a whisper like she didn't mean to say them out loud. I consider calling her out but leave her to her thoughts.

Before I speak, she straightens her shoulders and morphs into a different person. A happier person. "Are *you* out here with someone?" Her lips curl into a wide flirtatious smile, flashing deep dimples I haven't noticed before at the edges of her mouth.

"I'm flying solo tonight."

"A good-looking man like yourself all alone?" Her lashes flutter. "You're not still pining for Chloe, are you? I think it's a safe bet that Kip's locked her down."

Everyone assumes I haven't dated anyone seriously since Loe because I'm hung up on her. She's a catch, I know, but is it so hard to believe that I'm fine with the breakup? Maybe not the way things went down, but it is what it is. We can be grown-ups about it.

I keep the bite out of my tone. "I'm well aware, but no. Loe and I are better off as friends. Even without Harris, we weren't a good fit."

"Hey, you want to go for a walk?"

The question jumps out of the blue. "A walk where?"

"Just around the yard. I can't bear to go back inside yet. I promise I don't bite." Something in her eyes says she might if I asked. She's lethal in the best way, but what's real, and how much is the act of a girl who likes flirting with a man? She seems lonely, and it's her loneliness that makes me cave.

Looking over my shoulder and verifying we're not being watched, I give in.

We walk the Harris property, moving further and further from the lanterns lighting the garden. The winter moon is bright enough that if someone looked outside, they could see two bodies wandering even if they can't make out who we are. With that in mind, I maintain a respectable distance from Mia. Every once in a while, she makes a comment about growing up on this property —playing with Brynn and Kip, a birthday party with pony rides —but most of our walk is silent.

Mia stops when the faint shadows of the fenced boundary of the land I work on comes into view. "I made a huge mistake in August, and I don't know how to forgive myself. I don't know how to forget it."

Swiveling my head to see her expression, I try to make sense of what she's talking about.

Her voice is subdued. "I thought I was so smart, keeping him away from her."

My eyes trail her frowning profile, shame tinging her far-off stare. "You might have to be a little more specific if you want me to know what you're talking about."

"I'm the reason Brynn was attacked." Her eyes avoid me as she continues staring at the Lockwood farm. "Her ex-boyfriend kept calling, and I screened the calls without telling her. I didn't want him to enter her life again. If she'd known he was trying to get a hold of her, she would've been more cautious. She never would've been hurt."

Heaviness presses on my chest. Is this why she feels like an outsider? All of this misplaced guilt? I'm not sure why she chose me to confide in, but Mia obviously needs someone to talk to.

"There's something my dad used to say. *Give yourself permission to be human.* I'm sure he was quoting someone else, but sound advice nonetheless. I don't know much about that situation, but I know it wasn't your fault, Mia. You couldn't have known the extremes that guy would go to. You were trying to protect Brynn. No one is to blame but the man who hurt her. Even if you did tell her about him, there's no telling he wouldn't have gotten to her anyway. From what I've heard, he was determined and a little unhinged."

She flicks her hand through the air, her sad smile attesting to my words doing no good. "Nothing is the same. Maybe it's the shock of coming back after being gone for a few months." Twisting around, she peers toward the treeline in the distance and chokes on a stifled laugh. "God, I must sound so dramatic. Forget I said anything."

Shaking my head, I reach for her but think better of it and tuck my hand back in my pocket. "It's not dramatic to have feelings. Some heavy things went down last summer. You're just trying to figure life out. Give yourself time."

Mia's smile is forced. Nothing I say will penetrate the guilt she's encased herself in.

We head back to the house, keeping a small distance between us, though holding back takes self-control. After her broken confession, there's a piece of me that wants to give this girl some comfort.

When we reach the garden bordering the stone patio, we stop. "I should probably go inside," she says. "I imagine I've been missed by more than a few people."

I doubt I've been missed. "You do that. I'm going to head out." I hang back to give some space between the two of us entering the house. Better to avoid everyone seeing us together.

"Hey, Reid?" Her hand catches the sleeve of my coat, and I still. My eyes dart around as this beautifully sad girl closes the space between us and presses a kiss on my cheek. "Thank you for walking with me. And for listening." She drops my sleeve and turns toward the garden path without a backward glance.

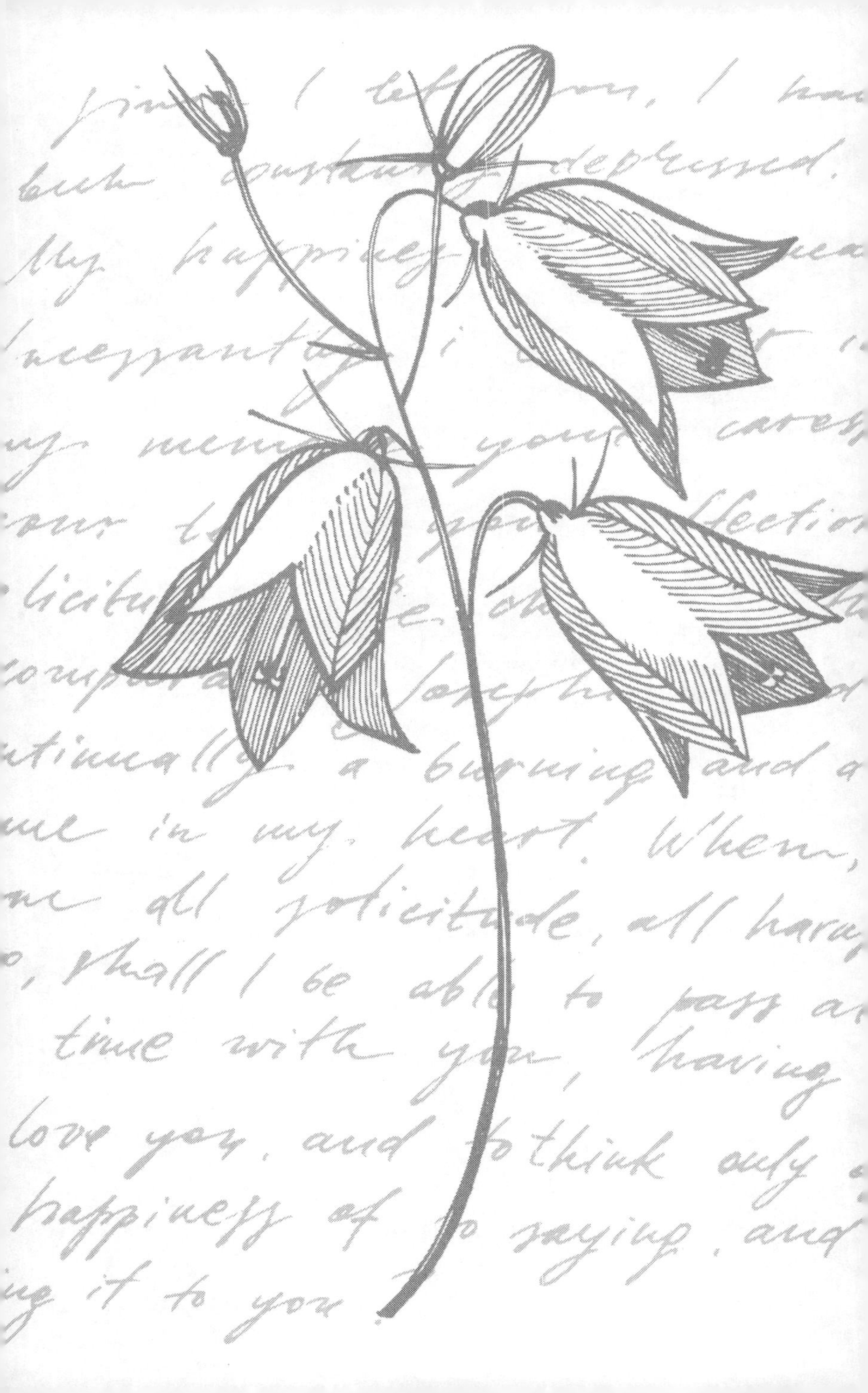

2

Grace

THE HOUSE ERUPTS in booming cheers and clapping. I join in, lifting my glass of merlot to congratulate Brynn and Hayden on their engagement. Brynn's smile stretches from one ear to the other as Hayden nuzzles the top of her copper locks.

I'm happy for her. Really, I am. She's had a rough go in the love department. After I opened Fig, Brynn came in frequently and we grew close, meeting up for lunch and such. I didn't know the extent of Preston's ill treatment toward her, but I knew enough about what kind of jerk he was. And if anyone deserves to find happiness, it's Brynn. Hayden is the perfect man for her.

I just wish it was me.

Not with Hayden. But I wish I was the one announcing I found the love of my life and we were going to live happily ever after. Oh, the clichés our heads are filled with as little girls. They never fade.

First Chloe and Kip—who might as well be engaged—now Brynn and Hayden. Most of my other close friends are either dating someone, engaged, or married. One of my roommates from college recently found out she's pregnant. With twins.

Lucky party of one. *Ding, ding, ding!* That's me.

The cheers grow louder as glasses chime with forks and knives. "Kiss her! Kiss her!" Everyone chants.

Is it hot in here? My rose gold romper has long billowy sleeves, a plunging neckline, and the bottom half is shorts, cutting across mid-thigh. All things considered, I should be freezing. Am I sweating? Trying to be discreet, I fan out my armpits, but it doesn't help. Heat rises up my neck, my head dizzying. I need air.

I head out the back door, but chanting follows me. The deck isn't far enough. Darting down the garden path in my stilettos, I run into Mia on the way.

Her head cants as her dark gaze moves beyond my shoulder to the boisterous house. "What's all the fuss about?"

"Oh, you missed the announcement. Brynn and Hayden are getting married!" I smile. It's genuine. Or as genuine as I can manage.

"What?!" Without saying another word, she bolts for the house.

Watching her go, I keep walking and slam into a hard body. Cool liquid drips down my bare chest between the gap in my romper, soaking me from the neck down.

I jump back, arms out with an empty wine glass in my right hand.

"Oh, crap." A hand darts out and stops short of touching my skin. "I thought you saw me. I'm sorry, Grace."

My eyes lift, and a crimson-stained white dress shirt stretched across a broad chest fills my view. Rising higher, I meet Reid's light green gaze. "Your shirt. Reid, I am *so* sorry."

He looks down and tugs at the row of buttons, pulling the

shirt away from his torso. "It's no big deal, but here." Slipping out of his suit coat, his eyes fall on my exposed cleavage dripping in red. Clearing his throat, he says, "Take this."

"I'll get wine all over it."

Reid holds the dark blue blazer out, waiting for me to slide my arms inside the sleeves. "I really don't care. Use it to dry off. I think you got the worst of it. You must be freezing."

"Thanks." I accept his offering because, while I was burning up seconds ago, the splash of liquid shocked my system. Tugging the coat around me, I dab my front.

"Red wine is a pain to get out, but try using some white vinegar and detergent. It should come clean."

"I was looking for a reason to toss this old shirt anyway." One of his shoulders lifts in a shrug as his mouth curves into something between a smile and smirk. "Every time we've bumped into each other, you've been fleeing the party. Is this a sign that I should leave now before it's too late?"

"Well, it's after eleven, so I think you're stuck now. You have to stay at least until midnight. Ringing in the new year by yourself is unacceptable."

And if I have someone by my side who wants to be here less than I do, it'll make enduring to the end bearable.

"Who says I'm by myself?" He arches a brow.

I tilt my head and peer around him. "Did you bring an invisible date?"

"No, I have her tied up in the bed of my truck for safekeeping. I didn't want her to get any ideas and run off with another guy before the clock strikes twelve."

His self-deprecating humor pulls a short laugh from me. "Smart. How embarrassing not to have a New Year's Eve kiss."

"Exactly." His eyes light with amusement. "I take it you're all paired up for the night and don't need to hold your date hostage in your car."

"If I had anyone to tie up, that would have been my first

order of business." I spread my arms out. "Alas, merlot was my date for the night, which we're both now wearing."

"I made you spill your date. Let me get you another one." Reid moves to step around me.

I wave him off with a chuckle. "No, it's fine. I'm better off without it. Wine hangovers are the worst, and that was my second glass. Drunk Grace might be fun, but she is mortifying."

"I wouldn't say mortifying. Obnoxious, maybe."

I shove his shoulders. "You've seen me drunk like once."

Reid laughs. "It was enough. Loe shared many stories to back your *spirited* antics of that night."

It's not often I get Chloe to let loose with me, but after James's stroke, the woman was close to having a nervous breakdown herself. We might've tipped back one too many shots at The Taproom. I remember very little from that night.

"What can I say? A woman's got to let her hair down every once in a while."

Reid scratches the scruff along his cut jawline. "Did I hear you right? Brynn and Hayden are getting married?"

Tugging his suit coat tighter, I fold my arms across my chest. "Yeah, those crazy kids are making it official."

"That was quick."

"Kind of makes sense for them, though. I've never met a couple who fell as fast and hard as they did. With as noncommittal as Hayden was in the beginning, Brynn needed to take him off the market," I joke.

"I don't know. You haven't been working alongside him all summer and fall. The guy is crazy about her."

What that must be like.

Reid cocks his head to the side with a furrowed brow. I said that out loud, didn't I?

If Reid were a prospect to date, I might be embarrassed by how vocal I'm being about my pitiful love life and lack of men lining up.

All I manage is a shrug. "As happy as I am for them, I came outside to avoid the engagement excitement. What are you doing out here?"

Unease flashes across his face before he replaces it with nonchalance. "Just checking out the land, seeing what Lockwood missed out on. I've never been here before."

"There's not much to explore in the dark and in the dead of winter. You should see it during the summer. I came for a couple of parties, and it's no wonder the Harris family bought it all up. I would have, too."

The corner of his mouth tugs up. "Seeing the view from our side, I can only imagine." A slight shiver tenses his arms, and Reid's hands shove in his pants pockets.

"This is stupid. You shouldn't suffer because I'm a klutz." I move to slip my arms from the sleeves of his jacket.

"I'm a big boy." He reaches out, moving closer, and holds the lapels shut. "I can handle a little cold."

And just like that, there's an uptick in my heartbeats, the chill receding from my chest. *Huh?*

I shake my head, knocking it toward the deck. "Not necessary. I can go up by the heat lamps."

"Same as me." Reid takes a step to the side and gestures for the stairs, silently encouraging me to go first.

Giving him a slight smile, I surrender and make my way up the garden path. One heat lamp stands in each of the four corners of the deck. We take the unoccupied one on the far left, furthest from the house.

"Do you think people actually like parties? Or is it one of those things that, in theory, it's a good idea, but when it comes to planning one or showing up and partaking in all of the small talk, we instantly regret it?"

I chuckle. "Maybe I'm crazy, but I love parties. Don't get me wrong. I'm one hundred percent a homebody after talking to customers at work all day, but when the party consists of people I want to be around, count me in. Call me an extroverted introvert."

"So, this shindig." He gestures to the random people milling around the deck. "Happy to be here or counting down the minutes until you can leave?"

About ten minutes ago, I was ready to peace out. I'd had my fun and enough fifth wheel time with Kip and Chloe and Hayden and Brynn, but things are looking up with Reid's help. "Both?"

His nod bounces from side to side like he's gauging my answer.

"Since I practically forced you to stay, what about you? Are you looking for a way to ditch me now?"

He pulls an exaggerated cringe before shaking his head with a laugh. "Nah. I wouldn't say I'm happy to be here, but you're not terrible."

An amused grunt leaves me. "Thanks for that."

The rhythmic countdown to midnight filters through the back door. "Ten, nine…"

Is it midnight already?

"What do ya say, Embry?" Reid leans into me with an impish turn of his mouth. "Since my date is bound in the back of my truck and yours is coloring our clothes… Spare us the humiliation and be my kiss at midnight?"

He might be on my off-limits list of men to date, but a kiss wouldn't mean anything. Just a peck between friends. It'd be nice to not be solo for once when the New Year's countdown ends.

"Why the hell not?"

The chorus of shouts continues from inside, giving us our cue. "Three, two, one."

Playfully, Reid grabs the front of his suit coat in one hand and brings his mouth down on mine. The kiss doesn't last long, but long enough that I notice the softness of his lips pairing with the roughness of his scruff. He plants one more short one before my eyes open.

When we pull away, there's a crease between his eyebrows. It matches the one indenting my face. And then laughter bursts out of the two of us.

"Happy New Year, Pruitt."

"Happy New Year, Embry."

CURLED into my couch's corner with a sketchpad propped against my knees, I sketch a dress that's been running through my mind all day. I finish off a high, ruffled neckline, but the design doesn't feel complete. I tap the eraser of the pencil on my chin. Could add a ruffle on the hem, maybe? No, that might be too much.

My phone buzzes beside me. There's no picture, just a number. A recognizable Seattle number.

Drew.

Like every other time he's called, my stomach tenses and my breathing stalls. Rather than hit *Decline*, I silence it and continue with my sketch.

Over the TV's droning in the background, the deadbolt on the front door clicks and Chloe walks through. "Honey, I'm home."

"It's about dang time," I tease. "I assume you're grabbing clean clothes to head over to Kip's for Valentine's Day weekend."

"You guessed correctly."

I glance up at the swoony tone of her voice. She's so in love—it's sort of disgusting. "A gift from Kip?" I chuckle, nodding at the poppy-covered sweatshirt I've never seen before.

"Correct again." She tugs the white-lettered *I love it when you call me big poppy* away from her chest with a grin.

Toeing off her boots at the door, Chloe sinks down next to me and peeks over my shoulder. "Drawing up a new one?"

"Yeah, I had a thought about these long lantern sleeves with this short two-tiered skirt."

"It's pretty. I could see it hanging in Fig."

If only. "That'd be a dream."

"Doesn't have to only be a dream. Are you ever going to do anything with your designs?"

"I'd love to. Maybe someday, but finding the right materials and manufacturer won't be cheap. Can I afford to do it in the states, or would I have to outsource? There's also typically a minimum order quantity. I don't know. There's a lot to learn and consider. While trying to run Fig, it would take a lot of time to make this happen."

"Well, you should bump it up the priorities list. I'm not kidding, Grace." She pulls the sketchpad from my lap for a closer look. "If not Fig, you could honestly sell a line to Nordstrom or something. I love everything about this dress. It's very feminine, very you."

Resting my head on her shoulder, I say, "It's still missing something. Maybe a skinny belt or row of tiny shank buttons down the center?"

"Why not both?"

I tilt my head, eyes tracing the lines of the design. *Both.* "That's actually not a bad idea, Loe. Look at you with fashion ideas."

"I may not be designer knowledgeable, but I've hung around you long enough to pick up a thing or two about style."

Slipping the sketchpad from her grasp, I pencil in a belt with a simple oval buckle. "Did you get lunch with your mom today?"

She works her jaw. "Yeah, we went to Pizza Pie Café, but I had to get back to the farm, so we didn't have a ton of time together."

"How's she doing?"

A heavy sigh falls from Chloe as I add dainty buttons. "Miserable. When my dad isn't giving her the silent treatment, he's snapping or giving her grunts for answers. And I'm sure there's more she's not telling me."

I pause, setting my pencil down. "Do you think he's gotten physical with her?"

"What? No. Nothing like that. He's acting unreasonable, that's all. I don't know what to do for her."

"He hasn't softened even a little?"

Her head shakes. "At this point, he never will."

"And she's going to stick around? Put up with that?"

"Where else is she going to go? Is she supposed to give up on a thirty-seven-year marriage?"

"I'm not saying she give up on the marriage, just…" I angle my body toward Chloe. "My house is tiny, but you're rarely here as it is. She could move in with us for a bit, just for a little break."

"Stay with us? I don't think it'll come down to that. My parents have been together since high school. They're…" She fingers a curl, covering her unease. "This is a rough patch. Certainly, it's just his health and this issue with Kip, and—"

"It was a suggestion, Loe. I'm sure it's a non-issue, but if it becomes one, the offer stands."

She pauses, studying my face. "You'd be okay with my mom crashing your single lifestyle?"

An uncontrollable laugh spits out. "Do you see any men lining up at my door? It's a Friday night, and I'm in flannel pajamas watching home renovation shows."

Though, if I answered one of Drew's calls, would this still be the case? What does he want? After all of this time, and nearly two months later of avoidance, he remains persistent.

His unexpected gift from Christmas is tucked away in my nightstand. I haven't opened the popcorn or lemon drops. I haven't even unwrapped the plastic on the DVD case, leaving everything enclosed in the package it arrived in.

It took me weeks to listen to the first voicemail he left. Though his voice was benevolent, the message was short and to the point, like him. *Grace, I really want to talk. Please, call me back.*

I don't want to call him back. Drew broke my heart. It took too long to put myself together. My biggest fear is what if inviting him in unravels all that I accomplished?

"You choose to stay in," Chloe says, bringing me back. "We have plenty of single friends you could go out with."

"Really." I raise an eyebrow. "Plenty? Name one I'd have a good time with."

She opens her mouth, then falters, closing it.

"It's fine." I wave her off. "Run the idea by Robyn. It's not forever, but if she needs some space, I'm happy to provide it. She shouldn't have to suffer in her own home. I'm gone most of the day, so she could still have her privacy."

"I don't know that she'd take you up on the offer, but I'll mention it." Chloe circles her arms around my shoulders. "You're a good friend, Grace Elizabeth."

"Right back atcha, Chloe Mae."

since I left you, I have
been constantly depressed.
My happiness
incessantly
my memory your caress
your
licitude
Josephine
ntinually a burning
me in my heart. When,
all solicitude, all harass
, shall I be able to pass a
time with you, having
love you, and to think only
happiness of saying, and
ing it to you.

3

Reid

WE'RE NEARING the first official day of spring—our busiest season of the year.

In my rain gear, I crouch alongside Charlie and Eric in the daffodil patch, harvesting blooms. There's a faint mist in the air, but rain or shine, the flowers can't wait. The flowers wait, and we lose our window. We lose our window, and we lose money.

"Why isn't Denise with Meredith?" Eric peers over his shoulder at the brunette kneeling in the mud a few rows down.

"I sent her to help out Loe today."

God knows Loe wasn't going to ask if I didn't make the decision for her. She's so bound and determined to get this Lockwood extension operating, but she's going to run herself into the ground in the process.

Eric shifts down the line, snipping stem after stem. "In a few weeks, we'll have our work cut out for us when the trees and shrubs arrive if we're down a person."

"At least having them will slow the constant wind that barrels through the valley," Charlie says, always the peacemaker. "The flowers have been getting a beat down."

"Chloe needs the help. I get it." Eric pauses, cutting Charlie off. "But if Denise or you keep leaving us for that new land, we'll need to get a couple more sets of hands. It was hard enough losing Chloe. We can't keep up with the demand shorthanded."

I cross my arms. Of course, none of us want to leave Loe hanging at her new site, but I understand the guys' frustration. It's unfair to any of them when they have to work twice as hard because we're dipping out on them. Plus, here, we all work for Lockwood Blooms. The new farm is Chloe's Blooms. Sure, it's an extension of LB in her mind, but I'm not so sure James feels the same.

"All right. I agree. Loe and I will get together and discuss some solutions."

It's hard keeping James out of it, though. Now that Loe doesn't come around and he's eighty-five percent physically recovered from his stroke, he's a lot more present. He can't hack working in the fields like he used to, but he sure wants his hand in the rest of the business, which I understand. In all fairness, Lockwood Blooms *is* his company, even if it'll be Chloe's someday. But ever since their falling out, things haven't been the same. Loe had an aggressive model for moving the flower farm forward, and since she's gone, James is reverting everything to the way things were.

I mean, I get it. He doesn't like the Harrises, but to shut out your daughter because of it? I was wronged by a Harris, too. You don't see me quitting and leaving Chloe hanging. Some things aren't worth the trouble and grief. Some people are more important, and she's not even my blood.

Grabbing his bucket of one of the trial variety daffodils, Eric says, "I'll go help Meredith with the anemones and hyacinths."

"He's not going because she needs the help," Charlie whispers.

I chuckle under my breath. "Good luck to him. Mere has her sights set on Caleb McCarthy."

"She told you that?"

Shrugging, I say, "I overheard her and Denise a couple weeks ago."

Now that Denise is engaged and Chloe's practically engaged, Meredith feels like a spinster who will wind up old and gray and single. Girl talk. I can't escape the gossip on this flower farm.

He snorts. "Poor Eric."

"I played ball with Caleb. Meredith is better off without him, but I'm not getting in the middle of that one."

Caleb was a piece of work in high school, and he's only made more of a name for himself as Seaside's eternal bachelor, hopping from one bed to the next. We're friendly, but Meredith is too good to be chasing after him.

"You want to head to Shooters later? I could use a night to let off some steam, and something tells me you could use one, too."

Is it that obvious? Running this farm, pitching in with Loe, and playing mediator between her and James, I'm exhausted.

I sigh. "Yeah. Why not?"

I WALK through the thick wooden door of Shooters and take in the locals mingling at the bar and around the dimly lit pool tables. On the far side, the dance floor is crowded. It's a Tuesday night, but that's not stopping anybody.

"Let's grab some drinks and play a round of pool," Charlie says.

We make our way to the pool tables, beers in hand. One table is unused, the other is surrounded by a small group of women. I check out the group and find myself staring at a pair of tan thighs attached to toned legs bent over in a short skirt. Not a terrible welcome. My eyes scan from the high-heeled boots on her feet all the way up as she rights herself. One toss of her long dark hair gives me a glimpse of her profile.

My gut somersaults.

Mia Mason.

I blink away the lust-haze. She's back in town to tempt me. With it being mid-March, it must be spring break.

Mia peers over her shoulder as we approach the tables. Recognizing me, her mouth curves into a coy smile. "Well, hey there, Mr. Pruitt."

Internally, I groan. *Please don't call me that.* It makes me sound like a pervy old man. I'm not *that* much older than her, but I am old enough to know better.

"Mia." I tip the top of my bottle toward her.

"And who's your friend?" She offers Charlie the same flirtatious grin she gave me, spinning all the way around to face us. Her charms aren't reserved for me, and for some dumb reason, that bothers me.

"Charlie, Mia. Mia, Charlie. He works on the farm with me."

"Hi, Charlie. These are my friends. Halie and Andrea."

Each of them lifts a little wave and a smile, eyeing both of us. They look the same age as Mia. Shooter's is an eighteen and over bar, so I wouldn't doubt if they graduated the same year she did.

"How do you two know each other?" Charlie tips back his drink as he eyes me with piqued curiosity. Mia might look physically mature for her age, but she still appears too young for me.

"Through Kip and Chloe," I answer before she can. With Mia's unpredictable mouth, who knows what she'd come up with? "Her mom works for Harris Development."

Behind the back of her hand, Mia pretends to whisper to Charlie. "He thought Kip was robbing the cradle when he caught us grabbing lunch last year. When really, Kip's more like my older brother."

I sigh, but a small chuckle leaves me. "You're never going to let me live that down, are you?"

"You're just too fun to tease."

And I like her teasing too much.

I back away toward the other pool table. "Well, you ladies have fun. Charlie and I are going to play a game."

Holding the cue stick at her side, Mia pops her hip. "Why don't you boys join us?"

Yeah, that's *a good idea.* It's bad enough she's in the same bar as I am. Hanging around her is asking for trouble. The happy couple probably doesn't go out much during the week, but if word gets back to Harris somehow that I'm with Mia at Shooters, we can say goodbye to our shaky truce.

"We don't want to crash your girls' night. We've got a guys' night all of our own to have."

Her dark brow raises. "Scared of losing to a girl, Reid?"

It's the first time she's used my name, and I hate how much I like it. Maybe I need to remain Mr. Pruitt. Put my head where it belongs.

I look to Charlie for backup, but he shrugs, and Mia notices, an impish smile pulling the corners of her lips.

"Fine. One game." I hold up a finger as I set my bottle at the corner of the table.

Friend One and Two—I really should have paid attention when Mia introduced them—whisper back and forth before the brunette excuses herself. "I'll let you four play. I'm going to interrupt our buddies over there."

She saunters her way toward a table of guys who look more their age, which makes it so glaringly apparent we're not.

"Rack 'em up." Mia slaps the triangle against my chest. "Ladies break first."

"What are we playing for?" A mischievous smirk stretches wide as Charlie eyes the girls.

"What do you want?" Friend Two asks. Mia rolls her eyes and

smacks her girlfriend's butt, making Charlie's eyes gleam and my lips twitch as I rack the balls.

"I don't think it would be fair to make a wager with these two, Halie. They've never seen us play."

Oh, girl's got swagger.

Mia steps directly beside me as I remove the triangle from the table and move back, needing to keep space between us. "What are you doing home for spring break and not partying at the beach?"

"If you want to see me in my bikini, you're welcome to join us at the beach tomorrow." She leans over the table and breaks the balls with precision. A stripe sinks into the left back pocket, and Mia offers a coy bounce of her shoulders.

"Unfortunately, some of us have to work," I say as Halie lines up the next shot and misses.

I motion for Charlie to take his turn first as Mia steps closer, leaning against her pool cue and peering up at me.

"That is unfortunate." Mia's full bottom lip pouts. "I've heard a lot of stories about how working on the Lockwood farm turns men into steel. I wouldn't mind seeing the proof for myself."

Stories about Hayden, no doubt. I hear similar things from Meredith and Denise. My fingers tighten around my cue. She's amped up her flirting since Christmas. I still can't decide if I'm a fool for liking it.

Mia chuckles as Charlie misses the pocket with a curse. She circles the table, her brown eyes flitting from the green surface to my face with each step. She picks a shot and bends low, the neck of her top gaping and giving me a peek at the swell of her ample cleavage.

The crack of the cue ball hitting the blue striped ten is sharp, sinking the ball into a side pocket. She's good. Better than Charlie and I combined.

"To answer your question about why I'm here in Seaside

instead of some exotic location is simple; I'm here to pick out my dress for Brynn and Hayden's wedding."

"You're skipping spring break for your family?" Charlie asks while Halie sinks another ball. *Damn, that's three down for them—zero for us.*

Mia looks at him. A fiery little spark in her eyes makes me jealous. Does she look at all guys that way? Maybe I'm nothing special? "I love my family." She gives him a pointed look then knocks another ball down.

Pool shark.

"Besides, I go to school on the Georgia coast. You think this little body doesn't see the beach every other day?"

When I catch Charlie eyeing her sun-kissed curves, I punch him in the shoulder. Maybe I shouldn't be looking at her, but it doesn't mean I'm okay with him doing it, too.

Halie tugs on Charlie. "C'mon, we should let Mia clean the table. You weren't getting another turn anyway. Wanna dance?" She's a pretty blonde. I'm not surprised Charlie follows her without a second glance back. *Some wingman he is.*

Mia playfully wiggles her fingers at her friend and rounds the table to stand by me.

"Are you not going to give me one shot?" I eye the seven solid balls still spread across the table before us.

She nudges between me and the table and bends her behind into my pelvis. I take a step back. Looking over her shoulder, she smiles. "At this game? No." *Thunk.* The green fourteen sinks.

Leaning against the wall, I wait for a turn that doesn't come. True to her friend's prediction, Mia wins.

"Well, that was fun." I lay my cue on the table. "I believe I've been hustled."

A long stare stretches between us, the tension building as the music drifts around the room.

Mia fans her shirt. "Want to get some fresh air? I worked up a sweat beating you." Her cheeks are flushed red.

"A bit of a sore winner, are we?" I shake my head, and Mia laughs. The sound is musical. She's such a compelling mix of innocence and sensuality. I can tell myself I'm not interested, but I'd be lying.

I take her palm in mine with a sigh and lead her out the back doors where Shooters opens to a large patio and grassy area. There are party lights strung from the building into trees, keeping the grounds lit but not blinding. Dropping her hand once we're out of the crowd, we walk further.

"I never would have guessed you were a little pool shark."

She twists her long thick waves around her hand, cooling her neck. "Thank Kip."

What is it with those two?

Her eyes narrow as though she can read my thoughts. *My jealousy?* "You certainly must know the story of how the Harrises took me and my mother in when she first arrived here?"

"Vaguely," I admit. Everyone knows the basic story. Mostly because Denton Harris is known to most as a ruthless businessman. The only soft spots he has are for his family, Carrie-Ann and Mia Mason. Last year he added Chloe to that list when Kip fell in love with her.

"You know you weren't wrong to imply something improper between Kip and me."

I'm sorry, *what?*

Her small hand grabs my forearm. "Oh, no. No, not like that," she rushes, her face blanching at where my thoughts went. "What I meant is, I crushed on Kip for years. I promise you he has *never* been inappropriate toward me, no matter how much I dreamt he might. He's been the best big brother a girl could have. He taught me how to drive, surf, throw a curveball…"

"And play pool?"

"Exactly." Her fingers tighten on my bare arm. "I can also shoot some mean darts and have quite the poker face. Or so I'm told."

She leans up, pressing closer toward my body, and I find myself bending forward. "All things a smart girl should know before going off to college."

"Don't worry. He also taught me how to throw a proper punch." Her free hand brushes my waist, drawing me even closer.

"Hopefully you don't feel the need to demonstrate that as you did your pool game."

"Only if you chicken out."

"Chicken out?" I repeat, and she pops onto her toes, bringing us inches apart.

"Aren't you curious?" Her full lips lengthen into a beguiling smile. Chickening out is the furthest thing from my mind as I brace her with my palm on the base of her spine.

I'm a red-blooded man, and she's a beautiful girl. Of course I've wondered. My pride took a lashing when Chloe tossed me aside for Kip. Maybe Mia is the cure. Just this once, our lips brush.

Her mouth is full and soft. I could sink into a long kiss with this girl and enjoy the hell out of it, but Mia Mason isn't a band-aid for my ego. I can't use her that way. Stepping back, I pull off my ball cap and comb my fingers through my hair before replacing my hat.

What did we talk about last time? What can I possibly ask her to redirect us? I clear my throat. "How are things with you and Brynn?"

She looks down at her hands, spinning the silver ring on her middle finger. "I still hate myself. You know Preston pled guilty and is rotting in prison for at least the next ten years, right?" I nod, and Mia grunts with disgust. "You'd think the sentence for premeditated attempted murder would be harsh, but nope. The screwed-up rich man who makes a deal gets some leeway. Too bad the Harris family knows a lot of judges in this state. I doubt he'll ever see parole." She leans against a tree outside of the light's reach. "So anyway, the fear of a trial was a big deal for Brynn, and

Hayden, too. Preston being sentenced helped things. They picked their wedding date, started making more plans for their future. I guess you already knew these things. You work with the man. I forget about that."

"I've heard things here and there, but I don't work with Hayden every day. I don't know much. I didn't even know the ex's name." Hayden is a private guy, and he only referred to the offender in expletives. Understandably so.

"You found a way to change the subject quickly." Mia chews on her bottom lip, cocking her head. "Was the kiss too much?"

"I wouldn't say that." I wish I knew how I felt. I want to protect her and devour her all at once. "But don't pretend you don't see the obvious complications."

"What ever are you talking about? Yes, your boss, who also happens to be your ex, is practically married to my almost brother. And sure, you were ten when I was born. Oh, and fine, I'm a college student in Georgia, and you live on the Washington coast." Her face pulls in mock horror. "You call those complications? I thought you were braver than that."

I chuckle. "Bravery doesn't have anything to do with it." More like logic and decency.

She sobers. "It's probably best this way."

I tuck a strand of her hair behind her ear. "Yeah, let's quit while we're ahead. Another round of pool? But maybe you let me play this time."

"You want me to go easy on you?"

"At least something to let me leave with a little bit of my dignity intact." I wink.

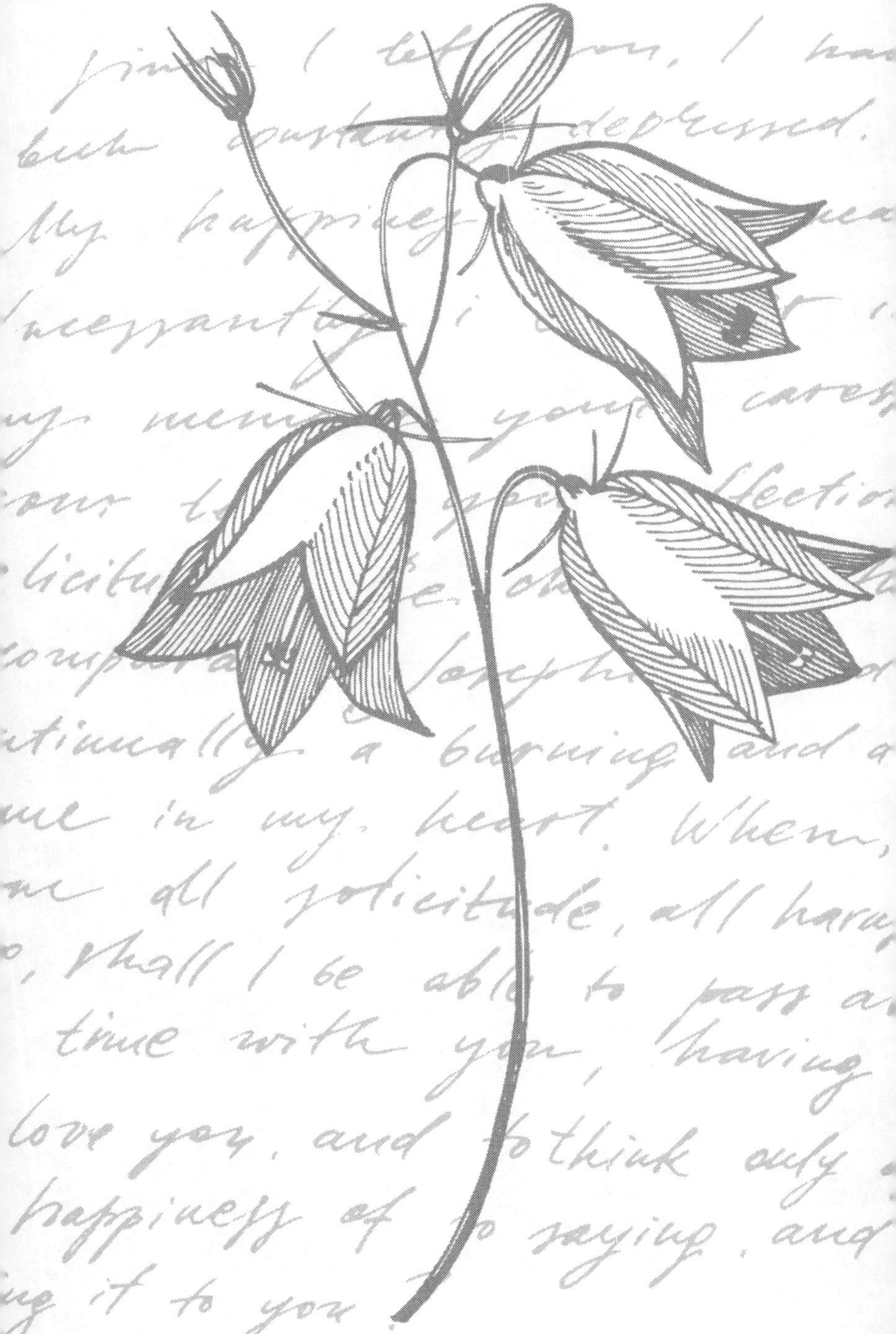

4

Grace

MARKET.

Quite possibly my favorite place to be, surrounded by like-minded people and hundreds of clothing vendors, waiting to discover my summer finds for Fig. It's day two, so I've already done my rounds and narrowed my list of wants. Today is buying day. With the success of the shop, I've got more money to work with than previous years, so my fingers itch to snag my favorite pieces. A few bold and breezy tops as well as delicate and dreamy floral dresses. There's a salmon fit and flare eyelet shirtdress that I cannot wait to get my hands on. And the daintiest rose gold necklaces and rings that must be mine—and Fig's.

Last night I enjoyed the L.A. nightlife and grabbed drinks with a few seasoned boutique owners I met my first year at market. They took me under their wing after finding me with my deer-caught-in-the-headlights stare, clueless on where to begin with so much to look at. I'll never forget their mercy and kindness, offering the most valuable advice. And I've never felt more seen than last night after sharing stories about nightmare vendors they'd never work with again and impossible-to-please customers.

I stick an address label with all of my information on another order form as my phone buzzes from my shoulder bag.

"Thank you so much." I wave to the vendor and back away, digging my phone out. I check the screen.

DO NOT ANSWER displays across the white backdrop.

Yeah, I renamed the number in case I get any bright ideas.

Like every other time, my gut seizes, my chest constricting. I silence the call. This is the fifth time Drew's called. I still haven't answered. He's bound to give up at some point, right? His last voicemail was on the verge of begging. I'm half-tempted to answer to tell him to stop calling, while the other part of me fears engaging because I'll cave. Whether he's good for me or not, I'll hear his voice and fall into old habits. His charm was one of the reasons I continued going back to him over and over again, no matter how bad he was for my heart.

As I slip my phone back into my purse, it rings again. He wouldn't call twice in a row, would he? I breathe a sigh of relief when Chloe's wild curls fill my screen.

"Hey, Loe. What's going on?"

"How serious were you about my mom moving in with us?"

I pause, taking in her words. "Why? What happened?"

Her voice is subdued, near defeat when she says, "I'm not sure. She didn't want to go into details. When I told her about your offer, she didn't hesitate for long, which has me more concerned. It's so unlike her."

"Are you all right?"

"I don't know. I don't know what I am. All I know is last spring my dad hung the stars and moon, and now he's shattering every last piece of our family."

I've always been a fixer, someone good at listening and giving advice. This situation leaves me speechless. I have no idea what I'd do if my dad became a man I didn't recognize. I'd be beside myself, completely heartbroken.

"I'm here for both of you. Whatever you need."

"Thanks, Grace. I'm going to help her pack up and move her in tomorrow morning."

"I'll be back tomorrow evening, so the extra bedroom isn't ready. The bed's not made and it's covered in a bunch of my crap." Miscellaneous things. Fashion magazines, swatches, used sketchpads. Unwearable articles of clothing I sewed from the designs I've drawn. I don't want anyone to see those.

"Don't worry about it. She can have my bed for the night. I'll probably stay with Kip anyway. He's trying so hard to help. He even offered Mom his spare room." Chloe huffs a dismal laugh. "Can you imagine?"

Though it seems entirely out of character for her father, with Brynn's experience with Preston, and James's erratic behavior, my mind can't help going to dark places. "Loe, is Robyn okay? He hasn't…"

A heavy sign flows through the phone. "Yeah, she's been pretty tight-lipped, but I don't think he's laid a hand on her. She's more fed up than anything else. I'm hoping with time away from him, she'll open up a bit more. Or maybe he'll see what his actions have caused. Before, I thought maybe the stroke was the cause—and it could be part of it—but I don't know at this point. He's not my father. I don't know this man."

"Time apart may do them both some good. He might need to hit rock bottom, losing you both before he sees the error of his ways."

Chloe is silent on the other end before she murmurs, "Hopefully. And not that you would, but can we keep this between us? My mom doesn't want anyone to know yet, and you know how Seaside gets."

"You don't even need to ask."

As soon as I open the front door of my little bungalow-style house, warmth radiates from inside. All the lights are on with cars in the driveway: Chloe's truck and Robyn's hatchback. Italian spices and garlic permeate the air.

"Welcome home." Robyn lifts her head from where she sits at my kitchen island, facing the living room where Chloe lounges on the couch. While Robyn smiles, it doesn't quite reach her eyes. Maybe even a hint of embarrassment tinges the hazel irises, which I hate seeing. She has *nothing* to be embarrassed about.

"Robyn, this place smells amazing."

"Oh, it's nothing. I just wanted you to have a home-cooked meal to return to after your days of eating out."

"That's so sweet of you. Thank you." I round the counter and give her a hug. There's an extra squeeze in her touch, and I reciprocate. A silent exchange of gratitude.

"It's no problem." She pulls away, back to assembling the dinner—lasagna. "And don't think this is a one-time thing. I'll earn my keep. You'll never go hungry with me here."

I chuckle. "Robyn, there is no earning your keep. You do not need to cook every night. I'm a big girl. I cook, so can Loe. You're not responsible for us."

"Oh, I know that," she swats the air before wrapping foil across the casserole dish, "but I'd like to. It'll help keep me busy."

I don't want to remind her why she's trying to stay busy or take away the woman's need for an outlet, so all I do is nod.

Bending down to slide the glass dish in the oven, she says, "It needs to bake for about forty-five minutes, so I'm going to take a shower and put on some comfy clothes."

"Now we're talking," I say. "Come join the girl time when you're done."

Her smile brightens as she leaves the kitchen, down the hallway. It occurs to me that Robyn probably never had this before she married James, considering their wedding was only a couple years out of high school. She didn't go to college or live on her own. Not that there's anything wrong with that, but a little female time is good for the soul.

I settle on the couch beside Chloe with a relieved sigh. Traveling is the worst. Nothing beats the comfort of my home.

"How was market?"

"Amazing. I can't wait to have the items in Fig. Plus, I found a few things you won't be able to resist. You'll look incredible in them."

"My dad asked Reid to take over Lockwood Blooms."

I rear back. "I'm sorry, what?"

"The farm. My future legacy."

That's utter bull. "What did Reid say?"

"He's conflicted, of course. He doesn't want to turn down the offer, but it's obviously a family business. Reid knows it should be mine. How hard I've worked for it."

"What did he tell James?" Please tell me he didn't say yes. After hanging out with him on New Years, he burrowed a small space in my mind, a niggling sense of curiosity. And that kiss. That unexpected kiss. It wasn't much, but it was enough for my brain to return more than once over the last few months. Most likely because I haven't been kissed in years.

"He said he'd think about it. Reid wanted to talk to me before making any decisions."

That's respectful of him.

"While I want him to turn the offer down, he's worked just as hard as me over the last few years. He's really stepped up with my dad's stroke and then with getting my farm up and running. He's undertaking so much more responsibility. It makes sense that he'd get a piece of the pie."

I rest my hand on her knee. "I mean, sure, Reid is deserving of a lot, but this is your birthright, Chloe. Not just because of your Lockwood blood. You've poured your heart and soul, blood, sweat, and tears into these farms. You've given everything to not only keep it thriving but expanding. Lockwood Blooms wouldn't even have this new land if not for you."

Chloe gave up college, for goodness' sake. Though she never talks about it or views it as a sacrifice. If she could've added a horticulture or business degree to her resume, imagine what more she could've done for Lockwood Blooms with all that knowledge. But James wanted her here, made her believe she didn't need it, that being hands-on was going to teach her more than any classroom could. And maybe that's true, but maybe not. He's been running on the same business model that his father did and his before him. The world is constantly evolving. Marketing isn't the same as it was even five years ago. Change and development are essential, and Chloe knows that. She's the one who got them online, created their social media pages, and keeps them updated. James should be on his knees thanking his daughter, not handing the business to someone else out of spite.

"I'm trying not to resent Reid because it's not his fault my dad is offering him an amazing opportunity on a gold platter."

It is hard to blame him, but he hasn't earned a stake in the business the way Chloe has. "What are you going to do if he accepts?"

"Hope that he wants to keep Chloe's Blooms under the Lockwood umbrella and continue a partnership, I guess."

"Does Reid know how you feel about it?" I may not know him that well, but surely if he knew, he'd refuse James.

Her smile is dry as she snorts a laugh. "I didn't need to say a word. He read the expression on my face quite clearly."

Poor Reid.

Poor Chloe.

Damn you, James Lockwood.

...jim, I left you, I have
been constantly depressed.
My happiness... ...ua
Incessantly... ...
...my mem... your cares
...our l... ...flection
...licitu... ...se ch...
...compa... ...longhi...
...tinually, a burning and a
...me in my heart. When,
...e all solicitude, all haras...
..., shall I be able to pass a...
...time with you, having
...love you, and to think only ...
...happiness of... ...saying, and
...ing it to you.

5

Reid

MARCH AND APRIL bring endless hours of work on every flower farm, but add in opening a second location and planning and decorating the Lockwood Blooms float for last week's annual May Day Festival, and I was anticipating not setting the alarm for this morning. Or I was until Loe wakes me with a text asking me to help out for a few hours. There goes my first Saturday off in months, but Kip has construction meetings for Riverfront and Hayden needs the day to help with wedding plans. A tux fitting? Or cake testing? I don't know, and it doesn't matter. They're not available, so I'm working. It's probably a good thing. Loe and I haven't worked together alone since James floored me with the idea of my taking over the business. I told Loe I'd put off James to give her time to work things through with him, but he wasn't pleased with my lack of enthusiasm.

Morning always comes too quickly after five full days at the farm, but the sun is out in full effect for the first time in days, so I guess there's a silver lining. Tugging on my ball cap and grabbing my coffee, I head out the door.

"Hey, you remember Mia Mason? The Harrises—I don't even know what to call her." Chloe chuckles. "You know, the underage girl you accused Kip of cheating on me with last spring?"

It takes everything I have to keep a straight face as I help Loe unfold the landscape fabric for the freshly prepped zinnia beds. "What about her?"

"She's coming home for the summer in a couple weeks and needed a job, so I hired her to work at the farm with you guys."

My head whips up.

"That's not a problem, is it? You guys are still in need of help, even after you hired Julian and Vanessa in March, right?"

I school my features. "Yeah, no. That's great, but why isn't she helping on your farm?"

Chloe stiffens, and I curse under my breath. Lockwood Blooms and the newly named Chloe's Blooms both belong to her, but it's easier clarifying them as hers and James's or Lockwood's when we're discussing work.

"Hey, Loe." I stop working and wait until she meets my gaze. "Just because you aren't at LB's daily doesn't make the place any less your legacy. No matter what James says, I'm not taking over ownership. You're a Lockwood. We'll work it out." I want to step up running the farm and handling business, but I won't steal her first love from her.

"I know. I really appreciate your understanding. It can't be easy being stuck in the middle of our family drama." She brushes a stray lock of hair from her face with a smile and continues, cutting off any reply I might form. "Anyway, after you and I talked, I hired enough help for the spring and summer to keep from pilfering from your crew."

Canting my head, I cock a brow. "And yet, I'm the one you had come out on a Saturday."

"That's because you don't need to be trained. We can knock this out in a few hours. My newbies would take all day. I want a Saturday, too."

Yeah, yeah. I'm not even mad.

"Mia will have more to do on the Lockwood farm. And you guys have more hands to train her. I'm still teaching my new crew. Really, we're taking on Mia as a favor."

I kneel down as Loe does on the opposite end of the bed, laying the fabric over the irrigation lines. "Why isn't she working at Harris Development with Kip and Brynn?"

"I don't know." Once the fabric is secure, she stands. "Brynn's building her design business up, and I guess Mia wanted something different. Didn't want to be stuck in an office all summer."

Or maybe things are still strained with Brynn. Either way, this is a gift and a curse. Working alongside Mia all summer, I both can't wait and dread it.

Loe picks up another folded sheet of landscape fabric and I help her unfold it. "You're okay with her helping you, right?"

I need to learn a better poker face. Apparently, mine sucks. "Yeah, yeah. Thanks. Meredith and Denise will love the extra hand, too."

I'M STACKING the new shipment of t-posts in one of the supply sheds when gravel crunches under feet.

"Knock, knock."

I turn to find Mia standing at the entrance. Straightening, I flip my ball cap backward. I wasn't expecting her today.

"Hi." Mia tucks her hands into the pockets of her cropped

jean jacket and steps further into the shed, her gaze scanning the space filled with tools and supplies, most of which have littered this building for longer than I've been alive. "Um, I wanted to drop by myself and make sure you're all right with me working here this summer."

Professional. Be professional. Don't take notice of the way that hot Georgia sun has blessed her skin and it's early May. You're her boss now. It's like a triple whammy: teenager, Kip's bonus sister, employee. The kiss never happened.

"Yeah. Why wouldn't I be? We can use all the help we can get in the summertime."

"Right. Summer's busy. Of course." She captures the corner of her lower lip, abruptly cutting the forced laughter following her words. Her shoulders lift with a heavy sigh. "I just didn't want to make you uncomfortable because of the... our..."

"Nothing to worry about here." I shrug to put her at ease. "Unless...will you be uncomfortable with me as your boss?"

With the slightest smirk, she tilts her head. "I suppose I can handle you bossing me around."

Why am I not surprised she went there? I like the idea more than I should, but I need to set a precedent. If we have to work side-by-side, there's no way the two of us won't be the talk of the farm if I don't keep some semblance of professionalism between us.

I clear my throat. "I didn't know you were interested in the flower business."

She bends down and retrieves a rusty spade from where it fell on the floor. "Actually, Kip suggested the job. He reminded me how much I loved helping Mary plan and plant her gardens when I was little. I took the agriculture classes my senior year for fun, but I never really considered flower farming an option for a job until now."

She inches a foot closer and lifts one hand to the edge of her mouth. "Probably because I grew up thinking Lockwood was the devil."

I laugh. "While James has his flaws, he's a decent man. You won't be dealing with him much, though. Any questions or concerns can come my way. He stays out of the fields for the most part. It's no desk job, but there's something special about this farm. I think you'll enjoy working here."

"So, Monday, right?"

"Yeah. Be here at six in the morning. You'll want boots that can get wet and dirty and clothes you don't care much about. I don't think there's rain in the forecast, but come prepared with a jacket. We work rain or shine. Here we don't dress to impress, just to get the job done comfortably."

"Chloe dropped off some Lockwood Blooms tees, and Kip bought me boots. I even have a baseball cap now." She tips her chin toward mine and grins. "It's the Atlanta Braves."

I adjust my navy Mariners cap with a teasing scowl. "Wow, how quickly you can be swayed. Traitor."

Her eyes sweep over me before she spins around, her dress fluttering around her knees, and she tosses a wave. "I'll see you around ten Monday, boss."

"Six," I call after her.

"Fine, eight." Her musical laughter lightens my mood.

She better be kidding.

"Be here at sunrise, Mia," I holler as she saunters out of the supply shed. "Or you won't be cutting blooms, you'll be turning the compost pile."

I'm only partially joking, but she won't get any preferential treatment from me. I can't. No one can see my fascination with her. It'll be bad enough that Charlie will sense it, especially after we played pool with her and her friends. He doesn't have a loud-mouth like Eric does, but it'll only be a matter of time before the news spreads if I'm not treating Mia like everyone else.

I need to stop beating myself up about my mixed emotions.

It's not a crime to find someone attractive. And Mia's an adult. Chloe and I managed to have, and lose, a relationship as boss and employee, and things worked out.

It might be a stupid idea, but a relationship isn't impossible.

Relationship? *Don't get ahead of yourself, Reid.* It's one summer.

...... I tell you, I have
been ...... depressed.
My happiness ......
Incessantly I ......
my memory your caress
your ...... affection
solicitude ......
compare ......
...... a burning and a
...... in my heart. When,
...... all solicitude, all hara...
...., shall I be able to pass a..
time with you, having
love you, and to think only ..
happiness of ...... saying, and
...ing it to you.

6

Reid

Cars churn gravel, taking the unmarked parking spots around an unfamiliar just parked decade-old blue hatchback as Lockwood's employees arrive for work. It's Monday morning before six, and today is Mia's first day on the job.

I step out of the garage with coffee in hand and close my eyes, taking a deep breath and willing my pulse slower. *You can do this, Reid. You can work with this girl and stay in your lane. No flirting, no touching, no kissing!*

Meredith and Denise greet our new crew member before her booted foot hits the ground as she steps out of the blue car. Mia returns their warm welcome, her voice too low for my ears, as the other workers continue into the buildings spread over the farm or further into the fields. I acknowledge Charlie when he passes by, but I stick to the entrance of the workshop, waiting for Mia, Meredith, and Denise. When they arrive, I send them out to snip the last of the ranunculus in the eastern hoop, then have them move onto the peonies. Keeping them busy and Mia far away from me for the day.

"It never occurred to me how many people and hours it takes to weed acres upon acres of flower beds even with the landscaping fabric." I overhear Mia talking to Julian when I walk by the pansy beds after lunch on her second day. A transplant from Utah, Julian's a struggling musician who moved to Seattle to work the bar scene then ran out of money to pay the rent and ended up in Seaside Pointe. I intend to walk by but pause when Mia begs him to sing her a song.

She's not the first to make the request. The guy has a crazy deep timbre to his speaking voice, hinting at great vocals lying beneath. We've all forced him to perform in the two months he's worked here. Tossing a fistful of weeds into his bucket, Julian looks around before putting his touch on a familiar hit currently playing all over radio.

"You're a star," Mia gushes, and I can't stop the touch of jealousy her awe sparks. I can pinpoint the emotion now.

Julian ducks his head, still humming the tune and picking up his pace. Clearly, Mia's embarrassed him. I turn to leave as Mia throws herself back into her work, but not before she lifts her head and spots me.

"Keep up. I need someone to harmonize with," Julian pulls her attention his way, his smile wide as he jerks his chin toward the flowers.

Flashing me a tentative smile, she turns back to Julian. "Ha. What makes you think I can carry a tune?"

"Well, can you?" Julian asks.

He's flirting with her, and I'm unsure how I feel about that.

Running late on her third day, Mia attempts tiptoeing up, as if I won't notice, behind everyone gathered at the base of the fields while I'm assigning jobs. I should have her work with Denise and Meredith again. Or send her out with Julian since she enjoyed being by his side yesterday, but I can't continue ignoring her. Keeping my attention focused away from Mia, I ask Denise to fill a supervisor role this morning and assign Meredith to the garden roses. The women wave, and Mia turns at the waist, her long braid swinging over her shoulder, watching them leave.

"I..." Mia's lips tighten into a straight line as she looks about the empty gravel space. *Yep, you're the last one.* "Am I in trouble for being late?"

"For two minutes? Please, do I come across as that rigid of a boss?"

She circles the toe of her boot in the gravel, and I smile. The only vulnerability Mia Mason shows is when she talks about Brynn. This is new.

"You're with me today. We're going to string sweet peas." I run my fingers along the brim of my hat. "We've got about fifteen hundred feet to do, so we need to get started."

"String them?"

Making my way down a lush row of towering lilac bushes, I explain, "We have to train the sweet peas to grow up and straight, give them nice long stems. The only way to do that is tying the vines to the trellis."

"That seems tedious." The gravel crunches beneath her boots as her pace quickens.

"It is." I flash a grin over my shoulder.

We arrive at the sweet peas, and I pull out a spool of green wire from my tool belt and hand it to her. "C'mere so I can show you what to do."

With as dense as the foliage of the vines are, Mia has to stand shoulder-to-shoulder to see. I pull another spool of wire from my belt and ignore her warmth at my side.

"The tighter you can get them to the trellis, the more upright you make them, the better." Snipping off a piece of the wire, I gently wrap the twist tie around the long green stem, tying it in place. I bow my head into hers, lowering my voice and pointing to one of the thick vines. "Try to tie the wire where it's strongest, right before it branches off."

"Easy enough," she matches my hushed tone, and my head swivels, our faces inches apart.

This was a bad idea. Temptation wars with sense. I step back and clear my throat while digging a second pair of shears from my belt.

"We'll start going down this row and make our way up the other side."

Mia's wide eyes rove the length of the sweet peas. Fifteen hundred feet of flowers in three identical rows back up to the edge of the Harris property.

"Do we have to have all of this done today?" She plucks the shears from my palm.

"That's the goal. Denise and Meredith will join us later, so it'll get done faster."

"Is it my hat?" Mia asks randomly, and I look at her with a confused frown. "I'm wondering if your lack of attention over the past two days was due to my hat choice. I knew my defecting to something so anti-Pacific Northwest as the Braves would get a rise out of you, but I didn't think you'd ostracize me because of it."

I snort. The only words I've spoken this morning have been related to our current project, and most of them have been correcting her work. It's been ten minutes since I last grunted. Obviously, she feels ignored.

"The hat's the least of our problems. I do have a job that needs to get done."

"I'm too tempting. Is that what you're saying?"

My hands fall to my side as I face Mia. Her smile is flirtatiously sweet, and I'm so frustrated. "If you think I didn't meticulously choose the tallest patch of flowers to remain unseen and team myself with you on purpose, you're not as sharp as you seem." A storm wages within as my stare settles on her flushed face.

Antsy, I flip the bill of my baseball hat around, then swap it back when the sun blinds me. Mia slaps a length of wire against her jean-clad thigh, then winces. We're a mess, the two of us. Locked in this strange battle of will and want. Should and shouldn't.

"If you didn't realize my showing up last Friday was about more than my getting your permission to work here, then you're not as sharp as *you* seem."

My tongue traces my bottom lip. "Okay. Then let's hear it. Why did you show up last Friday?"

"I..." She blinks. "I needed to know if things had changed since March. If I could work beside you without wanting to," her face turns a deeper shade of crimson, "without wanting more."

Swallowing, I inhale through my nose. "And what was your conclusion?" My voice is huskier than intended.

Mia's jaw snaps shut, and I get it. Admission is a painful thing.

"You want to know what I've learned?" Her gaze falls to where I'm gripping my shears so hard my knuckles turn white. It's not anger that has me so twisted, but restraint. My chest heaves as I say things I possibly shouldn't. "I'm your boss, Mia, but I'm also a man...who's maybe overly territorial. I didn't like seeing you with Julian yesterday. And while there are a million other things I should be doing today, I couldn't focus knowing you might be charmed by someone else." As hard as I try not to, my words come out like I'm ashamed.

"So, you snagged me for yourself," she says, not moving her stare from my hand and the shears.

I lift a shoulder with resignation. "I'm not proud of it, but this is a less labor-intensive task I thought you'd appreciate after pulling weeds yesterday. It seemed like a win-win. I get you to myself, and you get a break from other grueling tasks."

"While I appreciate the break and like the company, I can't help wondering what your point is. You say you aren't proud. Is that your plan? Hide me from the other guys, but hate yourself for doing so?"

Clenching my jaw, I tuck the wire and shears in my tool belt. "I'm not hiding you. It was meant more as a protective barrier in case something happened. What happens between us isn't their business."

"So, you haven't made your mind up about what will happen between us. Are you standing by the excuse that you're my boss when you were clearly involved with Chloe last year?" She crosses her arms with a frown.

I roll my shoulders and crack my neck. "Chloe and I were in a different situation. It didn't look like I was taking advantage of her, and she definitely wasn't taking advantage of me. While you might want to ignore the age difference between us, it exists all the same."

Mia moves into my space, her chest brushing mine as she reads the irritation on my face. "Answer a question for me. If you didn't know me. If we were two people who met in some random place, would my age stop you?"

Well, hell. I rear back. In another place and time, no. Age shouldn't matter if you're consenting adults, but... "That's the thing, isn't it? We're not two random people. It's a nice fantasy, sure, but it's not reality. I'm trying to do the right thing. *I'm* the older guy. *I'm* the boss. *I'm* not exactly Kip's favorite person."

"You can't want me, but not use me, Reid. And you certainly can't keep me from others if you don't want me." She shifts back, adjusting her traitorous Braves ball cap the way I so often adjust mine.

"No one should ever *use* you." Why is she pushing this? Why am I bending to it? My hand lifts of its own accord. "I never said I didn't want you." I swipe at a smudge of soil on her cheek. "Just that we can't jump into something without considering the consequences."

"Well, good." She bobs her head, her tone serious. We stare in silence for one beat, then two, before her lips wobble and mine part, and we're laughing like two crazy people.

"Glad we got that out of the way." More laughter fills in the spaces between my words as I lock my fingers behind my head and take a step back.

"We should get to work, huh? Denise and Meredith are going to show up and wonder what we've been doing all this time. I don't want to be blamed for distracting the boss." Her palm taps my chest.

"No worries." I chuckle, pulling out my wire and cutters and sidling beside her once more. "They'd fully blame me."

I remain by Mia most of the day, even after Meredith and Denise show up to help. When I finally leave, midway through the last patch, to take a call from Chloe about an issue at her property, I shoot Mia a private smile. One that says we'll figure things out.

An hour later, Mia finds me in the main workshop. "Hey."

"Hey." I turn from the table I'm hunched over, more at ease than I've been since Monday. Though I'm still stuck on what to do about our attraction, this afternoon's tension breaker in the sweet peas offered me breathing room. "I figured you'd be out of here the moment the others were."

"Yeah, I was on my way, but I was wondering." She twines her fingers together in front of her waist, twisting them. "We're having family dinner tonight. Do you think it'd be okay if I threw together a bouquet for the table? Chloe will be there, so I can pay her whatever she says is comparable."

I wave her offer away. "Don't worry about paying. That's a perk of working on the farm. You might not get health insurance, but you're welcome to take a bouquet any time." He smirks.

"Thanks." Mia moves to leave then stops. "You were right, you know. About Brynn and Preston. What he did wasn't my fault. I miss my family. I've kept a distance between us these last nine months, but it's time I take down the wall."

I never thought of myself as a white knight, but once again, her vulnerability weakens me. Something about Mia Mason makes a person want to save her. "Have you talked to Brynn about it?"

"Not like I should. Hence the flowers."

"Something tells me it'll work out."

in my heart.
all solicitude, all
shall I be able to
time with you, having
love you, and to think
happiness of so saying,
it to you.

7

Grace

"I HAVE A FAVOR TO ASK." Brynn slides into the booth across from me at Mac's, a whirlwind of red hair and perfume as she joins me for dinner Tuesday after work. I suggested the casual barbecue joint since I'm a bit of a mess, coming straight from spending my day cleaning Fig's storage room, while she looks every bit the pulled-together businesswoman she is.

"Well, hi to you, too." I snatch our water glasses from the center of the table to keep her giant handbag from knocking them over as she pulls out her ever-present wedding planner.

Brynn huffs her bangs from her eyes and flashes a harried smile. *Make that semi-pulled together.* "Hi." She settles into the maroon vinyl seat. "I'm sorry, I think my nerves have finally hit."

The concept of Brynn Harris having nerves about her big day with Hayden is absurd. Despite my initial reaction to their announcement at the New Year's Eve party, I'm all on board.

Especially when she asked me to be one of her bridesmaids. I love wedding planning. She deserves the best, most memorable day.

Hayden and Brynn are a dream couple, with the kind of love everyone hopes to have, and the man is beyond handsome. It's ironic how her ex—the one who abused and tried to kill her—was a preppy poster boy for country clubs. While Hayden Fox, despite looking ready to pummel anyone who looks at him wrong with his pierced and tattooed muscular body, is possibly the most genuine and protective man in love I've ever seen.

I push her ice water across the table. "You're nervous?"

"Mmm-hmmm." Her fingers tremble as they wrap around the glass, and she nods vigorously, shiny eyes blinking as she downs half the liquid.

My stomach turns to lead. "Brynn? Why are you on the verge of tears?"

She sets the glass down and blows out a long exhale. "Hayden and I had an argument."

I spot a waiter approaching and send him away with a discreet wave as I reach across the wooden table and cover Brynn's hand. "What happened?"

"I had a GYN appointment today, and since she knows about the wedding, we got to talking about kids and birth control, and she offered to remove my IUD."

I can't help but check our surroundings. This isn't a conversation most people want to hear over lunch. "Okay, this isn't what I expected, but continue."

Slipping her fingers from mine, she rolls her eyes. "I'd been considering removing it for a while, and since the strings were right there and she offered, I went ahead with it. It was too convenient not to. The only reason I had the damn thing in the first place was that Preston required it." She says the last bit with a sneer, and my breath catches. *Required it?*

"Such a piece of—" I mutter a curse. Prison is too good for him. He should be six feet under.

"So, anyway, I called Hayd afterward, admittedly not my smartest decision since he was working and all, but I don't know. I was so happy to have that last piece of my past out of my body." She sniffs, her emotions welling in her eyes. "I was telling him how I got a birth control prescription I could start, or we could just...not."

"Not use birth control? Are you two ready for that?" Excitement blooms in my chest at a sweet Brynn and Hayden baby, but I think better of it. "So soon?"

"Why wait?" She rests her elbows on the table and sags. "I mean, that's what I thought anyway. We've discussed it. There's nothing I want more than to be married to that man and give him a million babies—"

A choking laugh snags in my throat. "You've made it clear the sex is good, but a million?"

Her smug grin tells me she'd be happy doing just that, and I'm hit with an odd sense of envy at how much she loves that man. "He doesn't agree with you?"

"He wants me to focus on my business now that I've stepped away from working property management full time."

I nod. Of course, he does. It's what she went to college for, her passion. "It's what you love. He knows how good you are at it."

"It's silly, really." She groans, sliding the wedding planner in front of her and picking at the corner. "It's just...he accepted that job teaching history at Kingston Prep next year. With him back to a school schedule, starting a family works perfectly."

He'll likely be a teacher for the next twenty or more years, especially at a high-profile boarding school like Kingston. Why is this an issue? As if she senses my confusion, Brynn stares at the table as she asks, "What if he's changed his mind?"

"About marrying you?" She's straight-up insane for even considering the thought.

"No, about having kids," she hisses. There's no joking on her straight face. She really thinks that's a possibility. "I know I must sound crazy, but you don't know Hayden. He struggled with the concept of living a happy life for years. His sister's death filled him with such guilt, he didn't think he should be allowed to enjoy love and family. Maybe—"

"Maybe you're overthinking." I kick her foot under the table, and her hazel gaze snaps up. "Brynn, you've gotten yourself all worked up over nothing. Hayden hasn't changed his mind. That's your insecurity talking."

"How do you know?"

I don't, but I do, and I'm working on figuring out some way to prove my point when the man of the hour walks through Mac's double glass doors, his green eyes narrowed and scanning the restaurant until they land on me. Like a heat-seeking missile, his gaze sweeps to the back of Brynn's blazing hair, then he's moving our way.

"I think you're about to find out," I warn with a grin a moment before Hayden stops at the end of our booth.

Brynn's yelp is low and her eyes wide as her guy bends and puts all his hard-earned muscles to work, dragging her by the waist along the booth until she's on the edge and he's squatting between her knees.

His name is all she manages to gasp before he takes her face between his hands and kisses her. I look away, meeting the stares of other patrons when Brynn wraps her arms around her fiancé's shoulders and presses closer.

"Baby, we can start making babies right now. I'm ready. Whatever you want."

Hayden's gruff whisper draws my eyes back, and I can't help eavesdropping. The possessive way his tattooed fingers grip the back of her neck, holding her face close as he speaks into her ear, stokes a pang of longing in my core.

Brynn's auburn brows arch. "But you seemed upset."

Hayden withdraws, studying Brynn before he glances at me

and winks. His position is awkward, crouched between her legs at the end of a table in a restaurant. He must realize he's drawing a crowd. "Scooch." Jerking his chin, he stands tall.

Obliging, Brynn slides, and Hayden slips into the seat, drawing her against his side when she moves too far. Their bodies angle toward each other as he brushes his thumb over her cheekbone.

"You caught me off guard, Duchess. I didn't know removing something like that was so simple. I was upset because you'd had what I thought was some medical procedure, and I didn't know you were doing it."

"Nooo, it was simple," Brynn snaps her fingers, "Barely felt a thing."

"I know. I looked it up on my phone the moment our call ended. I'm glad that's taken care of. I'm sorry I wasn't more supportive. I was in the middle of spraying compost tea; I didn't expect to start a conversation about birth control and babies with my fiancé."

Brynn's lips curve down as she swipes her left hand across her face, her engagement ring sparkling in the lights overhead. "I'm such an idiot. I should have waited."

Hayden snatches her hand and kisses her finger right below the ring. "No, you can call me whenever you want. Just maybe give me time to catch up with your rambling before turning into a crazy woman and hanging up."

A choked laugh falls from my lips. *Oops.* Two pairs of eyes swing my way.

"You hung up on him?" I ask for clarification, no point in pretending I'm not part of this conversation now.

Brynn's shaking her head, but Hayden answers, "She sure did."

Shooting a glare at Hayden, Brynn turns to me. "I'm hormonal and have wedding planning stress. Give me a break, huh?"

"Okay. Give me this." I drag the wedding planner across the table. "There is no need for you to have wedding jitters. You've got everything figured out." As if the women in her life haven't made sure the day would run perfectly. She's a Harris, for Pete's sake. "We're ready."

"Actually, there is one thing I want to change, but it shouldn't be an issue." I arch a brow as Brynn shares a look with Hayden. "I'm going to see if Mia will help Chloe create our flower bouquets."

Chloe will be ecstatic. "Mia?" She does flowers?

"Yeah, just the one for me and the bridesmaids," Brynn rushes to explain. "She brought this perfect bouquet she threw together at the farm to dinner the other night. I thought it would be special to have both my sisters be a part of putting together our flowers. I'll still have Alice at the Flower Patch put together the centerpieces and boutonnieres, but Reid confirmed he could have the stems for our bouquets delivered to the site the morning of the wedding."

"That is the sweetest thing."

"Really?" Brynn nearly jumps out of her seat as she grabs my hands across the table. "You don't think I'm crazy changing things up with less than a month to go?"

"Not at all. I know Chloe will be touched, and I'm sure Mia will be, too. I'm just glad you aren't asking me because *that* would be crazy."

Brynn gives a massive sigh of relief. "That's the last touch to making our day perfect. I'm so excited."

Hayden smiles at me, his eyes shining at how happy Brynn is. Curving his arm around her shoulders, he tugs her in and kisses her temple. "I should get out of here and let you two have dinner."

"What? No, stay and eat with us," I insist. I've spent very little time with Hayden recently since Chloe keeps him so busy, but I already love the guy. It's impossible not to with how happy he makes Brynn.

"You sure?" He looks between the two of us.

"Of course." I slide the planner to the side. "We don't need to talk about the wedding right now. Tell me about your honeymoon. Where are you guys going?"

"It's a secret." Brynn pouts, and Hayden laughs. "He expects me to pack for nearly two weeks, and I don't even know where we're going." The waiter's appearance quiets Brynn.

"I can't believe you're still complaining about this." Hayden pokes Brynn's side once the waiter leaves with our order. "I gave you enough weather information to pack, plus I promised to make sure you have whatever you need."

She slaps at his chest. "That's not the point. I want to know where we're going, you stubborn man."

"It's not like you'll need a whole lot of clothes. It is your honeymoon, right?" I tease.

"My thoughts exactly." Hayden takes a sip of Brynn's water. "Especially since my fiancée has made it clear that she wants a baby."

I bite back a smile as Brynn spins on Hayden. "Really? You're ready?"

"I've been ready to make babies with you since the first time we met. If you don't want to wait, I'm not arguing. The only reason I said anything earlier is because I never want you to give up on doing what you love again. If you'd rather grow your design business, I'll wait. I'm on your time frame, baby. Always."

What it must be like to have a man take your time frame into consideration. Granted, time frames are unpredictable. Nothing is certain. Maybe if I'd been more patient, Drew would've caught up. Just because he wasn't ready for more when I was doesn't mean he never would've been. Is that why he's calling? He's ready now?

"Coincidentally, this conversation leads me to the favor I have to ask and why I wanted to meet for dinner."

"Flowers, honeymoons, packing, and babies." I tick the items off on my fingers as I look at Brynn across the table. "Girl, the only area of expertise I have in the realm of conversations we're having is packing. Please tell me that's what this is about?"

"You aren't supposed to hear his part." Brynn looks at Hayden, batting her lashes.

"Oh, no?" The man holds her stare long enough to make me sweat before chucking her chin and slipping out of the booth. "I'll just go over to the bar and order a drink. Let me know when I'm allowed to return."

It's no wonder the soon-to-be-bride glows. "He's the perfect man, isn't he?"

"So perfect." She agrees wholeheartedly. "You'll find yours soon, Gracie Lou. I've got a feeling."

I chuckle. "Only Kip has permission to call me that." And only because he's been doing it since we were kids. "I guess I'll give you a pass on account of you being so deliriously happy. Now, what's this favor?"

"I was hoping you'd help me plan my wardrobe for the honeymoon."

"So, like two outfits since you'll be naked the rest of the time?"

Brynn's porcelain cheeks pinken. "Maybe a few more things, you know, just in case."

"I would love to. Think I could get Hayden to spill the secret locale?"

"You could try, but I doubt it. My man is a vault when he wants to be." She snags the wedding planner and flips through the pages. "I do have a list with the weather and his idea of possible clothing needs."

I take the paper from her. "Casual site-seer, sexy dinner, activewear, lots of barely-there lace things and bikinis." I roll my eyes—*such a man.* "I like how he specified very tiny next to the bikinis. And green." My eyes narrow on a scribble next to the color. "Did he draw a tractor?"

"It's his favorite color, and mine since it matches his eyes." She shrugs with a Cheshire grin. "I know you're not a personal shopper, but I love Fig, and I want to wow him."

"Not a personal shopper, don't be silly. I would love to help you plan. This will be fun. We have such great things in the shop right now, too. I made some amazing summer buys at market."

a burning and
in my heart. When
all solicitude, all
shall I be able to pass
time with you, having
love you, and to think only
happiness of so saying, and
it to you

8

Reid

IT'S BEEN two weeks since Mia started working with us. There's been so much work; I've paired her with everyone but me to keep myself on task. There have been weak moments where I've thought about cornering her or calling her in the workshop under false pretenses, but then I get a hold of myself and remember what's at stake. No matter how tempting Mia Mason is, will acting on urges make us happy? Is she someone I see myself with years from now? Or would she serve as a temporary fix?

She's been lighter since her dinner with the Harrises. I've seen the change in her countenance, her eyes brimming with an air of contentment. The last thing I want is to bring her down by asking her to keep secrets. And that's precisely what we'd have to be—a secret. For now, anyway.

I might not know a ton about women, but I know Mia doesn't want to be hidden like a dirty little secret.

I don't leave the Lockwood farm often for lunch unless I'm already out because it takes up half my break to drive to and from town, but I'm hankering for an oyster po' boy from Saltbox. Nothing else will satisfy the craving.

I head to the seafood joint after parking on Main Street, but my anticipation for deliciousness deflates as I come upon the wooden-planked building. Saltbox is packed. People loitering on the sidewalk and loading up the benches outside. I'll be lucky to get a table before I have to head back. *Man.*

On the benches nearest me, white-blonde hair flutters in the breeze, catching my eye. Grace pulls her cell phone away from her ear, tapping the screen with a rose-polished finger, and sets it in her lap with a sigh. She stares across the street, her lips pursed, shoulders sagging.

"Hey, stranger. What's the wait looking like?"

Almond-shaped eyes find me, and a sincere smile broadens her mouth. "Hey. I'm not sure what it is now, but I've been waiting for about twenty minutes. They're supposed to call my name any minute."

Dang. I check my watch. I have little more than thirty minutes before I need to turn and head back.

"Are you in a hurry?" she asks.

I mean, technically, being the farm manager, I've got some leeway, but I don't like taking advantage. And I want to set the right example for the rest of the crew. Eric and Charlie would definitely give me crap.

"Yeah, I'll have to eat somewhere else. It was good seeing you, Grace."

The door to Saltbox opens, and a woman in a navy blue polo peeks outside, glancing at the waiting crowd. "Grace?"

Grace stands and opens her mouth but then stops and turns to me. "Chloe was supposed to join me, but I just got off the phone with her. She's held up with a seed emergency. Why don't you take my table?"

"I can't steal your table after you've been waiting for so long."

"It's no biggie." She shrugs, her eyes warming with genuine politeness. "Take the table, Reid. I'm going to grab a burger from Perry's and head back to Fig."

Before I know what I'm saying, I ask, "Why don't you join me?"

Her thick full lashes blink, a contemplative upturn of the corner of her light pink lips.

"It *is* your table, after all," I say. "I don't mind sharing. A burger is not going to suffice when you have seafood on the brain."

She chuckles and hikes her purse onto her shoulder. "I really did want an oyster po' boy."

With a grin, I hold the door open, letting her pass in front of me. "You've got good taste."

After the hostess seats us, Olivia takes our order immediately when I mention I'm on a time crunch. I flip my ball cap around and relax back.

Grace smirks from across the table. "After I mentioned it, you just couldn't resist, could you?"

"Actually, I think you were reading my mind. I saw a seafood commercial last night and haven't been able to stop thinking about the po' boy since."

She laughs, and the melody makes me want to draw out the sound again. "I haven't seen you since we rang in the new year. Lockwood keeping you busy, I assume."

Damn. Has it been nearly six months since our friendly kiss under the heaters at the Harrises'? I kick the memory of Grace's soft lips against mine to the curb and focus on her question. *Now, what was it? Oh, am I busy?* "Understatement. Losing Loe last summer was hard, but with the spring season, her absence is glaring. No matter how many we hire, it doesn't fill the hole she left."

"It's a lot when you lose someone with as much knowledge and experience as she has. If James wasn't so hard-headed, maybe you guys would be able to function better."

I choke on my soda, pounding on my chest with a laugh. "Tell me how you really feel."

"Sorry, but it's true, isn't it?"

"I try not to have an opinion on the matter." At least not a vocal opinion.

"Understandable. Caught between boss and owner. Not to mention one being your ex. Speaking of…I hear James offered you the business."

I blow out a heavy sigh. "I'm really trying to stay out of it, Grace. I know damn well that James Lockwood wouldn't have offered me jack if it weren't for Chloe choosing Kip."

"That's not true; even Chloe thinks you deserve more for all the work you do. It's just—"

"It's her family. I'm not the type of guy who steps on someone else's toes. If James gets it in his head to truly sell to some outsider, then I'll make a deal with him, but I'm hoping—maybe against hope—that he'll come around sometime soon."

"I get it." She leans forward, resting her elbows on the table. "It's been a year, though. And they've talked maybe once. Now that I think about it, it was at Christmas. Chloe was hoping they could put aside their differences for the holidays, but he couldn't even do that."

I knew things were bad, but I didn't realize their relationship had deteriorated *that* much until James was hinting I take over for Chloe. They avoid each other at the farm, but I figured they'd talked here and there outside of work. To be civil for Robyn, if nothing else.

As if reading my mind, Grace says, "I hate it for Robyn the most. How do you choose between your husband and daughter?" She shakes her head, eyes falling beyond my shoulder.

It must tear Robyn apart being in the middle of that. She

rarely comes out to the fields anymore. After James had his stroke, she stayed by his side. The flowers used to be her happy place. Are they nothing but a source of pain now?

"Do you think there's more to it?" I ask. "Disowning your daughter just because of the man she chose to be with—feud or not—it doesn't make sense. If Kip was a criminal or treated Loe terribly, I'd get it, but even *I* have to admit he's not a bad guy."

Grace studies me, her lips puckering as she tilts her head. "You're not still interested in Chloe, are you?"

I toss my hands in the air. "Why does everyone keep asking me that?"

She chuckles. "Sorry. It's the best friend in me."

"Well, best friend, I got over Loe a long time ago."

"Have you dated anyone since then?"

Well, that escalated quickly. I scratch my neck. "Not really. One date here and there, but no one steadily." That's a lie, there's been no one, but I can't sound like a total loser in front of the pretty woman I kissed in the new year with. "Just looking for Mrs. Right at this point, but I haven't found her yet."

"Ah. The elusive Mister and Misses Right. I know a thing or two about that."

"What? Our little kiss didn't bring you luck?" I tilt my head. "You're not dating anyone?"

Grace wraps her lips around her straw, takes a long sip of her water, and then shakes her head.

Come to think of it, I don't think I've ever known Grace to be attached with anyone. We might not be close, but we still run in the same circles. A few high school buddies have shown interest, but whether they struck out or even bothered asking her on a date, I can't say that I know.

"Do you want to be dating anyone?" Dumb question. "I mean, is there a reason you aren't dating anyone?"

Her hand goes to her earlobe, taking the flesh between two

fingers and rubbing. "Guess I'm picky." A light chuckle trickles past her lips.

"Or really busy."

She taps her nose like we're playing a game of charades, and I smile at the gesture. "I guess you know a thing or two about that, huh?"

Being too busy to take the time to find the right girl? Yeah, I do.

Olivia steps up to our table. "Two oyster po' boys." She sets the plates in front of us, and we thank her.

Checking my watch, I scoot in. I've got five minutes to eat and pay.

"All right, Grace." I pick up the po' boy with both hands. "You're about to witness an extraordinary feat. Two minutes and this thing will be gone."

Her smile brightens her whole face as she laughs.

since I left you, I have
been constantly depressed.
My happiness
incessantly
my mind your cares,
your affection
licitude
Josephine
tinually a burning and
me in my heart. When,
all solicitude, all harm
, shall I be able to pass a
time with you, having
love you, and to think only
happiness of saying, and
ing it to you.

9

Grace

AFTER A LONG WEEK—WELL, all except for bumping into Reid for lunch on Tuesday—Chloe, Brynn, and I slip into comfy clothes on Saturday for a night in. With Robyn visiting her sister in Spokane for a couple of weeks, it's just us at my place.

Four days later, and I'm still thinking about those thirty minutes in Saltbox with Reid. I like spending time with him more than I should. I haven't been able to stop replaying things he said and did that made me laugh and the feel of his mouth on New Year's. I must really be hard up. Not because it's Reid. Reid is more than good-looking, but he's not a path I should go down. And if I'm willing to put myself in that complicated situation, I must be desperate.

Brynn lifts her legs to sprawl across the loveseat. "I'm getting married in a week."

"Lucky wench." I smirk, sipping my merlot.

Her eyes hold a shred of panic. "What if Hayden backs out? Or decides not to show, and I'm left in my wedding dress without a groom?"

Chloe rolls her eyes, stretching back against the armrest of the couch, facing Brynn next to me. "Hayden is not going to leave you standing alone at the altar."

"You don't know that. A year ago he never thought he'd marry anyone."

"Then he met you." Chloe's eyebrow climbs as if to dispute her claim. "You have nothing to worry about."

"We already went over this, Brynn." I snag a handful of popcorn. "Are you getting cold feet?"

"No, no. Of course not." She breaks off a piece of the chocolate bar in her lap, worrying her bottom lip. "I know you're right. It's just my insecurities getting in the way."

"Understandably so." I hold her gaze. "You've been burned, but Hayden isn't going to run out on you. We've all witnessed the kind of man he is. He's not Thou Who Shall Not Be Named."

"Definitely not. And I don't actually believe he'd humiliate me like that. Everything is all so real. Sometimes he seems too good to be true."

That was Drew, showering me with gifts and extravagant dates. Until he'd fall off the face of the earth or ask to put on the brakes before crawling back months later. When he broke things off after my senior year at Seattle Central, I truly thought I'd seen the last of him.

Though I haven't heard from him in a couple of weeks, now that I think about it. Has he finally given up?

I nudge Chloe's bent knee. "Do you remember Drew?"

"The hotshot who swept you off your feet and treated you like garbage?"

Snorting, I swallow the last of my merlot. "That's the one."

Setting her wine glass on the coffee table, she pulls her hair up into a wild bun. "That's a name I haven't heard in a long time. What about him?"

"He sent me a Christmas present and has been calling me almost every week since the New Year."

They both sit up straighter. "He what?" Chloe says over Brynn asking, "Who's Drew?"

I turn to Brynn. "He's this guy I dated in college."

"More like, used you when he felt like it." Chloe hides behind her chardonnay.

"Excuse you." I shove her legs off the couch.

She laughs, but her eyes widen with conviction. "Don't act like it's not true."

She's not wrong, but it doesn't mean I like others pointing my foibles out. It's a period of my life I regret but wouldn't change because Drew taught me a lot about what I deserve.

"So, what did he send you?"

"A new *Pride & Prejudice* DVD, a box of my favorite microwave popcorn, and some lemon drops."

Chloe groans as her head rolls back in aggravation. "He always did sway you with that nickname."

Leaning forward, Brynn asks, "What nickname?"

My heart wakes from the Drew hibernation as I recall seeing him at that bar. "He used to call me Lemon Drop. It was what I was drinking the night we met."

"That is kind of cute." Brynn's nose crinkles as her eyes soften.

Chloe jabs a finger in her direction. "Don't you say that. It's not cute. He screwed Grace over after wasting some of her prime college years, led her to believe he was the one, and then tossed her aside when she asked for more than spurts of his time."

A hint of outrage burns in Brynn's eyes. "And what's the significance of *Pride & Prejudice*?"

"My favorite movie," I admit, the sweeter moments of our past tickling my memories. "I used to make him watch it with me all of the time. When we broke up for the last time, he took my copy to remember me by."

"So, he didn't want to be with you anymore, but he wanted a movie you watched together? Why is he trying to come back now? After how many years?"

"Like four." I sigh. "I don't know. He left a note with the present saying he wanted to talk, but I haven't answered any of his calls or texts."

Intrigue replaces anger. "You're not the least bit curious?" Brynn twists a lock of red hair around her finger, watching me intently.

"Of course I am, but what if hearing his voice reverts me back to the naïve twenty year old, willing to take any scraps he offers?"

I've grown since then. What if he's really changed this time? We've both had time to mature. Though, he was twenty-seven when we met, so he should've known better. But at thirty-four, surely he's a different man, one who's ready to settle down.

No, it doesn't matter. There's no sense in going back, in letting that part of my life back in.

"You're not that Grace anymore," Chloe says. "Maybe you need to talk to him to prove to yourself you can say no."

Maybe. But at this point, after not hearing from him, after all the ignored calls, I don't know that I'll hear from him again.

"He's been calling since January?" Brynn asks. "That's some determination."

"More than he ever showed before," Chloe says. "But that doesn't mean he's good enough for you."

"Let's talk about a more important question. How about we finalize that honeymoon wardrobe?"

since I left you, I have
been constantly depressed.
My happiness ~~~
incessantly ~~~
my mind ~~ your cares
your ~~ your affection
licitude ~~ ob~~
compare ~~ ~~
tinually, a burning ~~ a
~ in my heart. When,
~ all solicitude, all harra~
~, shall I be able to pass a~
time with you, having
love you, and to think only
happiness of ~ saying, and
~ing it to you.

Reid

Violet's, Hollow Tree, and Petals. Today's going to be a longer delivery morning. It's only three stops, but they're our farthest buyers. We tend to rotate the routes. Heading past Mt. Luna can be a pain. It takes a patient, careful driver to get the blooms that far through all the sharp curves.

The only thing that would make the drive better is some company. I spot Mia walking alongside Julian toward the fields. There's only a select few of us that make the deliveries each week. Since it's a one-person job, I haven't assigned her any routes. She's supposed to be extending the T-posts for the sweet peas this morning, but I have a better idea.

"Mia," I call out and she turns. "How about you join me on deliveries today."

She pauses, almost like she's waffling with the idea of telling me no. It's funny because I wasn't asking. Though, if she did tell me no, I wouldn't force her. I might be her boss, but I want her to *want* to spend time with me.

After a beat, she waves to Julian and makes her way to me next to the delivery van.

"I figured you might want the full Lockwood Blooms employee experience, and that's really not complete until you make the deliveries and see the faces of those receiving them."

A confident smile tugs the corners of her plump lips. "Is that right? It's not because you want to keep me to yourself again?"

"Or spare Julian the mini concerts you force him into?" Winking, I round the hood of the van to the driver's side, and Mia swings open the passenger side.

"Singing makes the work fly by." Her cheeks flush. "Plus, he's really talented." She's as enamored with the guy's voice as the rest of the women on the farm, but I wonder if there's something more.

As we buckle up, I crank the engine. "We're going to make our way north. Round trip, it'll take us around three hours. We can grab an early lunch on the way back if you want."

It'll be after ten before we return, so I guess that's a really early lunch. When Mia doesn't comment, I say, "Or a late breakfast, if you'd rather."

She tilts her face my way, not entirely, but enough to allow her gaze to sweep over me as she rubs her lips together. "Sure. Whatever works best, boss."

That might give another guy an ego boost, but it only reminds me that I'm taking advantage of my position today by bringing Mia with me just because I want to. We actually need her on the farm this morning. I'm being selfish. In truth, it's a last-ditch effort to figure this thing out between us.

"Let's stick with Reid, yeah?"

"Okay, *Reid*."

It's forty-five minutes of companionable silence, listening to music before we arrive at Hollow Tree, our first stop. Well, primarily companionable. I've been silently waging a battle. I've got her alone. We're away from the prying eyes of the farm and Seaside. We have a chance to be what we want for a few hours, but I can't bring myself to step over the line.

When we pull up in front of Hollow Tree, I point out the buckets we need to haul, and Mia follows me inside as the florists gush over the blooms.

After the first two buckets, I lose Mia. When I return, next bucket in hand, without her, she's caught in an animated conversation with the owner, Carla. Mia plucks a peony from one of the buckets and prattles on about how gorgeous an arrangement of the pink blooms would be with classic ivy. It's such a Chloe thing to do, carry on with the florists like she's known them her whole life. It's the kind of rapport Lockwood Blooms strives for with their patrons. Mia might be young, but sometimes the way she handles herself is beyond her years. Another confusing aspect of this enigmatic girl-woman.

"It's pretty up this way. Quieter, too." Mia inhales the cool air through her nose while glancing around the small town before climbing into the van. "Seaside has grown so much in the last few years. It seemed like such a tiny town when I was a kid."

"Yeah, I mean, growth is good for business, but I miss what Seaside used to be. Just the other day, there was a thirty-minute wait for a table at Saltbox." My comment is a tad tongue-in-cheek.

"The horror."

"Tell me about it." I chuckle. "When I was a teen we could walk into any of the joints off Main Street and never wait."

"I've heard the same complaints from Kip and Brynn, but they're quick to point out how even as it grows, Seaside maintains its small-town personality. I thought I was sick of it, but living in Georgia this last year taught me how much I took home for granted." She tightens her ponytail and sighs. "Or maybe it was the comfort of having people who looked out for me that I took for granted."

"Yeah, there's something to be said for growing up with the same people your entire life. I can't turn my back without bumping into someone I know. I've never hated it."

"I asked you at the party if you regretted never leaving Seaside. Somehow you never answered my question, but I'm pretty sure your answer would be no. You fit here." It's not a question but a statement, so I let her continue. "What they say is true, you know? The grass isn't always greener."

It's on the tip of my tongue to ask what she means, but then she hops out as soon as I park at our second destination. Mia does the entire delivery with a smile on her face, so when we climb back in the van, I don't pick up the conversation where we left off.

I lean forward to turn up the music when she touches my arm, stilling me. "Not that I don't enjoy the music, but can I ask you a question?"

I sit back and pull onto the road. "Shoot."

"I've been back for weeks, and you haven't made a move. Why?"

This topic was bound to come up. The temptation is there. Every time she smiles. Every time she laughs with the crew. Every time our eyes meet. Hell, every time I see her.

"Cat got your tongue?"

"I'm just trying to figure out how to answer. I think it's important we see what this is before diving headfirst. Things have finally smoothed out with Kip. Getting into it with him again isn't something high on my priority list."

"We're talking about Kip, who dated Chloe in secret."

"And I'm not Kip. I don't want to hide you. I just want to take things slow. Maybe spend a little more time together on the farm." *Rather than avoiding you, so I don't do something stupid.*

She toys with the ends of her hair, a smile playing at her lips. "That's the first time I've looked at you and noticed our age difference." My forehead rumpling, she continues, "Most of the guys in my social circles aren't quite so careful. It's nice."

A smirk tugs at my mouth. "Most guys your age are morons. Don't mistake me for a gentleman. I was the same way when I was your age. I've just learned a few things over the years." I take a breath. "I don't want to hurt you."

Her face twists thoughtfully before she asks, "Do I look like someone who is easily hurt?"

Yes, Mia Mason. You look like you'd break with one wrong move. She catches the arch of my brow and waves her hand. "Don't answer that. I know what you're going to say."

Once again, she shows her maturity even as her youth shines through. So beguiling. "Look, Mia, I don't want to use you, and I think we both know that anything that happens between us at this point would be just that." We're not *it* for each other. I'm sure of it. I imagine she is, too.

She nods, looking out the window for a silent minute before turning back. "I do have one request. You have to save me a dance at Brynn and Hayden's wedding this weekend."

As much as I like Hayden and Brynn, I've dreaded their wedding since I received the invitation. Another fancy Harris event with a coat and tie—which I need to replace after New Year's—and a who's who list of attendees. Dancing with Mia would be something to look forward to.

"You won't find me on that dance floor much, but for you, one dance won't hurt."

Her wide smile makes the humiliation of my two left feet worth it.

THERE'S a different feel on the farm today. Maybe it's because with Hayden and Brynn's wedding tomorrow, my bright spot isn't here. After our much-needed conversation Monday, my relationship with Mia has settled. She's a breath of fresh air with her sweet smiles and teasing, and there's a spark—because, uh, single man here—but that's all it is: attraction and protectiveness. I hate seeing her light dim, even for a moment.

When a break for lunch comes, I don't stay at the farm. I make my way into town. It's been a bit since I've gone to Aunt May's, and there's nothing quite like some good fried comfort food.

The hostess walks me to a table when I spot Grace munching on a French fry, flipping through a magazine.

"Actually," I say to the hostess, "right here is fine."

Sliding into the wooden booth across from Grace, I smile when she looks up, startled.

"Mind if I crash your lunch?"

She closes her magazine and smiles back. "No, be my guest."

I relax as the hostess sets a menu in front of me. "I don't particularly like eating alone."

"I don't mind it as much as I used to." She shrugs, dipping one of her chicken strips in barbecue sauce. "After doing it for so long, you get used to it."

Grace is too beautiful to be used to eating alone. Since I was dating Loe, I didn't pay much attention to Grace. I mean, I have eyes, so I noticed her, but in a different, platonic light. And she really *is* beautiful.

"Reid Pruitt." Aunt May sidles up beside our table, her bleach blonde hair falling in waves around her shoulders.

I stand and wrap her in a hug. "Hey, Aunt May."

"You don't come to see me nearly as much as you should." She pats my cheek before I return to my seat.

"It has been a few months, hasn't it?"

"I was starting to think you were cheating on me with that new raw food place down the road."

I cringe. "I'd never. I've been buried at the farm. Can't seem to catch up."

"Nothing wrong with a busy business. It means you're doing something right."

Ha. "Something like that."

"Well, what can I get you?"

"How about your famous BLT with pimento cheese and homemade chips on the side."

"Coming right up, sugar."

Aunt May walks away, and Grace hums, setting her napkin over her now empty blue plate.

"What's that hum for?" I ask as she folds her arms and settles against the booth with a soft smile.

"I've been coming here since I was who knows how old, and May has never greeted me like that."

"Takes a special kind of charm to get the royal treatment," I joke.

"Ah." She chuckles. "Maybe I just have the wrong parts."

I can't help it. My eyes drift to said parts on her chest covered by a flowery dress under a cream sweater. Catching myself, I shift my gaze to the side, laughing.

"Maybe that's it." I rub the back of my neck. "Hey, don't feel like you have to stay on my account."

"After that pitiful confession, what kind of friend would I be to make you eat alone?" Her eyes light, then she shrugs. "I have some time to kill before I need to be back at Fig. I don't mind keeping you company."

"Are you going to Brynn and Hayden's wedding tomorrow?"

"Am I going? I'm in the wedding party." Grace presses two fingertips against her lips, unsuccessfully covering her laugh, and my skin turns hot. "Loe *has* kept you far too busy, hasn't she?"

Or I'm that out of touch with everything going on around me lately.

Taking pity, she continues without waiting for some lame excuse of an answer from me. "Yeah, I'll be there. I even helped Brynn pick out the bridesmaids' dresses, in my signature color, no less." She wiggles her rose-painted fingers at me, and I smile as it registers—I've never seen anything not a soft shade of pink on her lips and nails. "With Chloe and Mia's help on the flowers, it's going to be a stunning wedding. Seaside's social event of the season." She's playing, but she's not lying. Everyone will be there. If I thought New Year's Eve was extravagant, no expense will be spared with Harris's only daughter's wedding.

Promising Mia a dance might not have been my smartest move. There will be too many eyes. Too many chances for people to draw the types of conclusions I drew way back when I met Mia with Kip.

Or I'm paranoid. It's one dance.

I don't have many women as friends, not any I can go to about this without it spiraling into a gossip train. But there's something about Grace. She gives off this trustworthy vibe like she's above passing around juicy stories and judgment.

"We're friends, right?"

Her eyebrow arches. "We're really sucky enemies if we're not friends."

I snort. "Can I ask you a question?"

Grace eyes me like it's stupid of me to pose and not outright ask the question.

"Right. Okay. Have you ever wanted someone you couldn't have?"

Tensing, she leans forward. "I thought you said you weren't still into Chloe."

"Loe? What? No, no. I'm not." I run my fingers through my hair and situate my hat.

"Are we talking like someone's wife?" She scrutinizes me. "Or mom, maybe?"

"Why would those be your first two choices? Do I look like an adulterer to you? Or on the hunt for a sugar momma?"

"Hey, I don't know your life. You could think Stacey's mom has it going on, and that's cool. You *were* awfully friendly with May."

That pulls a laugh from me. "All right, smart aleck. Let me rephrase my question because it's not that I want someone specifically. I just…do you ever worry you might want someone you shouldn't?" *Or that you'll push feelings for someone because you're tired of being alone?*

"Sorry." Her smile curves one side of her lips. "I'll stop giving you a hard time. To answer both of your questions—someone I couldn't have or shouldn't have. Yes. A couple times. One more recent than the other."

"And what did you do about it?"

"I…ditched the one I couldn't have, but the second one is still in question." Grace toys with an empty straw wrapper. "We text, and sometimes it feels like we could go somewhere, but then he ghosts me for weeks."

"So, is guy two the one you shouldn't want but do? Or are we talking more like an unavailable guy?"

She shrugs but gives a closed-off expression. "Something like that."

Doesn't really help my situation.

"Well, dish. Who's the unlucky girl because I know you're not asking this out of curiosity?"

My eyes narrow, unamused.

Grace is Chloe Lockwood's best friend. Anything I say could bite me in the butt. When I don't respond right away, she scoots forward, resting her arms on the table. "Do I know her?"

I clear my throat. "Yeah."

"Are you going to tell me who she is?"

"That depends." I brace my forearms against the table. "Will all of Seaside be buzzing about it tomorrow?"

"All. No. Half? Maybe." Matching my stare, she smirks. "I'm kidding. I won't say anything."

"And you promise this won't get back to Loe?"

Her shoulders square. "Does it have to do with her?"

"Not directly, no."

Grace cants her head. "Okay. I guess the better question is, am I going to feel dishonest keeping this from her?"

"I don't think so." How should I know?

"Okay. I won't say anything to Chloe. Unless you come out and say it's Robyn, then all bets are off."

Grace is funny. I never expected that.

"It's Mia Mason?"

"Is that a question, or are you genuinely interested in the recent high school graduate?"

"Not recent. She's a sophomore in college." Give or take two months.

"Defensive. So, that's a yes."

"Actually, it's not like that." Knocking my head back, I groan. "I mean, there's this crazy attraction between us, has been for a while, but nothing really came of it. Then she started working at Lockwood's. We flirted around the idea."

"Are you looking for a hookup? Because that's ruffling a lot of feathers for something that won't last."

I shake my head. "Hookups are the farthest thing from my mind. I got over those years ago."

"So, Mia is someone you see having a relationship with?" Her forehead creases.

This wasn't where I meant my question to lead, but now I can't help but wonder what Grace thinks of the situation. "Would I be asking you these questions if I didn't?"

Grace laughs. "I'm not trying to be snarky. It just surprises me. I'm genuinely curious. I want to know how much you've thought this through."

"Would that be a crazy thing? Considering Kip and Chloe, and our age difference."

Grace shifts, avoiding my eyes as she tucks her hair behind her ear. "Maybe I'm curious because I've sort of been in Mia's shoes before. I know a little about dating an older guy."

I don't know Grace that well, but I can't say I've ever seen her with a guy. We're two years apart, but Seaside isn't *that* big. Was her mystery man someone I know?

Before I can ask, she elaborates. "I dated one when I was in college, on and off. Didn't end so well. But I'm telling you because I'll be the last to shame you for dating someone that's not your age. No matter what it looks like from the outside."

"How much older was he?"

She chews on her bottom lip. "Eight years."

"That's not bad. About the same as me and Mia, but you weren't a teenager anymore."

"Actually, we began casually seeing each other when I was nineteen, so I was close to Mia's age."

"Why didn't it work out between you two?"

Hesitating, her eyes focus on the table as she crumples up the straw wrapper and tosses it down. "Different stages of life, I guess. Different expectations of the relationship." Her bluish-gray eyes lift to mine.

The urge to tell her I've already decided against pursuing Mia hits me. I'm not sure why. Maybe it's because she opened up to me, and I don't want her to think her confessions were for nothing. Or maybe I don't want her thinking of me like she does the older guy from her past.

"I have to be honest." I lean forward until she's all I see. "My intention was to ask if you ever find yourself trying to fit the wrong person into your life because you're tired of looking. Or, maybe tired isn't the word—"

"But it is, isn't it?" Grace cocks her head, understanding

dawning. "You're saying you looked at Mia—a beautiful soul, by the way—longer than you should have because you're ready to find future Mrs. Reid Pruitt."

Future Mrs. Reid Pruitt might be a bit of an overstatement, but finding someone to love? Yeah, I'm open to it. "You pretty much nailed it, Embry. I know Mia and I aren't right for each other, but I strung the idea along for months because, why not?"

Recognition flickers in Grace's eyes. "I swear that's all I do. Continue to be with or go after the wrong person because I want it to work so badly. I want to be loved…" Her last words are mumbled like she doesn't mean for me to hear them. Shaking her head on a laugh, she sweeps strands of her hair from her face. "So dumb. Time to make a change, Pruitt."

in my heart. When,
all solicitude, all
shall I be able to pass
time with you, having
love you, and to think only
it to you

Grace

IN A TWIST OF FATE, Brynn and Hayden chose Kingston Castle as their wedding venue before Hayden applied for his upcoming teaching job at the Kingston Preparatory boarding school located a few miles north of Seaside Pointe.

The manor, designed to replicate Tutor Gothic style, is bustling with activity when I arrive early Saturday afternoon. Chloe and Mia arrived mid-morning to work on the wedding bouquets, so I'm alone—and able to ogle the grandness of today's affair—as a staff member directs me to the changing room where the bridal party will get ready.

Though they're setting up the after-wedding cocktail hour outside, the ceremony and reception will take place indoors, thanks to the unpredictable Pacific Northwest weather. Or perhaps, predictable is the more accurate word. The risk of an evening summer rain shower was too significant for Brynn to consider planning an outdoor garden wedding on the property.

As I take in the rich mahogany floors and paneled walls throughout the castle, I can't say I blame her. The place is stunning and, paired with the vast amount of flowers Denton and Mary paid for to decorate every nook and cranny, the entire day will be a fairytale for Hayden and Brynn. Precisely what two people who have suffered so much deserve.

"Hey, Cinderella."

I spin at Bodhi's voice and the nickname he refuses to stop using.

"Hey, handsome." I pause and wait for him to catch up, admiring his careless swagger as he carries his sheathed suit hooked on his finger and slung over his shoulder. "You know every time you call me that I want to look in a mirror."

His piercing eyes twinkle, even from fifteen feet away, as laughter rumbles in his chest. "It's the blonde hair and dress, babe." His eyes skim my length. "You certainly don't look like the washed-up, ripped-apart girl whose evil stepsisters tore into."

Well, thank goodness for that assessment. Since meeting him a year ago, I've learned Bodhi rarely calls anyone by their first name. I guess I should be glad he saddled me with Cinderella. She was my favorite Disney princess growing up.

Reaching my side, he leans in and presses a kiss to my cheek. "How are you?"

"I'm good. Excited for Brynn and Hayden." We resume our trek toward the dressing area. "How are you? I heard you had a late flight in this morning."

Bodhi groans. "Yeah. I hate that I couldn't be here for the rehearsal last night. Some best man, huh?"

"When duty calls." I shrug. "We managed, but I'm sure the dinner would have been more fun with you there."

He wags his dark brows, his ridiculously full lips pulling into a flirty grin. "Of course it would have. No worries, tonight's party will make up for my missing last night."

A door up on our left opens, and Hayden's dark head pops out, his whistle cutting off any reply my brain was formulating. "It's about time you showed up, bro."

"Whatever, man. I've got the getaway car out front. You ready to cut loose?"

I smack Bodhi's shoulder. "Hush. If Brynn hears you, she'll flip. Don't you know anything about brides on their wedding day?"

"Can't say I do." Bodhi chuckles. "But I know Red, and Red knows Hayd. She's not worried one bit about that tattooed S.O.B."

I can't rein in my laughter, and Bodhi's ice-gray eyes, once again, rove over me. There's a crease between his brows and something thoughtful—maybe curious—about the way he looks at me. We seem to play this game each time we see each other, which is not often, thanks to his intense and secretive travel schedule.

Bodhi looks down the hall at Hayden impatiently propping the door open as he waits for his best friend, then back to me, his steps slowing. "Hey, let's make time to chat at some point this afternoon. Okay?"

I offer him a slow smile. "Sure, I think that's a good idea."

When we reach Hayden, he snatches Bodhi by the arm and shoves him into the men's dressing area—where Kip's greeting echoes—before he addresses me. "Hey, grab the girls and meet us on the front balcony for a pre-wedding toast."

My eyes narrow. "Is this sanctioned by your future wife?"

"Who do you think planned it?" Hayden backs into the room. "We were just waiting for you two to arrive."

"Then let me be on my way." I snap a salute and hurry for the women's changing room. More than ready for a drink or two and for this wedding to begin.

. . .

After two champagne toasts with the groomsmen and several hours of hair, make-up, and happy tears, we're slipping on our dresses in varying shades of pink so we can help the bride add finishing touches.

"Mia." My jaw drops at the stunning woman before me in a chiffon gown of deep blush pink. Mia and her friends did a lot of shopping at Fig after I opened the boutique. And I helped her choose a homecoming dress last year, but this is not the same girl. "College has done you good, girl. You look amazing, all woman now."

It's little wonder Reid fought an attraction to her.

She smooths her palms over her skirt as her cheeks flush. "I'm pretty sure I look the same, but thank you."

Chloe reaches out and adjusts one of the long dark curls resting across Mia's chest. "Nope, you're a knockout, sweetie. Kip grumbles about it all the time. I feel bad for the single men who look your way."

Mia's forehead wrinkles and a shadow flickers over her features before she smiles. "He should be worried," she teases. "You're very beautiful. And you, Grace. You're such an ethereal beauty. That dusty rose is perfect with your delicate features, that icy blonde hair, and long legs. I'm jealous of those."

I chuckle, and Chloe hip-checks me. "I'm with Mia. How were we best friends growing up? You're too pretty." Chloe links her arm through mine. "I don't know how Bodhi can ignore you looking like that."

My eyes cut to Chloe as I hiss under my breath, "Oh my gosh, would you stop with that?"

"You have a thing for Bodhi?" Mia asks, her smoky eyes wide.

Grace snorts. "More like Loe has a thing for setting me up with Bodhi."

Chloe rolls her eyes. "He texts you more than he does Kip."

"That's because we're friends, and Kip isn't nearly as funny as I am." I flip my hair over my shoulder. "Can we focus on the bride now?"

"Yes, please." Brynn whines, her hands fanning over her face as she fights tears for the who knows how many times today. "I'm ready to slip into my dress."

IN NO TIME AT ALL, Chloe, Mia, and I lead Brynn and Denton down the grand staircase and line up for the bridal procession.

Denton's shining eyes rake over the four of us as we wait for the wedding coordinator to open the doors. "I may be the luckiest man here, standing with you beautiful ladies tonight," he says, his voice thick as he gazes on his daughter with loving eyes.

Brynn's hand tightens on his arm. "Keep talking like that, Daddy, and you'll be the unluckiest when you're drowning in a pool of our tears."

I shift my eyes between Chloe and Mia, seeing what I imagine is my mirror image—rapidly blinking eyes, quivering bottom lips.

With that, the doors swing open and music fills the flower-shrouded ballroom. My gaze lands on Hayden, standing to the right of Bodhi and Kip as he awaits his bride. All three wear pale gray suits with crisp white shirts that must have the single women in the building fanning themselves. Fear of crying before the wedding ceremony begins has me looking down at my bouquet of peonies and taking deep breaths.

My gaze catches familiar faces on both sides of the ballroom as I work my way toward the front. They invited half of Seaside Pointe today. Shaggy dirty blond hair steals my attention on the right, and I meet Reid's eyes for seconds, catching the way they flare before I pass his row. I have the urge to turn back, to admire what looked like an actual fitted suit coat and tie covering his torso. To study the way he combs and parts his hair when he isn't able to cover the waves with a ball cap.

Sweeping the crazy thoughts from my mind, I continue to my spot instead and study the men watching me from the platform. I return Hayden's smile, loving the way he wrings his hands, his inked thumb rubbing against his palm. My gaze slides right, landing on Bodhi's warm smile. He's so tempting—all dark and mysterious—yet Reid's face pops in my mind. Then Drew's. *I need to get a grip on my hormones and feelings.* Thankfully, thoughts of the men in my life disappear when I lock gazes with the last groomsmen, Kip. My traitorous eyes give in to the tears as I picture the day—somewhere in the distant future—when it'll be him awaiting Chloe. Kip gives me a wink before I take my final steps and turn toward the back of the ballroom as Chloe, then Mia follows before trumpet blasts announce the bride's arrival.

As the newly coined Mr. and Mrs. Fox exit the ballroom to cheers, Mia meets the best man in the center of the platform, then Kip escorts Chloe and me behind them since we're an uneven party of five.

I stare at Bodhi and Mia's backs and attempt to ignore Kip's suggestive comments about Chloe's beauty. Bodhi's head dips close to Mia's, and I wonder what he's saying. They match beautifully together with their dark hair and eyes. Bodhi's complexion is a deep olive, whereas Mia is like Snow White reincarnated with her fair-skinned beauty, though working on the farm has given her a light golden tan. My lack of jealousy at their pairing tells me everything I already knew. My heart let go of any idea I had of dating Bodhi a while ago. Plus, I saw the way he covertly looked at her while we made toasts earlier. It was almost a relief.

Reid *was* right at lunch Friday. Sometimes we're so desperate to find someone, we hold onto the wrong one—or the idea of the wrong one—for too long. It's not the first time I've made this mistake. Does love operate on a strike system? Three strikes and you're out? Do I only get one more shot?

We step out of the ballroom and the wedding coordinator waves us to continue down the corridor to where the new husband and wife wait. I remove my hand from Kip's arm and lift the hem of my dress as Bodhi and Mia slow so we can walk as a group. We rehearsed the schedule last night. Chloe hits Kip's arm. "Seriously, were the champagne toasts not enough for you men? Did you do a few shots before the ceremony, too?"

I knew I smelled the tinge of strong alcohol beneath the mints when I took his arm.

Bodhi grunts. "Hayd was preparing to pledge his life to one woman. Shots were called for."

It's impossible not to steal a look at his strong profile. He wears a soft smile, and I note the way he holds Mia's hand hostage as she tips her head to look up at him.

"I guarantee you the prospect of marriage scares you a hell of a lot more than it does Hayden or Kip, for that matter." She bats her darkly-lined sherry eyes.

Bodhi and Kip share a glance and Bodhi tips his chin. "I guarantee you are correct."

There isn't time for a response before Brynn and Hayden appear, staring at each other and holding hands in an intimate bubble of two.

"Hell yeah, you did it." Kip's raucous shout startles me and interrupts their sweet moment before he shoves into Bodhi, and together, they attack the happy couple.

An arm weaves through mine as Chloe's flowery scent envelops me. "Men."

"You mean boys?" Mia clarifies as the guys exchange high-fives and hugs with Hayden like he's just invented the wheel.

Chloe laughs. "Exactly."

. . .

"I still think you two are perfect for each other." Chloe's stare drifts as she, Mia, and I join the cocktail party once we're finished taking group wedding shots. "I mean, look at him."

The three of us look up as Kip and Bodhi step under the covered loggia from the garden. The male beauty of those two men alone is off the charts. Throw in Hayden, and that best friend trifecta likely creates more fantasies than a romance author.

"Yes, he's gorgeous—"

Mia hums in agreement, then purses her lips when our attention swings her way. My chuckle remains under my breath.

"—but that doesn't mean we're meant to be. How many times has he told you he isn't looking for a relationship?"

Chloe cocks her head. "Neither was Hayden."

Shaking my head, I sigh. "I'm not pushing it, Loe. While it may appear so, I'm not that desperate. I don't..." I trail off as the guys make their way toward us. "Just drop it, okay?"

"You're not desperate. Far from it, but okay. I'm sorry. I just want the people I love to be happy. And maybe I'm a little selfish," Chloe whispers. "Those three are connected for life. I want to love whoever Bodhi winds up with. Think of all the fun couple things we could do together."

I laugh, giving Chloe's arm a squeeze. She has such a big heart.

"Ladies." The guys step into our circle, broad smiles and drinks in hand.

"Um, I'm going to go speak with my mom." Mia steps sideways. "I'll catch up with you guys in a bit."

"Hey." Kip's fingers snag her elbow before she escapes. "Save me a dance?"

"Of course." Mia agrees, but her gaze flits over the best man, and my heart rate ratchets a notch. Especially when I catch the way he lifts his drink, covering his smiling mouth, as she walks away.

That could get interesting.

depressed.
in my heart.
all solicitude, all
shall I be able to
time with you,
love you, and to think only
happiness of so saying, and
it to you

Reid

"Is this dance saved for me?"

Mia turns, a taunting smirk teasing her lips when she finds me at her side. "Kip on the dance floor with Chloe doesn't discourage you?"

I spot Loe in her light pink bridesmaid dress pressed against Kip, dancing cheek-to-cheek. With how lost they are in each other, I'd have thought today was their wedding day.

"Maybe I'm willing to take a chance tonight." I offer my hand. "Besides, we're friends, right?"

As I guide Mia toward the other dancing couples, I draw her against me by the waist, holding her hand out. We sway while Sinatra croons.

"You look beautiful, Mia."

Her fingers crawl along the back of my neck before she jerks them away and lays her palm flat on the curve of my shoulder.

"You don't clean up half bad yourself. Aside from New Year's Eve, I can't say I've seen you without a baseball hat."

I shrug. "It's easier out in the fields to keep the hair out of my eyes." My hair's getting longer these days. I should cut it before the ends reach my shoulders.

"I like it. It suits you."

A little rugged and untamed? I'm nearing thirty. Maybe it's time I clean up a bit?

"You know what's crazy?" Her brown gaze flicks from the dance floor to mine and back, soaking it all in. "This is actually the first wedding I've been to."

"Your first?" While I haven't been to many, I've attended a couple of my cousins' and my Aunt Joyce's second marriage. "And how are you feeling about it? Is it everything you imagined a wedding would be?"

"Oh no, are you one of those people who think all little girls dream of their big day?" She pats my shoulder like she's sorry for me. "Everything has been beautiful, and Hayden and Brynn are glowing. I'm happy for them, but this is a lot."

A lot might be an understatement, but I hadn't expected anything less from the Harrises. "So, you don't dream of your wedding day, I take it."

"Don't get me wrong, I believe in love, but trusting in someone to spend a lifetime with? I'm not sure I even want to get married."

Her confession tweaks something in my chest. There's a lot to unravel, but I tackle the last part first. "Not a believer in marriage, huh?"

Her fingers slide along the curve of my shoulder instead. She's withdrawing. "I don't know. Men haven't been too kind to the women in my life."

Before I think better of it, I ask, "How so?"

"There just aren't any, not biologically. Although my mother was adopted and doesn't know either of her biological parents' names, she was told the father was never in the picture." Her doe-eyed gaze shifts to the buttons on my shirt. "And my sperm donor wasn't one my mom wanted to stick around."

It's not a surprise to hear about her dad, but I didn't know Carrie-Ann's story. When there's no lasting couple in love to model your life after, why would you believe in marriage? My mom ditched us when I was nine, so it's been me, my dad, and my brothers for a long time. My grandparents on my dad's side passed not long after my mom left, and my mom's parents never liked my dad, so they didn't have any trouble abandoning us, too.

I didn't really know how much I wanted a family until I started working with James and Robyn, seeing what they've built. I want what my parents didn't have, a solid partnership. But marriage doesn't always equal a happy family. Plenty of people have kids and never get married, stay together and remain faithful. I can't fault Mia for her views.

"I'm familiar with the single parent bit. My mom didn't stick around either."

"No? You have siblings, though, right?" A flicker of recognition across her face. "Oh, my gosh. I'm an idiot. Wade Pruitt. He's your younger brother, isn't he? I'm not sure how I didn't put two and two together."

"Yeah." My little brother is a year younger than Mia. Just another reason we shouldn't be. "And an older brother, Ford. He's a big wig in Seattle. A broker and financial planner."

"Wade was a stud at Seaside Pointe High. Star on the baseball field. You played too, didn't you? With Kip? Were you like Mr. Big Shot back in school?"

"Kip was a sophomore when I was a Senior, but we played Varsity together my last year. *He* was the big shot. I was just a guy who loved playing ball until I was injured." With Kip's talent, he could have played in college, maybe even in the pros, whereas, as much as I would have liked making a career out of playing, I don't think I had the goods. Then the shoulder injury happened, and I never found out. "Wade's good, though. He got a scholarship to play for the University of Utah. Thank goodness. He's too restless for this town."

Kind of like Mia.

After our dance, I hang with Charlie, whose date ironically enough is Halie, Mia's friend from Shooters, and keep my distance from her for the rest of the night.

As I take another swig of my beer, my eyes wander the decked-out ballroom. When my attention returns to the woman in a dusty pink dress, something in me stills. Her white-blonde hair is in short waves, pinned on one side, like a classic movie star. Grace Embry.

Holding a flute of champagne, she watches Hayden and Brynn on the dance floor with a melancholy glint in her eyes, a faint smile on her lips. They kiss and smile and whisper to one another like they're in their own world.

Grace runs the edge of her glass along her plump bottom lip, her chest rising and falling on a deep sigh.

I pass Charlie my beer. "Hold this for me. I'll be back."

When I get closer, Grace's attention shifts off the dance floor. I follow her line of sight to Mia talking to one of the groomsmen. Brody, I think his name is? The final piece of Kip and Hayden's bromance. He's an intimidating guy, has the lean muscular build an MMA fighter would have. Mia is dwarfed by him even in heels, like a doll he could fit in his pocket. Though Mia is adding her coy natural flare, they're talking like old pals, and maybe they are. Being Kip's best friend, he probably knows Mia better than I do.

Unlike a few weeks ago when I nearly blew up watching Mia with Julian, I feel nothing when I see her with the best man, but Grace…the corners of her mouth dip, her eyes pinched in contemplation. With a shake of her head, she looks back at the newlyweds making eyes at each other and downs the rest of her champagne.

Does Grace know Brody? Probably through Loe. Determination propels my feet forward as I approach her from behind. I want to wipe the frown off her face.

"If your goal wasn't to steal the attention from the bride, you did a poor job," I whisper in her ear.

Grace's breath catches, her gaze whipping over her shoulder. When she sees it's me, the frown disappears, replaced by a soft smile. "Chloe never mentioned what a smooth talker you are."

"That's because I'm not one. I only tell the truth."

Her head falls back as she laughs. "Spoken like a real Casanova."

I had no intention of getting back on the dance floor, but I find myself asking Grace, "You wanna dance?"

After a couple seconds of eyeing me with something I can't quite pinpoint, she says, "Yeah, okay."

I take her hand, Grace's long, delicate fingers so soft compared to my calloused, blue-collar ones. When my other hand meets her back, my palm lands on the silky skin exposed by the low cut of her gown. The move wasn't on purpose, but I can't bring my hand to shift away.

"Some party, huh?"

She pulls away a fraction, bringing our faces close, enough so we can look at each other while we speak, but the distance is more intimate than friends would typically have between them. "Brynn has impeccable taste. I might have to enlist her help when I get married someday."

"Coming from the woman who owns one of the most popular clothing stores in Seaside."

"It's one thing to know how to put an outfit together. It's another to know how to style a room. Just because you can do one doesn't mean you can do the other. Brynn helped me design Fig, you know?"

"Can't say that I knew that. Can't say that I've even set foot in Fig."

She chuckles. "Unless you were shopping for women's clothing, you wouldn't have had a reason to."

Spotting Mia and Brody again, I knock my head to the side, gesturing. "Do you know him?"

"Bodhi?"

Bodhi. I was close. "Yeah."

One side of her pale pink lips curves. "You want the scoop on the guy entertaining your crush?"

It's pure curiosity. "She's not my crush." Anymore. "But also, how well do *you* know him?"

"And what makes you think I know him?"

"You know his name, and that's more than I know, but also, the way you were looking at them earlier before I came up to you."

Tilting her head, her eyebrow arches as she studies me. Not sure what I said to cause the examination, but she doesn't say. Instead, she moves in again, closing the distance so I can't look into her eyes that are more fiercely blue under the lights.

"We're friends, met at a Fourth of July party last year. We text on occasion."

They text. "Is he the current want-but-can't-have guy?"

"I—" She exhales. With how tall she is, in heels, her cheek grazes the stubble on my jaw. "Am I that obvious?"

I take a deep breath through my nose. She smells incredible. "No, but since we talked about it yesterday, it's fresh on my mind."

"I don't know that I actually wanted him or if I like the idea of him wanting me." Grace's fingertips brush the back of my neck before settling just below the collar of my suit coat. The faint touch pauses my lungs. "Is that weird? Like, I wouldn't turn the man down, but I'm not even sure that we'd fit if he was interested."

I clear my throat. "You really don't think he's interested?"

"An interested man doesn't text you to ask how all of your

mutual friends are doing, then ask about you as an afterthought. Nor does he go weeks without communicating. It also helps that he's vocalized his opinion about relationships a few times. Or rather, his lack of interest in them. Chloe just doesn't listen."

"Loe?"

"Chloe is the only reason we started texting in the first place. And I'm okay with being friends. I am. He's a good friend to have."

When I spare a glance at Bodhi and Mia, she's already watching me and Grace dancing with her head tilted, this pensive glimmer in her brown-eyed stare. There's no jealousy or longing. It's almost like she's deep in thought. *What's on your mind, Mia?*

The longer I hold her stare, the more her face morphs until it's like she's come to a conclusion and smiles. It's not her usual flirtatious smile. It's gentle. Friendly. I blink and she turns her attention back to Bodhi, who's talking with Mary Harris.

"Where does he live?"

"Seattle, but I know he goes out of town a lot for work. Everyone's very cryptic about his job, so I couldn't tell you what he does."

The guy's probably like the muscle for a mob boss. I laugh to myself. "Well, his loss. Don't sell yourself short. And just so you know, Embry." I lower my mouth to the shell of her ear as the music changes to a louder, faster beat. "Any man who you have your sights set on that doesn't return the sentiment is insane."

Grace steps back with a burgeoning smile and pats my chest. "You're good for the ego, Reid Pruitt. Maybe I'll keep you around."

since I left you, I have
been constantly depressed.
My happiness
incessantly
my memory your cares,
your
licitude
comp
tinually a burning
in my heart. When,
all solicitude, all harass
shall I be able to pass a
time with you, having
love you, and to think only
happiness of so saying, and
ing it to you.

Grace

I'm waist-deep in fifty electric violet sequined mini-skirts. I shouldn't be waist-deep in fifty electric violet anything. This isn't what I ordered for Fig. They're hideous. I should've checked the boxes when they came in on Friday, but with the wedding and the store busier than usual over the weekend, I haven't had time for inventory. So, now I'm three days behind on getting the correct order, which was supposed to be fifty powder blue A-line skirts.

Deep breaths. It's fine. I'll call Della and sort this out—scanning the shelves of inventory around me—as soon as I find my phone.

Ah-ha! There it is. Oh. A text from Chloe pops up on the screen.

Chloe: I saw you and Bodhi dancing at the wedding. I've waited long enough to talk about it. I'm coming by around 12. I'll bring lunch. Tell me what you want.

Well, at least with the mention of his name the butterflies stay dormant in their cage. That's a good sign—no more unrequited feelings.

The thing is, the butterflies have been dormant for him for a couple of months. It just never occurred to me until this weekend.

"What do ya say, Cinderella? I might not be Prince Charming, but how about a dance?"

Laughing, I accept Bodhi's hand as he leads me to the dance floor. "Don't sell yourself short. If not a prince, you're at least Maui."

He cocks an eyebrow. "The tattooed god with long hair?"

"Demigod, and the guardian of mankind, so pretty awesome, if you ask me."

"It's because of my heritage, isn't it?"

I chuckle. "A little too on the nose, huh?"

With a building smirk, Bodhi shrugs. "I'll accept it. So, was Kip's little sunshine a matchmaker growing up, too?"

Burying my forehead in his shoulder, I huff. "Oh, gosh, what did she do now?"

"She's persistent, is all I'm saying." He twirls me out and pulls me back in. "I can catalog all your finer attributes, in case you were wondering."

My cheeks heat. Mortified doesn't touch my level of embarrassment. "I'd apologize for her, but I doubt she's sorry. So, I'm sorry." I breathe a laugh. "No matter how many times I ask her to chill, she weasels her way out of it."

"Look, Grace..." The muscle in his jaw leaps as he swallows, and his eyes darken.

I press my palm to his firm chest. The last thing I want is for Bodhi to try and let me down gently when it's unnecessary. I'd like to save a smidgen of my pride.

"There's no need to say anything, Bodhi. I think we both know the only way this is happening is in Loe's mind."

"It's certainly not because you lack qualities any sane man would want."

"Are you saying you're not sane then?" I tease.

He goes crazy-eyed. "Not even the slightest bit. You're definitely better off without me."

"You might not be my *prince charming*, but you're certainly an amazing friend."

"Yes. What I lack in sanity I make up for with loyalty. There's nothing I wouldn't do for those guys." He motions in the direction of Kip and Hayden dancing. "That loyalty extends to you girls as well, you know."

I've overheard enough chatter between Kip and Hayden to know Bodhi's not talking to hear his own voice. He's not the type of guy who messes around. "Like I said, you're a good friend."

Me: Your choice.

I text, pulling out of the memory of my dance with Bodhi. Maybe if Chloe's eating something she loves, it'll ease the blow of letting her down.

Chloe: Are you dying?

Me: What are you talking about?

Chloe: The only reason my best friend Grace wouldn't have an opinion about lunch is if she's about to deliver bad news.

Caught.

Me: Oh my gosh. Just bring Pizzeria Limone or Pizza Pie Cafe.

Chloe: My comfort food? This is worse than I thought.

I laugh as I swipe the screen and dial Della.

An hour later, Chloe finds me finalizing inventory in the stock room. "Should I eat a piece before we start?"

"Stop being so dramatic." I laugh. "This doesn't affect you."

She pulls up the extra chair and sets the pizza box on the table. "Spill."

"Bodhi and I talked at the wedding, clearing the air a little bit."

"I don't like where this is going." She shoves a slice of her Margherita pizza in her mouth.

"It's not right between us, and it's time you moved on, Loe." My expression carries a hint of teasing, but she needs to know I'm serious. "Bodhi and I are best as friends. And we're okay with that. It was a mutual agreement."

"This isn't like one of those break-ups where one says it's mutual while there was clearly a dumper and dumpee."

"There was no dumping because we were never in a relationship to begin with. Not to mention: it *is* mutual. I don't want to be with Bodhi."

"You two are the worst," she says, shoveling in another bite. "I'm giving you a match made in heaven, and what do you do? Throw him away."

"It seriously feels like I'm breaking up with *you*." I chuckle. "There's no spark. What are we supposed to do with no spark?"

"Maybe you'd have a spark if you'd just kiss each other. Worked for Kip and me."

"It worked for you two because the spark was already there. You guys just ignited it into a freaking bonfire after you kissed."

"Yeah, we did." She smirks, stuffing her face with the last of her slice. "I concede. No more shipping Bodace."

Bodace? Forget it. I'm not going there. "Thank you."

She picks up another piece, her lips curving into a meddling smirk. "Something else I noticed Saturday night. You were dancing *awfully* close with Reid."

"Oh my gosh. Will you stop?"

"What? I can't notice you dancing with my ex-boyfriend?"

I curb my wince. "Did seeing us bother you?"

Rearing back, she eyes me, baffled. "Why? Because we dated for a few months? Come on, you know me better than that."

"Just making sure."

Not that it meant anything. It *was* one dance. Did he look delicious in a tailor-made suit? Sure. But so did Bodhi and lots of other men at the wedding. Were there warm tingles when his fingers grazed my bare back? Okay. But in my defense, it's been a while since a man has touched me. It doesn't mean I have a thing for Reid Pruitt.

"Should seeing you two together bother me?" Her ears perk up. "Are you asking me to give up on Bodace because you have a crush on Reid? Do I need to ship Greid? Race?" With her nose scrunched, she shakes her head. "Those ship names are not going to work for me. Graid? Reice? Reice. Reice I can work with."

I nearly choke on the diet Coke she brought me. "Stop it. Why do you have to make us sound like pre-teens?"

"You didn't answer my question."

Serious relationship or not. Girl code clearly states: One shall never date best friend's ex. Period. Not to mention sloppy seconds and all of that. But most importantly, I don't see him like that. I can't.

I laugh. "I don't have a crush on Reid, *Chlip*." Her mouth

pulls in consideration of the awful nickname, and I continue. "He's just been nice to talk to."

"Liar. You rubbed your earlobe."

"What?" I pull my hand away from my ear.

"Every time you don't tell the truth, you rub your earlobe. It's your tell. You used to do it with your parents all the time growing up."

I straighten my neck and square my shoulders. "I find rubbing my earlobe extremely comforting, so sue me. And this conversation is making me uncomfortable. Besides, I wasn't lying. Do I find Reid attractive? Yeah, but you already knew that. I said as much when you two started dating. Heck, we both said it back in school when he didn't give us a second look. We've bumped into each other a couple of times over the last month and had lunch. Same place, same time kind of thing."

"If this is about me, I'm fine if you like him. Honest to God truth. Hand over my heart. No, hand on my dahlia fields. You could date Reid, and I'd be perfectly okay, Grace."

Even if dating Reid interested me, it would get complicated, especially with Lockwood Blooms's future hanging over his and Chloe's heads. And he has his little hang-up on Mia, even though he says he doesn't. I'm not sure I trust it. That crush faded awfully quickly. I'm not touching that with a twenty-foot pole. No more unavailable men for me, thankyouverymuch.

"This doesn't have to do with you. Stop fixating. Just because Bodhi is out of the picture doesn't mean you need to shove somebody else in his spot."

"We never…you know…" Her head gives a subtle shake as a blush hits her cheeks. "So, it doesn't have to be weird. If you wanted. Reid's all yours."

My eyes widen. "You didn't bump nasties? How did I not know this?"

It's Chloe's turn to choke, and she slaps her chest to regain function of her lungs. "First of all, don't call it that."

I smirk. Serves her right for playing matchmaker. I already have one in my life I don't want. I don't need another. "Well, I can't call it getting jiggy, so I'm running out of options."

She rolls her eyes, ignoring me. "Secondly, you didn't ask, and I wasn't going to volunteer that kind of information. It would've made it all the more clear that I shouldn't have been dating him, but he was good for me at the time."

I can see that now, where she was in her life. He supported her in a way I don't think she even realized she needed.

"He was a good one for you. If there was no Kip, I'd have whooped your butt for losing him." I eat the rest of my slice. "Just cool it on the Yente front for a while. When I find the right guy, I'll know."

[...] I tell you, I have been constantly depressed. My happiness [...] incessantly [...] memory [...] your cares [...] your [...] affection [...] solicitude [...] completely [...] tinually a burning [...] in my heart. When [...] all solicitude, all harass [...] shall I be able to pass [...] time with you, having [...] love you, and to think only [...] happiness of [...] saying, and [...] ing it to you [...]

14

Reid

"Hey, my man! What's up!" Tony Stosich shouts from where he's already stretching on the diamond at Bingley Park.

I drop my bag in the dugout. "You're early."

"First practice of the season, baby. You know I had to get my lazy butt out here for some extra stretching. I'm getting old, and I don't labor all day like you do. Don't want to be tearing something."

After exchanging fist bumps, I join Tony in stretching my hamstrings and quads. "Eh, c'mon, sitting at a desk all day is dangerous on the body. All those paper cuts and the carpal tunnel from too much typing."

"Yeah. Yeah." Tony knocks into my side. "I haven't seen you in months. How's it going?"

"Busy."

"Don't I know it," Tony agrees. A former high school teammate of Ford's, Tony owns his own insurance agency, which keeps him as busy as the flower farm does me. When he isn't working, he's raising three kids and keeping his wife happy.

I swing my arms, warming up my shoulders as more of our team arrives. Their cutting up prods us into heading their way. Summer softball league. I've needed this.

"I missed catching up with Ford over the holidays. Did he even make it home?"

"You know Ford. He was here for two days. Too damn busy to take a vacation, as usual."

Tony slows and faces me, his face grim. "He's not back with *her,* is he?"

Her. I laugh. *Angelica.* Ford's ex-fiancée. "After what she did? Hell no. Besides, it's been almost two years. I think he's worked her out of his system."

"Good. She might have been easy on the eyes, but damn was she annoying."

I'm glad I didn't know her that well. Other than three random visits to town, Ford kept Angelica to himself for the first few years of their relationship. Once he popped the question, we made a big Christmas trip to Seattle—because she wanted to host us at Ford's fancy new digs—but things went south between them not long after our visit. According to Tony, who met her when he spent a weekend in the city to hit up a Seahawks game, Angelica was on her best behavior for our family. The woman he described—bossy, whiny, and materialistic—was nothing like the one I met. Though she always seemed a bit stiff, she fit the man Ford turned into after leaving Seaside Pointe.

Shoving my brother from my head, I join the rest of our team by the dugout. The co-ed softball summer league is one of the few things I do outside of work. Something I look forward to every year. And if that doesn't make me feel a tad pathetic, I don't know what will. Maybe it's time to look at my life and think about making a few changes?

I'M ON MY KNEES, laying down mulch around the perennial cutting garden when Mia kneels across from me and helps me spread the chips out.

"Hey, you got a sec?"

Using my shoulder to wipe the sweat running down my cheek, I pause. "Shoot."

"I'm heading back to Georgia."

I sit back on my heels and school my features, a slew of confusing emotions coursing through me. "Already?"

Her shoulders curve in. "Yeah, I...my friend Kaylee is having some issues, and I feel like I should be there for her."

I study Mia, curious. She seemed fine after our talks about being friends, but maybe I read her wrong? If I'm the reason she wants to leave...

"I don't want to sound conceited, but this isn't because of me, is it?"

Sifting a fistful of mulch through her fingers, Mia smiles. "No, I swear it's not. We're good, Reid."

I release a sigh. "So, how long will you be gone?" The way she talks about Georgia, it doesn't seem like she loved living there. For her to go back early feels off.

"I don't know." She catches her bottom lip with her teeth and looks at me through dark lashes. "I don't expect you to keep my job open or anything. Kaylee and Dana, my other floormate last year, have an apartment at the beach. I came home because I missed Seaside, but a few weeks on the beach doesn't sound awful either."

I nod. It's strange. Without the should-I-or-shouldn't-I hanging over us every day, it's like I can think more clearly. I stand by my choice to sever whatever was forming between us. I was lusting after a pretty girl who flirted with me and boosted a wounded ego, but that's all this was.

"Plus, there are a few loose ends back in Savannah I need to take care of. It's good timing." She glances around the farm. "For me anyway. I'm sorry if my leaving messes things up here."

"Nah, it'll be fine. You take care of your friend and enjoy some beach time." That's what she should be doing to begin with. "When do you leave?"

"Tomorrow."

Wow. Okay then.

For the next hour, Mia helps me finish laying the mulch, making things go twice as fast. At the end of the day, she lingers until we're the last few left on the farm. Pulling her into one of the supply sheds, I wrap her in a lingering hug.

"I hope things are all right with your friend, but just know, you have a place here if you need it. Okay?" Her grip tightens around my waist. "I mean it, Mia. If you need anything, you have my number."

"You're a good guy, Reid Pruitt." She sniffs against my chest. "I appreciate you humoring a teenager with a crush. Thank you for being the type of man who said no, instead of the type who takes what he wants."

What? I withdraw and tip her chin, and she reads my unasked question. "I'm fine. No one hurt me—at least not physically. Let's just say I learned a lot about myself, and guys, last semester, and leave it at that."

It's not my place to ask more. I want to, but I won't. Giving her one last squeeze, I release her with a smile. "Keep in touch, okay? Let me know when you're coming back, even if you don't want to get your nails dirty again."

"I will." Mia heads for the exit, her fingers untangling her long braid and sending her dark tresses whipping around her face as the breeze picks up. Flipping my ball cap backward, I turn for the office.

"Hey," Mia yells at the last minute, and I peer over my shoulder. "You should take a second look at what's standing in front of you, Reid. You deserve to be happy."

With a final wave, Mia disappears. I'll miss that girl, but what's standing right in front of me?

bit constantly depressed.
in my heart. When
all solicitude, all harm
, shall I be able to pass a
time with you, having
love you, and to think only
happiness of so saying, and
it to you

15

Grace

SUNDAY DINNERS. They're the best and worst part of my week. I get to spend time with my family, but my mom never misses an opportunity to meddle in my love life. Chloe ain't got nothing on Nanette Embry.

"Grace Elizabeth, just because you're twenty-six years old doesn't mean I'm not going to mother you."

Forget that I graduated magna cum laude or that I run a successful clothing boutique. Not to mention I bought my own house—it might be small, but it's still mine—and am perfectly capable of taking care of myself.

"I don't want you to set me up with Renee's cousin's neighbor's son or whatever he is. I'm perfectly capable of snagging my own dates." This is why I skipped last Sunday's meal. After Brynn and Hayden's wedding I knew I wouldn't be able to escape

Mom's meddling. It was wishful thinking that she'd leave me alone this week.

"Is that right?"

I am a strong, independent woman.

"You act like I never go on any dates."

One thin eyebrow raises. "Well, do you?"

So, it's been a couple of years. I've been busy building a business. Doesn't that count for anything? What if I never get married? It's possible I'll never meet the one. Some women don't even want to get married. Maybe I could change my outlook on life. Will my mom hound me until the day she dies if I never find a man to spend the rest of my life with?

You never gave me any grandchildren. In my head, she sounds like a decrepit old lady on her deathbed before she takes her last breath. Those would be her last words. I'd put money down.

"This isn't a Jane Austen novel, Mom. I'm not an old spinster. Women get married and have kids in their thirties all the time. I've got time. I'm not in a hurry."

That's what I tell myself anyway. I don't need a man. Do I want one? It wouldn't be the worst thing, but I've survived this long on my own. Getting burned in college didn't help matters, but that was four years ago. You'd think a girl could pick herself up after that.

I mean, I have. I've accomplished so much since I graduated. Sure, Gram's money helped, but I went for it. I turned the money into something great, something I love. I haven't wallowed in self-pity for years. And I've gone on dates since then. I just haven't wanted to go on second dates with any of them.

Bodhi would've been a real catch, someone I'd have taken a chance on, gone on as many dates as he asked, but he was opposed to a relationship from the beginning. Maybe I held on so tight to the possibility because it was the first in a long line of nos. Even though I knew Bodhi wasn't the one for me, I hoped eventually he could be.

"Boys are dumb, Mom," Lucy says, twirling her pasta. "Why would Grace want to be with one anyway?"

Lucy, my favorite. Twelve going on thirty. The little blonde is wiser than she knows.

"You only think boys are dumb because they haven't noticed you yet." Stella picks apart her roll, stuffing one chunk at a time in her mouth. "When they do, you'll change your mind real quick." Spoken like a true boy crazy rising junior.

Lucy scrunches up her nose, her freckles disappearing in the creases. "Doubtful."

"Even if you don't go out with Renee's best friend's nephew, it wouldn't hurt you to be more willing to put yourself out there. Don't close yourself off to possibilities just because they don't meet your high expectations."

I don't have high expectations. Do I have standards? You better believe it, but they aren't unreachable by any means. A man with a stable job, a car, and a decent place to live who treats me with love and respect. Oh, and not unavailable. Emotionally, mentally, physically. Is that too much to ask?

"Let Grace be, Netty," Dad says, cutting into his lemon chicken. "When she wants to find a guy, she'll find a guy."

"I know, Phil. I know." She tosses her hands in the air. "I just want you to be happy, Grace. And that store isn't going to bring you joy forever. It's not sustainable happiness. But you know I'm proud of you for what you've accomplished, right?"

"I do." Even if it's met with a side of judgment at every available opportunity.

"Good." She nods. "Good. You just would make such pretty grandbabies."

"*Mom*," my sisters chime in with me, all three of us groaning.

"I'm done." She guzzles her wine.

Four daughters. A family of five women. That's what my dad has to put up with. He tells us he never wanted sons, but only because he's nothing if not devoted to this family. He'd never want any of us to feel less than.

"Where's Autumn?" I ask.

"I'm not sure." Mom looks at the clock on the wall. "She said she'd be here, but you know how her timetable runs."

Autumn time. Late is on time for her. On time is early. And arriving before on time doesn't exist. If she were here, she'd have been the first to back me up. She's too caught up in her own love life to care about the lack of mine. And the older she gets, the more she embraces the independence of a woman.

Almost as if on cue, the front door flies open and my little sister, Autumn, stands there with a giant grin on her face and her fair cheeks flushed. Levi stands behind her, heart-shaped eyes pinned on the back of her strawberry blonde head. She holds her left hand up and wiggles her fingers. "I'm engaged!"

And just when I didn't think my night could get any worse.

THE LAST HOUR before closing tends to be my quietest. Some stragglers come in after work before they go home, but it's rare on a Wednesday. I sent Gina home an hour ago. So, when the bell dings thirty minutes before closing, the last person I expect is Reid.

"Excuse me, miss?" He looks around before meeting my gaze. "I was hoping you could help me. Someone recently told me I own too many flannels. You have anything that might look good on a man like myself?"

I come out from behind the counter and snatch the nearest blouse from a rack. Leaning my hip against the wood, I dangle the hanger from my fingers. "The cut might be a little off, but maybe you can pull it off."

Reid could probably pull anything off. He's got that rugged, don't-care-what-anyone-thinks vibe. I wouldn't put it past him to rock a pearl necklace like Harry Styles. Not that he would, but he'd make it look good if he did.

"I like it." He strides toward me in light gray pants and a denim button-down, the front quarter of his shirt tucked in, his sleeves rolled up his forearms.

"Don't worry," he says. "I changed my boots, so the mud and muck won't trail through your store."

The dark brown boots are laced up but not tied, his pant legs scrunched up behind the tongue like he slipped into them to come inside. And not to deviate from the norm, he's got a baseball hat on backward, his golden strands curling behind his ears and at his neck. A little sloppy and unintentionally hot. Why aren't more women going after Reid Pruitt?

"That's what vacuums and mops are for." I smile, dumping the blouse on the counter. "Can't really hurt concrete floors unless you take a sledgehammer to it. Don't do that."

"You're taking away all my fun." His curious eyes sweep around my shop, from floor to ceiling, wall to wall. "Not too shabby, Embry. A real store, quite the accomplishment. And this corrugated steel counter is pretty cool." His suntanned hand glides along the weathered wood surface as he peers at the metal base. While he washed his hands, it's clear he just came from the farm. Remnants of dirt are stuck under his nails that he couldn't quite get. Somehow it only adds to the appeal of his rough hands. Hands that see laborious work, that are utilized all day. Why does the sight of his hands make me flushed?

"*That* I can take credit for. Brynn designed everything based on it. I just love that industrial modern feel."

He squints like he's trying to understand what I'm talking about. "Yeah, that. So, why did you name the place Fig?"

With a gentle smile, I cross my arms over my chest. "My gram had these fig trees in her backyard, and for as long as I can remember, every time they were ripe, she'd call my sisters and me over, and we'd pick them together. We'd make fig jam and fig bars and all kinds of other delicious recipes. When she passed, she left me some money, and I used it to open the shop. It only seemed fitting to name it after one of my favorite memories with her."

"Sounds like you two had a really close relationship."

I nod but don't delve more into it because Reid looks as if he doesn't know what that's like. "So, what really brings you here? Something tells me you're not actually looking for women's clothing."

"You caught me. I was just on my way home, took a detour to grab a quick bite, and since I was in town, decided to rectify never setting foot in here."

"I'd give you a tour, but there's not really much to show except for clothes, dressing rooms, and a stock room."

"Dressing rooms seem like a fun place to tour."

He's not flirting with me, is he? Does he know what Kip and Chloe did to one of my mirrors last year?

"They're reserved for merchandise only, I'm afraid."

"So, I'd just need to pick up one of these blouses and try it on for you." Reid holds up an olive green peasant top with flutter sleeves.

"That color would do wonders for your complexion, matches your eyes perfectly."

He laughs and returns the hanger to the galvanized pipe rack.

Taking a step toward him, I say, "I lost track of you at the wedding after our dance. Did you have a good time?"

"Yeah, it was quite a party. Those Harrises know how to throw down. I can't complain, though. Open bar and all that."

"Yeah, it's fun to live like the other half, huh? How are things at the farm?"

"Not bad. I had a surprisingly restful weekend. I'd expected Chloe to beg me to come in, seeing as how Hayden is on his honeymoon, but I guess she took the weekend off for a change too." She did. Kip treated her to a surprise weekend getaway to belatedly celebrate their one-year anniversary. "I needed the break after the hell of last week. Our dahlias are blooming, and the cutting is never-ending. How about you? How was your weekend?"

"Well, I worked." I drum the top of the counter. "And my younger sister got engaged."

"That's fun." He smiles, but his expression contradicts his words like he knows how I really feel about it. "How old is she?"

"Twenty-three, but, truly, I'm happy for her." Just sad for me. "He's some musician she met like six months ago." I shrug. "But I guess, when you know, you know." I don't want to talk about Autumn anymore, so I ask, "How are things going on the Mia front?"

"Oh, you haven't heard yet? She left, went back to Georgia last week after the wedding."

"What, really? Why?"

"To be with friends and scramble away from me, probably."

"What did you do to that poor girl?"

Raising his hands in surrender, he chuckles. "Nothing. I'm kidding. We're good, on friendly terms."

"You broke her heart, didn't you?" I tease.

"I did not break her heart. We're too different, and while some opposites can make things work, we're not those people. It was clear to both of us."

"*Hallelujah.* I did not want to have to hide your body."

"What? You said you were on my side."

"Only because I don't like to stick my nose where it doesn't belong, but Kip would've murdered you, and as Chloe's best friend, it would've been my duty to help cover the whole thing up."

"Loyalty." He nods, a trace of amusement in his gaze. "I can appreciate that."

"The loyalest." I beam like I've been awarded a gold medal. "Are you really okay with the Mia thing?"

"Yeah." Reid swats the air. "It was never going anywhere, and at this point, I don't want to waste my time on something that I know from the get-go isn't going to last."

"You really don't think she left because of you?"

"God, I hope not. She thanked me when she said goodbye, so I don't think so."

"Thanked you?"

"Yeah, it was something like, thank you for saying no and not just taking. How would you interpret that?"

"Maybe thanking you for not leading her on? Or for thinking with the right body part." I smirk.

"It can be a challenge, but I do use the right brain on occasion." His eyes dance with mirth.

I brought it upon myself, but with his roguish gleam, my mind gravitates where it shouldn't, and warmth blooms in my cheeks. I check the clock on the wall over Reid's shoulder, and he notices. "Oh, are you wanting to get out of here? I should've looked at the door to see what time you close."

"I close in about five minutes, but you can stay. I don't mind the company while I balance everything out." I round the counter, and Reid rolls his neck with a yawn. "Unless, of course, you're probably dead on your feet. Don't feel like you need to stay."

Indecision flickers across his face, but he says, "Yeah, I really am beat. How about we meet up for lunch again sometime this week?"

"A set time rather than a coincidence?" I wink. "Sure. I'm always in town."

"I don't know what day will work best, but I can let you know."

"I'm down. A girl's gotta eat."

We exchange numbers before Reid leaves with a side grin and a wave. As the door chimes on his exit, it hits me.

Did we just set up a date?

since I left you, I have
been constantly depressed.
My happiness is
incessantly i
my mem your cares
our affection
licitu
compa
tionally a burning and a
in my heart. When,
all solicitude, all har
, shall I be able to pass a
time with you, having
love you, and to think only
happiness of saying, and
ing it to you

*R*eid

MOVING ALONG THE DAHLIA PATCH, snipping stems, Loe appears beside me.

"Hey. I wasn't expecting you to stop by today, though it is dahlia harvesting time, so of course you're here to visit your favorite patch." I smirk. "You normally call or text first."

She shrugs with one of her golden Loe smiles. "Yeah, things are running so smoothly today that I snuck away and met Brynn for a real lunch hour. Hayden's been keeping her all to himself since they returned home." *Ha. Yeah, I bet.* I'm tempted to give Loe a round of applause. Lunch breaks off the farm are few and far between, especially for her. "I figured I'd stop in on my way back."

"You're figured you'd stop by?"

Chloe doesn't just stop by. The risk of running into James is too high. She continuously checks with me to make sure he's not around.

"Yeah, why not?" She shoves her hands into her messy bun and tugs the knot tighter, the locks growing in volume. I cock my head, not buying her excuse.

"Fine, you caught me." She waves me to follow her. "I was thinking—"

"Oh, great. The last time you did that, you made the compost tea that smelled like the walking dead."

"Hey, it's not a bad idea to switch things up sometimes. I still don't know what I messed up."

"Let's not find out, okay? My nose didn't work for weeks."

"Yeah, yeah. We'll stick with our tried-and-true recipe from now on. Onto the reason I'm here." She stops walking. "How difficult do you think it would be to move this over to my farm?"

"This?" I glance around, unsure what she's referring to until she settles her palm against the yellow building we use as one of our many storage buildings. "The shed?"

Her smile grows wide, her wild curls bouncing about on top of her head as she nods. "I wanted my workshop, but with it being the old garage and immovable, that's not possible."

"I mean…" *Move the shed.* "Yeah, we could take it apart and rebuild it. It's just a kit. Time-consuming but not difficult. What are you thinking?"

She steps back and eyes the metal walls like she can see through them. "I need more storage on the back half of the new property, and since this is mostly filled with stuff older than me, I don't think it's needed here anymore."

The thought of sorting the junk is more overwhelming than tearing apart the building and putting it back together again.

"Plus, if we move it, we can build another bed for the dahlias." She walks along the gravel path surrounding the shed. "This takes up valuable planting property. All this space could be flowers."

"True, true. We never seem to have enough dahlias. I can get to work sorting through the stuff in here unless you want to do it yourself."

Her gaze strays toward her parents' house. "I trust you to know what's important and what isn't. There's a good bit of room in our blue shed to move things from the yellow, isn't there?"

I nod. "Anything I'm unsure of I'll keep so you can check it out."

"Thanks, Reid." Her fist taps my shoulder. "I better get back to it. Hayden's building our store this week. He's probably cursing me for leaving him with rookie builders."

Her face lights up at the mention of the store. She's always wanted a "you pick" farm and a place to sell her seed packs. The desire doubled after the camping trip where Kip took her to the lavender farm. That trip ended us, but it sparked her next idea. All she needed was Kip—with his background in development—to show her the demand for what she'd dreamed up. He's convinced a roadside gift shop will bring tons of publicity to Lockwood Blooms with free advertising she'll get from visitors posting on their social media.

"Does he need my help? Denise and Meredith can run this place in the afternoons."

"Nah, it's all good. He says he's using the experience to hone his skills for when he has to build playhouses for his future kids."

I choke. "They just returned from their honeymoon, and they're talking kids already? Should we start a pool on how long it will be until he knocks Brynn up?"

"You say that like it's a bad thing. You always said you want kids. Have you changed your mind?"

"Not at all." The one downfall in our brief relationship last year was knowing Chloe wasn't close to ready for a family. She used to say she wanted one, but growing the business came first. Another sign we never would have worked out, I suppose. Running my palm under my ball cap and smoothing back a wayward chunk of hair, I add, "I think I'd prefer a year of marriage under my belt before adding little monsters, but I'm flexible."

"We need to find you a girl, Reid Pruitt—"

"Ooohhh, no, you don't." I step back at the gleam in her eyes. "Grace told me about your matchmaking habits. I don't need your help finding a willing woman, Loe. For one, with our history it's weird. You should focus on Meredith and Eric. Leave me be."

She chuckles. "So, I had one failure in my pursuit to find happiness for Grace. Doesn't mean I'll fail with you. But fine." Her hands lift in surrender. "I'll stay out of it."

"Much appreciated."

"Okay." She rubs her palms together. "When I can come get the shed, let me know. I'll bring some muscle."

"I see how it is. You're going to make me do all the hard work, clearing it out."

"Sic Tyson on it." She walks backward with a teasing glint in her eyes. "He's good at getting rid of stuff."

My brain flashes back to the seed disaster of 2020. "Low blow, boss. Low blow."

"Too soon?" She laughs and turns, walking off toward old, reliable Betty.

Returning Julian's wave as he heads out for the day, I check the time. Four o'clock. Two hours until softball practice. Stretching my arms over my head, I glance at the yellow shed Chloe wants removed. *Might as well use my time wisely.* Pulling the doors wide, I take a visual inventory. The place is crammed with old tools, hoses, PVC for irrigation. Too many things James never dared throw out but are unusable at this point. The old hoarder.

About thirty minutes into it, and less than a quarter of the shed sorted through, I've got a good chunk that can be thrown away sitting outside the doors.

"What are you doing in here, Reid?"

I turn to James's shadow in the doorway. He steps inside and looks around with a deep frown.

"Oh, uh…Loe stopped by earlier and asked to move this shed onto the new land since we don't need it. We're going to utilize our land for more dahlias and get rid of all this stuff since we can't use it anyway."

He tenses, adjusting the waistband of his pants. "That's not happening."

"James, all of this stuff is rusted, cracked, or deteriorating. We don't need it. It's taking up valuable space."

"I don't care," he snaps. "Get rid of the crap in here, but the shed stays. We'll use it for other storage."

I wipe the back of my hand across my brow. "We could really use the land for more dahlias tu—"

James takes one step closer to me, a vein popping out of his wrinkled forehead. "Chloe can buy her own damn shed! She's not taking this one! Maybe I made a mistake offering you the farm if you're just going to let Chloe run things anyway." Tossing an arm in the air, he walks out without another word, leaving me shocked.

Well, okay.

This is why I didn't jump on his offer to take over Lockwood Blooms. James has never yelled at me before. Honestly, when I found out he lost his mind on Loe after discovering her relationship with Kip, I almost didn't believe her. In all the years I've worked here, he's gotten angry—who doesn't—but never raised his voice at a single employee, no matter how badly they mess up.

Something isn't right with him. How does a father carry that much anger toward his daughter he won't even let her have a shed? Not a brand-new shed we use regularly, but a rundown one we'd probably replace in a couple of years anyway. After all this time, I thought this family feud would blow over, that his heart would soften, but it seems to be getting worse. Robyn has all but disappeared. James is moodier by the day. Is it any wonder Loe stays away?

in my heart. When
all solicitude, all
shall I be able to pass
time with you, having
love you, and to think only
happiness of so saying, and
it to you

17

Grace

"How did I let Bucky talk me into this?" I ask my frowning reflection in the tinted window of an SUV in the Bingley Park parking lot while pulling the ponytail on top of my head tighter.

"C'mon, Grace. Vera broke her leg and can't play. We need another female on the team or we can't compete for playoffs." Bucky begged when he called last night.

Go on a few dates with a guy, and suddenly you're his go-to stand-in for summer league co-ed softball.

"Isn't the roster set? It's halfway through summer. You can't just add a new player."

"We can when it's a medical exemption," he replied. *"Don't pretend like you don't like baseball, Grace. You spent half of high school coming to our practices and watching games."*

"Blame my teenage hormones, Buck." And Chloe for her closeted crush on Kip. *"I hung out at the football games too, but you don't see me suiting up in pads and a helmet, do you?"*

Bucky chuckled. "We're practicing tomorrow at six at Bingley Park. Why don't you show up and see what you think? You probably know half the team. It'll be fun."

I might have said no if it weren't for Mom's complaints about all the time I spend alone or at work. That little bug in my ear made me second guess everything. All around me, my friends are settling down. Chloe's got Kip, Brynn has Hayden, my baby sister is engaged.

"Fine," I relented. Maybe it'll be fun, and if nothing else, I'll get some badly needed exercise.

I WALK through the bustling complex searching for my new team—the Stosich Agency Seasiders. There are two youth games taking place, one vacant field and one field with a group of adults spreading out across the infield. Clutching Stella's borrowed softball glove for her JV team between my nervous fingers, I head toward the adults.

The first person I recognize is Jackie, kicking the dirt around the first base bag. She's the one name Bucky mentioned from their team. Even if he hadn't told me she's their other female player, Jackie's tall frame and pink and black braids are unmistakable. Thanks to baseball hats, the rest of the faces are indistinguishable from my vantage point.

The faces are, but some bodies aren't. A smile plays on my lips as the *very* recognizable pitcher stands to his full height on the mound. *Reid.*

In a white form-fitting T-shirt and black gym shorts, his toned calves on display, he returns my smile. Who knew calves on a man could be so hot? They're just legs, but attached to Reid, my mind wanders to what his thighs look like. And higher, does he have the V? I mentally slap myself. I can't think about Reid like that. Chloe's blessing or not, he'd never want to be with me if he knew everything about my dating history.

"There you are," Bucky hollers, drawing my attention to home plate where he's slipping on a chest plate.

I wave half-heartedly. "Here I am."

Bucky flashes a bright smile and jerks his head—wordlessly telling me to get my butt on the field—as he turns. "Hey guys, we've got our other gal," he shouts as I slip through one of the dugouts and onto the dirt. "I think most of you know Grace Embry."

I'm not particularly shy, but having my name echoed by seven people simultaneously sends a wave of heat up my neck. Again, I lift a lukewarm wave, and Bucky shoots out introductions. The guys swinging bats at his side are Jackie's older brother Tony, who owns the insurance agency that sponsors the team, and Eric from Lockwood's. I nod my greeting and turn to the others in the field.

"Not all the guys could make it tonight, but I know you know Reid and Jackie," Bucky points out.

While Reid eyes me from the pitcher's mound with a peculiar grin on his face—of course he's the pitcher, that was his position in high school—Jackie jogs her way to my side.

"I haven't seen you in months." We hug. "How's that shop of yours doing? I've been meaning to visit."

"It's great. Busy and tiring, but great. You better come in. I offer a high school friend discount, you know." I wink. Only to the ones I'm still friends with, anyway.

"Now you're talking, girl."

"We've only got the field for an hour, ladies," a tenor voice hollers.

"I know that voice." My head pops up to the guys walking their way in from the grassy outfield. Scott Ketchum and… *Oh, Lord. I knew I knew that voice.* "Well, hell, if I'd known you were on the team, Rick, I would have refused to join."

Rick flips me off, but there's a smile behind the action. He stops at Reid's side and says something that makes him laugh softly before they both look my way.

"Tell me something, Buck. Did you purposely omit the fact that I've dated one-third of this team so I wouldn't say no?" Scott married Sarah Rinaldi last year, and last I heard, Rick was dating Chelsea Bray, Kip's old high school flame. At least I won't have to worry about them hitting on me. I punch Bucky's shoulder when he shrugs. "Dirty move."

With little to no remorse, Bucky sends me to the shortstop position. Eric, then Tony, take turns batting through the large bucket of balls Reid pitches before they switch places with Scott and Rick. I catch a hit here and there and field a few more, tossing them back to Reid per his request.

"All right, Jackie. Grace, you're up," Rick calls when he's done with his at-bat.

I'm up? I blink. Jackie jogs toward home plate and takes a bat from where it leans against the fence. *Oh, I'm up! Crap.* "Um, maybe I should stay out here tonight. With tonight being my first practice and all?"

"Considering we have a game Thursday night, I think you should take a few swings," Rick responds because he's the closest as he walks to take my place on the field.

"Oh, is that what you think?" I shoot him a mocking glare. It's not that I dislike him, but when we dated in high school, he cheated on me, which kind of sucked. What sucked harder was being too weak to turn down his request for a second chance when we ran into each other after I returned to Seaside once I graduated college. He was my rebound from Drew that lasted all of one week and two dates before he cheated again. We weren't really a couple, so it wasn't actual cheating, but obviously, my winner radar is horribly broken.

"Hey." A hand wraps around my elbow and draws me away. Turning, I look at Reid, allowing him to lead me toward home plate. "Watch Jackie, then take a few pitches of your own. Having two women on the team is a league rule, but we're only required to make one bat. Jackie holds her own—"

I cock my head. "Are you saying you don't think I'm good enough to play like the rest of you?" Which, come on, I'm not. I've never played softball in any official setting. I've thrown a ball around with Stella a few times throughout the years and joined in during recess or physical education.

Reid's eyes go wide under the dark rim of his trusty ball cap. "I said nothing of the sort."

"No? Then what are you saying, Pruitt?"

This time he chuckles. "Ummm, that you should take a few pitches and see how you feel?" He studies me like I'm a loose cannon, his eyes scanning across my face as his thumb soothes over the inside of my elbow, causing a shiver beneath his touch. With a jolt, he drops his hand.

"Okay, you're right," I concede with a shake of my head. I can't not bat. I'm too competitive to let the men skip me over. If I'm going to join the team, I'm going to play.

I stand to the side during Jackie's practice and swing each time she does. Working on my timing as Reid throws every pitch directly over home plate. Sure, he's throwing underhand and slow-pitch, but dang, he's still got the goods. Finally, it's my turn.

"Don't worry, Grace." Reid says while I'm positioning my feet and shaking my butt like the guys always do. "I'll take it nice and easy on you."

My mind goes blank. No witty comebacks, no jabs at his masculinity. Nothing. I'm nervous. My palms are sweating while the others actually call out encouragement.

The first pitch flies by before I move the bat off my shoulder.

"Just keep your eye on the ball. You've got this," Bucky says from his spot as our catcher.

Second pitch comes, and I catch air, swinging after the thud of the ball hitting Bucky's mitt sounds.

Ugh. I hate not being good at things. *You* can *do this. Eye on ball. Bat off shoulder.* Reid releases the third pitch. Once again, I miss.

"That was closer, girl. You've got this. Swing a little lower, waist level," Jackie encourages.

Swing waist level? Exhaling deeply, I test my swing. *Check.*

Shaking my butt and setting my feet in the dirt, I turn my head and meet Reid's eyes for the first time since I stepped to the plate. His nod of encouragement is subtle, a slight dip of his chin, as he holds the neon yellow ball with a wide grip before his face. I swear I hear him saying, "Watch the ball," as he tucks it into his glove. In the span of one breath, Reid's arm winds down and around and he releases. I swing the moment the leather leaves his fingers…

And BAM.

"Oh my—" I burst into laughter, my arms vibrating from the connection, as the ball flies over Reid's head and lands in the empty space between Bo and Tony. My heart pounds with pride as I revel in my new teammates' cheers for a full five seconds before I'm back in position and ready for the next pitch.

Reid cocks his head, a new ball in his glove. "Ready?"

Swinging my hips and adjusting my stance, I smile. "Show me what you got, Mr. Pitcher."

"See you guys Thursday. Oh, Grace, I'll have your uniform shirt."

"Thanks," I tell Bucky, waving to the others as we exit Bingley Park, splitting off at the parking lot. Reid remains at my side, following me toward my car. I open my mouth to call him out on his being a gentleman, then slam it shut when I notice his truck three spots to the left of my Accord. We slow our steps, and I dig in my bag, searching for my car keys.

"So, softball?"

I chuckle. We've been together for the last hour, but we've had little time to talk about anything other than what was going on on the field. "Yeah, I'm a bleeding heart for those in need, apparently."

Reid adjusts his bag over his shoulder—a genuine bag for baseball gear: cleats, helmets, two bats. He looks like a dang pro —before his hands go to his waist. "The needy appreciate it. We can usually fill our team with little effort, but this year…" He loses my attention as his fingers tie a knot in the drawstring of his workout shorts. The movement allows flashes of taut golden skin and hypnotizes my brain before two sharp blows of a horn startle me back to my senses.

Grace! Get a hold of yourself.

I catch Reid tossing a wave as Tony and Jackie drive by and do the same.

Reid's gaze returns to me with eyes one shade lighter than the olive green blouse he joked about trying on in Fig as their taillights fade from view. I've had dozens of conversations with him but never paid much attention to his eyes. They're beautiful. The kind of green people buy colored contacts to replicate. No wonder I have difficulty looking away.

"You did well tonight," he says. "Though, I might lay off the cockiness a bit when batting against the opposing team."

"I thought smack talk was part of the game."

"Sure, when you earn it."

"When I earn it? I earned it. I hit the ball."

He clicks his tongue against the roof of his mouth. "You hit three out of twenty, Grace."

Stopping my eye roll is impossible. "Whatever, Mr. Big Shot Baseball Player. Not all of us earned our letterman's jacket in high school."

Reid steps closer and rests his hip against my car, his sinewy arms crossing. Have I never seen him in a short sleeve shirt before? That can't be right. Have I simply never noticed? Flower farming did those bulging biceps good.

"No? Then tell me, what did you earn in high school?"

"A reputation that wasn't memorialized in the yearbook." I shoot a wink over my shoulder and open my car door.

Wrapping his hand over the door frame, he pulls it wide for me. "You're such a tease. This town has too many eyes and ears for that to be the truth."

Don't I know it. Reputations follow everyone in Seaside Pointe, and secrets have a way of always coming out. Or, almost always. I toss my bag into the car and turn back to Reid. "You caught me. I was an angel, and I earned a lot of awards in art. Lots of drawings of fashion lines."

He nods because that makes more sense. "I'm not surprised."

There's something about his answer that resonates with me. Just like earlier on the field, he seems to have faith in me when in truth, we've only just begun to get to know each other on a deeper level.

"Okay, well, I guess I'll see you Thursday for my first game?"

"I was going to head to Los Rancheros to grab dinner. We haven't grabbed that bite yet. You want to join me?"

"You and your aversion to eating alone. Or is it just my delightful personality?"

"Eating alone. Putting up with you." Reid holds his hands out at his sides, weighing his options. "You're right. It's a tough choice."

"If it weren't for the fact that I could marry a burrito right now, I'd force you to eat alone."

since I left you, I have
been constantly depressed.
My happiness
incessantly
my mind
your
licitude
continually a burning and a
in my heart. When,
all solicitude, all harass
shall I be able to pass a
time with you, having
love you, and to think only
happiness of saying, and
ing it to you.

Reid

OUR WORKLOAD at the farm is enough Wednesday and Thursday that I don't have a chance to revisit cleaning out the shed for Chloe. I should probably tell her about James's reaction, but she doesn't need more of his crap. Maybe he'll cool off by next week. He's walking through the farm daily now. He doesn't speak to anyone, just walks through the beds and stops and stares. We'll get the occasional approving nod or grunt, but that's it. Compared to the man he was a year ago, he looks frail and gray. Too weak for a man in his early sixties. That stroke took a lot out of him, but if I were a betting man, I'd bet a month's pay his estrangement from Loe is what's killing him.

"At what point do you think that man is going to accept his daughter isn't walking away from Kip?" Denise comes up behind me as I tie off a new dahlia from our breeding patch Loe wants harvested for next season.

"Never." My disappointment in the man who taught me so much about flower farming and life is hard to hide these days.

Denise tsks. "All because the Lockwoods and Harrises couldn't get along? I'm not buying it." Dropping my spool of string by accident, Denise bends and picks it up for me. "You know my aunt went to school in the same grade as Denton. She said there was a pretty big scandal between them back then."

"Scandal? With James and Denton?" James is several years older than Denton Harris. From what I recall, they would've been a sophomore and senior. They were never friends, like their fathers before them. Before the infamous cow incident.

"Yeah. She said it was all hush-hush. Everyone knew something happened because Denton was pretty vocal about his hate for James for a while, but no one knows why."

"Huh." I continue down the row, tying off another dahlia. "It's ridiculous either way. Harris has accepted Chloe into their family like she's already his daughter-in-law. I've seen it personally. The fact that James can't get over himself—"

"Unless James is the one who was wronged?"

Maybe. Even still, is a man's hatred toward another enough to justify cutting off his own daughter, his own flesh and blood? I couldn't do it. As much as I wanted to continue hating Kip Harris after the way we butt heads, I can't deny Chloe's never been happier.

"All right, enough with gossip. Let's head to the roses and help Meredith finish cutting. I've got a game tonight, so I don't want to be here too late."

"I heard from Eric that you guys added Grace Embry. I'm sorry I couldn't commit."

Psh. "You're not sorry."

Denise laughs. "Yeah, you're right. Everyone knows sporting is not my thing. You were obviously having a lapse in judgment when you asked me about joining."

"Clearly. Grace will be good, though." I mean, she can't hit the ball for nothing, but she looks cute trying, and she was decent at fielding. Plus, I got a pretty enjoyable dinner date out of the deal. "We'll be fine," I say with a touch more conviction than I feel. We'll see how she does for her first game tonight.

"So, you're predicting another league championship for the Seasiders?"

"Damn straight."

"For someone who struck out at each of her at-bats five days ago during her first game, you impressed me tonight." I open the door to Perry's for Grace after Tuesday's practice. We're starving, and apparently, eating together is becoming our thing.

"I don't think my first game should count. I should get a… what's it called?" She snaps her fingers, her forehead wrinkled as she searches for whatever word she's trying to recall. "A mulligan! I should get a mulligan."

I throw my head back with laughter. "You know that's a golf term, right?"

"I guess that explains why I know it. That's the only sport my dad watches and plays."

Again, laughter pours from my lips. While dating Loe, I never realized how fun Grace was to talk to, how easy. She's chill but witty. Time flies when we're hanging out.

After we order, I say, "This week, you watch, you're gonna get a base hit. I have a feeling."

Grace tosses a fry in her mouth as we find a table and sit. "From your lips to my bat."

"So, what did you do for the fourth? Did you go on that camping trip with Loe?"

"With Kip, Brynn, and Hayden? Yeah. She told you about it?"

"Only because she asked me to take any calls if there were emergencies." I unwrap my burger. "Bodhi didn't go?"

"Nope. I was the fifth wheel." Grace wags her brows. "It was fun, though. We had a boat for the weekend, and us girls drank and tanned while the menfolk caught dinner."

Now that we're under Perry's fluorescent lights, I note the pink tint across the bridge of her nose and cheeks from her weekend in the sun. "Man, I helped my dad repair a bunch of fence boards. Your weekend seems more fun."

"Aw. That's a good son, but not much of a weekend for you." She brushes my calf under the table with her foot, but was it on purpose? "Like you don't do enough physical labor at work, huh? I tell you what, next time I'll invite you along. You need a break, Reid Pruitt."

"I'll hold you to that." I don't know how Kip or Loe would feel about dragging me along on a weekend getaway, but I'm not sure I'd care if it meant more time with Grace. "So, tell me more about the weekend."

It's after nine, and the sun has set by the time we're done eating and chatting, so I take a detour and follow Grace to her car. She attempts to wave me off, swearing she's capable of making it to her car, but I refuse. The parking lot lights are dim, and I am a gentleman, after all.

Music pours from a bar down the strip center as the door opens and a group steps outside, their laughter carrying as they light up cigarettes by the curb.

Grace leans against her Honda's door and offers me a soft smile. "Once again, thanks for the dinner company."

Slipping my hands into my pockets, I rock on my heels. "I should be thanking you."

"For saving you from another solo meal?" She confirms with a nod. "It was my pleasure."

"Oh, I forgot to ask, did you get that issue with your supplier figured out?"

She showed up at our game last Thursday full of fire and sass because a shipment of new something—dresses with raw silk edging—was completely wrong from what she'd ordered. We teased her endlessly that all her wrath was the reason she struck out. The woman was swinging blindly, her only aim to kill.

Grace cocks her head, her teeth sinking into her bottom lip as she looks at me.

"What?" I wipe my palm across my mouth. "Do I have mustard on my face or something?"

"No." Her teeth release her lip. "I'm just surprised you remembered." *Why wouldn't I?* "I did get it fixed. They discounted what they did send, and they're shipping what I ordered as well. That's twice in one month. I should probably find a new supplier, which is too bad because I like Della. Thanks for asking."

"Yeah. I mean, of course." I glance over my shoulder, looking toward my truck, as the hairs on my nape rise, reacting to the softening in Grace's tone. "I'm glad you were able to straighten things out."

The smokers by the bar laugh and a car drives by with bass shaking its windows, but silence hangs between Grace and me. Her gaze lowers to the ground, then lifts, and her mouth parts...

"Hey!"

A deep-voiced shout pulls our attention toward the bar. A man breaks away from the group standing around smoking. He saunters into the street, causing a car to slam on their brakes, and heads our way.

"You're...you work for Lockwood," he slurs.

My eyes narrow, trying to pinpoint how I know him. He looks to be around fifty, in shape but gray hair feathers around his temples and shallow lines edge his eyes. I inch closer to Grace, putting myself between her and the man weaving toward us like he's had two too many drinks.

"You work for that haughty little girl," *Little girl?* "Harris's whore."

What the—

"Excuse me?" Grace pushes at my arm, shoving me out of her way.

I wrap an arm around her waist, pulling her back before the drunk man finds himself knocked out by a woman. "Easy, Slugger," I warn, tucking Grace behind me as I turn to the man. He's familiar, but not. Well dressed. The chunky gold watch on his wrist hints at money. "I suggest you find yourself a cab."

"You tell your boss to watch her back."

My muscles tense. The urge to wail on this drunk prick is overwhelming. "Are you threatening Chloe Lockwood?"

The man keeps his distance, not coming any closer than the grass median in front of Grace's vehicle. "Warn Harris, too. He screwed with the wrong man. That land shouldn't be in that girl's hands."

Ahhh. *This* is Joseph Sullivan. The crooked son of the man who owned the land Chloe—well, technically Denton Harris—bought for Chloe's Blooms. What the hell is his problem? Yes, the land was meant to be sold to another before Denton purchased it, then sold it to Chloe, but that shouldn't matter to Sullivan. They got paid either way.

"I'm not going to tell you again. You need to hail a cab and go."

"And think twice before threatening our friends, boozy." Grace clutches my arm, her soft curves pressed against my back as she yells at the man. *Feisty woman.*

Two men jog across the street, likely drawn our way by Grace's outburst.

"Is he bothering you?" One asks as the other places an open palm on Joseph's chest, pushing him back.

"Bothering us? He's making threats—"

"Grace," I hiss. My hand takes hers, squeezing her fingers.

The first man steps closer, his gaze raking over us as the other keeps murmuring to Joseph and shoving him back toward the bar. "I apologize. He threw back a few too many beers on the course this afternoon."

I give a curt nod. I'm not escalating this when Grace stands here, and there are three of them and one of me. "Just get him away from us."

A three sheets to the wind Joseph is no match for his buddies, and with another nudge and muted words, the group makes their way across the road and back toward the bar. Tension releases from my limbs with each step they take.

"This isn't over." Sullivan spins around and waves a finger through the air. "Screw with my life, my money, my land, and I'll —" His words cut off as his friends swing him around. I don't turn my back until they're inside and out of sight.

"You have three little sisters, right? That *is* what you told me?" I spin on the fighter before me.

Her head draws back. "Yeeaaah." She stretches the word out like she has no idea where I'm going with this.

"Then where in the hell did all that spitfire come from?" I force myself from not chucking her chin as her understanding dawns. "I'm standing here, blocking you and doing my best to keep you safe, and you're ready to throw down."

"You think only men can teach a woman how to stand up for herself?" Her full lips purse. "While I appreciate the white knight instincts, I've learned how to handle a prick or two over the years."

I shake my head. "You are not at all who I assumed you to be, Grace Embry." With a look back at the bar, I steal Grace's keys from her hand and reach around, opening her car door. "Come on, I'm going to follow you home to be safe."

It's been the longest week of my life and we've got one day to go, but today's Thursday. And Thursday is game day, better known as time I get to spend with Grace. The more Tuesdays and Thursdays that pass, the more I'm living for them. *For her.*

Most of the crew and a few extra are here weeding today, so I step away for the last of the day and head to the yellow shed. I consider roping Eric into helping me, but I don't want to drag anyone else into the middle of this mess with James.

Because you know what? Screw him. I've played Switzerland in this battle between him and Loe for long enough. I'm not going to let him win this one. It's beyond stupid. There's no reason she shouldn't have this shed. She put her own hard-earned money down and procured a loan out to invest in the new farm on her own when James wouldn't budge on offering more financial support from the business. Not only is he not supporting her, but he's trying to cut her out altogether. The least he can do is give up a useless shed.

As I haul out the last remnants of junk before I head to the softball game, my eyes fall on James's daily roam of the fields, but he's not looking at the flowers. He's glaring at me. I offer him a short wave, and he frowns but makes no attempt to stay my hand.

C'mon, old man. He's gonna either give himself another stroke or a heart attack. I'll break it to him later that the shed's not staying. He knows we could use the area for another patch of dahlias. More flowers mean more money. I just hope I can find time to take the building apart and get Loe here fast enough in the next couple of days to move it before he can stop me.

since I left you, I have
been constantly depressed.
My happiness

my memory your caress
your ... affection
solicitude

continually a burning and
me in my heart. When,
all solicitude, all harm
shall I be able to pass
time with you, having
love you, and to think only
happiness of saying, and
ing it to you

19

Grace

"To GRACE!" Chloe lifts her wine glass. "Who knew you could run that fast toward anything other than a garment sale."

Her toast echoes amongst the occupants of our oversized round table at Hannigan's Tavern as glasses and beer bottles clink.

I stick my tongue out at Chloe. "Gee, thanks. And thank you all for coming out to watch. You really didn't have to." I glance around the table. "Like, really, you didn't have to."

Kip snorts. "Not come out? Are you kidding? I'm mad Chlo didn't tell me you'd joined a team before last week's game."

"I agree," Hayden says. "I'm not sure I've ever seen a batter whiff so hard in my life."

Brynn shoves into Hayden's side, admonishing him, as Kip leans over the table. "Oh, I have. Back when I played T-ball."

Reid's mouth tenses, suppressing a smile, when I toss a sugar packet at Kip's head. He was surprised to see Chloe, Kip, Brynn, and Hayden sitting in the stands for our game tonight. The spectators of adult leagues tend to lean toward wives, husbands, and kids. Apparently, we don't have much of an extended fan group, but we did tonight. One would think those four were at a Mariners game the way they cheered. Especially when I connected with a pitch and sent a ball soaring down the third base line. Even as Reid ran toward home plate, he joined them in celebrating me. When I jogged into the dugout after Tony flied out to left field on the next bat, Reid's arms dragged me in for a hug that lingered longer than any other. Even when we pulled away, there was an air of reluctance.

Chloe throws her arms around my shoulders and plants a loud smacking kiss on my cheek. "Ignore them, Grace Elizabeth. You were awesome. You got a base hit."

"And scored a run," Reid points out. "When was the last time either of you did that?" He tips his beer bottle toward Kip and Hayden, and I join Chloe and Brynn in chuckling.

"Touché, Pruitt." Kip nods. "Maybe we should all join a league?"

Hayden sits back against his seat. "Don't look at me. I'm a soccer guy."

"Yeah, no thanks," Brynn chimes in. "I'm planning on babies, no sports for me."

Chloe and Reid share an amused look before Kip catches her eye. "Don't even bother asking me, Kipling." She laughs. "You can play, though, as long as you wear those tight pants you had to wear back in high school."

Taking Chloe by the back of the neck, Kip drags her close and kisses her quickly. "Anything you want, babe."

I can't help looking at Reid to gauge his response. Am I gauging for him or for me? It wasn't all that long ago their show of affection would've bothered him. Not anymore. He's told me several times all he sees when he looks at Chloe now is a woman he cares about as a great friend in love with the man she's meant to be with. And when I stare into his eyes, it's confirmed. There's no longing or bitterness. All I see as I look around the table is a group of friends and family with a tight-knit bond and how they're welcoming Reid into their fold. Life is crazy like that. Who would have thought?

And who would've thought seeing his lack of resentment would be such a relief?

It's nearing ten o'clock when Reid's truck pulls up beside my Accord at Bingley Park. Since the others drove to the game together, he offered me a lift to dinner. We both had to pass the field on our way home from the restaurant anyway. "That was fun." Reid pushes his door open and jumps out.

I waffle with staying put, then exit his truck on my own, grabbing my bag from the floorboard before he reaches the passenger door. *This isn't a date.* "It was." I toe the gravel. "This is becoming a habit, isn't it?"

"What is?" Reid asks.

"Us going out for dinner after softball."

He rotates his pitching arm like his shoulder aches. "Is that a problem?"

"No, it's not actually." Our dinners are my favorite part of the week. How did this happen? "It's nice."

Pausing his stretch, Reid drops his arm and slips his fingers under the duffle's strap on my shoulder and takes my bag. "Do you think maybe we could try going out when there's not a softball game?" He inches closer.

I gnaw on the corner of my bottom lip, my head tilting. I should say no, but I don't want to. I like Reid. I think I *really* like Reid.

"Yeah, I think I'd like that."

For the second time in one night, Reid draws me to his chest. My bag drops to the asphalt, and his capable hands fall to my lower back before traveling the length of my spine. Up and down, the path trembling every nerve ending. "You smell like perfume and red clay, Grace Embry." My nose wrinkles, and Reid cracks a grin. "It's a seriously dangerous combination for a boy who grew up on the ballfield."

So, not such a bad thing. I've never taken Reid for being smooth, but he sure knows how to lay on the charm. Genuine charm. Not sleazy I-just-want-in-your-pants charm. The kind of charm that's dangerous for the heart if not handled properly.

I like the feel of his strong hands on me way too much. *Hold me closer, my body begs.*

"I'm really glad Bucky convinced you to join the team."

I ran bases and chased a softball on the field, but this is what leaves me breathless as my arms tighten around his waist. "He got me to practice, but seeing you made me join."

"Yeah?"

I lean back, but Reid's hold stays firm, keeping me close.

"Yeah, I knew I'd have fun with you. It made the decision easy."

When Reid's head dips down, I roll to my toes. *Am I really contemplating this?* This isn't a friendly tradition at midnight. It's a choice. A choice that doesn't require much contemplation. I want Reid to kiss me. I want to know what it'd feel like when not in good humor or planned but with a hint of a thrill or in the heat of the moment because we just can't not.

Our gazes hold until his lips brush mine: soft and simple. *Brush, nip, brush.* The barely-there grazes coax my pulse to quicken. I fist the back of his shirt, pressing closer, and Reid hums in the back of his throat.

Strong, calloused fingers grip the nape of my neck as the tip of Reid's tongue traces the seam of my lips, memorizing their shape before retreating. And, just like that, the kiss is over. *Too quick*, my mind screams. It's a tease of what could be, like New

Year's Eve, but rather than asking for more, Reid kisses my forehead and steps back.

"For the record," he says, "I always have fun with you, too."

Tingles spread from my fingers to my toes. Walking away without kissing him again exerts serious self-control, but if we go there—and I'd really like to go there—I should be open with him about my past before we get too deep.

Looking in the mirror above my bathroom sink, I brush blush over my foundation and swipe on a hint of liner and mascara. The music blaring through my Bluetooth speaker pauses as a call comes through on my phone.

CHLOE

I accept and press the speaker as I swipe a light shade of nude on my top lip.

"It's only nine o'clock in the morning. Such a rough day already? You needed to call me before I head into work?"

"Reid was in a car accident while doing deliveries this morning."

Mid-stroke on my bottom lip, my breath catches. "Is he okay?"

"I don't know. The ambulance took him to the emergency room at Valley. Since it was one of the Lockwood vans, they called me, but they couldn't give me any information since I'm not family."

I rush down my hallway to my bedroom and slip into some flats. "When did they call?"

"About thirty minutes ago."

"I'm going to call in Gina, and I'll head there now." I don't stop to think what Chloe might make of that.

"I doubt they'll let you back there."

Right. Who am I to expect to see him? We're not even dating, but the truth doesn't stop the instinctual need to be there.

"Well, who can I call? Who will know more? What's his dad's number?"

Chloe pauses, and my toe taps the hardwood. *Give me an answer already, Loe.*

"You're gonna go see him?"

"I have to know if he's okay. Don't you?"

"I do, but I have a few things to tie up at my farm. I'll text Gregory's number to you. Let me make sure everyone at the farm is up to speed on what's happened, then I'll be there."

"There's no need, Loe. I know how much you hate hospitals after your dad's stroke, then with Brynn. Why don't you let me do the waiting?"

"I should be there, shouldn't I?" She sniffs, but I reassure her she's fine to not come right away. "Okay, send me updates if and when you get them."

Hanging up with my heart hammering in my chest, I look at my phone clutched in my fist and make a rash decision. Pressing *SEND* on my hastily worded text, I snatch my keys off the hook by my front door and book it to the hospital.

Just last night Reid's lips touched mine. I was all kinds of mixed up about whether I wanted more or not, whether it would've been a bad idea or not. What if we never get the chance again?

REID'S BEEN in surgery for over an hour, and I've been in the waiting room with his dad, Gregory. He's a quiet man, hasn't said but a handful of words to me. I'm sure a lot of it has to do with nerves and fear, though something tells me it's part of who he is. My dad would've been pacing the halls, walking off his worry, while Mom would've been talking to anyone who would listen.

Gregory sits beside me, one ankle crossed over his knee. The only indication he's anxious is the way his finger rubs the side of his phone as he aimlessly scrolls a news feed. With how quick the headlines pass his screen, there's no way he's actually reading any of them.

I'd try to make conversation, but I don't want to make him talk if he'd rather be alone with his thoughts. He knows my name and that I'm friends with Reid, and that's all he needed to know before he patted the seat beside him for us to wait together.

Other than the five minutes he stepped away to answer a call from Wade, Reid's younger brother, he hasn't moved.

"Mr. Pruitt." A dark-haired man in blue scrubs stands at the edge of the waiting room, and the two of us race forward. "We were able to get the bleeding under control and Reid's stable. He's being moved to recovery in the meantime before we transfer him to a private room. It'll be a little bit before he's fully conscious, but I can bring you back."

Hand over my heart, I take my first easy breath and back up a couple of steps to sit down in my seat to wait until Reid's awake.

"Where are you going?"

I stop walking. "I was going to wait here."

"Come on, honey." Gregory waves me forward. "I'm sure Reid would much rather see your pretty face when he wakes up than mine."

"I don't mind waiting out here if you would prefer the family time. It's understandable."

One side of his mouth lifts in a timid but honest smile, his light olive green eyes a mirror image of his son's. "I would rather not sit alone in there."

Unable to hold in a return smile, I step up to his side and pat his arm. "Okay."

I HAVEN'T TAKEN my eyes off Reid. He's been in and out but not coherent enough to know we're here. They moved him to a private room about thirty minutes ago when he started coming to, but he fell back asleep.

For the last two hours, my gaze has roamed every part of him not covered by a gown or blanket. Stains of dark red mark his cheeks and arms, blood that wasn't thoroughly washed clean. A couple of butterfly bandages cover a gash on his forehead, circled by a yellowish bruise surfacing. Apart from a few other cuts, he looks untouched. From what the doctor mentioned, my guess is the majority of his injuries are on his torso. That ruptured spleen is going to be painful for a while.

His eyelids flutter and a quiet, pained groan passes his lips. In seconds, Gregory stands at his bedside. Blinking, Reid's eyes open and remain, a little unfocused but awake.

"Don't look so frightened, old man. I'm alive." His voice is like the first sentence you try to form in the morning, raspy and sluggish.

"There he is. It's about time." Gregory takes hold of Reid's hand in both of his. "I know you don't get much sleep, but save it for another day. You had me scared, kid."

A garbled grunt escapes. "Sorry about that."

"Here." Gregory steps aside. "Let me make room for this patient angel."

And it's confirmed where Reid gets his charm. I step up to the foot of the bed. "I don't think I can accept either of those compliments. I've been more like an anxious chihuahua."

Reid's eyes ruffle in confusion, but then he cracks a smile. "Slugger?"

"You really messed with my day, Pruitt." Teasing lightens my tone, masking the genuine fear underneath. "My stomach's been in knots all morning, and everyone's lighting up my phone asking about you."

"I'll try not to get in another wreck anytime soon."

"I'm going to hold you to that."

Our stare holds, this unexpected pull still there. It wasn't a fluke.

Shuffling back, I sit down to give Gregory more room.

With a knock on the door, the same dark-haired doctor enters and checks Reid out. He goes over the surgery and Reid's injuries and prognosis. This all could've been so much worse. I'm so grateful for tender miracles.

As the doctor exits, a tall Reid lookalike passes him, rushing in. The pair of organs on either side of my chest refuse to deflate, the air trapped there. Even though I prepared myself for the possibility of him showing, my heartbeats stumble.

"Dad." His suit-covered arms encircle Gregory as he pats his back, then turns to Reid, not noticing me sitting in the corner.

"What in the world did you do to yourself?"

Reid shakes his head. "Ford, you really didn't need to come all the way here."

His hand grips the bedrail, angling his back to me. "When Dad calls and says you were in a car accident and are going in for surgery, yeah, Reid. I did."

"So, I had some internal bleeding and momentary memory loss. It's a ruptured spleen and concussion, not paralysis and a coma. I'm fine. They want to monitor me through the weekend, and then I'll be home." His words are labored by the time he finishes.

"Yeah, but you lost a lot of blood, bud. A big brother is allowed to worry if his brother is going to make it out of surgery or not."

Reid nods, but there's something more in his eyes he's trying to hide.

"What even happened?"

"I don't know." His tongue swipes out, moistening his split lip. "One minute I was cruising down Mt Luna, the next I was upside down."

"Mt. Luna? Reid, you could've died."

"Tell me about it. I thought I had until I woke up in the hospital and they were checking me over in the ER."

If moving wouldn't draw attention to me, I'd slip out. This is the last place I want to pull focus away from Reid.

"We're being rude." Gregory turns around and faces me. "Reid, introduce Ford to your friend."

No, please don't. Let me blend into the room. I'm part of the chair. I am the chair.

Ford peers over his shoulder, straightening as soon as his green eyes fall on me. "Grace," he says. "Thank you for sending me the text."

I stand. I don't know why. Maybe to escape. If I run fast enough, will it bring me back to five minutes ago, so I can leave before Ford—or Drew as I know him—got here?

Ford Andrew Pruitt: Breaker of Hearts.

"Yeah, hi. Of course."

"Text?" Reid asks. "You two know each other?"

I'll leave that for Drew to answer. I've kept my word all of this time. I don't plan on breaking it now. He's not going to come clean. I guarantee it.

"Grace and I…" Drew's eyes sweep from me to Reid and back as he clears his throat. "We dated a few years back."

Maybe I should've stayed seated, my legs nearly give out. He actually said it, admitted our association out loud. I'm sure he won't bother bringing up my ignoring his gift and calls the past few months, though.

Confusion clouds Reid's eyes, his eyebrows knit together.

Having spent time with Reid while he dated Chloe, I'd already gotten past the hurdle of him being Drew's brother. I didn't put much thought into it again when we started spending more time together because I wasn't expecting us to be anything more than friends. Until last night. But from the hurt he's attempting to mask, keeping the relationship from Reid obviously wasn't the right move.

"It was while I was still in college. Seems like a lifetime ago." Four years, to be exact, but who's counting? I was a different person.

"And you're here as Reid's…"

At this moment, I don't know what to say. We're friends, of course, but could we ever be more? If the kiss last night meant to him what it meant to me… Our eyes meet, the hurt and confusion replaced by curiosity. Is he wondering what I'd say?

When I don't answer right away, Reid shifts. "Friend," he says. "We're friends. I dated her best friend, Chloe Lockwood."

"Oh right, that flower farm you've been working at since high school."

A few seconds of hesitation pass before he replies, "Yeah." There's weight in that small four-letter word, but I don't know what it means.

Drew swivels away from Reid, fully facing me with a familiar softening of his eyes. "How are you, Grace? You look amazing."

I resent my heart for the rapid flutter. "Thanks. You look good, too." And he does. He looks like he came straight from the office, not a golden blonde lock out of place. Gray suit and navy tie still on and perfectly pressed. He fills the shoulders out nicely. Must still be hitting the gym every day.

"Your hair is lighter, shorter." Taking a step closer, he gestures around my face, and a frantic hummingbird flies through the ventricles of my heart.

His is shorter too, parted on the side with just enough volume like he walked off an Ivy League campus.

My fingers brush through the ends of the strands I curled this morning, just below my shoulders. "I got tired of the dark blonde. I needed a change."

A new me.

"I like it. The color suits you."

Why do his compliments warm me from the inside out? They shouldn't do that anymore. Not for as long as we've been over.

"Thanks." I pull my eyes away from him and focus on Reid. "Well, I was actually just about to head out. I'll update Loe, so they can have everything taken care of while you're out and you don't have to stress. How about I call you tomorrow?"

With a nod, a subtle smile curves Reid's lips. "Thank you, Grace."

I pat his foot, the heaviness of the day easing with his smile. "I'm"—*relieved, thrilled, thankful*— "really glad you're okay."

Drew leans in close as I pass by and lowers his voice in my ear. Spice and citrus infiltrate my senses, tapping into memory lane. "It was good seeing you, Lemon Drop. I'd still like to talk."

The nickname sends a shiver down my spine, flashing me back to our time together, but I conceal it. Ignoring his last statement, I say, "It was good seeing you, too."

It's the polite thing to say. Do I mean it? Yes and no. When are complicated emotions not involved after seeing the one who was your greatest heartbreak? I'm entitled to a miniature nervous breakdown, which I will succumb to as soon as I'm in the safety of my car.

I wave to Gregory. "Thanks for being my waiting room buddy."

He shakes his head with a gentle smile. "No, thank *you*. I was grateful to have you there."

I manage to make it through the halls of the hospital and parking lot, settling into the driver's seat of my car before throwing my head back with a frazzled groan. Being from the same town, it was always inevitable that I'd see Drew again, but I hoped I'd be married or in a serious relationship. Something to show him I moved on just fine without him. Yet, here I am. Twenty-six and single.

Might as well send me burlap instead of silk.

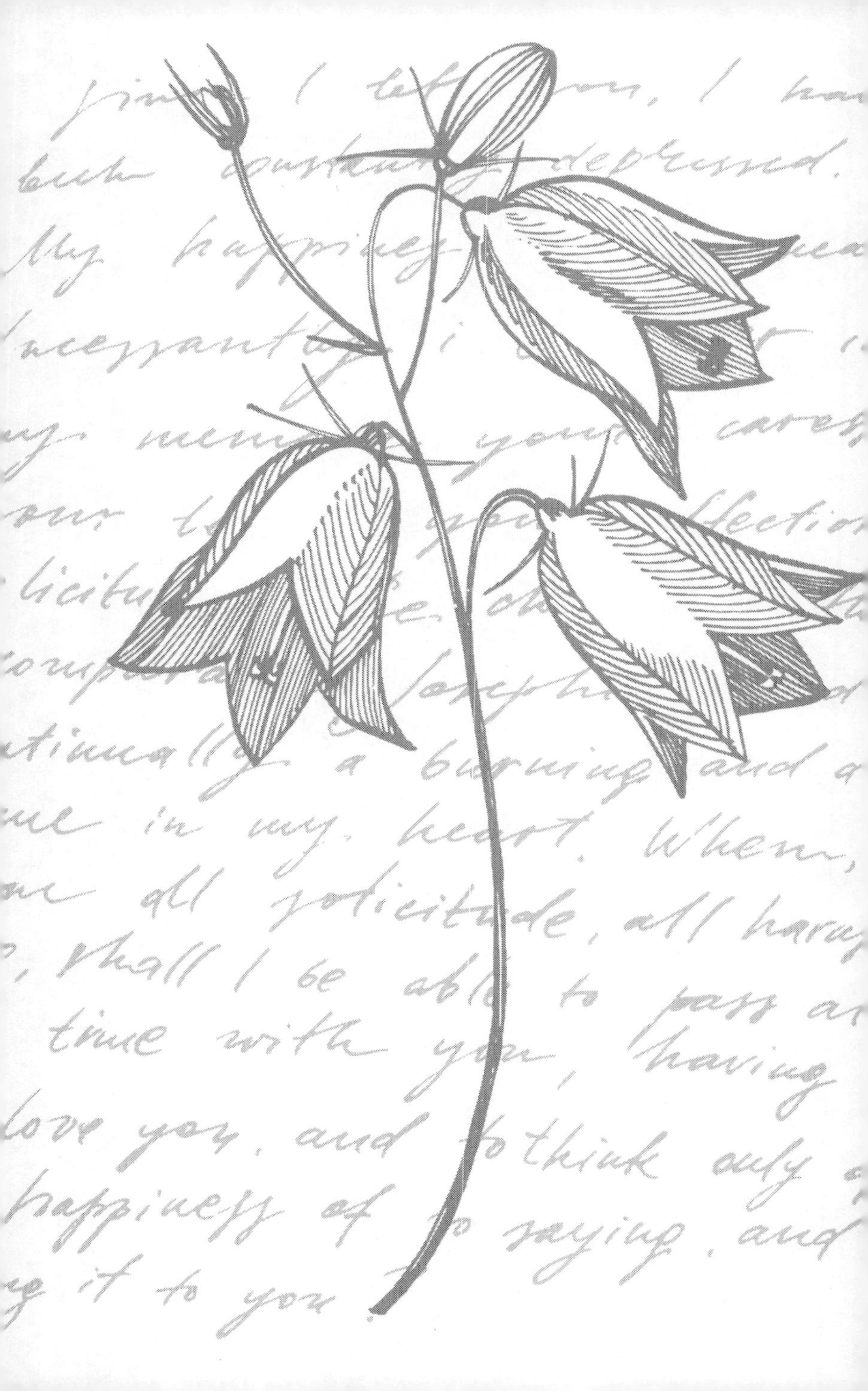

Reid

I'VE DONE nothing but lay in this hospital bed since yesterday morning, and yet, I'm exhausted. The police and investigators stopped by a couple of times, going over what happened, clarifying the cause of the accident, and it's taken every ounce of energy to deal with them.

Ford props his feet against the side of the hospital bed, tapping on his cell phone. "How long will it take for you to recover?"

"A month, maybe two. The doctor said it wasn't a severe rupture, thank God. I would've been out of commission for a few months if that were the case."

"Are you going to be able to do any work while you recover?"

"Well, I'm not supposed to lift anything more than ten pounds, no shoveling and such, so Charlie and Eric will have to do all the heavy lifting around the farm. But I've got plenty of other things to keep me busy." I'll have to back out of softball, which sucks. They should still make the playoffs in a few weeks, but there's no way I'll be in pitching shape by then.

Dad and Ford have been in and out of my room all day, grabbing us meals—so I don't have to eat the hospital food—and taking showers at home. It's not lost on me how the only time Dad's left me with Ford was when I slept. There hasn't been a moment where I can ask him about Grace. My brain was fuzzy after surgery yesterday, but Ford saying they dated rang clear as a bell. Dated? How could I not know? Why didn't she say something?

I stare at my older brother. While Dad is content to sit and read or watch television, Ford spends most of his time on the phone. Work never stops with him.

"Don't you need to head back to the city? Stocks to trade and rich people to make richer."

He looks up from his phone. "Well, in case you bumped your head harder than we thought, it is the weekend, but also, I took a few vacation days."

Today is Saturday. That's right. It's weird how time becomes irrelevant when you're bed bound. "You took days off, and yet you haven't put your phone down." With an arch of my eyebrow, I smirk. "When was the last time you used vacation days?"

"It's been a while." Ford chuckles, setting his phone aside. "But you're my little brother. Family steps up when family needs to step up."

Our gazes hold and a familiar gratitude seeps in. When Mom left us, Ford was fifteen. Dad did his best to meet our every need, but he still had to work to keep a roof over our heads. Ford had to grow up real quick to help take care of me and Wade. When it was time for him to graduate, I couldn't blame him for getting the hell out of dodge and never returning. He deserved to have a life after his teenage years were stripped from him.

"Did he call Wade, too?" I look at Dad snoozing in a corner chair, an open book abandoned in his lap.

"Yeah, he's keeping him updated. Wade wants to be here, but Dad doesn't want him missing training. Otherwise, he would've flown him in from Salt Lake yesterday."

I wave my hand. "No, I'm glad he's not taking time off. That would be a waste."

Wade's participating in a summer baseball camp for The U. He needs extra training and weight room time to prepare for his freshman season. That kid is going to be somebody someday.

AFTER SIX, the most welcome sight enters my room.

With a *knock,* Grace peeks her head inside. "Can we come in?"

"That depends. Who's we?" I joke.

Loe follows Grace inside, carrying a giant bag of Reese's Cups. "Your favorite boss."

"I don't care who's with you. If you bring my favorite candy, you can bring anyone you want."

As Loe sets the orange bag on the tray with a quiet chuckle and bends over to hug me, my attention doesn't waver from Grace and Ford exchanging glances and smiles.

Ford stands, his voice quiet when he says, "Hey, Lemon Drop." *Lemon Drop?*

"Hey." Grace's cheeks flush pink, the same color as the large flowers on her dress, as she bites back a smile and steps closer to the foot of my bed, shifting her eyes to my face.

A jagged ache pulses inside of me. It could be my spleen. It could be insecurity.

Loe doesn't react to their interaction. Did she hear him? Does she know about their relationship? Is she ignoring it?

"You remember Ford?" I ask Loe.

Still by my side, she waves with a polite smile. "Yeah, hi. It's been a long time, though. I was probably in elementary school."

Elementary school? So, maybe she didn't know either.

Ford chuckles. "Probably. Maybe with some braids and overalls."

"Most definitely both of those things." Loe's gaze leaves him abruptly, her smile morphing into sympathy when she looks at me. "How are you feeling today?"

"Like I rolled down the side of a cliff. Oh, wait." I smirk.

She tenses, her eyes narrowing. "Is that really what happened? You rolled down Mt. Luna? Were you speeding? I've told you to watch it around those curves countless times."

"I wasn't speeding. My front right tire fell off."

Loe's face pales. "Fell off... Didn't we just have an inspection? How—"

"Yeah, I'm not so sure it was a malfunction."

Their faces fall. "Did you tell the police?" Grace asks.

"They came this morning to hear my account of the details. I told them what might've happened, and they looked into it and came back about an hour ago. There isn't any proof of tampering, but all three tires on the van had loose or missing lug nuts. It could've happened sometime during the accident, so they need to do more digging."

"Tampering?" Loe crosses her arms. "That's ridiculous."

"Not according to Officer Davenport." My hands tighten to fists—the reality sinking in. "Tires on well-maintained vehicles don't just fall off, Loe. Davenport felt it was highly suspicious."

Out of habit, I reach for the baseball cap I'm not wearing, my nerves ratcheting, before lowering my hands to my lap. "If I hadn't been on Mt. Luna the tire would have fallen off, and I would have skidded to a stop, or maybe caused a little pileup. Instead, the right front side dropped with force as I came upon a curve, and I had no shoulder..." My eyes close, shutting down the memory of helplessness as my van flipped down the bank.

"But intentionally?" Loe says in a near whisper. I open my eyes as she presses her hand to my blanketed shin, her head shaking. "Who'd want to do something like that to you?"

Who indeed?

Grace gasps. "Do you think?" Her storm-clouded gaze meets mine. "Could it have been that guy outside the bar the other night?"

Sullivan's son. The incident hadn't crossed my mind since that night. Grace didn't even know who he was and when she asked after the fact, I told her he was a client of Kip's who was angry about losing the land to Chloe. I swore her to secrecy, not wanting to upset Loe. She doesn't need more drama piled on her.

Grace tilts her head, her eyes narrowing in a silent plea for me to come clean before she does. This is crazy, isn't it? Would the man really tamper with a Lockwood Blooms delivery van because Denton Harris sold Chloe the land? I can't believe he would, but what if…

"What guy?" Ford prods Grace, who looks guilty as sin. As if she did something wrong.

"What am I missing?" Loe asks.

"Grace and I ran into Joseph Sullivan last Tuesday night after softball practice."

At Sullivan's name, Grace's lips part with a sharp inhale and swatches of angry red color her cheeks. In hindsight, I should have told her who the man threatening her best friend was.

"You had a run-in with Joseph?" Loe's head whirls around with narrowed eyes. "Why didn't you tell me?"

I shake my head. "I didn't want to worry you. He was drunk as a skunk and spewing empty threats."

Her arms cross over her chest. "Don't seem so empty now."

Ford mimics Loe, his face drawing tight with anger. "Why would Joseph Sullivan have a beef with you?"

"He doesn't." I wave him off. Grace and Chloe are paranoid. Officer Davenport is bored and looking for excitement in Seaside Pointe. The idea that someone intentionally tampered with our van is ludicrous. "Sullivan wouldn't even know which truck I drove."

"Unless he was watching you," Grace argues. "Or if he was trying to get back at Lockwood in general. Send a message. What if he was trying to hurt Chloe?"

The skin between Loe's eyes pinch. "He's a money-grubber, but I don't think Joseph would go as far as hurting anyone."

Grace shakes her head. "You didn't see him that night. He said some awful things about you, Loe. Said something about watching your back, and Kip, too."

Her head shakes as her eyes close. "You guys should've told me."

"You've got enough on your plate without worrying about a nasty drunk."

"Well, obviously, he's something we need to deal with." Chloe goes about messing with her hair the way she does when she's nervous, and I hate dragging her into this. "Seriously, Reid, there's more to the story with Sullivan than you know. Stuff with him and Kip."

Touching Chloe's arm, Grace looks at me. "Did you tell the police about him?"

"No, I didn't think to. I'd forgotten about the whole incident until just now."

"I've got Davenport's card." Ford steps closer. "We'll call him. No detail is too small. If Sullivan didn't get his desired outcome, who's to say he won't try again?"

"Yeah, I'll get ahold of him tomorrow."

Ford's mouth parts, but I give him a glare that says we're done with the conversation. Thinking about the wreck and foul play has the drums in my head going to town.

I rub my temple and turn back to Loe. "How's the farm? I hate not being able to be there."

"Don't stress about it." She opens the bag of Reese's and hands me one. "It hasn't even been twenty-four hours. Denise has everything under control. We'll see how you're doing in a week. If you need more time to rest, we'll work it out."

"I'll be fine. Even if I can't handle the manual labor, Julian's a hard worker, and you know how I enjoy bossing Charlie and Eric around. They can pick up the slack." I smirk.

"They could use some tough love." Loe taps the bedrail. "All right. I'm meeting Kip for dinner, so I need to head out. You can bet your butt I'll be telling him about Joseph, so don't be surprised if he calls you for all the details."

"I'd expect nothing less." I'm glad I'm in the hospital. When Kip learns Sullivan threatened his girl, and I didn't think to tell anyone, he's going to lose his damn mind. "I really thought the man was blowing smoke."

"Let's hope so, but we're not taking chances, considering." Our gazes hold before she breaks a small smile. "I'm glad you're doing okay. We'll keep in touch, and don't think about work. Just get well."

"Thanks, Loe."

She gives Grace a one-armed hug and says something into her ear that makes Grace shove her away with a soft laugh.

"See ya!" Loe closes the door behind her.

Ford lowers back to his chair and rests his forearms on his knees. "For exes, you two seem to handle it pretty well."

I shrug. "She was first and foremost my friend. It's hard to stay mad at someone who you care about. All of our years working together, building this business, lots of sweat and tears. We have mutual respect for one another. And honestly, we're better as friends. We never quite clicked the way we should have in a relationship." My eyes travel to Grace standing at the foot of my bed. Her light hair is in a loose bun, strands falling down her slender neck and around her face. Why did it take me so long to notice how gorgeous she is?

Loe and I never clicked the way Grace and I do. But she dated my brother. Why did Ford have to find her first? And how long ago is a few years? Was he—

"Well," Grace cuts off my train of thought, tucking a lock of hair behind her ear. "I'm going to head out, too."

Ford rises to his feet. "Let me walk you to your car."

"You really don't have to."

"I want to."

"Reid needs you more than I do."

"Reid is surrounded by capable doctors and nurses. He'll survive without me for a few minutes."

She relents with a reluctant nod, but I can't tell if she wants him walking her out or if she's simply being polite. Her gaze shifts to me. "Are you being discharged tomorrow?"

"That's the plan."

"Is there anything you need at home? Some groceries? Milk? Frozen dinners?"

"Nah." The corner of my mouth twitches with a smile. "I'm going to stay with my dad for a few days, so he can keep an eye on me."

"Oh, good. Okay. That makes me feel better. But if there's anything you need—anything at all—you'll let me know, right?"

I want you to stay longer, but not while Ford is here. "Yeah, I'll let you know."

She hesitates, then rubs my foot over the blanket. "I'll text you tomorrow to check in on you. Rest up."

Ford follows her out, calling over his shoulder. "I'll be back in a bit, though Dad should be back any second if you need something."

"I'm fine, Ford. I can handle some alone time." I like alone time, just not when it means my brother is spending time with the woman I want to myself.

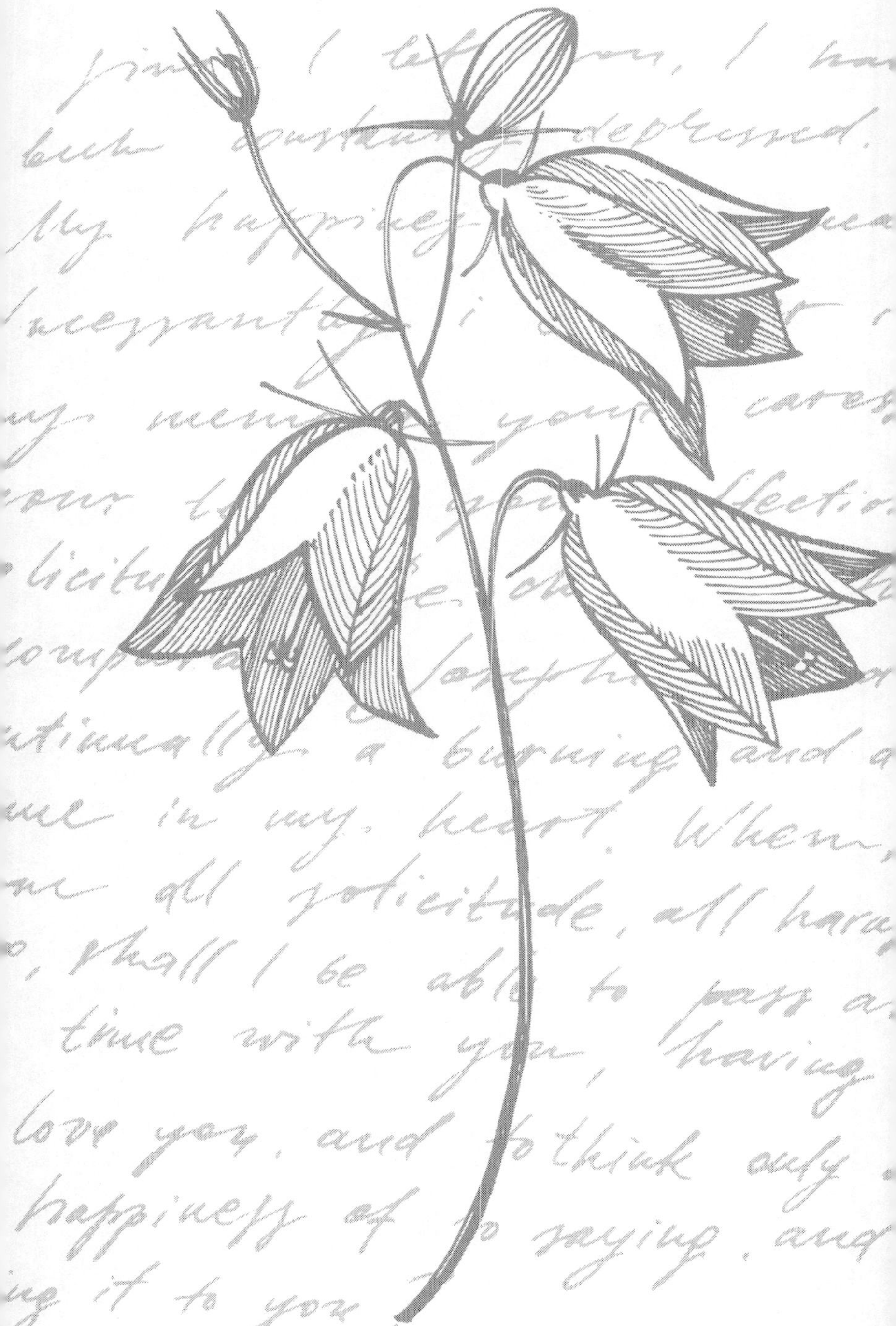
in my heart. When
shall I be able to pass
time with you, having
love you, and to think only
it to you

21

Grace

THE WALK down the pale blue hallway of the hospital to the elevators is silent, but Drew's large frame beside me can't be ignored. His muscles are leaner than Reid's, but he's taller, towering over me. His height was one of the first things that caught my attention. My five foot eight to his six foot two made me feel petite.

As we approach the elevators, the metal doors of the middle one open, and Gregory steps out.

His eyes light up when his gaze falls on me. "Well, aren't you a sight for sore eyes in this somber place? Did Reid run you off already?"

I smile. "No, I came here straight after work, and I need to get home." Or rather, I need not be in the same room as Drew and Reid. I honestly thought after finding out Reid was going to recover just fine, Drew would've headed back to Seattle today.

Nothing was more important to the Drew I knew than getting ahead at work.

He nods and looks at his son. "You're not leaving, are you?"

"I'm just walking Grace to her car. I'll be back up in a few minutes."

Gregory slowly nods as his eyes drift between the two of us, questioning, assessing. His stare is unsure. What is his conclusion? Is he wondering how we know each other, wondering about our history? Or is he wondering why I came to see one son but am walking out with the other?

Drew holds the elevator open when the doors start to close.

Another smile forms on Gregory's face, but it's not as cheerful as when he first saw me. "I'm glad I got to see you before you left. Have a nice evening, Grace."

"Same to you, Gregory."

Once inside, the elevator doors slide closed.

As we descend, Drew says, "I'll be frank, after all those unanswered calls, I'd finally given up and never thought I'd see you again."

"Your brother was in a car accident. Don't confuse my text as anything other than sharing important information about your family. And we're from the same town. You can't honestly think that, Drew. Or should I call you Ford like your family?"

"You always knew exactly who I was, Grace. Only my dad and brothers call me Ford and some people around town. Old habits die hard. As for us seeing each other, it couldn't have escaped your notice that I don't come home often."

"Avoiding me at all costs?" One corner of my lips turns up, teasing.

He chuckles, stuffing his hands in his jean pockets. "Maybe something like that. I think I knew if I saw you, I wouldn't be able to stay away."

That beating organ in my chest stutters. *They're just pretty words, heart. Calm yourself.*

"As it is, I haven't seen you in four years, and I still can't stop thinking about you. Why did you ignore my Christmas present? My phone calls?"

I exhale. "Let's not do this."

His forehead wrinkles. "Is there something going on between you and Reid?"

"What?"

"You and Reid. Are you two a thing?"

A thing? I mean, we've shared a couple brief kisses and we have a good time together. Does that constitute us as a *thing*? We haven't discussed anything official, granted that could be because there's been no pressure, no expectations of it being anything more than what it's been. Our pace has been organic, but a month ago, he was hung up on Mia, and I was still considering Bodhi and confused about Drew. Then there was Thursday night. Reid hugged me. He's never done that before. And I liked being in his arms. Then he kissed me. And I *really* liked his mouth on mine.

But am I drawn to Reid because of Drew? Aside from their height and style, they favor each other so much. Side by side, you'd know in an instant they were brothers. If not, mistake them for twins. How can I tell Drew something is going on if I'm not even sure Reid thinks there is? If Reid wants there to be?

The elevator opens and I rush out like my life depends on escaping. "We're friends."

"Are you sure that's all?"

So, what if it isn't? My head swivels in his direction. "I'm not sure why my relationships are any of your business."

"They're not. You're right. It's just…I'm going to stick around for a couple more days. I'd like to see you. Outside of the hospital, I mean. And I don't want to interfere with anything."

What would be the point? To rehash the past? To get my heart all confused? "I'm not sure that's a good idea."

He stops outside of the hospital's automatic double doors and takes hold of my arm, gentle enough to face him. "Just to catch up. Dinner, that's all."

How is it possible that after all these years, looking into his eyes still flutters my stomach? Love's not fair. He shouldn't hold any power over my body anymore. Breakups should give immunity. They should sever any and all strings.

While staring into his luring green eyes, I find myself saying, "I'll think about it."

"I can work with that. I'll call you. Unless…it's a Saturday night. Are you really going home?" His eyebrows rise, interest piqued. I sort of want to chide him for thinking of taking me on a date when his brother could have died yesterday morning. I shake my head instead.

"I've been working all day, and I'm exhausted, so yes, I'm going home and not doing a thing for the rest of the night." And I'm not even ashamed.

"That little boutique must keep you busy."

As much as I want to gloat about what I've made of myself without him, all I do is smile. "I have no reason to complain."

"That's really impressive, Lemon Drop. I'm proud of you."

I equally love hearing him call me that and want to demand he stop. "Thanks." I pull my keys from my purse.

"Okay. I'll let you get home and off your feet, but look out for my call. I'm not going to let you get out of seeing me that easily."

You had no problems letting me go before. The retort is on the tip of my tongue, but I hold back. I don't want him to know our end still bothers me.

I erased Drew from my phone years ago, wanting to be rid of any reminders of him, but I don't want to tell him that. No need to rub salt in old wounds. And I honestly don't know if I'm going to say yes. I'm torn, but tonight is not the night to dwell on it. I just want to grab some dinner, put on my pajamas, and binge on a show for the next five hours or more. Probably more. Maybe

Robyn will join me and we'll be scorned women together for an evening.

When I take a step away, his hand drops. "Bye, Drew."

"See ya, Grace."

I peek over my shoulder once I hit the parking lot, and he's still at the automatic hospital doors, watching me walk away.

Me: Are you still in the hospital or have you been discharged?

He responds quicker than I thought he would.

Reid: I'm here. My doctor wanted to run a few more tests before releasing me, so I'll be here until this evening.

Me: That sucks. Well I'm not working today. You want me to swing by and bug you?

It takes longer for him to answer this time. Does that mean he doesn't want me to come and he's trying to figure out the best way to tell me?

Reid: You want to come see me or my brother?

Ouch. Going to see Reid is more in spite of the fact that Drew could be there. I hate the thought of Reid thinking I'd use him as an excuse to see his brother.

Me: I deserve that. Is he there now?

Reid: No. He's not coming today since I'll be home later.

Me: Then I'll be there in twenty minutes.

AFTER KNOCKING and opening the door a crack, I wait for Reid's reply.

"Come in." His mouth curves up when he sees me. The colorful bruising on his forehead has spread.

"When people ask, you should give some cool story like how you stopped an armed robbery or rescued a baby from a runaway dumpster."

"Rolling down the side of a mountain because someone messed with my tires isn't cool enough?"

"Not nearly." I laugh lightly, taking the seat closest to his bed. "How are you feeling today?"

"When the drugs aren't working? Like I rolled down a cliff, but it's nothing I can't handle."

My fingers knot together. "When Chloe called, I think I had a mini heart attack. I was so scared."

"My dad said you called him and asked if you could come to the hospital. Though, he says you were obviously already on your way since you showed up a minute after the call ended. He says you stayed with him in the waiting room the entire time I was in surgery."

I nod. To deflect from my embarrassment, I say, "Someone had to keep the poor man company." It's easier to joke than admit nothing would've kept me away, and I don't even know why.

"Thank you, Grace. Not for me, but for staying with him. He's really good at hiding his emotions, but if he'd been alone, I know he'd have been a wreck."

"No thanks necessary. I did it for me, too." I add, "And Chloe, everyone at Lockwood and the Seasiders were worried about you."

His teeth run along his bottom lip as he nods. "Of course."

Clearing my throat, I scoot forward. "Look, I wanted to explain the thing with Drew, uh Ford, and me."

"You can call him Drew if that's how you know him. It's been his preferred name since he left Seaside. Dad, Wade, and I just refuse to get on board with it. He'll always be Ford to us."

I nod. "I'm sorry I didn't say anything before."

"Yeah, that was…that was a surprise." Reid pushes up in his reclined bed, sitting straighter. "Why didn't you tell me?"

"It's stupid, really." My eyes fall to my lap, picking at the skin around my nails. "We kept our on-and-off-again relationship quiet from everyone. It's what Drew wanted. Looking back now, it all seems so pointless, but nevertheless, it's been so long, I didn't want to bring up the past. I didn't want to make things weird between us. But after our kiss the other night, I was going to tell you. Then you got in the accident, and he came, and—"

"Ford was the older guy when you were in college, wasn't he?"

"He was." I lift my head. "The age difference now doesn't seem like such a big deal, but when you're newly nineteen and a guy who's nearing thirty shows interest, it feels like a lot."

"How long did you two date?"

"It started midway through my freshman year and ended when I graduated, but we broke up so many times, it was hard to keep track." The relationship sounds longer, more serious than it was. Or than it was to Drew. I planned a whole life for us in my head.

Reid's forehead creases. "Before you said you guys didn't work out because you had different expectations of the relationship. What did you mean by that?"

My fingers reach for my earlobe. "I—"

A knock echoes through the room and Reid's doctor enters.

"Reid, let's go over these test results and get you out of here."

Oh. This feels intrusive. I stand. "Let me just get out of the way. Do you need a ride home? I can wait in the hallway."

Reid shakes his head. "My dad will be back soon. He was just taking care of some errands."

"Okay. I'll check on you tomorrow."

With a slight nod and smile from him, I leave, but going feels wrong. I shouldn't be there for the results, but he shouldn't be alone. I didn't have nearly enough time with him. Maybe it's because I've grown accustomed to our long lunches and dinners. For the last three days, I've had—combined—fifteen to twenty minutes with Reid. And aside from today, the time has been shared with other people. It's not enough. I'm greedy for more. I want to be around to make sure he's okay.

This is ridiculous. Gregory is going to take good care of Reid. He doesn't need me.

Why do I want to be the one to take care of him?

I'M WALKING into Fig after lunch on Monday when my phone rings. *DO NOT ANSWER.* I've ignored his calls so many times it feels odd to accept now.

"Hello?"

"Grace?"

My name. One syllable. Five letters. And yet, his voice is unmistakable. "Hey, Drew."

"I was worried you'd change your mind and go back to ignoring me."

Yeah, we'll pretend the idea didn't run through my mind. "I guess you lucked out."

"I'm heading back to Seattle tomorrow. I held off and gave you a day to adjust to the idea. So, what do you say? Will you let me take you out tonight?"

Why does the thought of saying yes feel like I'm cheating on Reid? I touched base with him this morning now that he's settled at Gregory's, needing to know how he's doing. I wanted to stop by after work, but after avoiding Drew for this long, I need to put this to rest once and for all.

"As friends?"

"Yeah, friends," Drew agrees after hesitating for a beat. "I just want to reconnect. See how you've been. What you've been doing with your life for the last few years."

"Okay. I'm not closing the store tonight, so what time do you want to go?"

"Five work for you? Los Rancheros?"

"Sure, but how about Baja's? It's a new place across from Mac's. You'll like it." And it's a place I haven't been to with Reid. Not sure why that's important to me, but it is.

When Drew agrees, I tell him I'll meet him there. I won't let him pick me up. There will be no room for misinterpretation tonight.

a burning and
in my heart. When
all solicitude, all
shall I be able to pass
time with you, having
love you, and to think only
happiness of so saying, and
it to you

Reid

I TURN off the television when the fumbling of his keys sounds at the front door. I'd stand If I weren't so damn sore, making my face the first thing Ford sees as he sneaks back into the house. My irritation with whatever he's doing boils my blood.

"You snuck out while I was in the shower," I say before he's even closed the door and locked up. My back is to him as I sit on the couch, but his reflection freezes on the black television screen. "You can't tell me that was a coincidence."

Ford huffs. "That I went out to dinner while you were showering?" He rounds the couch and takes a seat on the edge of Dad's favorite chair. "Am I supposed to ask your permission to go out?"

"When you see Grace? Yeah."

With his elbows on his knees, Ford leans forward and drops his head. "This damn town never changes."

I don't correct him. He needs to assume he can't wander

around Seaside without the gossip mill spreading his every move back to me. In truth, his little dinner date with Grace reached my ears because they ran into Jackie at the Baja's, and she asked Grace how I'm doing. When Grace told her I was discharged, Jackie called to check in and bemoan the Seasiders' chances of winning the league playoffs without my pitching skills.

"You've both said you're just friends, Reid. Is that not the case?"

"This isn't about me and Grace." Not one hundred percent, anyway. "This is about Angelica."

Ford hisses and sinks into the wide cushion of Dad's recliner, his face contorting like the name is painful to his ears. Understandable after the crap his ex-fiancée pulled. Though, now I know he wasn't exactly innocent in that relationship.

"Look, Reid—"

"Grace mentioned she'd dated an older guy back in college. It didn't take a genius to do the math, Ford. You were seeing them both at the same time, weren't you?"

His hand runs through his perfectly gelled hair, ruffling it. "It was complicated."

"Complicated?" I punch the pillow to my right and wince. Curse that damn accident and my ruptured spleen. If I wasn't in pain, I'd be on my feet and in his face. "What in the hell is wrong with you? You were dating a girl just out of high school and making her keep secrets while you brought Ang home to meet us."

"Oh, get off your high horse." Ford shifts, his eyes darkening as they meet mine. "You have no idea the kind of stress I was under back then. You've stayed here in this little bubble of a town your entire life. I'm not saying what I did was right, Reid. I'm saying it was complicated."

"Right." I snort. "The stress of your high-paying financial career was so much you had to be a womanizer. Give me a—"

"Really, little brother?" Ford leaps to his feet, pacing in front of the chair before turning and exiting the living room. The clang of his keys hitting the kitchen counter and the clatter of bottles knocking into each other as the refrigerator door yanks open keeps me apprised of his whereabouts.

"When Mom left, I gave up everything to keep you and Wade from feeling Dad's misery. To keep you from missing her. That time sucked for me too, you know." He returns to the doorway between the two rooms, a beer in hand. Clearly, he noticed Dad's car missing from the garage if he's willing to bring her up.

"What does *she*—" I will never call her Mom out loud again — "have to do with this?"

He laughs bitterly. "Her betrayal changed the way I saw women. You're right, I was a womanizer. They were good for one thing and one thing only through my college years."

Sawdust coats my throat. Picturing Ford with Grace. His using her.

Ford's brows furrow, my brother quickly reading my anger. "That's not how I was with Grace. Angelica either. I'd let a good portion of my hostility go by then, but things were still—"

"Complicated?" I use his damn word, and he takes a swig of his drink as his answer. "Then uncomplicate it. Explain to me what happened."

"Why do you care so much?"

I want to hide my reasoning, but he's my brother. He helped raise me. He discerns my emerging affection for Grace in everything I say and do. I could cop to them, but regardless of romantic feelings, she's still my friend first. The same as Loe.

"Because I care about Grace, Ford. She's a good person. We share the same friends. We hang out. This is my town and my people. My life. If you screw that up… Grace doesn't know she was the other woman, does she?"

"Do you think she'd have gone to dinner with me tonight if she did?"

Yeah, that's highly unlikely. I didn't think so, but I had to ask. I can't see Grace being that girl, even if she was only nineteen at the time. Plus, she didn't mention Ford being a cheater yesterday when we talked. She's as clueless as we—his family—are about the life Ford lives.

A low chuckle leaves my lips. "I've seen her swing a bat. I think if she knew, you'd be hiding your fancy car in the garage right about now."

Ford's muted laugh joins mine, but his smile is temporary. "Please don't tell her." He straightens from the door and returns to Dad's chair. Propping himself on the edge of the seat, he bounces his knee like he can't decide if he's going to stay or run.

"It's not really my place to tell Grace something like that, but it's not exactly my place to keep secrets either." Damn, I wish I'd stayed clueless. "Like I said, she's my friend."

"And I'm your brother."

A brother who helped raise his younger siblings. Who drove home the moment he heard about my accident. Our relationship was never strained, it was just pushed to the background once he left for school. Life sucking up all his time, or mine, until here we are—grown men who rarely talk or share feelings.

"Okay, brother, tell me what happened between you and Grace and Ang." I grab the medicine bottle on the end table and fish out a pain pill. "Explain complicated to me." I swallow the tablet with water—while wishing it was a stiff drink—and settle deeper into the couch.

Head down, Ford rolls his beer between his palms. "Everything you know about Angelica is the truth."

"You say *everything* like we know so much."

I envision his ex-fiancée. The future trophy wife. She was his supervisor's little sister, visiting her brother at the office when she ran into Ford. Literally. My distracted brother crashed into the gorgeous blonde while he was leaving his boss's office and she was heading in. Not only that, but he somehow gave her a fat lip during the collision.

His grip chokes the bottle in his hand. "I hate talking about her."

Understandable, considering.

"She was sweet at first. We had fun. I'd mostly let go of my anger toward Mom by that point, so I let myself contemplate a relationship with her. Something more than what I'd done through college." He takes a swig of his drink before continuing. "It was good for a while. I was working long hours, proving myself. Ang didn't complain. She encouraged me to work as much as I needed. She was happy to be there when I had time for her. I think we used each other for what we could offer."

Ford curses beneath his breath and lifts his head for the first time since he began. "You know this story, Reid. She stroked my ego. She was a gorgeous woman who looked good on my arm when we had client dinners and parties. She knew exactly how to work a room because she'd been raised to be a charming woman on the arm of her husband." His upper lip sneers. His disgust is something new because a few years ago all Ford wanted was a trophy wife. "And because I watched our mother walk out on our family like we were nothing…I found I was okay with the idea of having something pretty on my arm and in my bed. I was okay with keeping my heart out of the equation."

What that must be like, to stay with a woman without feelings getting in the way.

A deep exhale leaves him. "Then I saw Grace Embry."

My breath catches as a low-key smile tugs Ford's lips.

"I'd left a client dinner and was walking down the Ave when I saw her through the window of an Irish pub. She was laughing so hard, she'd turned her head toward the street and covered her mouth." *Likely masking the little snort she does when she laughs too hard.* "Probably to cover that obnoxiously adorable snort she has."

My hands fist in my lap at sharing knowledge of Grace's quirk with Ford. At sharing any part of her with him. Not that she's ever been mine, but...dammit, he knows her. Like biblically knows her. I rub the back of my neck and focus on his story.

"—so I sat at the bar, and I waited and watched, hoping for a moment to speak."

"Wait." I think I missed something. "You stalked her?"

Ford chuckles. "No, you idiot. I saw a beautiful girl who mesmerized me, so I made a move. She was with her girlfriends, eating nachos, and drinking."

"Did you recognize her?" What are the chances of him running into her like that? Sure, a lot of kids from Seaside wind up at school in Seattle, but still.

"I had no clue." He sets his empty bottle on the carpet between his feet and continues. "Nor did I know how young she was. We were in a bar, but she had a fake ID. So, no, I didn't know she was a nineteen-year-old from Seaside, but she knew me. I'd been biding my time for maybe thirty minutes when she nudged her way out of the booth and walked my way. Bold as can be, she wedged herself between the guy on my left and me, ordered a Lemon Drop, and said, 'since I've never seen Reid without a baseball cap and boots, you must be the older brother.'"

Two things strike me. The first is her drink of choice— Lemon Drop aka Ford's nickname for her the other night in the hospital. With that question answered, I allow a self-satisfied smile to grow at the idea of Grace bringing me up the night she met him. Even way back then, Grace helped Loe out at the farm when she could. She knew me well enough to recognize my look-a-like brother at a glance in some dark Seattle pub.

"I'm not going to lie, Reid. I didn't think twice about flirting with her. I didn't even consider Angelica's feelings. Grace had me from day one. We sat in that pub for hours, long after her friends headed out, and talked about the city and college and home. Ang was out of town that weekend, so I asked Grace to lunch. Things grew from there."

"Things grew from there? Why didn't you break it off with Ang then?"

"Dump my boss's sister? God, I wish I had, but at the time I was scared. I was building a clientele and honestly, I figured Grace would be a fling. She was so young."

Clenching my jaw, I hold back my tirade. He thought Grace was a fling. I want to hate him.

"I didn't know I would fall in love with her."

"And that's why it was complicated," I surmised. He was in love with the role Ang played in his career, with the image he wanted to project like all the ambitious bastards he worked with. And, he was in love with the college student from his hometown —the woman who was real.

With his head down, Ford shoves his fingers through his hair and sighs. "I think I made a mistake."

Jealousy burns in my gut. "You think?"

"I know I did." He lifts his head and the manic energy in his eyes has me holding my breath. I read his mind before he speaks. "I want another chance, Reid. I think she could be the one. I should have dumped Ang years ago. The moment I knew I was in love with Grace, I should have come clean. I could have saved myself all this crap I've dealt with."

Yup. Called it. He wants Grace. "All the crap you've dealt with? What about Grace, Ford? Do you really think whatever you put her through didn't affect her?" She barely revealed her dating story to me, but the bits she shared when we discussed Mia were enough to know my brother did a number on her. "And how do you think she's going to feel when she learns the truth?"

He has the decency to wince as he asks, "Does she have to?"

"You're joking, right?" I ease my feet off the coffee table, ready to knock his teeth in, forget my injuries. "Your engagement wasn't a secret, idiot. You think Dad isn't going to put two and two together? What are you going to do, ask Grace to lie about your past with her?"

Messing with his watch, he works his jaw. "I'll tell her, I swear. I'll come clean about everything, but I need a little time. I need to get her to give me an opening."

"Wasn't that what dinner was about?"

"Tonight? Nah, tonight was strictly platonic. Nothing happened. We were like two old friends catching up on lost time. She was nervous. I didn't want to bring up our past and give her any reason to cut me off and walk away."

"I don't know, Ford." I should tell him how I feel. How Grace worked her way into my life over the last few months in such an unexpected and perfect way. How I kissed her the night before my accident and wanted to ask her out. I should, but...

"I loved her, Reid. And she loved me."

That. That is the one thing I need to keep in mind in the whole situation. Grace was in love with Ford four years ago. Does she love him still? Is whatever was sparking to life between us just Grace settling for second best? Settling for the brother of the man she wanted but couldn't have? And, if she could have him back, would she want him?

"I'd do right by Grace. I'd spend the rest of my life making my mistakes up to her if she'd let me. I'm not that man anymore. I swear, I'm not."

For his sake, I hope not, because brother or not, if he hurts Grace, I'll bury him.

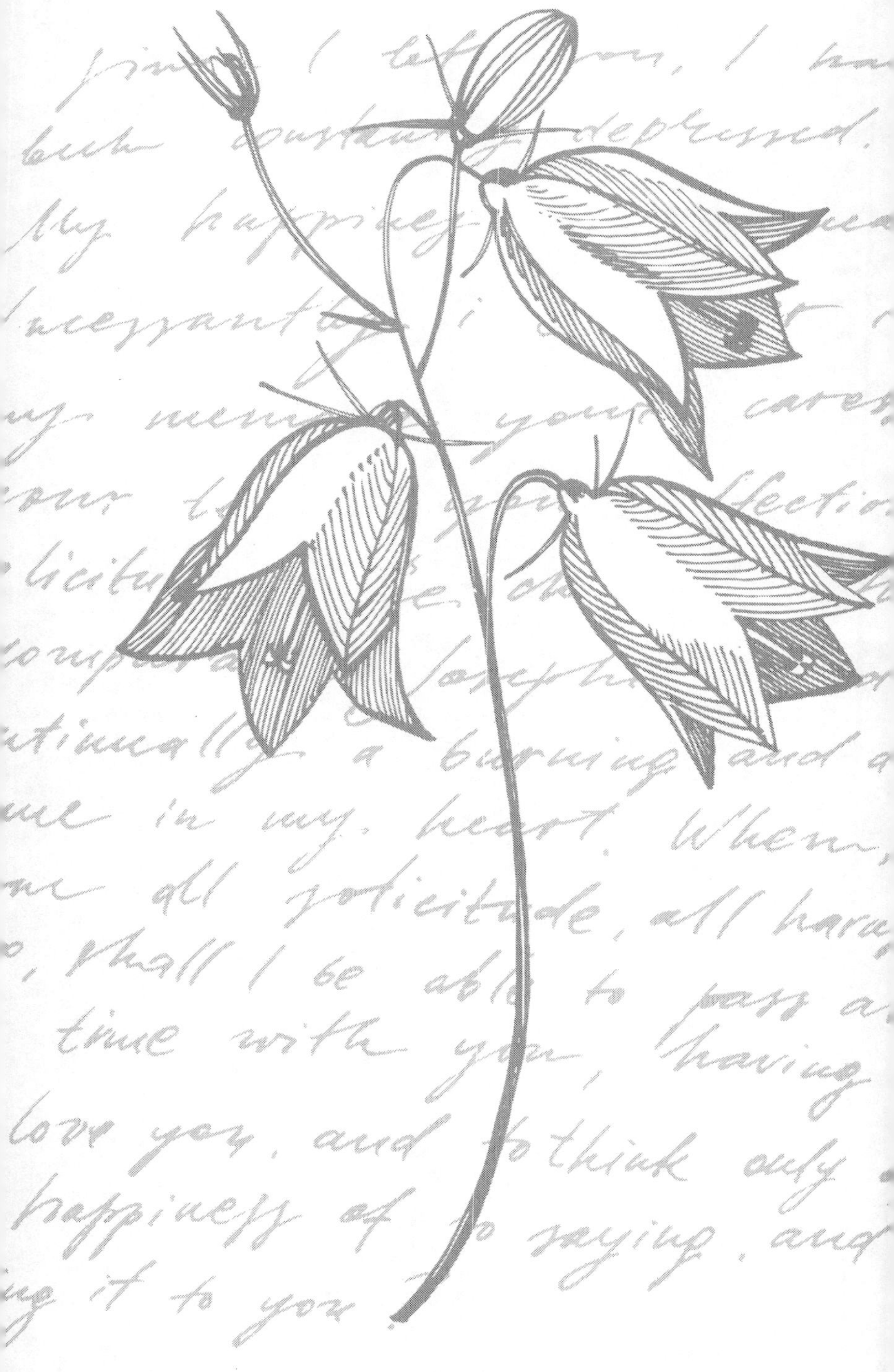

Grace

I SHOULDN'T BE STUNNED when Drew walks into Fig an hour after I open the store Tuesday morning, considering he hinted at possibly stopping by on his way out of town, but I am. We were together for over three years, and I can count on one hand the number of times he paid me a surprise visit.

"Wow, three sightings in four days. I think that's a record."

Slipping his hands into the pockets of his gray slacks, he pauses a few steps into the store. "I wasn't the greatest boyfriend, was I?"

"Oh. No, I shouldn't have—"

"Told the truth?" he interrupts, his shoulders dropping just enough that I know I hit a nerve. "It's okay. I should hear it."

"You were a very busy man back then." I swallow any further excuses. I won't make them for him, but I won't condemn him either. I don't want to go there. We need to let the past rest. "You know what? Let's not do that. It was years ago. I'm not that young naïve college girl anymore, and I'm sure you've changed."

Drew winces. It's slight but hard to miss as he walks further into the store. "I have, Lemon Drop. That's why I came by."

I hug the peplum blouses draped over my arm tighter to my chest the closer he gets.

"I'd like a second chance."

A metal arm from a display stand jabs into my back and I spin on my heels, heading to the checkout and dropping the blouses on the counter. "I'm sorry, you…"

"Want a second chance," he repeats, clear as day.

"I don't…I can't." *What, Grace? What are you trying to say?*

"You're right, Grace. We're not the same people we were four years ago. You can make excuses for me, but the truth is, I was never good enough for you. I was too ambitious and too…" He shakes his head, blowing out a deep exhale. "I don't know. I just wasn't what you deserved."

Hindsight is twenty-twenty, am I right? If I knew now what I knew then, I'd have kicked Drew to the curb before he had the chance to break my heart, but I was in love with his drive and his charm, with his mature worldliness. I had this silly young-minded fantasy that we were going to live happily ever after. Oh, how wide-eyed I was.

"But now you are?"

"I'd like to think so." His head cocks, and that little look—a lift at the edge of his mouth and the narrowing, almost wink, of his left eye—that separates him from looking too much like an older version of Reid appears. It's sexy and charming and ensnared nineteen-year-old me in a dark Irish pub one long-ago winter night in Seattle.

Drew shared more about his career and current lifestyle last night than he did in all the years we dated. While his new open book policy doesn't make up for what he put my heart through, he has grown, and I did love him once.

When I don't reply, Drew steps back and glances around the store. "This place is amazing, G." He circles a rack of blush miniskirts before returning to stand before me. "I'm not at all surprised you accomplished opening your own place so quickly."

My chest inflates. "It wasn't without help, but thank you."

"I'm asking for another chance. We can start small. Let me call you this week? Can you make time for me?"

Can I? Memories of the pain from when we ended things says I can't. I gave him most of my college years. Years that should've been spent dating and exploring and discovering. Was that not enough of a chance? Then again, I was so young. So idealistic and in love with the concept of marriage—something Mom never stops browbeating. I tried pushing my ideals onto Drew when he wasn't ready. He wasn't perfect, but neither was I. A few phone calls can't hurt. If nothing else but to know for sure there's nothing left between us.

"You know my number."

With a full smile, Drew reaches for my wrist and draws me into a loose hug. "I need to get to Seattle for a meeting this afternoon. I'll call you tonight. Thanks, Lemon Drop."

I watch Drew leave the store, my chest tingling from his use of my old nickname and the touch of his lips on my temple, but it's the phantom scent of soil and flowers that fill my nostrils.

WHEN I WALK onto Chloe's new land, I'm reminded of what the property looked like a year ago and how far she's come. Rows and rows of richly colored flowers speckle the twenty acres, hoop houses lining the far side. It's like stepping into a different world. If fashion wasn't my life, I'd trade fabrics for flowers easily. But maybe I'd just let someone else grow them for me so that I could enjoy the beauty without the labor.

"Woman, even with unfamiliar soil, you nailed your dahlias this year."

Chloe looks over her shoulder, a camera in hand. "Are you saying I don't nail them every year?"

"I'm just proud of you for getting the blooms going on this land so quickly and crushing it. Sticking it to the man." I fist bump the air.

Chloe nods and smiles, but the joy doesn't reach her eyes.

"What's with the fancy camera?"

"I'm trying to get our social media up and running, so I'm practicing my photography skills with the magic hour. Gosh, I love this golden lighting. Since we're opening the pick-your-own fields and seed shop next year, I want to get this location out there as much as possible. Spread the word about a second location of the most stunning blooms in the Pacific Northwest."

"And naturally, the dahlia patch is where I'd find you taking pictures."

"Duh. I only get these beauties for like four months out of the year, five if I'm lucky." She bends at the waist, taking another shot of the colorful patch. "What are you doing here so late?"

"I could ask you the same thing, but I know there's no rest for the wicked."

"Damn straight. Kip's working late, so I'm not in any rush to get out of here."

"Do you remember when I was in school and I ran into Reid's older brother at that little pub?"

Chloe hesitates at my abrupt change in subject before snapping another picture. "Ford? Yeah. I figured that's why you two didn't need any introductions at the hospital."

I nod. "That, and I might've dated him for a bit back in college."

"I'm sorry, what?" She whips around, the camera lowering to her waist.

I wince. "Ford *Andrew* Pruitt."

It takes a moment for realization to set in. "Oh my gosh, he's Drew?"

Lifting my hands, I say, "In my defense, you and I didn't talk a ton while I was in school. You were neck-deep in Lockwood Blooms, trying to learn the ropes of management, and I was buried in schoolwork and exams."

"So, you couldn't shoot off a text with, hey, best friend since we were five, I'm dating Ford Pruitt. Oh, and by the way, he goes by Drew now."

"It was more than that. Drew was weird about dating a girl so much younger than he was. With his job, appearances were everything. And because we're both from Seaside he didn't want the rumor mill circulating gossip about us."

"So, you lied to me about him instead." Her shoulders droop.

"I'm sorry. I wanted to tell you, but I figured breaking his trust wasn't the best way to start an honest relationship."

"Honest? There's nothing honest about lying about who you're dating. You didn't mind being a secret?"

"I did, but you know how it is when you're in love. I had on blinders. And I was an inexperienced teenage girl, enamored by his maturity, good looks, and fancy career."

"Don't take this the wrong way because I love you, but you didn't question why an almost thirty-something-year-old was interested in dating a college student?"

"Sure, but not enough to care in the beginning. At first, I think I was lured in by superficial things. His car, his suits, the money he was able to throw around to take me on dates. So, treating us like a secret wasn't hurtful because we weren't something deep to begin with. But not long after, I got to know him. He treated me with a certain level of respect and passion that guys our age did *not* know. He wasn't trying to impress me with his beer pong skills or keg stands. We had meaningful conversations and…"

Chloe's head cocks when I falter. "You can say it, Grace. The sex was good."

My cheeks heating, I nod because thinking about Drew in that sense now is strange, let alone talking about it. "By then I was in so deep, I didn't care about the secrecy because I just wanted him. I loved him."

"But he kept breaking things off. Why did you continue to let someone back in who didn't even want to parade you around or introduce you to his family? Forget the fact that you already knew Reid."

"I don't have a good enough answer. It was like hypnosis. He'd come back and I'd think, okay, this is the time he'll be ready to make us official. There were so many empty promises and what I thought were understandable excuses at the time. I allowed myself to believe in what could be, rather than the reality of the situation."

"So, what happened? Did you eventually tell him to claim you in public or go to hell? Is that why you two broke up?"

Kind of. I run a hand through my hair. "When I graduated, I thought things would be different. I was twenty-two and a college grad. I wanted to get married and have kids, to start a life together." Looking back, I'm not sure if I just wanted those things in general, or if I wanted them with him. Or, maybe I caved to the pressure of a mother who never stopped force feeding her daughters outdated expectations. "Drew wasn't anywhere near ready for commitment, so he ended things."

Her head shakes "So, that part was true, which makes him an even bigger fool. You came back to get stuck under your parents' roof, hardly able to function."

"God, I hated living with my parents again. Having Gram die was devastating, but the timing was a blessing so I could get out on my own and open Fig."

"And you've done nothing but put every ounce of time and energy into that business."

"To make it successful."

"And to drown out your heartbreak." She takes a deep breath, staring around the flower patch. "It makes so much sense now. All because of freaking Ford Pruitt. It took you like a year or two before you went on a date with what's his name."

"Geoff Gunderson."

"Oh my gosh, yes. G-off Gunderson. I still can't believe you let your mom set you up with that neanderthal."

That date was the first, but unfortunately not the last time I agreed to one of her setups.

Chloe laughs then sobers. "Grace, why didn't you just tell me? After things were over. After he ended your relationship, why didn't you open up?"

"Because I'm not that person. I made a promise, and I wasn't going to betray Drew just because he broke my heart. What would've been the point? We were over anyway."

"Dang it, Grace. And here, I was going to suggest you go out with him, but all I want to do is drive to Seattle and punch him in the nuts."

I laugh. "Please don't do that."

"I saw the way he was looking at you at the hospital, and now it's all coming together. He knows he messed up. That man couldn't take his eyes off of you."

I tug on my earlobe. "I went to dinner with him last night."

"Please tell me I did not hear what I think I just heard."

"You just said you thought I should go out with him," I point out.

"That was before I knew the truth. He doesn't deserve you."

"Well, it wasn't a date, just dinner. I kept things completely friendly. We met at the restaurant and said goodbye at the restaurant. There were no kisses, not even a hug, nothing."

"But…"

"Then he showed up at Fig today."

"No…"

"He wants another chance. Asked if he could call me sometime this week."

"And you said no, right?"

Maybe I should have. "I said yes."

"Grace Elizabeth."

Saying yes might not have been my brightest moment, but what if it is? I won't know unless I hear him out. "I'm not saying I'm giving him a second chance, but I'll talk to him. It's been four years. I'm older and wiser, and I'm sure he's changed."

Her free hand plants on her fitted overalled hip. "So, he's willing to parade you around in public now?"

"We went out to eat in Seaside, didn't we?"

"That's true." She nods, but skepticism is written across her face. "What about Reid?"

A knot forms in my chest. "What about him?"

Her eyes widen, her eyebrows rising up her forehead. "Did you tell him about you and Drew?"

"Yeah, he picked up on it on Friday when Drew walked into the hospital room and saw me."

She winces. "What does he think about it?"

"We talked a little bit on Sunday. He seemed okay, more annoyed that he was in the dark, which is understandable."

"He doesn't care that you dated his older brother?"

I could play dumb, but she'd see right through me. "I thought he might, but if he's bothered by it, he didn't say anything to me."

"Why would he? You've basically marked yourself as off-limits now."

"How do *you* know he'd want me in-limit? Unlimited?"

Chloe laughs.

"Shut up. You know what I mean."

Chloe doesn't even know about our New Year's kiss, and I'm not about to share the kiss in the Bingley Park parking lot. I'm confused enough without Chloe tossing in her two cents.

"Only because you asked, not because I'm meddling like your mother." She slips the camera around her neck. "Let me name the ways. One, the wedding. Maybe he didn't realize it at the time, but that man was enchanted by you. The way he looked at you while you were dancing... He *never* looked at me that way. And with the softball game, how he hugged you in the dugout after your base hit. Even from the bleachers, I could tell he didn't want to let go. Then at dinner, the way you two interacted. I was surprised I didn't catch you two holding hands or snuggling into one another at the table."

It's like sixty degrees out, but I'm burning up, my heart pulsating double-time, pounding so hard my chest aches. The things Chloe mentions sparked something inside of me, but I didn't know anyone else noticed or read it the same way I did. He dated my best friend. I dated his brother. We were both in limbo with someone else when we started hanging out. It was hard to gauge what that made us. Our attraction just sort of...happened.

"Well, even if you're right. That probably all changed once he found out about my history with Drew."

Chloe swats the air. "It was years ago. As long as you don't still have feelings for him, I don't see a problem."

Oh, really. "If you had an older sister and you found out Kip was in a serious relationship with her at one point, knowing he likely knows what she looks like naked, would you be able to look past it?"

"When you put it like *that*." She pauses, nibbling on the corner of her bottom lip. "But at the same time, I can't imagine my life without Kip. If I knew he felt nothing for her anymore, I'd figure out how to get past it. It might take me time, but I wouldn't be able to let him go."

If Reid wanted something more, wouldn't he have said something? Granted, we were interrupted by the doctor in the hospital. He didn't have much of a chance to tell me how he felt with our conversation cut short.

"Okay. On that note, I'm going to be late for softball practice, so I need to go. Since you were on the way, I wanted to stop by, but this has turned into a much longer chat than I anticipated."

"You thought you could just drop the Drew-slash-Ford bomb on me and I wouldn't pry every last detail out of you. That's on you."

"Well, I knew that, but this has turned into a completely different conversation than I intended."

"I'm surprised you're still doing the whole softball thing even without Reid."

"I didn't join for Reid to begin with." Or rather, I didn't initially agree because of him. He just came as an added bonus.

I back away from Chloe through the row of coral dahlias. "I made a commitment to Bucky and I plan to keep it."

"You and your loyalty." She smirks. "Sometimes it's okay to do the right thing for you, even if it means breaking a promise."

"It's softball, Loe. Not a lifetime commitment."

"I wasn't talking about softball."

I don't have time to dissect her riddles, so I toss a wave and walk away with a pit in my stomach.

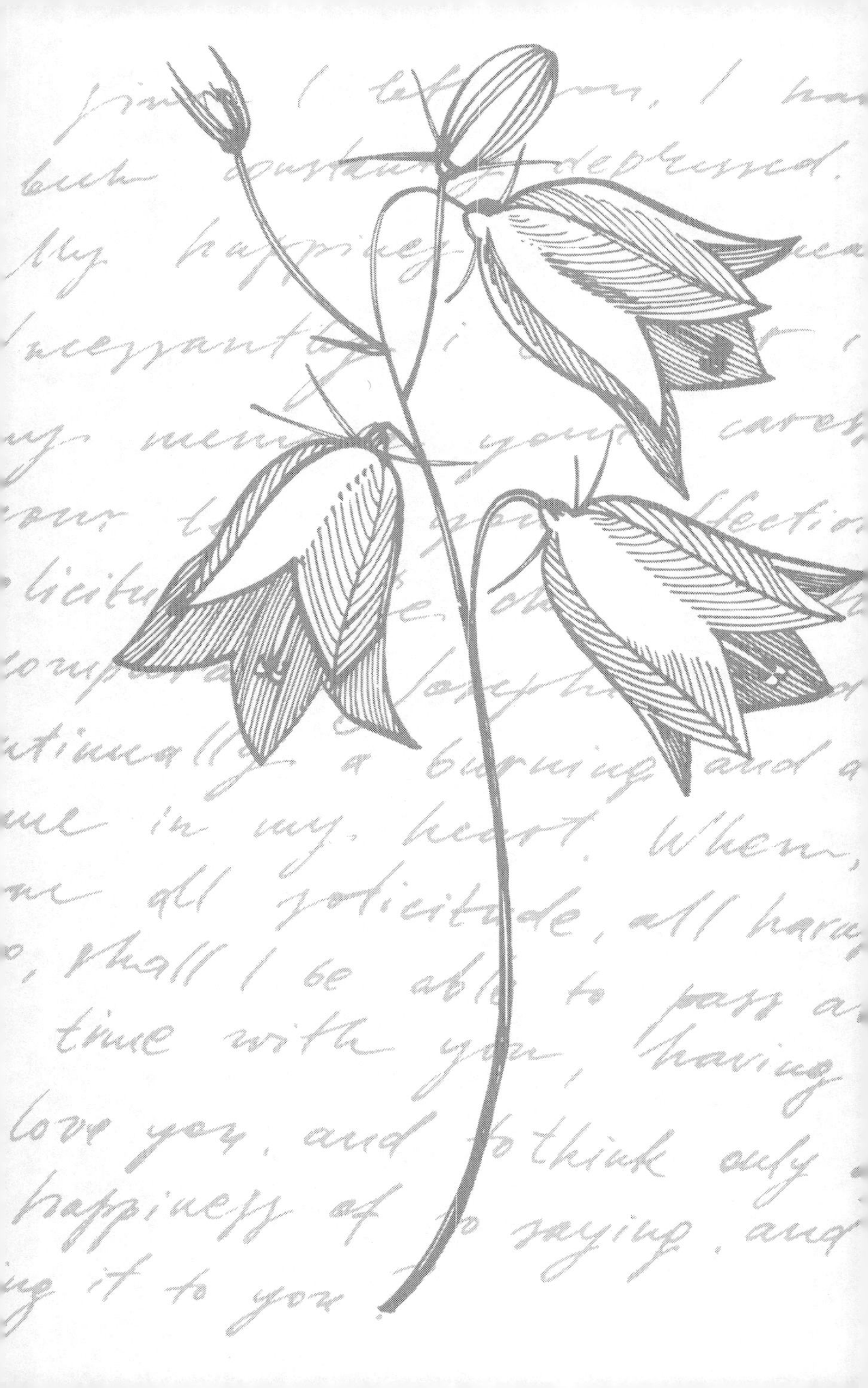

Reid

Me: Someone nailed a line drive and scored her first run in a game tonight. Proud of you, Slugger.

Grace: I'm not even in my car yet and you have the play by play? Didn't realize ESPN would show the highlights.

Me: Don't you know I've got spies everywhere? Really wish I'd been there to see it myself, though.

Grace: Those bleachers aren't exactly soft for someone recovering from stunt driving.

Me: Stunt driving, huh? There you go trying to make my brush with death seem glamorous again. Is that the only way for a guy to impress you?

I REGRET the question the moment it's sent. I pace an imaginary trench in the worn planks of my living room floor while awaiting a reply. My mind returns to making a list of home improvements—too many things. Being on enforced vacation and stuck at home will not be good on my wallet. I stop and eye a wall, debating for the hundredth time if it's load-bearing because knocking it down would open up the living room to the kitchen and make my little matchbox house appear larger. *I should have stayed at Dad's a few more days.* One day shy of a week since the accident and I'm losing my mind with boredom.

Lights flash across the front window as a vehicle pulls into my driveway. When the headlights cut off, I move to the front door, flipping the lock and pushing my storm door wide.

Eagerness tugs at my gut as Grace opens her car door and steps out, her hair flying around her face. A storm's moving in off the coast tonight and heavy clouds cover the sky, veiling the setting sun.

"You drove all this way to answer my text in person?" I call when her gaze meets mine.

"Oh, you were looking for an answer?"

I shrug, biting back a smile as she ducks into her car before reappearing and closing the door. "Aren't you supposed to be on bed rest or something?"

"I've been lazing around for six days."

She hums her disapproval as she makes her way up my driveway and down my sidewalk. With the last of the day's weak sunlight illuminating her way, it's impossible not to stare. Though she's replaced the dirt-stained sneakers she typically wears on the softball field with sandals, she's still wearing her Seasiders jersey and game day leggings. A gift to mankind: her black spandex pants cling to every inch of her long legs, hips, and rear.

"You've got to eat dinner with me."

Her words draw my gaze from her body. *Wait. What did she say?* I stare at her mouth like an idiot.

Grace smiles. "One way to impress me, Reid Pruitt. You eat dinner with me." She rattles the brown bag I'd paid no heed to in my face.

"You brought Perry's?" I shift sideways and hold the storm door open, inviting her inside.

Bouncing onto the porch, Grace stops inches away. "This is all your fault, you know. Thanks to you, I can't eat alone anymore."

I don't miss the way her eyes scan my ratty maroon and white Seaside Pointe High Varsity baseball tee and baggy gray sweatpants. Gray sweatpants on men: a gift to womankind, or so I've been told.

I tilt forward until we're eye-level and take the bag, my fingers lingering with hers. "I'm not even apologizing for that."

With a flair of her nostrils, our stare locks before she releases the bag and replies, "I'm not asking you to."

Turning, Grace walks inside and I follow. Stepping around her after locking the door, I nod toward the kitchen.

"I realize it's nearly nine o'clock at night, and you've probably already had dinner, but I wanted to see how you were doing coming back home and all."

I set the bag on the table and remove two glasses from the cabinet. "You know I can always eat. Though, I'm bummed you didn't bring milkshakes."

Grace rolls her eyes. "Next time."

I fill the glasses with ice water while she moves to the sink and washes her hands. "Jackie and the guys asked me to say hi. They miss you pitching. It makes it harder for us to win when Tony allows the opposing teams so many runs."

I settle across from her at my kitchen table. "You actually sound like you know what you're talking about. You're a softball pro now."

"I guess I have you to thank for that, too." She hands me a

wrapped burger with a red number *three* sticker—my favorite—and a large box of their famous seasoned fries.

"It was Bucky who invited you."

"Yeah, but you're the one who made it easy to say yes, and you're the one coaching me up Tuesday and Thursday nights over dinner."

My gaze follows her tongue as she licks a glob of ketchup from the edge of her burger. *Ford was in love with her. Ford wants her back.* Reining in the impulse to say things I shouldn't, I dig into my food. "Well, you're welcome. I'm glad you're enjoying the team."

Grace fills me in on the rest of tonight's game while we eat. She's not a woman you would look at and peg as an athlete, but she talks animatedly about the plays like she's officially become a fan. Her enthusiasm and competitiveness is sexy as hell.

"I should go," she says when I've yawned for the second time in five minutes. Crumbling her wrapper and tossing it in the paper bag, she stands and leans over the table for mine.

My fingers grip her wrist. "I miss you."

Oh. Hell.

Grace stills.

"Sorry, it's the pain meds. They make me sleepy and loopy." Releasing her wrist, I recline in my chair. "I meant that I missed our Tuesday night dinner, so I'm really glad you came tonight."

She chews on her lip, her eyes scanning over my face. "Drew asked me to give him a second chance." The words rush from her lips like if she doesn't spit them out she might lose the nerve altogether.

Composing my features is an all-out effort. I won't betray my feelings for her or about her and Ford. I can't. Her cheeks flush pink the longer I sit silently. Finally, I push back from the table and swipe the bag up, walking it to the trash.

"That's cool." *It's so not cool and neither is my response.*

Grace's laugh at my back is light. "Yeah, sure. *Cool.*"

Her tone is flat. I press my palm into the counter and practice deep breaths as she crosses the kitchen and dumps her water in the sink before loading the glass in my dishwasher like she's been here a million times. I like her comfort level with being in my house. I want her here, but it doesn't matter what I want. What I like.

"It really is the meds, Grace, I swear. Once I take my evening dose, it's best I lock myself away because I spew all kinds of crap. Ask my Dad. I argued with him for thirty minutes over the best way to cut onions while watching a cooking show the other night."

A somber chuckle leaves her.

"If you want to give Ford another chance, then I'm happy for you both. He's my brother, and you're..." *The woman I somehow fell for over lunch breaks and dinners.* "You're an amazing woman who deserves the best."

"So, you're okay with it?" She crosses her arms, rubbing them like she's chilled. "You think I should? It won't affect our...friendship?"

I can't keep from closing the space between us and settling my hands on her shoulders. "Never," I whisper, pressing a kiss to her forehead.

Withdrawing, I find Grace's ashy blue eyes lingering on my mouth. Tomorrow I'll blame this on the drugs. Sliding my hand up her slender neck and cupping the back of her head, I lower my lips, and Grace reciprocates. Her palms land on my chest as I press closer, slanting my mouth and allowing this kiss to connect fully, unlike the first two we shared. I nibble at Grace's bottom lip, tasting the saltiness from our fries, and I want to delve deeper, but I hold back.

"I'm sorry." The words fall from my lips without thought. "I really hate that Ford had you first."

Her fingernails lightly rake across my pecs, her eyes lowering, watching my T-shirt shift with each graze. "I've missed you, too, you know."

"Grace—"

Raising her long, full lashes, her piercing eyes strike me in the heart. "Is there even a possibility for us? Did I screw everything up by dating the wrong brother?"

"I…" My head tips to the ceiling, my Adam's apple bobbing as I swallow hard and weigh my reply. "It's not that I have an issue with you being with him first. I mean, of course, I don't like the idea, but the past doesn't change what I feel for you."

Grace blinks. "You have feelings?"

"You know my family history, Grace. Considering your past with him, you must know exactly what Ford gave up when our mother abandoned us. He stepped up big time for Wade and me. He held us together whenever Dad broke down."

Sinking my fingers deeper into her hair, I drop my forehead to hers, detesting what I have to say. "He regrets the way he acted toward you, Grace. I don't know the details of your relationship, but I know Ford hates the man he was back then. He wants a second chance, and I…" I withdraw. "I can't be the guy who comes between you two. I owe him more than that."

Her lips part, a breathy sound eking past, but she can't seem to form whatever words she wants to say. I know the feeling. I'm forcing my refusal of us becoming more.

"He still loves you." *Whatever possibility there was with Grace and me stalled when Ford admitted his feelings the other night.* "Maybe you should give him another chance."

"Another chance. Yeah. Right." Her hands falling from my chest, Grace turns away with a nod. "I should go." She gathers her keys and phone, heading toward the door without a second glance. "I'll text you tomorrow to see how you're doing."

The sound of the front door shutting resonates, her quick exit an agonizing loss.

I'M WALKING past the front windows of my house Friday, after waking from a mid-morning nap—Why not? I have nowhere to go and nothing but sitting around and healing to do—when I spot Mrs. Lockwood's car parked in my drive. Returning to my bedroom to grab a T-shirt, I open the front door as Robyn comes up the porch steps with oversized shopping bags in each hand.

"Hi."

Robyn skirts away from me, shaking her head when I reach for one of the bags. "Hi, sweetheart." Her gaze assesses me from head to toe. "You look good. How are you feeling?"

She doesn't wait for an answer before stepping inside and heading for my kitchen like she owns the place. She's visited a few times in the two years since I bought the house. Robyn Lockwood is Seaside Pointe's favorite mother hen, always delivering homemade meals to those in need. I still have dreams about the chicken noodle soup she brought me when I came down with the flu not long after moving out on my own.

"I'm good, and I have a feeling I'll be doing even better once I see what's in those bags." I'm nearly salivating at the prospect of a home-cooked meal for lunch.

I sat at my counter and shared the last of a box of Honey Nut Cheerios with Dad when he dropped by around nine this morning like he hasn't missed enough time at work this week. It's the only reason I insisted on returning to my place yesterday. The man can't stop hovering, and Lord knows I love him, but I'm twenty-eight.

"Well, you're in luck." Robyn digs into the bags, pulling out container after container of food, each tin lid with cooking instructions taped to the top. "I'm sorry I didn't get these to you sooner, but Chloe's been so busy with both farms, she forgot to tell me you weren't at Gregory's anymore."

"Are you kidding? Robyn, this is amazing." I mentally divide the portions, figuring she's brought enough to feed me for an entire week. "You didn't have to do so much. Thank you."

"Of course, I had to do this. You've been with us for ten years, Reid. You're like a son, you know that." She squeezes my arm, pursing her lips as her eyes water. "Plus, you were driving our van. I feel so responsible. If something more…"

"Uh-uh. Don't do that." I draw her into a side hug and walk her back into the living room. "Lockwood Blooms is not responsible for my accident, Robyn. That van was recently serviced. I know those vehicles like I know my own. It was—" I hesitate. "An accident. Plain and simple."

If Chloe hasn't told James and Robyn about the tampering, I'm not going to. There's no need to cause alarm within a family already struggling.

"I hope James hasn't tried working in the field with my not being there?"

"You know James…" Her voice catches as she settles on the couch. "I'm sorry he hasn't visited. He should have gone to you while you were in the hospital."

I wave off her apology and sink down on the opposite end of the couch. "Don't." James is a homebody, more so over the past five years. I didn't expect him to come see me. Though I'm surprised he hasn't called, considering not long ago he offered me his family business, but I bet he's still pissed at me for promising the shed to Chloe. "Your cooking more than makes up for him."

Her frown lessens at my tease, but stress wrinkles her brow.

"Is everything all right?" Clutching my side at the lingering sting from my surgery, I turn toward her. "Chloe's told me a lot about her argument with James. I understand if you'd rather not discuss it, but if there's something I can do…"

Robyn is an older version of her daughter. Soft, friendly, open, but today the woman before me looks nothing like the one I've known for so long. The cheerful motherly figure who chided me for forgetting my raincoat more than once when I first came on at Lockwood Blooms as a recent high school graduate in need of a job is gone. Replaced by a woman on the edge of sanity. Tension lines her lips, her hands wring in her lap, and those warm hazel eyes are dull. Unhappy.

She swallows, her gaze flitting about the room before settling on me. "I'm worried about James."

"How so?"

"He's become…manic?" She tests the word as though she's searching for the right one. "Moodier." Tears build in her eyes.

"Has he lifted a hand to you? Are you afraid of him?" Maybe I'm jumping to conclusions, but James's behavior at the shed comes to mind, and I wouldn't be able to forgive myself if I didn't ask and he'd turned abusive.

Robyn sinks back, her lips parting, but no words come.

"It's not completely uncommon after strokes for personalities—"

Finally, her hand touches my arm. "No, Reid. James hasn't hit me. In our thirty-eight years of marriage, and even before that, he's never laid a hand on me. It's only recently that he's even raised his voice."

"Since the stroke?"

"No, since Kip." She releases a heavy sigh and rubs between her brows. "Not that it's Kip's fault. He's such a good man for Chloe. He's…" Her face pales. "Oh, sweetheart, I'm sorry."

I can't help but laugh softly. It's been over a year now. "There are no hard feelings, Robyn. I'll always love Loe, but as a friend. She belongs with Kip. Don't feel bad for me."

"Well, I would have been happy had she chosen you. That was never an issue. Just so you know." Her assurance is sweet but misplaced. Chloe and I weren't meant for each other. I have no doubts about that, and neither does Loe. "It's that stupid feud with Denton. I just know it. There's no other reason for him to hate Kip."

"I know Loe was really hoping he'd come around, but that's not going to happen, is it?"

Robyn shakes her head. "You know, when we were in school, they just ignored one another. Denton's three years younger than us. They didn't have classes together. They didn't act like the enemies on those television dramas people watch. They just didn't speak." She smooths her palms down her thighs. "Then something happened between them the summer before we married. A fight that left them both bloody. After that, the hatred grew."

"Why did they fight?" James and Robyn were married when they were twenty. Chloe shared their love story with me when we were dating. So James would have been nineteen fighting a sixteen-year-old Denton?

"He would never tell me. He said the only thing that mattered was the last name Harris, but I know his hate for Denton goes deeper than fights over pies and cows and gates. Denton hasn't blocked Lockwood Blooms growth by preventing access to available land for over twenty years for no reason."

With a sigh, Robyn sits taller and forces a smile. "I'm sorry, I shouldn't burden you with my thoughts. Please, don't tell Chloe about this. She's dealing with enough."

After promising my secrecy, Robyn walks me through the meals she's made before she leaves, but I can't stifle my growing curiosity at everything she mentioned. The Lockwood-Harris feud has long been the stuff of legend in Seaside Pointe, but it was based on silly things that mostly spoke of the two families' egos. What happened between James and Denton to turn mild animosity into a hate so consuming?

a burning and
in my heart. When
all solicitude, all
shall I be able to pass
time with you, having
love you, and to think only
happiness of so saying, and
it to you

25

Grace

GINA and I are folding shirts at the back of the shop when the door chimes.

Keeping my attention on creasing the sleeve just right, I ask Gina, "Will you take care of that?"

"Sure thing." She ambles off.

Muffled voices travel across the way, one much deeper than Gina's. Men are always a challenge when they come in, typically shopping for a girlfriend or wife. They rarely know the proper sizing and, most of the time, want lingerie, which I don't carry yet.

"You know, it's hot being able to call you the boss."

I suck in a quick breath and turn, finding Drew in dark jeans and a mint green T-shirt that forms to his pecs and long, trim waist. "What are you doing here?"

"I couldn't stay away. I was going to call you when I got into town but figured I'd take a chance on finding you here."

"Are you here to see Reid?"

"That, too." He smiles, displaying his straight, white teeth. And an image of Reid's crooked bottom teeth comes to mind. The perfection of Drew's somehow less appealing.

Enough. I need to quit comparing them. And I should stop thinking about Reid altogether. It's clear after the other night, he'll never see me as anything but his brother's. I may have said I didn't regret dating Drew because I learned about my worth, but if dating Drew means losing a chance with Reid, I'd have thought twice about going up to him at that Irish pub.

"I already stopped by his place, but I wanted to take you out again, on a real date this time. You think you can swing it right now?"

My eyes touch on the other shoppers browsing. "It's four-thirty. I might be the owner, but I can't just leave whenever I feel like it. There are things that need to get done."

"I can wait until you're off."

"It'll be close to seven." Saturdays are our busiest day of the week.

Gina pops up beside Drew. "I don't mind closing up tonight, *boss*."

The way she says boss leads me to believe that's exactly how Drew asked for me.

His brow arches, like what's your excuse now?

"I can't leave you by yourself on a Saturday."

"I can handle it," she says.

"I'm not dressed for a date."

Drew smiles. "You look beautiful to me, but I'm not either. Go home, change, and I'll pick you up around five-thirty. None of this meet me at the restaurant nonsense."

"You're serious."

He nods. "We've got reservations at Briar's at six."

Briar's. It's on the outskirts of Seaside, and they have a dress code. "You don't even know if I'm going to say yes, and yet you already made reservations."

"I was feeling lucky."

"What if I say no?"

"I'll walk away like a bronze medalist and hang out with Reid for the night. So, what do you say, Lemon Drop?"

Why am I so conflicted? We've talked on the phone a few times this week, and for the most part, our conversations were effortless. We eased back into a groove, but that's how it's always been. Falling back together was never our problem.

The problem is Reid keeps popping into the forefront. He says he isn't bothered by the idea of me giving Drew another shot, but even if he's lying, it means nothing. He was practically shoving me back to his brother like he owed him a favor. Whatever was building between us was sabotaged by my history with Drew, which was another reason why I continued to stop myself from pursuing something before. Or maybe it wasn't sabotaged because there wasn't much there to begin with. We ate together and played softball and shared a couple of kisses, but no declarations were made or expectations set. I probably made more of it up in my head than there was.

No. That's not true. Reid said he felt something for me. I should have pushed for more of an explanation. Why couldn't he just say what he wanted? Dang him and his loyalty to his big brother. What a double-edged sword because the very thing that might keep us apart is another trait that makes me want Reid Pruitt more.

He may never consider more with me, especially with his loyalty to Drew. I need to accept that.

"Okay. Five-thirty. I'll be ready."

STARING at my reflection in the full-length mirror of my bedroom, I take a chance on a mustard wrap dress we got in this week. The tight hem rests a few inches above my knees, the neckline dipping farther than I'm generally comfortable with.

I don't know what I'm going for tonight. An 'eat your heart out, this is what you've been missing' vibe. Or simply, 'I never go to fancy restaurants, so I'm going all out because I can' vibe.

The doorbell echoes through my tiny house. Slipping into some strappy nude stilettos, I make my way to the front door. Drew stands on the other side in a tailor-made navy suit and baby blue shirt sans tie, the top two buttons undone. *The flawlessly styled businessman.*

With a suave smile, he holds out a bouquet of golden yellow roses tinged with pink. "The perk of being in Seaside is Lockwood sells locally."

My hand clutches my rose gold necklace before I reach out. "You remembered."

"There's not much about you I don't remember, Lemon Drop."

In the beginning, Drew brought me red roses. The cliché flower choice. I never complained because if a man brings you flowers, at least he's thinking of you. One random day we were talking about home and Lockwood Blooms came up as I told him about Chloe. I mentioned Lockwood's Honey Dijon roses—my favorite variety and never thought about the conversation again. Until one weekend, months later, Drew returned from visiting his family with a bouquet of—you guessed it—Honey Dijon roses.

I bring the flowers to my nose and inhale. *Perfection.* "Let me put them in water. You can come in."

The door closes and Drew's footsteps follow me down the short hallway to the kitchen. "Quaint little place you've got here."

"Yeah, I don't need much. Chloe technically lives with me,

though she's rarely here anymore. The place fits us fine." And Robyn, but she's hiding out because she still doesn't want anyone realizing she's left James.

"I like it. It suits you. All the original architecture and character. It's a good starter home."

"I can't tell if you're genuine or..."

"I'm serious. It might not be the right size for a bigger family, but for a newlywed couple, it's perfect."

I don't want to dig deeper into what he's implying, so after arranging the flowers in a white vase, I gesture for Drew to head toward the front door.

A charcoal Porsche Cayman waits at the foot of my driveway. "New car, I see. The Jag wasn't doing it for you anymore?"

"Oh, don't remind me. The engine blew, or I would've driven that baby another hundred thousand miles."

I smirk. "A Porsche isn't exactly a downgrade."

"No, this girl is a beauty. What can I say? I love a fast car." He opens the passenger side door and helps me in.

With how low to the ground the car is, my dress hikes up my thigh, and I have no extra length to pull down, so I rest my purse across my lap.

Drew's eyes immediately zero in on my legs when he slides in. His gaze trails up my body until he meets my eyes. "If I didn't tell you before, you look incredible, G."

I reach for my earlobe. "Thank you. You don't look too bad yourself."

The drive to Briar's is quick, probably because Drew doesn't know what a speed limit is. I suppose what's the purpose of a sports car if you can't test it, right?

After we've ordered and our server brings over our drinks, I take a sip of my merlot.

"No fruity drinks for you?"

My fingers glide up and down the stem of my glass. "I like

them on occasion, mostly when I'm out to have fun," not that that happens often anymore, "but wine tastes better with food."

Drew's eyes wander the packed restaurant, every table and booth occupied. Unsurprising since it's a Saturday night.

"I've come to Seaside a few times over the years, but I haven't really paid as much attention to how big it's gotten as I did last weekend. It's becoming quite the destination place."

I nod. "It's crazy how much it's grown even since I came home after college. Kip Harris, if you know Harris Development, he's Denton's son and Chloe's boyfriend. He has some massive riverfront complex going in soon. Shopping, restaurants, condos, office buildings, you name it. It's going to bring in a ton of people."

"Interesting. I bet that got a ton of flack from the locals."

I chuckle. "Yeah, probably, but growth is good. It needs to happen."

"I guess Seaside isn't the sleepy, small town it once was."

"Definitely not. It's one of the reasons I was able to open up Fig. There's a larger demographic I can reach, not just the natives who shop and eat at the same places over and over again."

A familiar look glazes over Drew's features. The wheels in his brain are turning, but I'm not sure what's going through his mind. Then his head tilts as he studies me, not saying a word.

"What?"

The edges of his mouth curve. "Nothing. It's just you're different, but the same. Our years apart have been good to you."

"You mean because I'm not an immature college student anymore?"

"You were never immature." His mouth forms a straight line as he bobs his head side-to-side. "Young and idealistic, maybe, but we never would've worked if you acted your age. You're just even more, *you*, if that makes sense. More sure of yourself, accomplished in the goals you strived for, even more beautiful. It's hard to take my eyes off of you."

Warmth blossoms in my belly. "Now you're just trying to get on my good side."

"Can't it be both? Honesty and a little buttering up."

"Only if you're sincere."

"I am. With you. I want you to know I'm serious about this, Grace. About us. I screwed up. Big time. I know that. I knew that the moment we broke up."

"You mean when *you* broke up with *me*."

He taps his index finger against the white tablecloth twice. "Yes. You're right. I'm sorry. I made a gigantic mistake, and I wasn't man enough to fix it. For years I paid for letting you go."

"So, why now?"

"Because I have everything I thought I wanted, but I'm miserable. I haven't been happy since you, G." His hand reaches across the table, curling around mine. The touch is so familiar and yet, strange, like a reliable pair of pumps that no longer fit quite right. "I've thought about you so many times over the years, but when I woke up one morning in December and wondered when the last time I felt true happiness was, my answer was with you. I don't know what it is about the holidays that get me reflecting on family and life, but I know one thing—I'm missing you, G.

"Having you be friends with Reid, close enough to know about his accident, to text me, to be in his hospital room. This feels like fate."

Well, fate sure knows how to mess with a person's head, that's for sure. And speaking of Reid's accident, I hate that we don't have any answers about the cause. We don't know if someone messed with the van.

"I think maybe we just didn't have our timing right the first go around. Our lives were in different places. It's why we never stuck, why we kept falling apart, but now, I think we're ready for each other. Ready to give this another shot."

Or we kept falling apart because we didn't fit. But maybe

Drew's right. Maybe it was the timing. If he hadn't ended things once and for all, would I have opened Fig? Would I have returned to Seaside? Would we have lasted?

"I'm not saying no, Drew, but I don't want to commit to anything, either. You really hurt me, and it's going to take time to trust that you're a man who will protect my heart."

"I'm willing to take things slow. I can come to Seaside on the weekends, and we can hang out, reacquaint ourselves. I'll do what it takes because I truly believe we have something special here."

Words. They're nice words, but are they true? Are they right?

I nod with a small smile, and the server drops off our dishes. We pick up where we left off after our first dinner, spending the rest of the meal chatting more about our current lives and what we've missed out on over the years. It's light and pleasant, no rehashing the past or placing blame for where we went wrong.

By the time he pulls up to my house, my barriers have thinned, and I haven't wiped the smile from my face in hours. It's like we haven't missed a beat.

As he puts the car in *Park*, Drew places his hand on my knee. "Wait here." He hops out of the Porsche and rounds the front before opening my door. Offering his hand, he helps me out and doesn't let go of my hand as he walks me all the way to my door.

"I'm not going to say yes if you ask me to come in, so just save yourself the humiliation." Drew's eyes flicker with teasing.

"Good thing I wasn't going to ask."

"Oh." His free hand thumps his chest. "Right in the heart."

"Thank you for tonight, though. I had a really nice time."

"And I'll be happy to show you more if you let me."

With a subtle nod, I smile at Drew. His head bows, and without meeting him halfway, I let him kiss me. Our lips mold together like they used to, a familiar connection. It's gentle and sweet and doesn't last as long as I expected.

"Have a good night, Lemon Drop," he says against my lips and pulls back.

There's a smoldering ember in my heart as my fingertips touch my mouth. With time, will the ember ignite into an uncontrollable wildfire again? Or gradually extinguish?

It's not until I've unlocked and closed my door behind me that he walks away.

a burning and a
in my heart. When
all solicitude, all
shall I be able to pass
time with you, having
love you, and to think only
happiness of so saying, and
it to you

Reid

"You're not coming into work this week."

Her voice is firm, and I sigh. I shouldn't have bothered calling. I should have shown up tomorrow morning and had one of the guys call her and let her know I was there.

"I can't take another week at home, Loe."

"I don't care. I know you all too well, Reid. You say you'll take it easy, but there's no way you'll be able to keep yourself from overdoing it. I don't need to feel more guilt over your injuries than I already do. A second week of rest won't kill you." *Does she not know me at all?* "Besides, Denise is loving getting to be boss, and Meredith enjoys being second-in-command." Her tone is no-nonsense.

"Oh, great. Keep me at home so the girls can't complain about fairness." I raise and lower my left arm, testing the sore muscles. "I'm pacing circles around the house and talking to myself for hours a day."

Chloe giggles. "You really need a hobby."

"The flower farm *is* my hobby, you know that." That and sports. My life revolves around two damn things I'm currently not allowed to do.

"I know, and we miss you there. I miss your leadership with the crew, but if you're gonna pick a time to take a few weeks, I guess now is the time. We're well-staffed, and while things are busy, it's nothing they can't handle. Take this break to rest up, so I can abuse you when it's time to get ready for fall and winter."

She's right. August is dahlia season, plus the hydrangea and roses are blooming, but at least we have our summer helpers to work the harvests. If this was September or October, poor Chloe would be in trouble, especially since she won't have Hayden's help at the second farm anymore come fall.

I give in. "My follow-up is Thursday."

"Good. You get me a doctor's note saying you can come back and I'll think about it." Grace's laugh sounds in the background.

"You're impossible, and tell your best friend I heard her. It's not nice to laugh at a man when he's down."

"Mmm-hmmm," Chloe hums. "I'll do that. We love you, Reid. We want you to get better. I know it sucks, but take it easy, please."

"Fine," I relent. "It's a good thing your mom delivered me a week of meals Friday. I'll get fat on her amazing food and binge crappy movies."

"You do that. Call if you need anything."

CONSIDERING Grace's laughter in the background during my phone call with Loe last night, I shouldn't be surprised she's shown up at my front door this morning with her arms full of bags.

"Let me guess." I yawn and push the door wide, letting her

in. "You felt bad for laughing, so you brought food to make up for it?"

Her glossy lips twist in a way that says, 'sure, buddy' as she brushes by with a sarcastic, "Close."

I eye her long tan legs shown off by jean shorts. Along with her hair curled in short waves and simple emerald-colored tee, she looks casual and summery. "Day off?"

"Yup." She glances around the space. "I guess the kitchen is the best place. Follow me."

She crosses the living room, her hips swaying naturally, and disappears into the kitchen while my feet remain glued to the floor. It's not that I'm unhappy she's here, but I'm fully aware of her date with Ford Saturday night. Ford hasn't made a trip home two weekends in a row since…well, ever. But he visited for Grace. I urged her to consider him, but part of me hoped his desire for a second chance would fade after he returned to Seattle Tuesday. Apparently, not. At least he held back the details of their night when he and Dad came to the house for lunch yesterday. Better than that was the way Dad slipped in the information I found most pertinent: One, Ford returned home at a reasonable hour. Two, he'd looked much the way he had when he left the house. In other words, Ford did not score a home run on his second chance first date with Grace. Not that I thought Grace would give in to him so easily. She'll make him work to win her heart.

Or so I hope.

"Are you coming?" Grace calls over the crinkling of plastic bags shifting around.

I run my hand through my bedhead and join her. "Yeah, but…uh, what are you doing here, Grace?"

With a bright smile, she holds up a fistful of paintbrushes. "I brought you hobbies."

I scan the table where she's unpacked the contents of her bags. I think a craft store threw up on my kitchen table.

"I couldn't help but overhear…" I level a gaze on her, cocking my head in disbelief. "Yeah, okay. Chloe repeated your conversation to me last night after she hung up, so I figured I'd come over and keep you company on my day off."

I move toward the table and pick up a box with a picture of some sort of mosaic tile stepping stone. "You didn't have to do this." I swallow the lump working its way up my throat and shake the box. "Especially after the other night—"

Grace removes the kit from my hand, drawing my focus to her face. "I know I didn't have to. I wanted to."

Fighting the need to grasp her by the arms and spill everything she doesn't know about Ford, I grip the back of the closest chair. "I had big plans to eat junk food and watch movies."

"We can do that, too. Later." She smirks. "First, we'll do these." She picks up a second box with a stepping stone on the cover.

She's serious? "You want me to make a garden stepping stone with you?"

"Yes?" Her answer is more of a question as her arms lower until she's set the boxes on the table. "You work at a flower farm, I didn't think it would be that huge of a deal to make something fun for the garden, but I mean—"

"No." I move forward, settling my hand over hers and easing the uncertainty creeping onto her face with a smile. "It's fine. It'll be fun. It's just…"

Grace rubs her lips together as she looks up at me through her lowered lashes.

"Can I eat breakfast first?"

"Breakfast?" Grace snags her hand from beneath mine and checks her watch. "It's after eleven." For what must be the first time since she arrived, she looks me over. Her blue-gray eyes running from my bare feet up to my slouching sweatpants and over a faded and ripped MCR concert tee from 2010 before resting on my two-day-old stubble and unkempt hair. She slaps a palm over her mouth. "Did I wake you up?"

"I'm on vacation." I straighten to my full height, like that will somehow make me feel less like the bum I am.

"I can go." Grace jerks back, stumbling over her own feet. "I should have called first. I shouldn't have—"

"Grace." I grab her wrist when she snatches her keys off the table. "I'm glad you're here. Please, stay."

She stares at me, a silent question in her eyes, and I answer with a nod.

"Okay, but if you want to shower or something."

My arms fall to my sides. "Are you saying I look bad?"

"No, you look perfect. Or, I mean good. Fine." I catch her gaze straying over my body for the second time. "You look fine."

Hooking my thumbs in the pockets of my sweats, where her eyes seem to have stalled, I grin. "So, I stink then?"

Grace turns like she's been caught, which she has. "I didn't say that. You don't look bad or stink. I just meant I didn't want to stop you from doing whatever you usually do in the morning." Her fingers toy with her hair, swiping the strands behind her ear over and over and over again. "You know what, I really should go."

Instead of going around, she steps toward me, and I stand my ground until she bumps into my chest and stops. Her head remains lowered so I can't see her face, but her shoulders rise and fall with each breath she takes.

Doing what I wanted to do earlier, I take her by the shoulders, then let my hands slip down to her biceps. I wet my lips before finding my words. "What you really need to do is stay, Grace." Her face jerks at her name. "I want you here. Let me grab a quick shower, and we'll make stepping stones, eat a crap ton of food, and spend the day watching movies. Sound good?"

Indecision flickers behind those gorgeous eyes of hers before she smiles wide enough to show a flash of teeth. "Yeah, sounds like a perfect day."

Giving her arms a squeeze, I leave her in the kitchen and go wash up.

When I return, country music blares from my Bluetooth speakers, bacon and eggs are waiting in my cast iron skillet, and Grace is smoothing over what looks like gray mud in molds on top of my newspaper-covered table. I step behind her as she concentrates on running a spatula-type tool over what I assume is the cement for our stones while she hums along with an up-tempo Ridley Goss country song dominating the stations these days.

Grace stills as I near. "I lied before," she says without turning and resumes working. "You totally stank earlier."

"Psh." I press closer, hovering behind her without touching. "I stank, huh?"

She peers over her shoulder, the bridge of her nose crinkled. "Maybe a little." When she takes me in, her expression slackens.

I soak up every inch of her fresh face as she holds my gaze: The curve of her light brows, the beauty mark at the edge of her right eye, the deep bow in her top lip. Yeah, watching her and Ford date isn't going to work for me, but could I live with my actions if I came between them?

"I smell better now, I hope?" I tease, slipping back and running my hand through my damp hair.

Like a spell is broken, Grace clears her throat. "I can't lie, you smell amazing now. Showering was a good choice."

"Ha. I try to clean up every once in a while."

While I eat my eggs and bacon, Grace sorts the glass tiles for our art project, explaining each step. She pulls up some examples of designs on her phone, but in the end, neither of us uses them. I become absorbed in coming up with the perfect creation, going so far as to grab a pen and paper to sketch my thoughts, while Grace is more abstract in her process.

When we're done, Grace has created something resembling fireworks mid-explosion, and I've made a sun with multiple layers of rays. I'm damn proud of myself, even if my side aches from bending over the table for so long.

"You overdid it, didn't you?"

I meet Grace's worried frown with a wince. "Maybe a bit."

"That's it." She claps her hands, shooing me from my seat. "Movie time. These have to dry, anyway."

We wash up and grab snacks, and I settle on the couch, propping my feet on an ottoman as Grace draws the curtains around the room closed, blanketing us in darkness.

"Blackouts, I didn't expect that."

"With the direction the house faces, the sun glares right across the television. I can't watch anything when it's too bright. I had to buy them."

She flops down on the couch—not directly beside me, but not at the far end either—and pulls one leg beneath her. "I like it. It's more fun watching movies in the dark like at the theater."

We choose a murder mystery neither of us has seen though the film released a few years back, and midway through, Grace sits a little closer to my side with her legs drawn to her chest and a throw drawn to her chin. Every time the music changes, she sinks lower into the couch, her breath catching.

"Do you hate this?" I finally ask, my arm itching to wrap around her shoulders and pull her in.

She lowers the plaid throw a notch, whispering, "No, I love thrillers. I just hate the suspense."

"Well, I have a shoulder if you need to snuggle close and hide your face." I say the words playfully, but I'm dead serious. *C'mon, Grace. Use me for protection.*

Grace scowls before her lips curve with her grin. Eventually, she glides closer, her shoulder pressing against mine, and I adjust into the corner of the couch, giving her space to relax into me. Her warmth soaks through my cotton shirt and into my skin as she leans against my body more and more. This is all I want. This woman in my arms.

If only I'd found her first.

THE ROOM IS DARK, the movie is over, and my neck is killing me. I fell asleep. Blinking away the ropes of exhaustion clinging to my mind, I stretch. The throw Grace used for protection lies over my lap, and I smile before realizing she's no longer sitting beside me. *Did she go?* The aroma of garlic and tomatoes hits me, prompting a low growl in my stomach. *She didn't leave.* My relief at her still being here is troubling, but I ignore the obvious issue and seek her out.

She's not at the stove where I expected. Instead I catch a glimpse of her emerald shirt through a crack in the blinds of my back door. Curious, I shift one slat and peek outside. Grace is painting—a flat canvas laying on the table with brushes sitting in a cup of discolored water and tubes of paint scattered about—and my tongue is all kinds of tied at seeing her looking so comfortable at my home. Backing away before she catches me stalking, I use the bathroom and rinse with mouthwash before taking a look at the meal Grace put in the oven for me. The timer still has thirty minutes, so I pour some iced tea and finally feel composed enough to step outside.

"I guess you're gonna have to tell me who lived and who died."

Grace startles at my voice, spinning around with a blue-tipped brush in her hand. A flush of pink colors her chest visible at the scoop of her neckline. It's cute she feels the need to blush when I'm the one who fell asleep.

"You should have woken me up."

"You're still recovering from a traumatic event and surgery. You fell asleep because your body needed rest."

"Well, thanks for not complaining about my terrible company. Also, thank you for starting dinner. Does that mean you're staying?" Grace turns back to her painting, swirling her brush on the canvas without answering.

"What's this?" I move closer for a better view of what she's painted. It looks like a random pattern of swirls, maybe flowers, but her vision of flowers, not the worlds.

"Just me playing." She taps the end of the brush's handle to the tip of her nose, cocking her head one way then the other while staring at the picture before dipping the bristles into a glob of white and mixing that into the blue she just laid down.

"Playing with what? What are you painting?" I prod. "I like it."

"Yeah?" Her gaze snaps to me, her eyes focusing on my mouth like she expects me to laugh any moment. I nod with encouragement instead. "It's an idea I have for fabric I'd like to have made someday. I think for a fit and flare dress or maybe a tiered, ruffled maxi skirt."

"A fabric? You can do that?" I study the design with a new purpose, envisioning the pattern wrapped around her body. "How do you do that?"

Dropping her brush into the paint, she turns. "Do you really want to know?"

"If it's something you want to do, then of course I want to know."

Grace runs the tip of her tongue over her bottom lip. "Okay, then. I'll tell you over dinner. Let me clean this up."

I learn everything I need to know and more about how an independent clothing designer can make custom fabric and clothing over dinner. Grace's dream of designing her own pieces blows me away. I never would have guessed she had such ambitions beyond owning her boutique. She impresses me more and more with every new facet I uncover.

When dinner is finished and the dishes are loaded and leftovers stored, I can find no reason to keep her here any longer. I walk her to the door and wrap her in a hug.

"You are an angel for today. All of it. Thank you." I rest my cheek on top of her silk head and close my eyes, savoring her in my arms.

"Of course."

I need to let go, but once again, I'm struck with the truth: no one has ever felt so right in my arms. As much as I want to explain myself to Grace, I can't. We've ignored the complication known as Ford all day. I want to preserve today as one of perfection.

"I won't hold you to our Tuesday after practice meal since you spent your entire day with me, but I hope you'll write me in for Thursday. Hopefully, the Doc will allow me to drive, or I can get Dad to come to watch you guys play."

Sinking back from my embrace, Grace gives me a frown. "First, I seem to recall you saying you can't drive until you're off the pain meds. So, don't rush it. And second, I have you on my calendar for Tuesdays and Thursdays. It's our thing, remember."

I'll take every moment she'll give. "Okay, then I'll see you tomorrow night. Drive safe."

"I will." Rising up, Grace kisses my cheek, pausing as she pulls away like she's been caught doing something she shouldn't. I fist my hands to keep from taking more and she turns away, her voice a little cooler when she says, "Goodnight" over her shoulder.

in my heart. When
all solicitude, all
shall I be able to pass
time with you, having
love you, and to think only
happiness of so saying, and
it to you

27

Grace

STRAIGHTENING my hair in the bathroom, I talk to Chloe on speaker. She might as well move out because she's always at Kip's these days, especially with Robyn sleeping in her bedroom.

"Another date, huh? Dinner wasn't enough last weekend to say, 'See ya, Drewy'?"

After talking on the phone almost every night this week, Drew texted me and said he got us tickets to see Ridley Goss. "How could I refuse Ridley?"

"You say, 'Drew, it's unfair to use the hottest man in country music against me, but I'll take both of those concert tickets as penance for your misdeeds and take my best friend Chloe instead.'"

"Yeah, I'll say just that to him."

She laughs. "I'll give it to the man, he knows how to win you over."

It helps that he knows all my favorite things; our history gives him an edge. "He's taking off work early and coming this way to pick me up. Actually, he should be here any minute."

"Make sure to wrap it up."

"*Chloe Mae Lockwood.*"

She chuckles.

"There will be no wrapping because there will be no getting jiggy. He's still got a long way to go before he's getting anything from me." If he ever gets anything more from me.

"I thought we agreed you'd never say jiggy ever again."

I laugh. "But you love jiggy so much I can't help myself."

"You're the literal worst."

Three knocks on my front door resonate through the small house.

"He's here. I've gotta go."

"You tell him to announce to everyone you pass that you're with him and that he's the luckiest man in the world."

"I'll do just that," I fib.

"No, you won't. You rubbed your earlobe, didn't you?"

I remove my thumb and index finger from the meaty part of my ear. "Gotta go. Bye!" I hang up and adjust my loose crop top over my high-waisted jeans. Cowgirl boots on, I grab my camel leather jacket and answer the door.

Drew's hair is less styled than usual as he runs a hand over the short, tousled strands. "I was about to ring the doorbell. Thought you were going to stand me up."

"Sorry. I was on the phone with Chloe and she wouldn't let me hang up."

His gaze sweeps up and down my body, darkening when he meets my eyes. "You look hot."

In a black henley with the sleeves shoved up his arms and light, distressed jeans, he's nothing to scoff at either. Dressed down, it's hard not to see Reid in Drew's eyes and his smile. All he's missing is the baseball cap.

I shove Reid aside and address Drew's comment. "I haven't been to a concert since college, so my wardrobe was a little lacking."

"Could've fooled me. You look like you belong on the stage right beside Ridley's backup singers."

"Okay. That's a blatant lie." I laugh.

"A stretch of the truth, maybe." He joins in my amusement. "So, what do you say we go have our eardrums blown out and lose our voices?"

It's after midnight by the time Drew drops me off. Unable to get the song lyrics out of our heads, we sing all the way to my doorstep. I'm sure my neighbors love me.

Drew squeezes my hand and swings me to face him, our bodies a foot apart. "I can't remember the last time I had so much fun."

I suck in a breath at our proximity, my eyes shifting between his. It's on the tip of my tongue to lie, but what good would that do us? It's not as if I can say I've had a lot of fun with my softball team—and your brother—this summer.

Before I get a chance to make up a response, he says, "We should make it a regular thing."

High off the adrenaline of the music and the crowd and the lights, I weaken. "I'm open to more fun."

One second we're smiling and the next, Drew's arm hooks around my waist and his mouth is on mine, his tongue taking advantage of my parted lips. My hands grip his shoulders to steady myself as his other hand sinks into my hair, holding the back of my head. With one step and another, my back is pressed against my front door. This kiss is the opposite of the one last weekend in every sense. Drew is uncontrolled and frantic like if he doesn't devour me now, he'll never get another chance.

Breaking the kiss with a nudge and turn of my head, I take a breath.

His clean-shaven cheek presses to mine, his voice husky. "As much as I want to, I'm not going to beg you to ask me to come inside. Though, I won't turn you down if you ask."

With a quiet, breathy chuckle, I shake my head.

"But at least say you feel it, G. This undeniable pull. Say you'll give us a chance. I'm dying here."

Undeniable pull? There might be a lingering connection, but is it something I can't live without? "That's not really taking it slow, Drew."

"I know, I know. I'm sorry. I have no patience where you're concerned."

The man doesn't have patience where anyone is concerned. He's a businessman. Whatever Drew wants, Drew gets.

"There's so much to take into consideration still." Apart from my lack of trust in Drew's ability to take care of my heart, Reid pulses like a crucial artery. How can I be with one brother when the other can't be forgotten? Even when he shoots me down.

"One thing. Name one thing and I'll ease your mind."

"Jobs. What about your career in Seattle? I'm happy in Seaside, and I have Fig. If you're looking for this to go somewhere, the distance is a bit of a challenge."

"We don't have to worry about that now, but I'm open. I could commute. It's not that far of a drive from Seaside. A little over an hour, but it's doable. Or I've considered opening up my own investment firm here to be close to my family again. I'm flexible, G. If you'll have me, I'll do what I can to make this work, to make up for how I treated you."

Drew in Seaside. While excitement should be my first reaction, panic sparks in my veins. What about Reid?

What about Reid, Grace? He made his stance clear. I still went to see him Tuesday and Thursday night after work this week, even after he told me about his relationship with Drew. I don't expect anything from him, but I don't want to lose our friendship. Especially if I try to make things work with Drew, the last thing I want is to have things be uncomfortable between us.

"Can you give me a little more time? It's barely been two weeks since we reconnected. I just...I need a little longer."

Drew nods, backing up a step, poorly masking his disappointment with a crestfallen smile. "Whatever you need, Grace. I'm not going anywhere."

Guilt eats at me for rejecting his efforts, but forcing this isn't going to help us build something lasting. If it's right, it's right, but for now, my head is too muddled. "I think maybe...we should take a little break for a few weeks. This might be too much too soon."

His throat clears, eyes darting away. "Okay, sure." Swiping the back of his hand across his mouth, he nods. "I've been blowing off too much work, so it'd probably be good for me to do some catching up."

Even if it's true, something tells me Drew would've continued prioritizing work below me, which is something he never did before. That counts for something.

"Can I still call you? Or send a text here and there?"

"If you call, I can't promise I'll answer, but if you want to drop a text, I won't ignore you."

My reply must appease him because his usual smile returns as he backs away. "I'm not giving up on you, Lemon Drop. I won't make the same mistake twice."

in my heart. When
all solicitude, all
shall I be able to pass a
time with you, having
love you, and to think only
happiness of so saying, and
it to you

28

Grace

AFTER TELLING Drew I need space, I send Reid a few texts checking in on him, but for my sanity, I don't go back to his house, making up excuses about Fig being too busy and getting backlogged with the numbers side of things. I can't see him either. I need a break from the Pruitt men. It grows more and more challenging to keep things affable, and for Drew's sake, I need to at least try to make an effort. I might not owe him anything, but what if this is our time and I'm blowing it off because of a man who will never look twice at me again?

The only issue with being alone with my thoughts, my brain circles an endless loop of irrational questions and fears. What if I was initially drawn to Reid because of Drew? They might be polar opposites, but hearts don't know the difference. Was my heart seeking the lost connection, searching to revive what once was with the possibility of replacing him for a similar version? Even as my mind speculates, my heart knows it's wrong, completely asinine. Everything I feel with Reid is new, authentic. Things I've never experienced before. Oh geez, does Reid see it that way? Wanting him at first because I couldn't have the other? Is that another reason he ended us before we began?

Skipping our after-softball meals is tough, but Reid doesn't mention anything. The way he goes right along with my absence makes me wonder if Drew told him about my asking for a break. It would be a Reid thing to do, respecting my boundaries.

Does time away fix everything? Not even a little bit. But subjecting myself to them wasn't doing me any favors, either. Chloe told me Reid went back to work at a reduced capacity, and she found it strange I didn't already know. Right there is reason enough for why I needed time apart. Drew put forth all his effort while I spent my evenings having dinner with his brother and every spare moment thinking of him. Even still, I can't help wondering where Reid's head is. Can I convince him to be with me despite his older brother?

When Drew mentions he's coming back to Seaside for the weekend, three weeks apart seems reasonable enough. If time hadn't made a difference, no amount of taking things slow is going to magically mend all of our problems. We haven't even exchanged many texts. True to his word, Drew didn't give up, but he didn't hound me either, which I appreciated. While I'm no closer to deciding if giving him a second chance is the right choice, a clearer head helps.

Even though he said he'd be in town, inviting Drew to Kip's twenty-sixth birthday dinner might not have been my brightest idea. I wanted to introduce him to my people, the life I have now. If he's serious about us, they're a big part of it. And he keeps coming back to Seaside, he's making an effort, and I probably should, too.

It's not until Drew and Reid show up together that I want to crawl under a rock and never come out. The other day Chloe mentioned he might come since he's feeling better, but it didn't register what it might mean with them in attendance.

They arrive together, side-by-side, striding through The Taproom with their unique forms of confidence. One with the self-assured presence of a man who knows what he wants and knows how to get it; the other with an easy air, who's comfortable in his skin and doesn't need the approval of others to be confident.

My initial reaction is to hug Reid. I've missed him these last few weeks, but I stall when it hits me: I'm technically dating his brother. Drew should probably be the one I hug and greet first, considering I haven't seen him either. Is it inappropriate of me to embrace Reid? Will my friendship with Reid bother Drew? I'm likely alone in my turmoil. Reid's just hanging out with his friends and big brother for the night.

As they approach our table, Drew runs a hand over his side-parted gelled hair, tugging on the collar of his thin-striped button-down, his pressed dark chinos hugging his thighs.

Bending, he kisses my cheek and whispers, "Hey, gorgeous. It's good to see you." Resting his hand on my waist, his thumb caressing my exposed midriff in my cropped peasant top.

His touch probably didn't have the intended effect when I shy away with a nervous smile. "Hi."

As he turns to the table to introduce himself, Reid moves around him and pulls me in for a hug. His arm hooks around my shoulders, drawing me into his body in a tender hold, lingering.

We do that a lot. Linger. Torture. They're equally the same in our situation, holding onto things we're not quite sure are okay to want, but can't help ourselves.

"Lookin' good, Slugger."

Earth and spicy body wash and man. It takes everything in me not to press my nose to his neck. "Thanks." With one arm around his back, I pat his white T-shirt-clad chest. "It's good to see you out of the house and those sweatpants."

Okay, maybe not the gray sweatpants.

He pulls away and shoves a hand in the pocket of his ripped jeans. "Yeah, about time, huh? I'd never been so happy to see the farm than I was my first day back." Reid's hair curls out from under his hat and around his ears, the strands damp, like he'd stepped out of the shower and they came straight here.

He and his brother couldn't be more different, and yet somehow the same.

"Reid!" Brynn's cry parts the crowd, and she drags Reid from my side, where she's standing with Hayden and Kip. "You're a sight for sore eyes. How are you?" She wraps him in a hug, then takes his face in her palms like he's a child she's checking for injuries. "You scared the crap out of us."

I miss Reid's response over the noise in the bar, but whatever he says has Brynn's worried frown flipping upside down. My feet carry me closer, curious at their conversation, as Hayden presses against his wife's back and eases her away from Reid, one hand settling across her stomach as the other claps Reid on the shoulder. "Good to see you, man."

"It's good to be out." Reid turns to Kip. "Happy birthday, Harris."

"Pruitt. Glad to see you're in one piece still. Chlo's been driving me mad with talk about the farm. When are you cleared to work at full strength?"

Reid's eyes go wide. "When am I—"

"Kipling!" Chloe hisses, shoving her way around me and slapping Kip's shoulder. Since I'm well aware it's Chloe's orders keeping Reid from doing much more than bossing the crew around at the farm, I can't help but laugh. Reid's head snaps my way, a secret smile flashing seemingly for my benefit.

Chloe wraps a hand around Kip's arm and rolls her eyes. "My bothering him about work has nothing to do with you. He'll find anyone to blame for me working too hard."

"That's because you working too hard keeps you away from me. Can you blame a man?"

"Ugh." I take Reid's hand and pull him back. "Their PDA is getting ridiculous. Come sit."

Reid's gaze flicks to our hands joined together and I hastily withdraw, catching Brynn's wide-eyed stare. *Grabbing him was a friendly reflex, nothing more.*

Liar.

"Let's all sit," Brynn agrees, nudging the others into motion. "I'm starving."

While the couples take the opposite side of the long rectangular table, Reid and Drew sit on either side of me. I've never been more aware of my body than at this moment. My lungs think they ran a marathon while my heart kicks into high gear. I slip my hands between my clamped thighs to keep from fidgeting.

I need to get a grip and get out of my head. I'm not torn between two men. This isn't some soap opera. I'm friends with one man and trying to give his brother a second chance. Do I have feelings for Reid? Yes. I can admit that to myself, but I need to get over them. He friend-zoned me, and I can't hop from one brother to the next. That's so much worse than dating your best friend's ex. They're blood. There is no escaping them.

Drew slips his arm along the back of my chair as he relaxes in his seat, sipping his beer like he's perfectly comfortable surrounded by a bunch of people he's not familiar with. He laughs at something Kip says. Then Drew brings up the Riverfront Complex and it's all over from there. If Chloe didn't cut Kip off twenty minutes later, they'd talk business for the rest of the night.

For hours the drinks and food and conversation don't stop.

When Chloe opens the cake box, she leads us in a loud, obnoxious version of Happy Birthday while Kip wears a wide grin, staring at her. When he blows out the candle, she shoves Kip's face into the cake—payback from her twenty-sixth birthday—and Kip grabs her in a kiss, smearing the frosting all over her mouth and nose. Quietly, against her lips, he tells her he loves her.

As we're finishing our slices, a guy with a flawlessly dark complexion pauses by our table. "Ford Pruitt! No way! Long time no see."

Drew slaps his hand in the guy's outstretched one. "Eddie? Yeah, it's been a few years. How are you?"

"Good, man, good. Is this your fiancée? Or did you two finally tie the knot? I've been waiting for my invite, but it hasn't shown up yet." He winks, holding his hand out to me with a bright grin, and rocks pile high in my stomach.

Drew opens his mouth, but when his eyes rove over my face, not a single word comes out. He has a fiancée? I'll kill him. I'll shank him right here in front of everyone.

My expression must reveal my assumption because Drew's eyes widen and dart between me and whatever his friend's name is. Once the man mistook me for Drew's fiancée, I forgot everything he said before that.

"No, no." Drew's hand moves to my thigh, holding tight. "That's over. Long over. This isn't Angelica. This is Grace Embry. She's from Seaside."

"Oh, I'm sorry. I hadn't realized. Talk about shoving my foot in my mouth."

Every other word they exchange goes in one ear and out the other, and I gulp down the rest of my lemon drop, licking the sugar from my lips.

I will not explode in public. That's not me. I don't lose my cool or storm off in dramatic exits, but if I don't get out of here right now, I might make a scene, and I do *not* want to make a scene. Not in front of everyone, not at Kip's birthday dinner. Tonight is his night. I won't ruin it.

"Excuse me for a minute." I force a smile and try to scoot my chair back.

"Grace," Drew utters, holding me in my seat by my thigh. "G, let me explain."

"You have a fiancée?" I hiss.

"I did. I don't anymore. It ended a couple of years ago."

Two years ago? My anger eases, but only a fraction until reality hits me. While I was licking my wounds during those two years following our breakup, he met, fell in love, and planned a future with another woman. When he broke my heart and said marriage wasn't what he wanted, what he meant was a marriage with me. Was I not good enough? Every insecurity I'd thought I'd moved on from over the years rises to the surface.

All this talk about regretting ending our relationship and it being the biggest mistake of his life. Am I just the next best thing because his engagement to this other woman was called off?

I push to stand again, dislodging his hand.

"Wait, Grace," he says under his breath. "Let's talk about this."

I match his quiet volume. "Now is not the time, Drew. I need air." Let me save my dignity. "Stay here, please." With that, I snatch my purse and leave the bar. I planned on stepping outside to catch my breath, but my feet continue moving. One after the other, I make it to my car and start the engine. Before I think better of it, I'm backing out of the parking lot and on my way home.

My phone goes off halfway to my house, but I ignore it. I don't know that I'm mad at Drew so much as I'm mad at myself. Reid obviously knew about this Angelica and didn't say anything. To him it was two years ago. Why would it matter? It shouldn't. So, why do I have this knot in my stomach? Why does it feel so wrong?

I check my phone when I walk in the front door. Three missed calls from Drew and a text asking me to call him. Another text from Chloe making sure I'm okay. My heart stills when my last text is from Reid telling me to let him know I'm safe.

I respond, letting them know I'm home safe and I'll call them tomorrow. Tonight I just want to get my conflicted head on straight.

I DIDN'T HAVE the energy to call Drew first thing in the morning, so I dial him when I walk in the door after work.

He answers after the first ring. "Grace."

"Hey."

Like he wasn't sure I'd call, he exhales. "I almost came to your house straight from The Taproom, but I didn't want the door slammed in my face."

"Smart move." There's not a hint of teasing in my tone. If he'd shown up last night, I'd have left him outside. Not to be petty, but so I could cool off. I hate saying things in anger I don't mean. And even though Reid and I didn't spend much time together these last several weeks, I haven't told Drew how much we hung out before. Outside, it's innocent—well, all except for that last kiss—and we were friends before Drew came back into my life, but with what's in my heart, it's not as innocent on the inside.

Maybe I'm feeling a bit guilty, too.

"And I thought about coming to Fig before I left this afternoon, but it didn't seem right bringing personal stuff to your place of work."

It would've been Seaside gossip for days. "I appreciate that."

"I'm so sorry that's how you had to learn about Angelica. I was going to tell you about her, but like you said, it'd only been a couple of weeks. I was trying to find the right time. And then you asked for space, and I didn't want to jeopardize what little I had with you."

Yeah, being blindsided sucked, but I don't think that's what's bothering me. "You told me that you've thought about me so many times over the years. So, does that mean while you were with your fiancée, you were thinking about me? Or were you lying about that?"

He releases a low curse. "Both. Neither." Another swear is muttered under his breath. "Angelica...she seemed like the right choice at the time, but it got complicated, and then..." He pauses. "She was my boss's sister, and I broke off the engagement after I caught her bent over my intern's desk."

Oh.

"Even before I found out she was cheating on me, I debated on ending it. I shouldn't have asked her to marry me in the first place. In the end, I realized I loved the idea of her, but not her. Never her."

His explanation only lessens the weight on my chest a fraction. I don't even know why I'm so upset. I don't love Drew. Not anymore, but I think I hoped I could, and this throws a wrench in that. But there's more. *Why does my heart hurt so much?*

"I want to tell you the whole story. I want the air clear between us so we can move forward with a clean slate, but I'd prefer to explain in person. When I come up next weekend, let's sit down and talk. I'll tell you everything. I swear."

"Okay."

"Just keep in mind..." His voice is strained when he says, "I don't think I ever stopped loving you, Grace. Angelica might seem like a roadblock, but she's nothing. Nothing compared to you."

Why don't his words fill me with reassurance and peace?

in my heart. When
all solicitude, all
shall I be able to
time with you, having
love you, and to think only
it to you

29

Reid

I THOUGHT my situation with Mia had my heart in my throat; that was nothing. Whatever mild feelings I had were but a drop of paint compared to the broad strokes Grace has made on my life. Stress hangs over me like a thundercloud as I pull into a parking space at Bingley Park and cut my engine. With an exhale, I climb from my truck and head for the field, where practice ends in fifteen minutes.

I was too anxious to stay home and wait for Grace to possibly not show for our usual Tuesday dinner. Too heartsick from missing her to allow another day to pass without seeing her. I wouldn't have blamed her if she bailed. She'd been bailing the last few weeks. I had plenty of opportunities to tell her about Ford's engagement. Even without spilling the rest of his secrets. We haven't spoken since she ran out on Kip's birthday gathering Saturday. I have no idea how she feels about me, or Ford, at this point. I've tried staying out of whatever's going on with them.

Clearly, I can't be objective—I'm pretty sure I've fallen in love with the woman. The woman my brother wants. The woman my brother cheated on for over three years.

After two days back at work at one hundred percent, my stride is labored, and my side aches. Cleaning out the yellow shed was too much too soon, but I needed an outlet after Saturday night. Chloe was right when she ripped into me after Denise called her and ratted me out for breaking a sweat yesterday morning. I don't know when to rest, and I *am* a glutton for punishment.

When I arrive at field four, the team is huddled around the pitching mound and calling it a night. *So much for watching.*

Scott's the first to notice me making my way to the bleachers outside the home team's dugout. He backhands Tony and shouts, "You back just in time for the playoffs?"

Everyone turns.

I raise a hand, waving. "I wish."

My friends and teammates surround me, offering hugs since I haven't seen most of them in the month since the wreck. Leaning against the end of the bleachers, they force me to retell the story of flipping down the side of Mt. Luna. Sweat peppers my brow every time I think about that morning. I was so damn lucky. I drove off the side of a cliff and lived to tell about it.

"That's pretty badass, dude." Bucky offers his fist, bumping mine before he takes off, and the others follow until Tony and Jackie are the last two standing with me.

"I don't know if I'd call it badass, but I'd say you have someone watching over you." Jackie gives me a hug, her glaze sliding toward the dugout—where Grace lingers over her duffle —as she pulls away.

"You coming to watch us Thursday?" Tony asks.

"I'll be here."

And then there were two. Sinking to the second row of the bleaches, I prop my feet on the first row and lean my elbows on my thighs as Grace zips her bag and finally steps out of the dugout. There's a breeze blowing in from offshore, dropping the temperature quickly as the sun lowers on the horizon, and Grace tugs the cuffs of the hoodie she's slipped on over her hands.

I flip my ball cap backward, wanting Grace to see my face when I speak. "I didn't know he hadn't told you about the engagement."

"You think I'm mad at you?" Grace drops her duffle on the bleachers and climbs up to sit on the metal bench beside me, hunching over in her seat to keep warm.

I stare at my keys, dangling from my fingers between my knees. "I don't know."

"Why didn't you tell me?"

My fist closes around the keys until the teeth bite into my palm. "As I said, I figured he would have told you. Why wouldn't he?" *Probably because he's hiding something more.*

"We haven't talked about you," I admit when it's too quiet for too long, my eyes memorizing her profile as I stare. "Other than him explaining the past and how you two met. I don't ask about your dates or phone calls or whatever. And I don't tell him about the time I spend with you."

Grace turns, tucking strands behind her ear, when a gust whips around us and swirls over the field, sending dirt flying in our faces. Grace ducks into my side with a squeal, and I huddle over her back as grains of sand sting my neck. As quickly as it came, the wind dies.

"This weather is crazy." Grace chuckles as she looks at me, her body still pressed against my side. My left hand resting on her thigh. I should move it, but I won't. She probably doesn't realize it's there.

I laugh with her, taken aback by the wind's speed. Gusts like that are more typical of fall and winter. "Want to go eat somewhere safe and warm?" I swipe a hand over one grit-covered eye.

"It is Tuesday, isn't it?" She arches a brow, her fingers covering mine on her thigh. *Okay, she knows it's there.*

"It is, but the last few weeks we've missed our dinner dates. I wasn't going to assume."

"Well, it's a new week."

We stand together, and I twist my hand until I'm holding hers like it's the most natural thing as we hop off the end of the bleachers and Grace tosses her duffle over one shoulder.

"I thought you weren't supposed to drive while on pain medication?" she asks as we near the parking lot.

"I'm not. I stopped taking them." Her footsteps slow, and I catch the worry wrinkling her forehead. "I needed to wean off them. It's been a month."

"But with all the moving around you do at work… Are you sure you're ready to—"

"I'm fine, Grace." Using my hand holding hers, I swing her around until she's leaning against her car, then release her. "Thank you for worrying about me."

The need to touch her hurts a hell of a lot worse than the scar tissue healing within my body. I believed myself to be falling in love with Loe last year. I thought myself attracted to Mia last Christmas. I was an idiot where they were concerned. Grace has taken every nerve ending and synapse that computes feelings in my body and redirected them straight to my heart. Well, and to another lower region. But nothing connects to my brain. That much is clear because I wouldn't be here right now if I were using my brain. I wouldn't torture myself with these feelings and this guilt.

"Why don't you talk about me with Drew?" she asks

I curl my fingers over the hood of her car and shift my gaze to stare just left of her face. "Because then I'd have to accept that you're seeing him."

"But—"

"He's my brother, Grace. And he cares about you." I shove

away from the vehicle and resituate my hat, needing the bill to hide my emotions now. "Let's not do this again, okay? Let's grab food just like always. Friends." I add the dirtiest f-word I know to get my point across.

She wavers.

So I push. "Please?"

Sighing, Grace nods. "Yeah, that's a good idea." She rubs her earlobe and pulls her key fob from the side of her duffle. "Feel like sushi?"

"Perfect."

EVEN THOUGH I missed two weeks of work and have a to-do list two pages long, I leave Lockwood Thursday afternoon earlier than I ever dared to leave before the accident. I still shouldn't lift anything over fifty pounds, but most of the pain around my fancy new scar is finally gone, making walking and working around the farm easier. I'm more than ready to resume life as I knew it before my trip down Mt. Luna.

"You left work early? Everything all right?" Dad's prepping dinner when I arrive at his house.

"Yeah, I figured you could use the help." I wash my hands, then move around the kitchen island and take a seat. "What time will they get here?"

"You know your brothers. Wade's flight landed twenty minutes ago." He pushes the cutting board he's using across the granite countertop, along with a knife. "So five-thirty or six, I guess."

All four Pruitt men in one house for four whole days. Ford drove up for one day this spring when Wade graduated from Seaside Pointe High, and before that he hadn't been home since the two days he spent with us at Christmas. Damn, I've seen more of him since my accident than the previous six years combined. Silver lining, I guess? Granted, now we know he stopped coming home because he was hiding a relationship with Grace. Then he was just hiding *from* Grace.

Dad drops a handful of garlic cloves in front of me, nodding for me to mince. "Has Davenport called with any updates on the accident?"

Had I expected any sort of foul play in my wreck, I never would have allowed Dad to sit in the hospital room while the police questioned me. "Nothing. If those lug nuts were loosened by Sullivan or someone else, it's doubtful we'll know for sure. It's not something you can prove without video evidence, you know?"

What I don't tell him about is my conversation with Kip. After Chloe told Kip about Grace's suspicion that Sullivan's threats outside the bar that night could have been more than drunk ramblings, Kip gave me a call. Last year while working on closing the deal between Old Man Sullivan and Chloe, Kip discovered Joseph Sullivan went behind his father's back to broker deals and stole money from Melvin Sullivan's estate. Because of Kip's discovery, Melvin stripped Joseph from his will and replaced him as executor of the estate. The revelation shows the man has a motive—to hurt Kip. Tampering with a Lockwood Blooms van as a way of revenge seems a stretch, but maybe Chloe was his target. Hurting Loe is the quickest way to ruin Kip.

"Hey, Dad? You went to school with James and Denton, right?" Dad turns from where he's stewing the tomatoes at the stove. "How much do you know about their relationship with each other?"

He gives a half-shrug. "The Lockwood and Harris families weren't friendly. Everyone knows that."

"Yeah, but there's got to be something more. Some reason for it." Ever since Robyn Lockwood stopped by my house, I've been curious about the past. James stopped by the workshop this morning, the first time he's spoken to me since the accident, and acted out of sorts. This afternoon I found him telling Julian—who isn't a native of Seaside and therefore isn't familiar with the stories—about the land to the North of the farm that Denton Harris stole from under his nose when both men were in their twenties. It's like the man can't help rehashing the past, as if to secure his justification to continue his grudges.

"James was the quiet type, same as he is now. Not a bad guy, he just kept to himself. Was only ever on the flower farm or with Robyn, from what I remember. Denton was...well you know how he is now—"

With a snort, I scoop my freshly minced garlic into a pile and unwrap the French loaf to prepare next. "I imagine Denton was a lot like his son. Mr. King of the World?"

"Yup, that pretty much nails the Harris men. He and James were complete opposites. Though..." Dad pauses. "There was this girl in my class. I remember murmurings about them fighting over her. Sound familiar?"

I give him a mirthless laugh. "Kip and I didn't fight over Loe, Dad. There was nothing to fight about. She ended things with me, and she was right in doing so. We weren't meant for each other."

"Don't groan. Even the gods started a war over a woman." He moves to stand opposite me and steals a tablespoon of minced garlic for the spaghetti sauce. "Look at you and your brother."

He's whirled around and back at the pot when my head snaps up. I drill holes in his back, deciphering his comment. Not that it takes much thought to understand what he's implying.

I set my knife down. "If you have something to say, just say it."

A hush falls over the kitchen. Nothing but the sound of his homemade sauce bubbling and my pulse pounding in my ears before finally he leans his back against the counter next to the stove, and his faded green gaze holds mine.

"Something was going on between you and that sweet Grace.

I saw the sparks with my own two eyes at the hospital, and you let your brother waltz in and steal her away." He crosses one foot over the other like we're talking sports. "You think I can't do the math, son? I'm an engineer. I know he did her wrong."

I can't hold his stare as I lie through my teeth. "I didn't let him do anything."

"No? Did you tell him about the two of you?"

A man who loves me will be willing to wait for the forever part. Mia made the comment during one of our conversations and her words have remained with me all summer. She's right. A man in love can wait. I'm waiting, because if Grace and I are meant to be together, it'll happen.

"No, I never told him. I'd just come out of surgery. I'd just found out they knew each other, let alone dated in secret for almost four years. What did you… I mean… It's like you said, wars have started over a woman. I didn't have the strength for that."

"When it's the right woman, you start the war, son."

in my heart. When
all solicitude, all
shall I be able to pass
time with you, having
love you, and to think only
happiness of so saying, and
it to you.

30

Grace

DREW HAS BEEN BURIED in work all week, so we haven't talked much since Kip's birthday dinner. I'd wonder if he's ignoring me if it weren't for the random texts he sends throughout his days. A shot of the flowers blooming at the park where we used to meet up for lunch, a tidbit about something annoying from one of his meetings, a question about which tie he should wear with his new dress shirt. He's giving signals he's committed to this relationship—not that we're actually *in* a relationship yet. Drew's showering me with more attention now when we're apart than he did through our time together. He *has* changed. His attentiveness makes my wavering feelings even more difficult to sort out.

I'd been looking forward to a quiet weekend to do just that until my phone blew up this morning. Wade Pruitt is coming home for a few days before the fall semester starts, and Drew's bringing him into town from the airport. And because Reid already made plans to come and watch our softball game, Drew and Wade jumped on the train. Drew's texts say he can't wait to see me play, though he keeps asking if it's all a joke. Like he can't fathom me playing sports. I suppose I can't blame him; I never pictured myself loving the game as much as I do. I never played sports when I was younger since I didn't have much of an interest.

So, here I am slipping on my team T-shirt and touching up my make-up, getting ready for a game that all the Pruitt brothers —all baseball players themselves—are coming to, and I might puke.

The last time Reid and I talked was Tuesday night. Even with the slight tension after practice, we ate sushi like Drew never came back into the picture. If he's struggling to accept the idea of my seeing his brother casually, he's doing a good job hiding it.

If I could go back to my nineteen-year-old self in that pub seeing the Reid look-alike, there isn't a hint of doubt. I'd tell her to turn her butt around. She'd thank me later.

While the war between my head and heart regarding my feelings for Reid leaves me with a deep hollow ache in my chest, it's a relief that our friendship isn't suffering. We've lived in the same town our whole lives. I don't know why we never connected like this before.

Tonight, more than anything, I'm dreading seeing Drew. Even without talking much, I haven't missed him. I'm not counting down the hours until he comes back to Seaside. No matter what he has to say about Angelica, it won't make a difference. I already know what needs to happen.

"That's some personal cheering section you have tonight." Jackie wags her brows and tosses a wave at the Pruitt brothers—it's like looking at triplets, if not for their age differences and Wade's very noticeable height advantage—sitting near the top of the bleachers behind our dugout. My sisters are here tonight, too. Well, Stella is along with a few of her giggly friends.

"They're not here for only me." Well, I suppose Drew is, but this is Reid's team too, and Wade's a ballplayer. He's probably here to support the Seasiders more than a woman he doesn't know. And Stella is here to stare at Wade and not support her sister. Seems I'm not the only Embry sister with a thing for Pruitt men.

"Sure, honey, you keep telling yourself that."

Glancing over my shoulder, I offer the men a smile before picking up Stella's glove I'm still borrowing and head onto the field. This is our last game of the regular season. Win and we're the number one seed in the four-team playoff next week.

I keep thoughts of Drew and Reid from toying with my mind, for the most part, throughout our hard-fought game, but when the last strike of the final inning is secured, I can ignore them no longer. Their deep-pitched cheers are easy to pick out over the rest of the crowd as the Seasiders meet the Tigers along the baseline for the customary sportsmanship handshakes. Once the teams break, we duck through the gate in the fence to greet family and friends, everyone celebrating.

"Who knew my athletically challenged sister wasn't so athletically challenged after all?" Stella raises her hand for a high-five which I match with a snarky smile.

"Oh, don't act like you were paying attention to anything but the youngest Pruitt."

She clasps her hand over her chest with a mock-gasp, her high ponytail swishing from side-to-side. "I am thoroughly offended. An Embry sister never chooses a boy over a sister."

I tug her into a hug and lower my mouth to her ear. "In this case, I approve, and no offense is taken."

A suppressed smile spreads across her face, her cheeks tinged in crimson as she nudges my shoulder and walks away with her friends.

I find a way to dodge not one but two attempted hugs from Drew by continuously moving around the crowd. Getting the picture, he turns to chat with Tony and the others while Reid joins me.

He slips his hands into his front pockets rather than making a move to touch me. Figures the guy I want to hug would avoid contact. "Who would have thought a few weeks ago you'd be scoring all those runs."

"Certainly not Rick." I look at my ex with a grimace as he attempts to eat Chelsea Bray's face off. "Praise the Lord, this is the first game she's shown up to. I'm losing my appetite."

Reid chuckles. "Speaking of appetite, I know it's customary for us to eat together after a game, but Dad cooked a big meal for Wade's arrival earlier."

I assumed our regular dinner date was out of the question since Drew and Wade are here, but I'm not ready for how disappointed I am with losing our weekly time together. We have one week left before the season is over. Will that mark the end of our Tuesday and Thursday nights together?

"Yeah, no big deal."

"But, Wade had a great idea," he says.

Pushing aside my disappointment, I give Reid my full attention as Drew and Wade join us.

"Growing up, Dad did this thing where we'd have this huge ice cream party at the house after one of us played in a big game. We'd go to the store and he'd let us buy out half the junk food and ice cream aisles. Then we'd compete in making the craziest sundaes."

A hand thrusts before me and I shake it with a smile. "I'm Wade, by the way."

Drew speaks up. "We figured I'd go with you to grab you something for dinner since Reid said you never eat before softball…"

I can't help but meet Reid's gaze. Did he tell his brother why I never eat before games? That I look forward to my time with Reid just as much, if not more, than I do the games and practices?

"…and we'll get the ice cream and head back to our Dad's place. You game?" Wade finishes.

Three pairs of green eyes in varying shades await my answer. "Wow. How can a girl say no to an offer like that? But I have one change to the plans." I turn to Drew and touch his arm for the first time tonight. "Why don't you go with your brothers, and I'll meet you guys back at your Dad's place." His brows furrow, and he opens his mouth with the apparent intent of arguing, but I push forward. "How often do you get to raid the dessert aisle together? It's fine. I can drive myself through a drive-thru. I'd rather you three have the time together."

That settled, we say our goodbyes to the others and head for the parking lot, me sticking by Wade, though Drew sneaks a kiss to my cheek before we part near my car. I purposefully take my time grabbing dinner and eating in my car before plugging the address into my GPS and heading to Gregory's house. By the time Wade greets me at the front door and leads me to the kitchen, there's a full-fledged ice cream shop covering the ivory kitchen counter.

"Wow." I greet Gregory with a hug and step closer to the sugar bounty before us. "You weren't kidding when you said you guys buy half the store out."

Reid catches my gaze from across the island. "I never kid about dessert, Gracie. You should know that by now." He pops a handful of chocolate chips in his mouth.

It dawns on me that Reid referred to me as Gracie—something he's never called me, and I love it—without a care in the world to what the others think, judging by his smile. Drew's pursed lips declare his opinion of the nickname. Rubbing my arms to ward off the chill creeping up my spine, I feign a fascination with the dessert bar. There are six—yes, six—gallons of ice cream, every flavor of drizzle topping made, and a ridiculous assortment of candies, chocolates, nuts. Plus, cereal.

"Cereal?"

"Yeah, that's mine." Wade nudges up beside me with a bowl in each hand. "You ready?" he asks, his grin so contagious I smile as I take one bowl and look at the others.

I nod, and Gregory barks the order, "Let's dig in before the good stuff melts."

I'm DYING of sugar overload, but Lord, it's so good. Fighting with four grown Pruitt men over snow caps and cherries and gummy bears was almost more fun than the eating part. Wade takes over most of the conversation, telling his father and brothers about the baseball and weight training he did all summer at the University of Utah in advance of his freshman season with the Utes.

"No wonder you can eat all of that." I nod to his still heaping bowl since he spooned out double the ice cream the rest of us did.

"I'm a growing boy." He smirks. He's six-foot-something and all muscle—he could give the Avengers a run for their money if he grows any more.

"I wish I could use that excuse."

Wade laughs. "Ford sure traded up. You're so much better than Ang." He shovels a spoonful of cereal and strawberry sauce-covered ice cream into his mouth. "She talked to me like I was five. I mean, I was twelve when I first met her, but I wasn't a freaking toddler."

Twelve? In my head I do the math. If he's a freshman in college, he's probably eighteen. Six years ago. That little spark of woman's intuition that's made itself known since I heard about this woman pulses. Why would Wade have met Angelica six years ago?

"Do you remember at my fourteenth birthday party how she—"

"Wade," Gregory cuts him off, his spoon clattering against his bowl.

Fourteenth birthday party? Blood drains from my head, and my hands grip the edge of the table, keeping me upright. My eyes trail from one Pruitt man to the next. From clueless Wade to Reid, who looks guilty as hell, past Gregory whose gaze fills with remorse and lands on Drew. His head hangs, one hand cupping the lower half of his face with his eyes lowered to the kitchen tabletop.

My stare fixates on his bowl of mint chocolate ice cream melting into a pool at the bottom. The gradual faith I've rebuilt in him is crumbling, but I can't stop staring at the floating chocolate chunks.

"How did I never see it before?" My voice is barely above a whisper. "All of the secrecy. Breaking things off when it got too serious and showing back up out of nowhere. The unpredictable work hours and late-night emergencies."

Red flag, red flag, red flag. But there I was, rationalizing every breakup, every excuse, every disappointment.

"Grace."

I don't know who says my name with the room closing in on me. Oxygen? Where's the oxygen?

"While Angelica was meeting your family and friends, you were keeping our relationship a secret, not because you were worried about the Seaside gossip or my age, but because *I* was the other woman."

Drew's head whips up. "No. It's not like that, G. You always came first. I never loved her."

I stand on shaky legs. "But you loved *me*, right? Loved me so much you were dating another woman at the same time. Were you engaged to her then?"

"Ohhhh..." Wade's mouth drops with a drawn-out four-letter word. The kid has no idea the size of the bomb he dropped.

"No, no. I didn't propose until after we ended. I accepted that letting you go was the right thing—"

"The right thing? The *right* thing?" I want to keep a level head. I don't want to be the unhinged woman who erupts in front of his family, but I can't contain my pain. "The right thing, Drew, would've been to not date two women at the same damn time!"

He bows his head, his eyes slanting in contrition. "I screwed up. I know." He reaches for me, but I step back. "It's just the moment I saw you, I couldn't stay away. You were everything I didn't know I wanted. I couldn't—"

I shake my head. I don't want to hear it. I don't want to listen to any of it. Another shattering realization slams into my gut.

"And you all knew." My stare falls on Gregory, his mouth pinched with sympathy, his shoulders sagging in defeat. "You... and *you*." I glare at Reid, tears welling up in my eyes, my jaw trembling. "You knew, and you said nothing. You let me give him a second chance, encouraged me to. All the while, I was trying to protect my heart, learning to trust him again. You made me a fool."

"Grace," Reid tries, his chair scooting back.

"No." My hand slices through the air, aimed at him. "Nothing you say will help you right now."

"G, please let me explain." Drew gets up. "I think if you give me a chance to—"

My eyes close. I can't even look at him, my hands tensing at my sides. "Drew, if one more word passes your lips, I swear it'll be your last."

Leaving my half-finished ice cream bowl on the table, I snatch my purse from behind the couch in the living room and race for the front door. Footsteps follow close behind, but I slam the door before they reach me.

since I left you, I have been constantly depressed. My happiness… incessantly… my memory, your cares… your… affection… licit… complete… Josephine… continually a burning… me in my heart. When… all solicitude, all harm… shall I be able to pass… time with you, having… love you, and to think only… happiness of… to saying, and… ing it to you…

31

Reid

BETRAYAL WAS WRITTEN all over her face when she turned to me, blaming me for not telling her what I knew. I shove back hard enough to shift the table as I go after Grace. Ford's growl registers, along with Dad's harsh warning for him to let things be, but I ignore them. I need her to understand.

I fly out the front door. "Grace, wait. Please."

"Reid, I can't talk to you right now. Just let me go home." Her voice cracks. Tears or anger? It's hard to tell as she hurries to her car parked at the end of the driveway. She doesn't even bother looking back in her haste to leave. My pace quickens.

"Then don't talk." I slap my palm against the driver's side window, trapping her, and she flinches as she fumbles through her purse. "But at least listen to me. I can't let you leave without explaining."

She mutters a little curse before finding her keys.

"Please?" I implore, pressing one step closer.

Her shoulders tense before her arms fall to her sides—purse clutched in one hand, keys in the other. As much as I want to touch her, I don't. Grace isn't one to show her emotions. She mentioned once how she hates people seeing her upset. As the oldest of four girls, she prefers teaching them strength. And she's so damn strong, such a role model for her sisters. To honor that part of her, I stop my hand from tipping her chin up when she averts her head, looking at the ground. Since she stopped trying to run, I'll take that as a win.

"I'm sorry you had to hear it like that. Wade didn't know you two dated. He wasn't…" God, I could punch Ford for not just telling her weeks ago. For putting us all in this position.

"How long did it take you to figure it out?" she asks the driveway. "How long have you been keeping it from me?"

I stare at the top of her head. "From almost the moment you confessed to dating him in college."

Her head falls back, looking up, and while the anger is there, it's her hurt that cuts deep. "So, the whole time. You let me open myself back up, only to let him blindside me."

"When was I supposed to say something? I'd just come out of surgery. You can't put that on me. How was I supposed to know you would allow him in?" She'd kissed me less than twenty-four hours before Ford arrived.

Her jaw drops. "I'm not—"

"At first, I thought I was wrong, so I confronted him about everything after he took you to dinner that first time. The night after I was discharged? He snuck out of the house without telling me he was seeing you."

"You confronted him before it even became anything. So, what about after? After telling you he wanted me to give him another shot, you didn't think that was the right time to clue me in? No, instead *you* were the one who told me to give him a chance. I thought we were friends. Why? Why would you put me through that?"

How do I get through her anger? Can she not see my side? "Do you not think I wanted to? Of course, you deserved to know. I debated spilling his secrets a hundred times."

"You said you wanted me to be happy." She laughs bitterly. "Did you think returning to a cheater was going to make me happy? Every day we spent together, you didn't think I deserved to know?"

I shove away from her car, putting space between us, and Grace takes advantage, opening her door and dumping her purse and keys into the front seat.

"Grace, he swore he would tell you. It didn't feel like my place." Not yet, not when they were still casual, reconnecting. Maybe I was wrong? Maybe I should have spoken up, but I trusted Ford when he said he'd never stopped caring for her. I trusted that he wouldn't let her fall too deep without coming clean.

She whirls around. "It's not even about Drew. Does it hurt to know he did that to me? Yes, but more than anything, the truth gives me clarity. At least I know we didn't end because he was ashamed of me. He was ashamed of himself. Now? Now it's about *you*, Reid. I've been—" She swears, shifting her stare away. "Maybe it wasn't your place, but you telling me would've been a hell of a lot better than finding out like that." She points to the house, the tears collecting in her eyes finally spilling over.

Dammit. "You're the one who agreed to see him again." I press closer, wedging her between her open car door and the vehicle. "What would you have me do, Gracie? Ruin your illusion about him, just so I could win?"

"Don't." Her breathless whisper still has bite. "I only agreed to see him again because I didn't think we were a possibility."

Tipping her chin, I swipe a tear with the pad of my thumb and hold her stare.

"What are you really mad about here? That Ford was a

cheating jackass, or that he didn't tell you before he asked for a second chance?"

"Why can't you see this isn't about him? I'm pissed as hell at Drew. No woman wants to be cheated on, but *you* are the one who hurt me."

"This is too about him. One hundred percent."

She smacks my arm away. "I trusted you and you let me carry on like a fool. You had so many opportunities to tell me and you didn't."

"I never meant to hurt you. We were... Hell, I barely knew what was happening between us before my van went barreling down a cliffside. Something about Ford returning to your life sparked interest in you. I wasn't going to be the guy who threw my rival under the bus."

"Drew didn't spark *interest*. He sparked confusion and second-guessing and buried hurt. You have no idea the amount of turmoil I've gone through since he showed up." Her breathing quivers as she inhales. "So, tell me, as his *rival*, is that what this was to you? A competition? Who will win Grace?"

"That's not at all what I meant. I told you weeks ago, he's my brother. He said he still loves you, and you seemed to reciprocate that in some way. I..." I grit my teeth, taking a calming breath before admitting something that shouldn't be said tonight. Not at a moment like this. Grace cants her head, waiting for me to finish, and I struggle with an explanation, but something she said niggles at the back of my mind.

"While we're on the discussion of trust. Just how much trust did you have in me when you couldn't even tell me you dated, no, that you were in love with my brother for years? I woke up to the secret you two had withheld from me. So, I suppose we're all to blame for the way this unfolded."

She sucks in a breath. "You realize I didn't tell Chloe he was your brother. I didn't even tell my parents, my sisters. I hid years of my life from everyone I loved. Seven years and I never told a soul. He never met any of them. Maybe if you'd given me a reason for telling you to be necessary, then I would have, but I'm not sure what the point would have been."

I chuff. *What the point would have been?* What if I had told her I wanted to be with her before Ford came around? Would she have told me then? Or would he have remained a secret between us forever? Maybe she didn't plan on anything to come out of the friendship we'd formed. Maybe it *was all me.* No, she asked if there could be a possibility of us. She wanted this, too, until I chose my brother's feelings over mine.

Twin tears stream down her cheeks. "You made your family loyalty clear. And I get that. I respect it, but this is different. If not tell me about Angelica, you could've at least told me to be careful rather than pushing me toward him."

"I didn't *push* you toward him. I asked you to consider giving him a second chance. I asked you to understand why I couldn't step into the middle. If you didn't think there was a possibility, you could have said no."

"He's a huge part of my past, Reid. How could I not try? Especially with his fervent apologies and your faith in him being a different man. If you weren't going to be with me, why shouldn't I give him another shot?"

For the record, I think Ford is a different man. I think he does love Grace, and he'll punish himself for a long time for screwing this up. I also think Grace never would have taken him back once she learned about his duplicity. I could have made this easy from day one, but then I would be the guy who ripped his brother's heart out by abusing his trust. She had to find out from Ford, or someone else, for me to have absolution for what I want.

"But the fact that you were willing to let me open my vulnerable heart, to fall for him again, knowing what you know."

Rubbing my neck, I finally step out of her space and turn toward the house. "If you think I would have let you fall in love with Ford without knowing the truth about his relationship with Angelica, then you don't know me very well."

"How do you know I haven't fallen back in love with him?"

Her question stops my retreat. "Because if you loved my brother, you wouldn't have kept our time together a secret from him, Grace. Or, maybe you would have, but if that's the case, your anger is entirely misplaced."

Her nostrils flare with an infuriated inhale. "I think we've said enough tonight. I'm going home."

"Gracie?" I take in her set jaw and raise the white flag. *Dammit.* Someone should kick my sorry butt up one side of the street and down the other for my last comment. I step back, giving her the space she so desperately needs.

"Why did you kiss me?" She startles me into standing still. "Why did you kiss me that night after we all went to The Taproom after the softball game then push me away if you didn't want more?"

"The night before my wreck?" I clarify, and she chews on her lip. "Grace, if I could go back…" Massaging the back of my neck, I blow out a frustrated exhale. "I thought we'd have all the time in the world to see what was happening with us. After all our discussions about the missteps we make when finding the right person? I didn't think either of us needed to rush into something. Who knew I'd be rolling down Mt. Luna twelve hours later? Or that your ex, my brother, would walk back into your life declaring his love?"

Her brows knit like she's thinking over my explanation.

"I kissed you because I couldn't help myself, not because I wanted to hurt you. Had I known…"

"Stop." Her hand lifts, and I swallow my apologies. "I should go. I can't do this anymore tonight."

Noting the trembling of her jaw, I ask, "Are you sure you're okay to drive? Wade could take—"

"Just because a woman is angry doesn't mean she's incapable

of driving." Moving her purse from her seat into the passenger's side, she slips inside.

"Will you at least send me a text when you get there so I know you're safe?" I grab the frame to the driver's side door, holding it wide when she attempts to reach for the handle.

With a heavy sigh, she relents. "Fine."

Her hands go to the steering wheel as I close the door, her gaze never turning my way as she starts the engine, backs up, and takes off, leaving me watching her long after she's gone.

...since I left you, I have been constantly depressed. My happiness ... incessantly ... my memory your caress ... your ... your affection ... solicitude ... change ... comparable ... continually a burning and a ... me in my heart. When ... all solicitude, all harass ... , shall I be able to pass a ... time with you, having ... love you, and to think only ... happiness of ... to saying, and ... ing it to you ...

32

*R*eid

When I return to the house, only after her one-word text declaring "home" comes in, Ford and Dad are missing, and Wade is cleaning up the mess in the kitchen.

"I saved you the Reese's." He tosses a miniature cup across the kitchen, and I snag it mid-air and lean against the doorframe.

Unwrapping the gold foil, my gaze scans over the messy counter. "Where are they?" I pop the chocolate in my mouth.

"Dad pushed Ford out back when he got tired of keeping him from chasing after you two. Want to talk about it?"

I shrug one shoulder, unsure of what I'd say.

Wade presses into the counter, balancing his body weight on his palms as he hovers. "I know you guys think I'm still a kid, but I'm not an idiot. I saw the way her eyes watched you. Ford talked about her most of the drive home, but she's not his girl, is she?"

"She was watching me?" I frown. How did I not notice?

Wade drops his feet to the floor with a thud. "Yeah, you were too busy staring at anything but her to see it," he says like he read my mind. "Obviously, she and Ford dated while he was still with Ang. What's your part in it all?"

"I don't want to ruin your visit with this crap." Wade drops his chin, his lips a straight line as he levels me with the same look Dad used on us boys for years. Adequately put in my place, I move to the sink, grabbing a bowl to rinse and load in the dishwasher. "Dad should be proud. You're good at that whole guilt trip thing. Just don't say I didn't warn you if crap hits the fan, and you wind up sprayed by debris."

I explain most of what happened with Grace and Ford and am finishing the story of how my friendship with Grace deepened this year when Ford follows Dad through the back door. Dad dips his head in recognition, his eyes assessing me, like looking me over will clue him into my feelings, before he heads to the refrigerator.

Ford, on the other hand, glares. "What did you say to her?"

Bristling at his tone, I snatch the kitchen towel hanging from the stove and dry my dripping fingers. "I don't see how that's any of your business."

"I should have gone after her, not you." He crosses his arms, his eyes thinning as he stares me down. "Why in the hell was Dad dragging me out the back door so you could chase her down?"

Wade scoffs, and Ford's head snaps toward him. "Dad did you a favor. Grace looked like she was ready to permanently affect your ability to create kids, dude."

He's not wrong. If she hadn't been so hurt, I would have been turned on by the fire she breathed Ford's way.

"Stay out of this, Wade." Ford turns his glare on me. "You told me you were friends, but why am I having a hard time believing that?"

I inhale through my nose. I don't want to fight with him right now. I love my brothers. I wanted a good weekend together.

Mimicking Wade—who did nothing more than snicker at Ford's hot-headed reply. *The kid isn't fazed by anything*—I lean against the counter at my back. "Believe whatever you want."

Ford throws his hands in the air, shoving them through his hair as his neck turns red. "What in the hell did you say to her, Reid? Did you at least tell her how much I care about her?"

So much for not wanting to start a fight. "How much you care?" I glance from Wade to Dad's set jaw and grim eyes. "How much is that? Please enlighten us. Was it enough to admit the truth right away?" I step forward and wave my hand in the air. "No? Well, for sure you care so much about Grace that after she heard about your engagement—from another person—you came clean, right?" I slap the counter separating us. "Oh, wait. No. No, you didn't. You had weeks to spill your ugly indiscretions. So don't expect me to talk you up, Ford. You had her, and you threw her away years ago. That's on you."

Head shaking, he shifts in place. "And what about this time? She's been distant for weeks, especially this last week. You wouldn't happen to know anything about that, would you?"

"Are you for real?" I could choke on his arrogance. "Maybe it has something to do with her finding out from *Eddie* about Angelica. You're not really accusing me of saying something to sway her feelings away from you, are you?"

Though his shoulders fall, there's still fury as he looks between the three of us. "I messed up. I never stopped loving her. I just wanted time to prove I'd changed."

I swallow my reply. Unable to belittle his feelings. No matter how wrong he is for the past and how he handled it, those actions don't change how he feels about her in this moment, when he's lost her.

Dad settles a hand on his shoulder. "A changed man would have confessed at the start, Ford."

Ford's eyes close, his chin dropping to his chest before he exits the kitchen without another word.

Regardless of the drama, the Pruitt men still have a weekend to get through. We charter a fishing boat out of Anacortes Friday and spend the day listening to Dad and our captain share fishing stories while we reel in salmon, halibut, and lingcod. Friday night, Wade provides most of the entertainment as we fry a fresh dinner and process the rest to freeze. Ford is quiet but present. That's all anyone can ask for, I suppose.

Saturday is less eventful. We spend the day helping Dad get work done around the house, and Wade sorts through his room for necessities he might want at school. Before Thursday night's debacle, I'd made the decision to spend the weekend at Dad's house to get the most time with my brothers as possible. It was a good decision, one that led to smack-talking over breakfast this morning, but it also led to Wade barging in my bedroom at one in the morning while I sat staring at my phone as if willing Grace to call would make it happen.

"You need to tell him." My head bounces off the headboard as he throws himself on the foot of my bed. "Tell Ford how you feel."

I grit my teeth. I didn't have to explain everything to Wade Thursday for him to know the truth. "There's no point in doing that right now."

My little brother, who is actually five inches taller and a hell of a lot heavier, thanks to a summer of bulking up, looks heavenward. "When are you going after her?"

My mouth barely opens before he answers his question. "The minute Ford and I walk out the door for Seattle tomorrow, you'll go after her. Don't tell me you won't. Ford's lit up her phone all weekend and she hasn't responded, but it's only a matter of time. I know you're not going to let him get to her before you do."

"It's not a competition, Wade." Grace mistook everything I said the other night as if I thought it was. "It isn't about one brother winning the girl over the other. My silence was always about Grace making her own decision."

"And what decision is that?" My cracked bedroom door pushes the rest of the way open, revealing Ford standing in the hallway. "Were you two seeing each other?"

Scrubbing a hand down my face, I push into a sitting position. "As friends, yes." It doesn't take a genius to read the skepticism on his face. "We had dinner together, Ford. We hung out, and I kissed her a couple of times, but nothing more than that happened."

He sticks to my doorway. "But you wanted more?"

"Since before you showed up. Yes."

"Did you kiss her after I came back? After I told you how I felt?"

It's my turn to show shame. "Once, yeah. But then I told her I couldn't be with her. I couldn't do that to you, not after all you gave up for us growing up."

Ford's face twists. "I don't—"

"You don't what?" I cut him off. "Understand how, after everything you did for us growing up, I couldn't admit to falling for the same woman you say you're still in love with?"

"First, everything I did for you guys after Mom left, I'd do again in a heartbeat. You owe me nothing, ever." He looks between Wade and me, glaring like he wants to drill his truth into our minds. "Second, I can't believe you. You should have told me. Had I known there was something between you…"

I shrug because what does it matter now?

"Dammit, Reid," he mutters under his breath. "That's why Dad gave me such a cold shoulder every time I mentioned her, isn't it? He took your side the other night. He forced me to let you speak with her."

"Dad and I never discussed her until we were making dinner Thursday. If he gave off a vibe, you'd have to ask him why—"

"I'd bet your Porsche his attitude was because he was pissed at you for being a two-timing womanizer."

I kick at my little brother's rock-hard thigh. "Shut up, Wade." But to my surprise, Ford laughs. It's self-deprecating, but it's a laugh.

"Since I actually like my Porsche I won't take that bet, but how about I let you drive her to the gas station when we leave?"

Clapping his hands once, Wade points to Ford. "Sold to the man in blue."

After a minute of staring, Ford walks further into my childhood bedroom and drops down on the old gaming chair sitting in the corner. "No matter your relationship with Grace, I shouldn't have put you in the position to keep secrets from her. She's completely ghosting me."

"Actually, bro, it's only ghosting if you have no explanation for the behavior. In your case—"

Ford throws my shoe at Wade's head. "Damn, you Gen Z's think you know everything."

since I left you, I have
been constantly depressed.
My happiness
incessantly
my mind your cares,
your affection
solicitude
comparable
continually a burning and a
in my heart. When,
all solicitude, all hara
shall I be able to pass a
time with you, having
love you, and to think only
happiness of saying, and
ing it to you.

33

Grace

SINCE REID SHOWED up last Tuesday night with his tail between his legs, I half-expect to see him on the bleachers after softball practice ends, but the only spectators here are Tony's wife and kids. Relief and disappointment mingle and set up camp inside of me, roasting marshmallows around the fire.

I'm not ready to talk to him, but I miss him. I hate the confusion. It's so discombobulating. Why did everything have to become so convoluted? Even with our complicated dating histories, what Reid and I had was familiar, second-nature, like we'd always been this close. Everything fell into place so seamlessly. We just...clicked.

And maybe Reid was right. While I'm upset with him and Drew, I'm mad at myself, too. Why didn't I tell Drew about hanging out with Reid? At first, it was because we were friends, who happened to share two friendly kisses. Nothing more was going on. Drew didn't get to decide who I spent time with. But then we kissed at his house, and it's all I wanted to do. The more I think about it, the more I realize our time together wasn't as innocent as I made it out to be in my head.

If Reid hadn't put a stop to us before we started, I would've forgotten Drew in an instant. No questions asked. I only contemplated getting back with him because his reappearance felt like fate intervening. Why would he return at the exact moment I was falling for Reid if not to set me on the right path? And when Reid didn't object, what was I supposed to do? Not try with Drew because of a man who would never consider me?

Even though I didn't realize it, my feelings for Reid began the first time we ate po' boys at Saltbox. We had the most natural interaction. Even with him being Chloe's ex and Drew's younger brother, none of that mattered to my heart. The past was inconsequential. My brain just hadn't caught up yet. It didn't see the truth.

And that's what stings so much about him keeping Drew's cheating from me. I never wanted Drew again, and if Reid had just been open and honest with me, I'd never have wasted my time. It's crushing realizing someone you trust knows something so humiliating about your life you don't. If he can keep something like that from me, what else can he keep?

Chloe's been ditching Kip and staying here since Thursday night, sharing a bed with Robyn. It's the longest stretch of nights in a row since she first moved in over a year ago. I spend Friday and Saturday away from Fig for fear that Reid or Drew would track me down. At least at home, I don't have to answer the door, and with Chloe the guard dog, she's willing to attack anyone I'm not ready to confront. God help Drew if he tries to show his face. I've left every text from him unread and every call unanswered. I'm over it. *So* done.

As I down a tub of cookies n' cream on Saturday night, I tell

Chloe I'm fine and that she can return to Kip, but she doesn't believe me.

I spend most of Sunday in the stock room of Fig going over inventory, ordering new items for fall, and handling the financial side of things while I let Gina and a new hire, Josie, run the front. There's very little desire in me to go to family dinner after work, but I have even less of a desire to raise questions from Mom. If she finds out I dated Ford Pruitt and kept him from her, I'll never hear the end of it.

Autumn spends most of the meal distracting Mom with wedding ideas, so I'm off the hook. It's both a blessing and a curse. While I'm grateful not to be the center of discussion, hearing Autumn gush over dress options and cake ideas is less than ideal in my current state of mind. Who am I kidding? It'd suck without being all torn up over Reid.

Stella keeps glancing my way across the table, questions in her sixteen-year-old eyes. If my ordinarily head-in-the-clouds sister can sense something is off, I must be doing a poor job of concealing my heartache. I should've just said I was sick and stayed home.

"Aren't wedding cakes fading out?" Lucy takes a bite of pot roast. "Aren't people doing donuts or cupcakes now or whatever?"

Autumn chuckles, an endeared smile on her delicately featured face as she nudges our youngest sister with her elbow. "You're twelve. What do you know about wedding trends?"

"It doesn't take a genius to know traditional is the new outdated." Lucy shrugs. "Be your own couple. Don't follow just because it's what everyone else is doing."

We all laugh.

"Solid advice, Luce," I say, and she beams, mashed potatoes at the corner of her mouth.

Monday I do much of the same at Fig, hiding out in the back where no one can find me.

I'd like to think I'm a strong, fearless woman capable of

anything, but avoiding my problems doesn't exactly back that up. Whatever. I deserve some space to work this all out in my head. I've been hit with a lot over the last several weeks.

Reid hasn't texted or called since I told him I got home safely last Thursday. Not that I expect him to. Drew, however, hasn't stopped blowing up my phone—I finally read and listened—with apologies and pleading to hear him out. I don't see the point. Getting an explanation won't change my decision to be done with him. I could never see his face again and be fine. I let him fool me too many times.

After softball practice Tuesday, I shower and change into black leggings and my favorite oversized sweatshirt, the torn neckline hanging off my bare shoulder. As I make my way into the kitchen, two sharp knocks echo through the house. Chloe is staying a little late at her farm, so I'm expecting her home any minute. She probably left her house key again because she's not used to staying here. Out of the last five nights, she's forgotten her key three times. Why not make it a fourth?

With my hair still wet, hanging straight down, and my face makeup-free, I open the door. "Maybe we should—"

"I'm in love with you." Reid's words rush out before the door opens entirely. He grips either side of my door frame like he's either holding himself up or barricading the opening so I can't leave. "I was figuring my feelings out when I got in the car accident. Then Drew arrived, and I learned about you two, and I couldn't figure out what to do. I didn't want to be second best again."

Blinking once, then twice, my mouth falls open. He steps into the doorway, pushing me to retreat inside and slides his hands down my arms until our fingers lock together.

"I'm so sorry I kept what I knew a secret. I was trying to save my relationship with Ford and a future with you. But we were all keeping secrets, weren't we? Ford should have told you about Angelica. You should have told Ford about all the time we were spending together, and when he asked me if we were truly just friends, I should have said no. I should have told him that he couldn't have a second chance with you because I wanted a first." He runs his tongue over his bottom lip. "I *want* a chance, Gracie. I want you."

I take what feels like the first breath since I found him on my doorstep. There are so many things to unpack, but the one neon-flashing confession my brain fixates on stumbles from my mouth. "You're in love with me?"

He grins. "God, yes." His head shakes. "I've known you forever. I kept thinking what I felt was our friendship growing stronger, but funny enough, my true emotions hit me when I went sailing off Mt. Luna."

I frown. The visual image tightens my lungs and twists my heart. When I got the call from Chloe, I've never known such fear. Fear of losing him, of never kissing him again, fear of never getting our chance. For hours, my heart was in my throat, praying he'd survive. Praying I wouldn't lose the man who could've been the one.

"Ironic, huh? Finally figured out what I wanted the moment I was sure I was going to die." Reaching out, his knuckles skim along my cheek. "I was thoroughly pissed as those flowers flew around the van and the world flipped on me."

Tilting my head, my forehead rumples. "You were pissed?"

"Hell, yes. I chickened out on kissing you *for real*, on showing you what I've been dying to do to you. Do you know how annoying that is? To think I'd forever missed my opportunity?"

Reid steps into me in one fluid motion, takes my face and covers my mouth with his in a hard peck. My brain and heart zing to life, but my body takes a second to catch up, stunned by his urgency. And then I curl my hands around his wrists, holding him there. It's strange how someone's lips can feel new and familiar at the same time. I don't know these lips, but they fit. They are the perfect match for mine.

One of his hands slips under my damp hair to the nape of my neck, slanting his mouth, deepening into a softer open-mouthed kiss. I melt into Reid, releasing the hushed moan trapped in my throat and his tongue takes advantage, sweeping inside. He runs it along my top lip and I whimper. I'm so embarrassed by the sound, but my desire only encourages him. A heady exhale pours from his nose, and he sucks my bottom lip in his mouth, his tongue caressing the length of it.

All too soon, Reid breaks the kiss, far enough that I feel the faint caress of his minty breath. With my eyes closed, I exhale. When I open them, Reid's thumb strokes my jaw as his eyes take mine in.

Dropping my gaze to his lips, I attempt to catch my breath. "What happened to not being the guy who comes between your brother and me? To owing him?"

"Screw that. My respect for his feelings only went as far as your feelings for him. If you're truly over and done with him, I will happily step in and claim what I should have claimed weeks ago."

Unsurprisingly, I'm turned on by that. "We have a lot to discuss, but I think talking can wait."

Reid doesn't argue as his arms slip around my waist and his mouth slams into mine. Backing me inside, he kicks the door shut, rattling the walls. Bending his knees, he gains leverage, hauling me against him, my toes lifting. His hands are on a never-ending hunt along my back, my waist, through my hair. He murmurs my name, and I wrap my arms around his neck and match the intensity of his mouth and tongue.

Finding the hem of my sweatshirt, his hands slip beneath. Skin on skin, his touch is the spark and I'm the coals. He sets me aflame. Someone open a window or remove the layers between us.

My leg climbs around him, and he hooks my other knee, hoisting me up until he catches my butt. I release a little yelp. "Oh, no, your injury. Put me down, put me down."

"I'll live." He laughs against my skin, his lips trailing down my jaw as he carries me into the living room. Sitting on the couch with me in his lap, Reid sucks on my neck, a frantic race along the curve of my exposed shoulder. Heat coils in my belly, radiating around my chest and down my legs. My thighs clamp around his hips as quivers course along my spine. I clutch the back of his neck to encourage his path across my skin, the ends of his hair tickling my fingers.

His teeth and tongue give extra attention to my collarbone before tugging down the neckline of my sweatshirt—descending fervent kisses on my chest. I tear off his baseball cap and latch onto the roots of his hair. The desperation and need thrumming become a physical being, wrapping around us and clinging. My hips roll into his, and one of his hands slides down my waist, spurring me on.

One by one, my sweatshirt goes, then his shirt. He flips me until I'm lying on my back on the couch, his body between my spread legs. Gently, I press my palm over the fading red scar below the left side of his ribcage. I've never desired another human being more in my life. His sounds of pleasure at every new sensation and his rough gasp at the sight of my body fuels my urgency to have him. Sanity and sense? Are those words in the English dictionary? Because nothing about how rabid I am for Reid is rational.

His fingers curl into the top of my leggings, tugging. Then he catches himself. Tightening his grip on the waistband in restraint, he stares into my eyes before he shuts them with his jaw clenched.

"Not like this." He lowers his head, pressing a tender kiss near my belly button.

I take deep breaths to calm my heart. The rejection stings,

but of course he'd stop us. It hasn't even been a week since I was seeing Drew.

"Yeah." It's impossible to keep the disappointment from my voice. I'm not that great of an actress. "Yeah, you're right."

His head lifts, his arms on either side of me, propping him up. "Don't think it's because I don't want to or that I'm backpedaling." Reid searches my eyes and lifts one of his hands to my cheek, his calloused fingertips grazing the shape of my face. "I want to take my time with you, and when I do, I want there to be nothing left unsaid, no room for regrets or second thoughts."

Nodding, I inhale another calming breath. "Who knew you'd be the sensible one in this?"

"I'm full of surprises, baby." Snagging my sweatshirt from the floor, he hands it to me. "But first, I need you to put that back on. I can't focus with all that on display."

A smirk tugs at the corner of my lips as I hold my top to my chest. "Maybe you need to work on your self-control."

"I'm a gentleman, not a saint."

Slipping it over my head, I say, "It's probably for the best. And as much as it pains me to say, you should put your shirt back on, too. Chloe is supposed to be here any second. If you hadn't stopped us, she'd have been in for quite the awkward steamy show."

Thankfully, Robyn already went to bed, and from what I've learned, she's a heavy sleeper. It's no wonder she can live with chickens, not even a rooster would wake her.

"Oh, Loe was getting out of Betty when I pulled up. She's staying with Kip tonight."

"You talked to her?"

"I didn't have to say a word." Reid yanks his T-shirt over his head. "As soon as I parked, she said, 'go get her,' hopped back in her truck, and pulled away."

Shaking my head, I smile. I'll have to thank her later.

"You're too far away. C'mere." He lifts my legs onto his lap as he scoots down, flinging his arms along the back of the couch, his fingers toying with my damp hair. I imagine it resembles Medusa's coils by this point.

"I am sorry I kept everything about Angelica from you."

I nod. "I get why you did. Drew should've told me. He put you in a tough position. Confessing his sins wasn't your responsibility."

"I needed him to fix the past or screw it up without my interference. Admittedly, I hoped he'd screw things up. And maybe, after everything with Kip and Chloe, I was a bit paranoid about you ending up with me because of what Ford did. I didn't want you second-guessing a missed opportunity later." Reid inhales deeply, releasing the air slowly. "Like my mother did."

Resting my hand on his jaw, my heart clenching, I stare intently into his eyes. "You were never a default choice or second best, Reid. You've been my first choice from the start. Things just got a little muddled." My thumb strokes his scruff, which is more of a short beard compared to when I last saw him. "Once my feelings for you became more apparent to me, I tried burying them. I didn't know if you'd be able to look past my relationship with Drew. We're not talking about a few dates and kisses. Over three years of on and off commitment—well, commitment on my part. It's a lot to ask of you."

"I won't say the idea of you two together gives me the warm fuzzies." His mouth twists. "Honestly, I don't know how I feel about you two, but your history doesn't change how I feel about you."

That's fair. "Just so you know...before the whole Angelica thing blew up Thursday night, I was going to end it with Drew. Even if it didn't mean being with you, I knew it wasn't going to work with him. What we had wasn't going to rekindle. Maybe I wasn't over the insecurities he left me with, but I fell out of love with Drew years ago."

He tucks a strand of hair behind my ear. "If I'd kissed you

like I wanted to on New Year's Eve, none of this would have happened."

"Why didn't you?"

His head falls to the couch as he twists his lips. "Three reasons," he says reluctantly, ticking them off on his hand. "Chloe, Mia, and my not knowing my own mind for a while."

What is that about?

"Don't jump to conclusions, Slugger." He presses the crease between my brows. "I doubted myself after the ordeal with Loe. She was this comfort swept out from beneath me and the loss left me stunned. Mia was a distraction. I think my ego needed a lift, and I let that buzz get the best of me for a while, keeping me from fully seeing you. But you became a friend who made me smile. Being with you is always so effortless, Gracie." His calloused fingertip traces over my jawline. "I fought the feelings you brought about because I didn't trust myself, not because they weren't there. Believe me, they were running me to distraction."

There's nothing uncommon about us. We were two people with baggage that made us gun-shy when the time came to leap. Two people scared of making a wrong decision with someone we respected and valued in our lives. This should have been easier, but falling in love never is.

"My heart decided its course that night on the dance floor at Hayden and Brynn's wedding." I place my hand over his on my face. "It just took the rest of me a while to catch up."

"We're a bit slow, aren't we? At least we finally made it to this point."

"What's going to happen between you and Drew? Did you talk to him about us?"

"We cleared the air. What he did to you isn't okay, but that's between you two. Trust me when I say Wade, Dad, and I all tore into him for how he behaved in the past." He flips his fingers around to hold mine, dropping our intertwined hands into my lap. "He's my brother, though. I told him how I feel about you, so he knows. I didn't think anything else was necessary until we talked. We can handle things, as they pertain to us and how much he knows, however you want."

I don't want to see Drew or discuss anything with him, ever, but Reid's right. This is his family. I want Reid, but not if it means he loses his big brother over it.

"Let me think on that, okay?"

Dipping his head in agreement, Reid brings his mouth to mine.

in my heart. When
all solicitude, all
shall I be able to pass
time with you, having
love you, and to think only
happiness of so saying, and
it to you

34

Grace

Okay, I lied.

I have to see Drew. I didn't know it until I woke up this morning with fire in my veins after spending the night talking and making out with Reid like teenagers. Even though Reid said he wasn't going to let Drew come between us, I don't want to be a wedge in their relationship. I can't imagine a life with a grudge against one of my sisters. Drew got us all into this mess, and he's not going to make Reid suffer because of his weak choices. Which is how I find myself behind the wheel of my Accord on I-5 southbound to Seattle after I close Fig, my angry girl playlist blaring through my speakers.

He moved sometime after we broke up, but I lucked out with the Christmas package I still had untouched in my nightstand, his address in the corner. During our dinner at Briar's, he mentioned he works out in his apartment building fitness center every Monday and Wednesday after work, so he should be home, and I don't want him to know I'm coming. I don't want him to have a chance to prepare what to say.

But it's just my luck that his building requires a keycard to enter. I don't know why I'm surprised. It's near the Puget Sound—with breathtaking views, I'm sure—and looks like it was plucked straight out of Manhattan. Of course, it has controlled access.

When his voice comes through the speaker, it takes all I have to keep my tone civil.

"It's Grace. Will you let me in?"

"Grace?" He pauses, fumbling. "Yeah, give me a sec."

The glass door unlatches and I pull, finding two sets of elevators in the cold, modern lobby. My white sneakers squeak across the tile floors, echoing through the vacant space. As soon as I wind up at his unit on the twelfth floor, I raise my hand to knock and the door swings open.

"You're here."

Before Drew can say anything else, I square my shoulders, clutching my keys and phone in each hand. "You're not going to talk. You're going to listen."

Snapping his mouth closed, he steps back and allows me to pass. In basketball shorts and a white sleeveless shirt, his hair matted by sweat, he must have just returned from the gym.

I glance about as he shuts the door and runs a hand through his dirty blond hair, standing it on end, so unlike his usual neat style. Before I lose my nerve, I whirl around.

"All of these years, I blamed myself for asking too much of you. I thought I let my mother's marital indoctrination screw up a perfectly good relationship because I felt like I had to get married or wind up alone. You allowed me to doubt my worth, my expectations, my heart. When all of that time you were screwing around with another woman behind my back."

"G—"

I hold up my hand, closing my eyes, on the verge of telling him to shush. "And even still, I can't let you shoulder all of the blame because *I* allowed you to make me feel that way. I let you come back time and time again, even though in my heart of hearts, something didn't sit right. I ignored my intuition for the chance at a possible life with you, a life I'm not even sure I wanted as much as I felt like I needed." I take a heavy breath, opening my eyes. "Were you ever going to tell me? If there was no Reid and your family never knew, would you have let me go on believing you were faithful and I was simply too young and naïve?"

Drew's shoulders hunch forward, his eyes darting to the hardwood floor. "I don't know. I'd like to believe I'm better than that now, but my fear of losing you again might've gotten in the way." Lifting his gaze, he takes a hopeful step toward me. "What good would come from telling you about a mistake made by a person I don't even know anymore? I'm changed. I swear I'm not that man. If there's even a slight chance you still care for me, I'll do whatever I need to prove I'll be better. I'd never hurt you like that again. I can be what you deserve."

"No, Drew. That's not..." To put more distance between us, giving him no room for misinterpretation, I move back a step. "I came here to tell you whatever you thought was between us is over. Once and for all. While I believe you're on your way to being a changed man, nothing you did was okay. Not making me the other woman, not keeping the knowledge of Angelica from me when you came back. But most of all, the way you've made Reid feel like he can't be with me because he needs to put your happiness first as some sort of repayment. None of it is okay, Drew."

"I agree. Reid never should've put my needs before his. When our mom left..." He pauses, his eyes shifting to the sleek leather couches near the floor-to-ceiling windows overlooking the Puget

Sound, and what do you know? The view is beautiful with the city lights reflecting off the water. "Can we sit?"

With a silent yes, I make my way to one of the couches, taking in the view. Drew doesn't attempt to sit on the same one, choosing the adjacent loveseat. Smart man, for once.

He perches on the edge, resting his forearms on his knees. "When she left us for her high school ex-boyfriend—her supposed soulmate with a hefty bank account and a second home in Park City—her betrayal changed all of us in different ways. I hated seeing the light diminish in my little brothers' eyes, and I vowed to do everything in my power to make up for her absence. Wade was too young to know better, but Reid was only nine, and he missed her so much. I gave up my Friday and Saturday nights with friends to hang out with them and fill their lives with as many good memories as we could cram in. While my dad was working his tail off, I was cleaning the house and making dinner. In between homework and studying, I was doing laundry and disciplining my brothers, but no matter how hard I tried, there was no way for me to replace her presence. I mean, how could an older brother replace a mother's love and attention?

"I never once resented them for it, but I sure as hell resented *her*, and I never wanted to feel the way she made me feel again. She rewired my brain to view women as nothing more than a means to an end...until I met you. I won't sit here and make excuses for my actions. If I had to do it all over again for them, I would in a heartbeat. I just want you to know there was nothing you could've done differently. This was me, all me, and I know that. I'll never forgive myself for destroying what we had. It's my biggest regret in life."

A sheen of moisture coats my eyes with the visual of those three young boys trying to get by. Of Gregory losing who he thought was his other half and struggling to support and provide for his sons independently.

"I don't want you to beat yourself up over it anymore. It happened. It's over. Let's move on."

His big hand lands on my bare knee below my linen shorts. "I'd like that."

For fear that he's not getting the reason I came, I need to make my feelings clear. Removing his hand from my knee, I level him with an earnest stare. "I'm in love with Reid, Drew. I don't know how it happened, but it did." Slow, and yet sudden. "And you can't be the reason Reid won't feel like he can be with me. We sort of sucker-punched him with our relationship. He's innocent in all of this." No matter what Reid says now. "I know he cares about how you'll view us together, how it'll affect your relationship. You can't let that happen. After everything you put me through, you owe me this. Reid is my happiness, and there's a good chance he always will be."

Swallowing, his stare drifts to the wall of windows. "You know…" He releases a humorless laugh, his tongue darting out to wet his lips. "I didn't want to accept it, but as soon as I saw you by his hospital bed, the way you cared for him and talked to him, I knew Reid was the one you wanted. Though I wanted to believe the two of you when you said you were only friends, the gut never lies." With a stoic gleam in his eyes, Drew looks back at me. "I won't come between you two. Reid has nothing to worry about. I love my brother too much to lose him, and I admire you too much to let my feelings stand in the way of something real."

Pushing past the lump in my throat, I say, "Thank you."

It's past ten when I make it back to Seaside. Instead of heading home, I drive straight to Reid's house. It's not much, but with all the work he's put into the place over the years to renovate it, his love for his home shines through.

Opening the storm door, I lightly knock on his front door.

It takes a minute before he opens it in the same pair of gray sweatpants he wore when I showed up with Perry's. Except this time, instead of his maroon and white Seaside High T-shirt, he's shirtless. With his living room dimly lit behind him, the ridges of his abs and pecs are spotlighted by the glow of the porch light.

"Hey, where have you been? I've been worried. You haven't responded to my texts, and Loe wouldn't tell me where you were."

To not alarm anyone, I informed Chloe of my whereabouts as soon as I got in my car. I swore her to secrecy because I didn't want Reid trying to stop me. I don't know why he would've, but nothing was going to prevent me from closure.

"I went to Seattle to see Drew."

"What?"

Curling my hands around the back of his head, I steer Reid's lips to mine, erasing the doubt written across his face. Pecking him once before breaking away, I meet his eyes.

"After everything, he wasn't allowed to hang over our heads like a giant gray rain cloud. I don't want you having any regrets where he's concerned. So, I told him I love you, and he's going to have to deal with it."

Reid's teeth glide along his bottom lip, a tilt to the corner of his mouth. "You told him that, huh?"

I shrug. "In so many words, yes."

"God, Gracie." With a smooth swoop, Reid lifts me off my feet, sealing his lips to mine. One secure arm looping around my waist, the other rising up to grip the back of my head. The need to be closer consumes and I jump, wrapping my legs around his waist, and savor the heat of my thighs skim over his bare torso. As he retreats into the house carrying me, he toes the door shut. And then he's moving me backward, the solid door holding me hostage against him. His hips roll, pressing me against the solid surface, his determined lips and tongue marking a path down my neck. "I love you, too," he murmurs against my sensitive collarbone.

"You're not mad I didn't tell you?" I sink my fingers into his hair, gripping the roots for stability. The tug pulls a resonant groan from his throat, and he latches onto the curve of my shoulder, sucking and nipping. I tremble.

"How could I be mad when it's so unbelievably hot that you fought for us?"

I yank his hair, dragging his mouth back to mine, and dive my tongue inside, releasing all my pent-up desire. Reid tastes like spearmint. Freshly brushed teeth? My thighs clench when he brings a hand to my waist, untucking my shirt and slipping beneath, his rough fingers stroking my skin.

"I will always fight for you," I say between panted breaths. "I don't ever want you to doubt what I feel for you."

When his hand skates higher and higher up my ribcage, a whimper escapes me. My chest arches into him, and he takes my not-so-subtle hint. Dipping down, he yanks the neckline of my shirt away, his mouth descending. My fingers lock at his nape, keeping him captive, right where I need him.

We might be frantic, but there's also an undercurrent of worship, of savoring what we've deprived ourselves of for months. This sense of rightness in our battle of affection colliding and clinging. Bodies, hearts, minds. Each uniting in its own form. It was always supposed to be Reid and Grace. The veil is torn back and we finally recognize the ties that bind.

Dropping my arms from around his neck, I tug the edge of my shirt. "Off. Take this off." I need to be intimately connected with him, indulging in his warmth, giving him full access to do as he pleases. *More.* I just need more.

"I can't do this." My feet drop to the ground, his large, capable hands no longer surrounding me, and my heart sinks until he drags me toward the couch. "I'd take you to my bedroom, but it's too far. I can't wait any longer for you." Tearing my shirt over my head, Reid lowers his body over mine as he guides my back onto the couch. Not a second later, his mouth returns to me, his hand snaking beneath. Faster than I can, he frees the lace from my arms and throws it across the room.

He pauses his assault, his eyes taking their fill. A soft mixture of awe and hunger glazes his stare. "You're flawless, Gracie."

Reid isn't the first person to call me Gracie, but he's the only person who reaches all four chambers of my heart with those six letters. The name belongs to him, no one else.

When our mouths connect again, my pulse quickens as his hand reaches between us, fighting with the tie of my shorts. The longer he takes, the more labored and frustrated his groans become. "Who *makes* this stuff?" He tugs and tugs, but the belt doesn't budge.

I shake with quiet laughter, easing his hand aside to help untie the knot. "Let me."

He kisses me, tongue devouring, wiping the smile right off as he works the zipper down.

"Next time, wear a dress," he orders, and never has a command charged me more. *Next time.*

Before my brain catches up, his hands and mouth stroke and handle my body until there's nothing more between us. Only our rawest forms, open and trusting. There are no more obstacles, no more confines. We're free.

Reid hovers above me, his forearm propped on the couch by my head, our faces inches apart. "I just need a moment." He takes his other hand and sweeps a lock of hair from my forehead, gentle and sweet. "Just a moment to grasp you're really mine." A tremor shudders through his limbs, dislodging my nerves. This is happening. We're not holding back anymore.

Blood rushes through my veins, our chests meeting with each fast-paced breath, hearts pounding with anticipation. My fingers trail up his warm, sculpted back, around his shoulder to cradle the side of his sturdy jaw. The shortened scruff tickles my fingertips.

"I'm really yours."

All at once, we're separate and then one. The way Reid moves against me, I come undone, unraveling all I thought I knew about love and passion. The hollow knowledge scatters around us as the meaningful pieces patch something new, something true.

I'm no longer just Grace, but Reid's Grace. As Reid is mine. Grace's Reid.

And I am changed.

in my heart. When
all solicitude, all
shall I be able to pass a
time with you, having
love you, and to think only
ing it to you

35

Reid

"I presumed my chances of having a champion athlete in the family were ruined when the Lord blessed me with four girls."

"Dad!" Stella punches her father's shoulder, her lips puffing into a pout. Mr. Embry waggles his brows as Grace's two youngest sisters rip into their father for his un-feminist remarks, and I hold back a laugh.

"Don't let him fool you," Grace says, sneaking up behind where I stand in the doorway between the Embry's dining and living rooms. "The man loves to tease, but he taught us we could do whatever we wanted regardless of our sex."

Turning, I admire my gorgeous Seaside Pointe Summer League Softball Champion girlfriend. "Knowing you as I do, I have no doubt he raised you right."

Smiling, Grace leans forward and kisses my cheek. "I'm going to help my mom in the kitchen. You don't have to be scared of her, you know."

"Who me?"

Grace tilts her head, calling me on my fib, and I shoot her a wink before she sets off.

Nanette Embry.

The woman doesn't scare me, per se, but she certainly has no boundaries, which makes for an interesting first meeting. Nanette quizzed me on my job, home, and plans for my future before she served me a drink, but Grace gave me the heads up for what I was getting into on the way here, so I was prepared.

Since the Seasiders party after winning the league championship Thursday night was more of a team thing at The Taproom, Nanette pushed for a family celebration as part of their usual Sunday dinner. Grace offered me an out, warning the real reason her mother wanted this barbecue was to inspect my potential as the possible father of her future grandkids, but I wouldn't hear of skipping out. First, what kind of future son-in-law would I be if I ignored a dinner invite? Second, maybe getting to know me is part of the woman's motive, but the house overflowing with balloons and baseball-themed decorations speaks of her pride in her daughter.

Plus, I've kept Grace holed up in my house, or more correctly in my bed, ignoring texts and phone calls since quitting time Friday afternoon. A family meal is the least I can do.

I haven't met the parents of a woman I'm dating since high school—not including the Lockwoods since I knew them beforehand. Being here makes Grace and me more real, which is fine by me. I'm embracing calling Grace Embry mine. We've crossed all the bases:

Ex approval—Ford gave his somewhat tepid blessing, while Chloe confessed she should have known I was meant for Grace from the beginning.

Family approval—Dad was at the game Thursday cheering Grace on with the rest of us. When they hugged afterward, *he* apologized for not blowing Ford's secret right away. Grace wiped her tears and promised him an ice cream party redo soon. As for the Embry's? I'm still in their home, so I'm on the right track.

Official coupledom—according to Autumn, the second eldest Embry daughter, the news of our relationship spread through Seaside Pointe like wildfire. The juicy tidbit of Chloe Lockwood's farm manager ex dating her best friend is too good to pass up.

We laugh at the naysayers. We know what we've found in each other. It's astounding how two people can spend years walking parallel paths, never intersecting, until they do. Then *boom*—the world finally makes sense.

GRACE GROANS when my alarm sounds before sunrise Monday morning. "Too early." She rolls, hiding her head beneath her pillow.

Chuckling, I ignore my usual routine in favor of spooning my beautiful bedmate. "You live with Loe, Gracie. You knew what you were getting into." I brush the satin strands from her neck and nuzzle.

Her body arches against mine as she murmurs, "Loe doesn't sleep in my bed."

Desire stirs and I creep lower, tasting her skin along her spine. "Too bad for her."

"You have to get to the farm." Grace's fingers clamp over my hand teasing around her curved hip. The huskiness in her tone says she's anything but mad at my wake-up call.

"Not for an hour, Embry. Let me offer you a proper good morning."

With a delicious sigh, Grace releases my hand and surrenders.

What a perfect way to start a Monday.

I'M surprised to see Kip's Audi parked in the gravel lot of Lockwood Farms when I arrive, albeit a little late thanks to Grace and our shared shower.

"Hey, man." Kip steps out of the shadows when I stop by Loe's old workshop I've taken over.

"What are you doing here this time of the day? Everything okay with Loe?"

"Oh, yeah, everything's good. Chlo could really use the storage the yellow shed would provide over at the second farm, so I volunteered to give you a hand with it."

"Give me a hand?" I repeat, noting his clothing for the first time. He's dressed in work pants, boots, and a solid tee instead of his usual male model meets millionaire dress code.

Kip's hands go up. "I had a free day and the boss lady is getting antsy about ordering the piping for the new beds we'll have ready by next spring since we have nowhere to store them. Plus, this is Hayden's last week."

I rough my hand over my jaw. We're two days from September. With the accident and everything afterward, I forgot she originally asked for the shed two months ago.

"Yeah." I nod and wave Kip to follow. "Yeah, this summer got away from me. Let me assign jobs and put Eric on deliveries, then we can tackle that shed once and for all."

WE'VE REMOVED and loaded the doors, windows, and shed roof onto a trailer when we decide a break is in order before pulling the interior shelving and taking down the walls. Grabbing some cold water bottles, we walk the rows of beds toward the property line between the farm and the Harrises'.

"I've learned more about flowers this last year than I ever imagined I could." Kip pauses to admire the dahlia patch. "What brought you here? To the farm?"

I flip my hat and swipe the back of my palm across my

forehead. "I wasn't much for school. Focusing on books and facts just wasn't my thing. Sometimes I think the only reason I did as well as I did was because I needed to keep up my average for varsity eligibility. If I hadn't torn my rotator cuff senior year…"

"Man, I remember that. It sucked. I honestly think seeing you go down was the first time I realized how fragile the hope of playing pro was."

What do I say to that? My dreams died young. "I liked working with my hands. I loved the freedom of being outside. James was hiring, so I begged him to take a chance on a stupid kid who knew nothing about flower farming." My gaze roams over the fields I know like the back of my hand. "And here I am ten years later."

"And I can't tell you how grateful I am for that," Kip says, almost offhandedly. I pull back, surprised by Kip Harris for the second time today. "No, really, Reid. This past year has been hell on Chloe. Knowing she can count on you to keep this farm running with everything—"

"Don't." I stop his unexpected spewing of gratitude. "This business is my life, almost as much as it is hers. I won't take it from her, but I'll work by her side for as long as she'll have me."

"So, you and Gracie Lou, huh?" he asks after a minute of awkward silence. The plastic bottle in my fist crunches as my fingers tighten at his use of *my* pet name for Grace. Kip laughs. "Easy, Pruitt. I've called her that since we were kids."

I could ask him if he blames me for my jealousy, considering, but I don't. What I once thought of as arrogance and high-handedness on the part of Kip Harris when he stole Loe away, I now see as the universe righting a wrong. He didn't steal my girl. He claimed his. Which left me to find mine. Grace.

"I probably owe you and Loe an apology." I chuckle, and Kip's head whips my way. "I didn't get it until Grace, man. There was never a choice. She just is."

Tipping his water bottle like a toast, Kip smiles. He understands.

"I hope you're ready for a million double dates. Our girls are—"

"She's asking me questions, James." The urgent hiss of words comes from nearby, and Kip freezes as he looks at me.

Who? I mouth, looking through the row of towering sunflowers for whomever we overheard.

"Stay away from my wife, Denton."

Denton? Kip pales and brushes his index finger across his lips, signaling for me to remain quiet.

"I've held the past inside because I respect Robyn, but with the way you've treated Chloe and my son." Denton releases a one-note chuckle. "I no longer have a reason to lie."

"Are you sure about that, Harris?" I've never heard that tone of menace in James Lockwood's voice.

There's a moment of tense silence, and Kip's foot lifts to step forward, halting only when Denton asks, "Are you threatening me?"

Landscape fabric crinkles, and the unmistakable sound of one of the men—my bet's on James—snickering reaches us. Kip and I crouch lower to keep from being caught eavesdropping.

"Our daughters found a picture of Traci and me. They're curious. The truth will come out eventually."

A flash of James's retreating form through the flower beds explains the rise in Denton's voice, followed by his rough curse.

I study Kip's profile as we remain kneeling, using the thick stems and giant leaves as our barrier. His brows are drawn, his jaw working as he stares toward where his father's voice resonated. After a full minute, Kip moves. Denton is no more than a speck on the horizon returning home when we reach the fence between the properties.

"What in the hell was that?" Kips asks himself more than me, kicking at the ground as he pulls his phone from his pocket.

I massage the back of my neck, dumbfounded. "I don't think I've ever seen those two men speak with one another."

"Me either."

"What's that about a picture? Do you know what your dad was talking about?"

Kip's shoulders rise as he inhales sharply. I fully expect him to tell me to mind my own business since this is between the Harris and Lockwood families, and I'm an outlier. "Yeah. Brynn and Chlo found a high school snapshot of my dad with an ex-girlfriend," he confides. "But that was last August. I can't see why they're arguing about it now."

Memories soar through my mind...

"You know my aunt went to school in the same grade as Denton. She said there was a pretty big scandal between them back then," Denise explained at the farm a few days after James tore into me about giving Loe the shed. *"She said it was all hush-hush. Everyone knew something happened because Denton was pretty vocal about his hate for James for a while, but no one knows why."*

Robyn's confession when she visited after my wreck holds new meaning. *"Something happened between them the summer before we married. A fight that left them both bloody."* Denton would've still been in high school at that time.

Then Dad's memories. *"There was this girl in my class. I remember murmurings about them fighting over her. Sound familiar?"*

"Even the gods started a war over a woman," I mumble as a piece of the puzzle unlocks. "Kip, they fought over a girl. The girl in the picture." *Can't we identify with that firsthand?* Kip shakes his head, but I forge on, repeating what Denise, Robyn, and Dad said over the last few months. "What else could etch hate so deeply on their souls other than a woman?"

Kip's eyes agree, but his head won't stop shaking. "James and Robyn have been together forever. Practically since they were kids. Why..."

"Maybe Denton wronged James? Maybe the girl was someone to him and your dad hurt her?"

"I need to see Chloe." Kip glances back toward his parents' home, then turns for the front of the farm. "I think it's past time we figure out our fathers' differences."

since I told you, I have been constantly depressed. My happiness ... incessant ... ... memory ... your cares ... your ... affection ... solicitude ... ... Josephine ... continually a burning ... ... in my heart. When ... all solicitude, all harm ... , shall I be able to pass a ... time with you, having ... love you, and to think only ... happiness of ... to saying, and ... ing it to you.

36

Grace

I LEAVE Fig before four to beat Robyn to the kitchen and make her dinner for once. My cooking skills aren't as seasoned as hers, but Mom taught me to bake a pretty mean chicken pot pie.

I'm rolling out the dough for the crust when the front door opens and closes. Robyn turns the corner of the entryway into the kitchen and startles before she smiles. "Grace, you're home early."

"I wanted you to relax for a night, thank you with a meal. It's long overdue."

"You're such a sweetheart." She sets her purse in the corner of the counter, sliding in beside me at the island. "Do you need any help?"

"No, I've got this." I shoo her off. "There's a cabernet in the fridge unless you're more on Chloe's level, then there's also a bottle of pinot gris. Kick your feet up and pour yourself a glass."

A gentle chuckle passes her lips. "Well. This *is* nice. Don't mind if I do."

After pouring a glass of the Cabernet Franc, she perches on a counter stool at the bar on the other side of the island. "How's Fig doing with the summer coming to a close?"

"With back-to-school shopping, we're not doing half bad. Our profits doubled from last year."

"That's so wonderful to hear. I bet your mother is so proud of your success."

I nod because even though her sights are set on me finding love and giving her grandchildren—no pressure, Reid—I know she's proud of what I've accomplished. "How are things in the flower land of Lockwood?"

Robyn shifts as she swirls her wine glass. "I'd never tell Chloe this because tensions are high enough, but we were doing better when she was able to be more hands on. Not that Reid doesn't do a fine job—we're lucky to have him—but you know Loe. Lockwood Blooms is in her blood. We thrived with her at the helm."

And it doesn't help that Reid has been pulled in a million different directions, not to mention his car accident. Chloe and Reid would be a dream team if James would just *chill*. They could join forces and take over the PNW. At this point, I have little faith that will ever happen.

The slam of the front door echoes through the house and my head pops up, waiting to see who's here. Though Chloe is the only one who makes sense, when she appears, I tense. Standing at the mouth of the kitchen, her usual sunny disposition is missing. With her arms dangling helplessly at her sides, her eyes are laser-focused with resolve.

"Hey, Loe." I pause the basting brush over the crust. "Everything all right?"

"Tell me who Traci is, Mom."

Traci?

Robyn stiffens before swiveling in her seat. Almost as if she was waiting for this question, her shoulders sag. "She was Denton's high school girlfriend. She was a year behind your father and me, a year ahead of Denton."

Why is Chloe asking about a girl from her parents' high school days?

"Yes, Denton told us that, though I never knew her name. What does she have to do with Dad? Why would Denton be fighting with him at the farm over a picture from forty years ago?"

I can't see Robyn's facial expression, but her head cocks to the side. "They were fighting? I don't…" She pauses, folding her hands in her lap before taking a deep breath. "I suspect maybe your father ruined their relationship."

"I'd ask why he'd do that, but Denton is a Harris." Chloe enters the kitchen, taking a seat on a stool beside Robyn. Placing the chicken pot pie in the oven, I grab the pinot and pour Chloe a glass. "Why would they be arguing about it now?"

"I doubt they've ever stopped. We're just typically not privy to their encounters."

"You don't know anything more? You were there. You were dating Dad at the time."

Robyn stares down at her wine glass in both hands on the counter, running her long fingers up and down the condensation. "Traci was a sweet and beautiful girl, but she was dirt poor. A girl from the other side of town. The side Denton Harris never would've normally stepped foot in. Her parents were zealots. Very devout. They never would have allowed their daughter to date, but everyone at school knew Denton was crazy about her. Her older brother, Leonard, worked on the farm sometimes for your grandpa and was friendly with your father."

"So, what happened?"

"I honestly don't know, darling girl. I remember hearing rumors back then. Comments about resentment between your father and Denton over Traci. I was happily in love and never paid them much heed, but..." She swallows. "Now I wonder if I wasn't wrong all along. I wonder if Denton's hatred for your father was more justified than we ever thought. I wouldn't put it past James at this point to have run her off to spite Denton. It would explain their deep-seated hostility."

"Why now, Mom? Why, after all these years, would you think that of Dad?"

Robyn takes a long sip of her wine before answering, "Because you found that picture, and it brought back memories. With the way your father has acted about Kip." She scratches below her ear. "I know there's a deeper reason for his behavior, but he's never let me in enough to share what."

My heart aches for Robyn. She's trying to explain the one-eighty attitude adjustment James underwent since Chloe and Kip fell in love. She's hurting because she's losing the man she's loved nearly her entire life and she doesn't fully understand why.

"Kip said Denton told Dad he didn't want to lie for him anymore." Chloe holds the glass of pinot but hasn't touched it otherwise. "If they hate each other so much, why would Denton Harris lie for him?"

"I don't have answers, Chloe Mae. Just speculation and hunches. And many, many questions only your father can answer."

"And have you asked him?"

"I tried. It didn't end so well."

"Does this have anything to do with you moving out?"

I note the hint of a lie in Robyn's eyes when she says it doesn't. Chloe must notice, too, because instead of pushing, she brings the glass of wine to her lips and guzzles it down.

WITH THE POT pie in the oven, I set the timer and leave, telling them to save me some. As I get into the driver's seat of my car, I shoot off a text to Reid, seeing if he's home yet. Cranking the engine, I head that way. Even if he isn't, it's best to give Chloe and Robyn some time alone. Though they didn't seem bothered by my presence, they were definitely having a private family conversation. I'll head back to Fig if need be. Business is never done there.

When the text comes in that he's not home yet, but he will be in about twenty minutes, I wait on his doorstep until his charcoal F-150 pulls into his inclined driveway. Reid hops down, slamming the car door, and rounds the hood of the truck.

"Well, if this isn't my favorite way to come home." His mouth spreads in a panty-melting grin.

I rise to my feet from the step, taking in the grit and sweat on this fine, *fine* man. "Can't say I hate the sight of you at the end of a long day."

Reid turns his black baseball hat backward by the bill, and as if my body knows what that means, my veins tingle in response before he bends his head for a kiss. Even the earthy musk screams virile man, feeding the hunger in my belly. I lift on my toes to match his ardor, wrapping my arms around his neck.

His fingers lock on my hands at his nape, angling his hips away from me. "I don't want to get my present dirty," he says against my lips with a sexy smirk. "At least I assume that's what this dress is."

"Maybe." I smile. Though it really wasn't on purpose. I hadn't even planned on seeing Reid tonight.

With a peck, he says, "Let me shower first. Unless, of course, you want to join me."

"As tempting as that sounds, I do have to head back home at some point. I don't want Robyn asking questions."

"Robyn? What is Robyn doing at your house?"

Every one of my muscles still. *Dammit.* I didn't even think twice. I've gotten so used to having her there, and with my trust in Reid, my mouth ran freely.

I try concealing my guilt and swat my hand through the air.

"She's just hanging out with Chloe tonight. Mother/daughter bonding and all that."

Reid's lips purse, reading my lie. "Grace?"

"Yeah, okay." I exhale. "You have to keep this quiet, no slipping like I just did. Robyn's been living with Chloe and me for a few months."

"What's a few months?"

"Since March."

He rears back, confused. "But I still see her at the farm."

"She's not being held captive. The woman is allowed to come and go as she pleases. And if I'm not mistaken, she still has a job to do handling the ordering and books for Lockwood Blooms."

Reid chews on his bottom lip, a contemplative shift in his eyes. "Let's head inside."

What does he know that I don't?

He unlaces his dirt-caked boots, leaving them on the porch, and opens the front door for me. I follow him down the hall to his bedroom we've frequented over the last few days. Opening his closet, Reid tears off his grimy white shirt and tosses it into a dirty clothes pile in the corner. No hamper. Such a man.

"Why is Robyn staying with you guys?"

"I don't know specifics. I'm not even sure Chloe does at this point. At first, I thought it was just a separation period to get away from James and his nasty new attitude, but now I wonder if it had more to do with James and his history with Denton. We got a little piece of the puzzle today."

Reid nods as he unbuckles his belt. "Kip and I overheard some stuff earlier at the farm."

"You were with him?"

His head tilts. "Yeah, what do you know about it?"

"Chloe stormed into the house about an hour ago after talking with Kip, demanding to know who some woman named Traci is."

He harrumphs, unzipping his tattered jeans. It's all so

domestic, watching him strip in a nonsexual way, talking like this is everyday business. Until his socks go, and then his black boxer briefs sliding down his muscular thighs. My stomach tightens, my heart rate picking up. *Oh, sweet mercy.* I must have done something right to be rewarded with a man as beautiful as this.

"Grace." Reid chuckles, saying my name as if he's trying to catch my attention.

My eyes dart up as I refrain from fanning myself. "Sorry. What did you say?"

A knowing smirk pulls the corner of his lips. "No apology necessary, but if I'm going to shower, you need to stop looking at me like that, or I won't make it, and I'll happily ruin your pristine dress with my filthy hands."

Heat flushes my cheeks as he turns toward the bathroom attached to his room, and I get an eyeful of his ripped backside. Maybe I don't care about the cleanliness of the dress. It's machine washable. Heck, I'd be willing to toss it in the trash at this point.

Following Reid inside, the shower runs as he snags a towel from the linen closet and hangs it on a hook.

"Denton and James were intense and all sneaky-like at the back fence line." Reid opens the shower door and steps under the warm spray. The water-speckled glass does nothing to conceal him from my view, even with the building steam. "We've all heard about the feud and the repercussions, but never have I witnessed their animosity firsthand. We always have a picture of what we think is the full story, but you really never know what's going on in people's lives."

Ain't that the truth. "What did you make of their argument?"

His hands run over his wet hair before leveling me with a stare loaded with ironic humor. "It all began with a girl."

I mirror his smile. "Surprise, surprise."

Reid squeezes body wash onto a black loofa, angled away from the spray, displaying every inch of his manly glory. "You sure you don't want to come in with me? I'll let you rub me down."

No, no, I'm not sure. If I were to check my pulse, my heart rate would surely be galloping.

"Just make it snappy, Pruitt, so I can jump you out here."

"Oh, I don't know. There's something about those big eyes on me while you can't do anything about it."

Slowly, Reid rinses off, taking his time running his hands over the suds on each ridge and groove. My fingers grip the counter behind me. I'd give in and strip out of my dress to join him, but I agree. There's something about watching him, watching him tease me, that excites me even more. The anticipation is almost as satisfying as the home run.

Our eyes catch as every inch of him flexes, standing under the steady stream. We don't say a single word, entangled in a battle of wills.

Loosening my hold, I hoist myself up and perch on the edge of the counter. "I could do this all day, Pruitt."

His sinewy arms raise, combing through his wet hair, squeezing out the remaining water. "Lucky for you, I don't have as much restraint." Reid shuts off the nozzle and steps out, droplets slinking down his tan figure, dripping on the rug.

"You'll learn very quickly I'm a patient woman, so if you want something, you'll have to take it."

Stepping between my legs, his adept fingers dig into my hips. "If you don't want to go home wet, I suggest losing the dress."

...since I left you, I have been constantly depressed. My happiness... incessantly... my memory... your care... your... affection... solicitude... comparable... continually a burning and... me in my heart. When... all solicitude, all hara... I shall I be able to pass a... time with you, having... love you, and to think only... happiness of... saying, and... ing it to you.

37

Reid

THE YELLOW SHED is no more. Finally.

Stacking the final wall panel on the trailer I'll drive over to Chloe's farm in the morning, I circle my arms, loosening my sore shoulders, and inspect the space left behind. An area we'll dig up and fertilize and grow close to five hundred dahlias a season. My gaze lowers to the soil and rust-coated planks that made up the shed floor. I've never been happier for James's frugality than I am as I look at that last remaining bit I need to dispose of. If James had poured a concrete base, I'd be heading out to rent a jackhammer. Instead, I can rip this platform up as easily as tearing out an old deck. Maybe I'll rope Charlie or Julian into it since the farm is slowing down. Save my back. I'm too young to ache this much.

The grinding of gravel under steps alerts me of someone's presence a moment before her voice wraps around my soul. "So, this is what you do when you work late? Stand around and stare at an old deck?"

"You caught me." I adjust my ball cap and turn, admiring Grace as she saunters my way, her hips swaying with invitation. I can't help but take in every inch of her shapely legs thanks to the way the flirty dress's hem flutters in the breeze. "Another dress, Miss Embry?"

She comes to a stop inches out of my reach, one thin shoulder shrugging. "I was under the impression you liked me wearing them."

Her coy eyes and siren grin have me seizing her by the waist and sampling the taste of her rosy lips. "Like is not a word I associate with you, my sweet Gracie," I murmur against her mouth, my fingers skating up the back of her bare thigh and rounding the curve of her behind.

"Reid!" Grace yelps when I pinch.

My palm soothes the sting, and Grace's hips roll, seeking my body the way mine seeks hers. "Gotta love easy access."

Grace's answering laughter thwarts my next kiss, and I give up. Leaning back while keeping her in my arms, I meet her hazel eyes. "What are you doing here? I was about to head out."

"It's Tuesday." Removing an arm from around my back, she pulls the strap of the soft-sided cooler I hadn't noticed her carrying off her shoulder. "I brought dinner."

Unable to staunch my smile, I accept the bag from her and brush a butterfly kiss directly on the beauty mark at the corner of her right eye. "You took your mom's advice to heart, huh?"

Grace's head tilts and I step back, reveling in the confused frown marring her pretty face. "My mom's advice?"

Clasping her hand in mine, I lead her deeper into the farm. "Didn't she tell you to lock me down?"

"Reid Gregory Pruitt!" Her breath catches. "Did you eavesdrop on my conversation with my mom?" She shoves against my side, but there's no malice behind the move.

"Gracie, your mother was *not* subtle that day. We all heard it. Lucy even asked Stella what locked down means." Grace covers her eyes and groans. "By the way, you might consider looking into what she's watching on television."

Horror flickers across her face as she drops her hand. "Lucy?"

"No, Stella. Her idea of locked down was not PG-13, sweetheart. I had to turn my back so they couldn't see me laughing."

"Oh, my… I can't with her." Her feet drag and I spin around, walking backward while she looks shell-shocked at her younger sister's antics. It's damn adorable.

"Did you know she seems to have a pretty hardcore crush on Wade?"

Grace perks up. "Yeah, I figured that out when she came to watch me play softball when he was in town. I can't believe she told you, though."

"Well, she didn't tell me so much as she quizzed me on him. Subtly, of course." I pause and break a hollyhock from a vine to soften that blow.

"Oh, geez." Grace takes the flower with a crooked grin. "I need a new family. I'm sorry."

"Sorry? I loved your family." I throw my arm around her shoulders, drawing her into my side as we resume walking. "If anyone should be apologizing about their family, I'm pretty sure it's me."

"Water under the bridge." Grace blinks up through long, black-coated lashes, brushing the pink petals beneath her nose. "So, is the dinner working?"

"At locking me down?" I verify, and Grace grins. Setting the cooler with our dinner in the grass on the back edge of the farm near the amaranth, I cup Grace's peach-hued cheeks between my palms. "You had me locked down the night you turned all feisty on Joseph Sullivan. I'm all yours, Grace Elizabeth Embry."

Grace's eyes darken with heat. "Maybe dinner can wait," she says, securing the edge of her bottom lip between her teeth.

Running my hands over her shoulders, down her arms, and

past her waist and hips until I'm teasing up the ruffled fabric covering her thighs, I wag my brows. "You *are* wearing a dress."

"Mmm-hmmm." Her fingers wrap around my wrist and steer my hand higher. "Easy access."

Dropping to my knees in the grass, I run my nose along her thigh, peppering kisses across her skin. "I love you, Gracie." Settling my hands on her hips, I fall back to sit and Grace sinks down and straddles my lap.

"I love you, too." She plucks off my hat, tossing it to the ground, and tugs my hair, angling my head as our lips meet.

I love kissing Grace. Even when we're frantically colliding in a fit of passion, the meeting of our mouths is smooth like satin. We simply fit like the perfect pair of jeans or a bouquet of ranunculus and freesia. I could savor her all day, but the longer we kiss, the breathier she becomes and the more insistent her hips roll. When her hands go to work tugging at my shirt, I give up holding off and give in to the need aching within my bones every time this woman is in my vicinity.

An hour later, I'm running my palm up and down Grace's shin, her bare foot locked beneath my thigh, as we sit facing each other, sated and enjoying our picnic dinner.

"Why do you keep giggling?" I ask when she breaks into whisper-soft laughter for what must be the tenth time since we resituated our clothing and dug into our meal.

Flashes of pink color her cheeks. "Brynn told me it was hot, but I didn't believe her until tonight."

My gaze drops to my club sandwich as though Grace means the food, and she giggles again.

Her laughter dies at my pointed stare. "Sorry, it's just..." With one tongue swipe across her top lip, she says, "Brynn and Hayden's first time was in Kip's old fort. I thought she was crazy. Having sex in the woods?"

Her disgusted snarl pulls a laugh from my chest. "I take it this was your first outdoor adventure, then?" The question comes out and I wish I hadn't voiced it. *Ford.* He shouldn't occupy one second of this moment, but the truth is, the woman I love slept with my brother for what I assume was years. I can't run away from that.

Grace sighs. Shifting forward, she grips my chin between her fingers and tugs my face to meet her gaze. "First, yes. You are my first outside adventure, Reid. And second, my time with him doesn't compare with you. Not one bit."

My hand slides up her calf. Using her for leverage, I rock forward until our faces are inches apart. "You loved him, and I'm okay with that. It'll probably take time for me to purge the idea of you two naked together, though."

"Were you a virgin before our first time?" Her hand secures behind my neck. "Of course you weren't, and neither was I. It doesn't matter who they were. They're the past. We're what matters. We're our future."

She's right. Those other times were merely moments with women who I might have cared about in some way, but the day I fell in love with Grace Embry, other women failed to exist in my eyes and in my heart.

"By the way, I'm having Lucy and Stella over for a sleepover Friday night," Grace says as we return to the front of the farm hand-in-hand. "It's sort of become a tradition since I bought my house. A back-to-school girls' night."

"So, nails and hair and boy talk?"

"Pretty much. And rest assured, I'll be chatting with Stella about her little locked down comment." Grace releases my hand and fusses with her tangled hair, finger combing the mess into a ponytail. "I'm afraid to know what kind of books that girl's reading these days."

"Oh, I don't know..." I tweak her side while her arms are up, causing her to yelp.

"Stop, you monster." She kicks out at my leg and puts a good six feet between us, glaring.

"You know, if we forget that the suggestion came from your little sister, I would consider the idea."

Stopping, Grace plunks her hands on her hips. "Are you asking me to do kinky things with you?"

I love the mischief sparking to life in her expressive eyes. "Would you say yes if I was?"

Tapping her chin with the tip of her light pink nail in contemplation, Grace hums a cheeky, "Maaaaybe."

My greedy body twitches to life. I had her an hour ago, but I'm primed for more. "You spending the night at my place tonight?" I bear down on her, erasing the space she placed between us.

"Absolutely," she says with her chin held high.

"Then, yes." My index finger hooks the scooped neckline of her dress and dips between the swells of her breasts. "Yes, I am asking you to do kinky things with me."

My attempt at a smoldering stare fails as Grace averts her gaze, laughing. "You know... Hey..." Grace's eyes narrow and her words pause as my finger toys with her ample flesh.

"Reid?" The uncertainty in her tone pulls my gaze from the vein pulsing along her slim neck. *Oh, the things my mouth will do to that neck later.*

The confusion on her face has me removing my hand from beneath her top. "What's wrong?" My gaze turns toward her point of focus.

"What...is that?" Grace stammers, and my attention lands on a dark shadow of a form on the ground near the trailer I stacked the pieces of the yellow shed on.

"A person." I hear my reply without realizing I said the words because I'm already running.

As the distance dwindles, the form takes shape, though its partially concealed by the trailer. Black shoes. Jean-clad legs.

"Gracie, babe!" I yell over my shoulder. "Get your cell." My pace quickens. "Call for help."

James must have come outside and had a fit after seeing the shed dismantled. If he's had another stroke, I don't know if I'll forgive myself. I skid to a stop and fall to my knees.

"Oh, God." I reach for the prone body. The red stain of blood covers the ground, sending my heart racing.

Grace trips as she rounds the trailer, her breathing labored, her gasp as audible as the emergency operator's voice.

"What's your emergency?"

"Yes, we need an ambulance at Lockwood Farms. There's been an accident, or I don't know what happened…there's a lot of blood…a head injury."

I pull my shirt off to staunch the blood flow, Grace's words muffled by the ringing in my ears. What in the hell happened? How…

"Yes, I know the victim." Grace's hand falls to my shoulder, squeezing. "Mia Mason." Her voice shakes. "Please hurry. She's only nineteen."

since I left you, I have
been constantly depressed.
My happiness [...]
Incessant [...]
my memory your cares
your [...] affection
solicitude [...]
[...]
continually a burning and a
[...] in my heart. When
[...] all solicitude, all hara[ss]
[...], shall I be able to pass a
[...] time with you, having
love you, and to think only
happiness of [...] saying, and
[...]ing it to you.

38

Bodhi

DIGGING my cell from my pocket as I slip my key into the lock and step inside my apartment, I recheck the date: Tuesday, August thirty-first. My sleep-deprived senses refuse to grasp anything beyond 'right foot in front of left,' but it's good to be home again. Securing the front door, I abandon my luggage in the foyer and fumble toward the bedroom, removing my shirt and kicking off my shoes on the way. Ten days of hell with three time zone changes and multiple debriefings have me landing face-first on my impeccably made bed and out like a drunk.

A VIBRATION TICKLES MY CHEEK. Burying my face against a ridged fabric, desperate to stay asleep, I slap at the nuisance. I expect an insect or rodent—in my line of work, it wouldn't be the first time a rat took liberties while I slept—but my hand connects with something hard instead.

Mumbling a curse as the vibration continues, I stretch my limbs and inhale, a familiar scent invading my nostrils. Home.

Home. My eyes pop open. I'm home and on my bed. The room is dark. It's Tuesday, my brain recalls, maybe early Wednesday morning by now. And the vibration? My fingers wrap around the cell I must've dropped by my head when I fell asleep.

Without thought, my thumb swipes *Accept*. "Yeah?"

"Bodh?" Kip's voice is hesitant. "I figured I'd get your voicemail."

"Nah, you got the real deal, man." I roll onto my back and scrub my hand over my face. Days worth of beard growth scratches my palm. "Everything okay?"

His prolonged pause prods me further into wakefulness. "Kip?"

"Yeah, man, I'm here." Another pause. "And no, everything isn't okay. Mia was attacked earlier this evening."

I jolt into a sitting position, dropping my legs off the edge of the bed. *Mia Mason.* I envision the little beauty, our introduction on Hayden and Brynn's wedding day playing in my mind.

I HUNT *people down for a living, but Kingston Castle's service area is a maze of hallways and doors no amount of direction from a well-meaning and highly flirtatious staff member could prepare me for. Finally, I come to a room packed from one wall to the other with floral arrangements and tables ladened with buckets of Lockwood Blooms flowers. I step inside the doorway.*

"Mia?" I ask when I spot a head of raven hair, and the girl yelps. "Sorry, I didn't mean to—"

"Holy...you are so lucky I didn't snap these stems." She lifts her gaze from the bouquet in her hand, her lips parting on a sharp inhale that barely reaches me.

My throat goes dry. I've seen pictures, but somehow we've never met in person. When I was in town after everything went down last year with Preston and Brynn, and Hayden was arrested, the family kept Mia away for her own sake, or so Kip explained.

"Or you'd what?" I ask, unable to avert my gaze from her round Bambi eyes.

"Excuse me?" she blinks, shifting. She's a tiny sprite hidden by the giant buckets of flowers sitting on the tables filling the room, some taller than her.

I release a breathy chuckle. "You said I'm lucky you didn't snap those stems. I was wondering what you were threatening me with, Thumbelina."

Her bee-stung lips quiver, a smile peeking through before she curbs it. "What am I threatening you with?" she repeats. "I don't need a weapon, Bodhi. I imagine your two best friends would handle you if you ruined Brynn's wedding day."

Ahhh, no introduction needed then, huh? I flash a flirtatious smile. "Glad to see my reputation precedes me."

Her lips tremble, but she continues containing the smile I know she's dying to release.

Crossing further into the room, I tilt my head. "Lucky for me, I love Red like a sister and wouldn't dream of ruining her day, but just so you know, if it came down to it," I lean closer to the flowers several feet down the table from her, whispering, "I could take both of them, easy."

My confession has her cheeks flushing and laughter bubbling up. Score.

"Wow, I thought Kip was full of himself. No wonder you two are best friends."

"And if I didn't know you were Mia based on the pictures I've seen, I'd know it from that sassy mouth of yours."

She gapes and her brows reach her hairline.

"Yes, Thumbelina, your reputation precedes you as well."

Her shoulders fall as she plops her free hand on her hip. "You've got me there." Mia laughs.

If I weren't aware of exactly how much she means to the people I love, I'd be tempted to step closer. To flirt harder. She's not some random girl in a bar. She's family. I step away from the table between us, fixing a soft and as innocent as possible smile on my face. "It's nice to meet you officially, Maid of Honor."

"Likewise, Best Man Number Two." Mia dips in a mock curtsy.

A curtsy. *Damn, she's going to make things difficult for me. And Number Two?* Psh, *I suppose that makes Kip Number One in her mind. Prick.*

"First, there is no Number One and Two. We planned this out. I'm Hayd's Best Man. Hayden will be Kip's, and Kip will be mine," I stumble over pairing myself with marriage, and Mia's head cocks. "Second," I rub my hands together, getting to the point of this meeting. "I was tasked with finding you. The others are upstairs, and we wanted to have a pre-event wedding party toast. So drop that bouquet"—Mia shoots me an evil eye—"carefully, of course, and come with me."

"WHAT HAPPENED? HOW BAD IS IT?" My mind goes straight to the worst when I hear a woman's been attacked. The worst is all I know.

"She's all right. Reid and Grace found her unconscious at Lockwood's. She had a head injury, so she lost a lot of blood and has a concussion. We're waiting for her CT results, and she needs stitches, but the doctor doesn't think there's any serious damage."

"What the hell? Knocked out?" *At a damn flower farm?*

Kip laughs humorlessly. "That's not even the start of what's been going on here this summer, Bodh. Someone is screwing with me, man. Or with my loved ones. I dunno. Reid nearly died in a crash at the end of June driving a delivery van the cops suspect was tampered with. We've had some vandalism at my properties—"

"And I've been out of pocket all summer. I'm sorry, bro."

"It's all good, but I was hoping you might have time coming

up to pay Seaside Pointe a visit. Hayd and I could use your expertise. Thinking about anyone else getting hurt…if Chloe…" He trails off with a choked sigh.

I check the clock. It's eleven p.m. I think it was around five when I got home. Six hours will have to do. Stretching and coaxing a kink from my neck, I stand and head for my bathroom. "Well, it just so happens I have some unexpected time on my hands. I'm on paid leave, so if you can spare a room, I can spare my expertise for the men of my two favorite women."

"Those women will be happy to see you. But, paid leave? What's going on?" Kip asks.

I flip the shower on, might as well wash the sleep off and head to Seaside tonight. "Oh, nothing much. I just killed two men."

Do we have your attention after that last line?
Find answers and dig deeper into Bodhi (yes, please!)
Learn everything in: ***Seaside Pointe, book 4***

FROM THE AUTHOR

As with every book we write, there are so many little pieces of us in these characters and settings. Read our books and get to know us. We're inviting you in.

If you enjoyed this book, we'd love it if you'd take a moment to post a review at the site of purchase or any other book site you like using. We especially LOVE seeing TikTok and Instagram posts. Please tag us so we can share for you!

https://www.instagram.com/mindymichelebooks/
https://www.tiktok.com/@michelegmiller
https://www.tiktok.com/@haymind

ACKNOWLEDGMENTS

MICHELE
To my husband and kids, Thank you for always asking about my stories and never making me feel bad for following a dream.
My amazing crew of readers, bloggers, and friends, you know who you are. The ones who like my posts and comment on my random musings. Those who encourage me when I'm pouting and help me when I ask. This world is so big, yet so small that I can have friends worldwide to share books with warms my heart. Thank you all for supporting my work and sharing it with your friends and family. I'm forever grateful for each of you.
Special thanks to author Cameo Renae and her family for helping me secure a proper middle name for Bodhi—Tupuolevasa—as mentioned in Blossoms & Steel.

MINDY
What a whirlwind the last year has been. I wouldn't have survived it without books and writing. Especially Seaside with

Michele. What a sweet escape it's been to be in a world we created together.

My readers and friends, I see you and your constant cheering. I keep writing because of you.

To my people, Ryan and Zoey Sue, I know having a wife and mom as an author means having someone who isn't always present because my mind is in other worlds half the time. Thank you for loving me anyway and supporting this passion of mine. I love you most.

KEEP READING!

ABOUT THE AUTHORS

We're pretty awesome! We like singing in the car, eating white cheddar popcorn, and going on road trips together. You'll find us sharing a table at a few book signings each year. We have a love of romance, New York, anything sweet, and great books.

To find out more you can hunt us down on social media. We're all over the place!

Track down Mindy:
Email: mindy.hayes.writes@gmail.com
Website: www.mindyhayes.com
Facebook: www.facebook.com/hayes.mindy
Twitter: @haymindywrites
Instagram: @haymind

Connect with Michele:
Email: authormichelegmiller@gmail.com
Facebook: www.facebook.com/AuthorMicheleGMiller
Twitter: @chelemybelles
Instagram: @chelemybelles
Website: www.michelegmillerbooks.squarespace.com

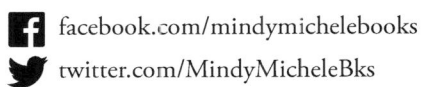

- facebook.com/mindymichelebooks
- twitter.com/MindyMicheleBks
- instagram.com/mindymichelebooks
- bookbub.com/authors/mindy-michele

Manufactured by Amazon.ca
Bolton, ON